The Crocodiles of Chibembe

The Crocodiles of Chibembe

A Natural History

David Ollier Weber

Kila Springs

Kila Springs Press is an imprint of the Kila Springs Group,
Placerville, CA.
E-mail: press@kilasprings.net

First Edition

ISBN 978-1-7338479-4-0
Library of Congress Control Number: 2020909909

For Sebastian, Carlitos, Bryce, James, Will and Roger,
when they reach maturity.

*W*hen *the terrible shrieks rose from the river and the fishermen burst from the copse of mopanis shouting hysterically in Chikunda and Kiswahili-laced English and the guides nursing* Mosis *in the post-and-thatch bar leaped to their feet and Simon ran to the HiLux to grab a torch and his .375 Brno... (all of this we pieced together later)... we were pitching our tents at the barricade near Nsefu, fifty kilometers southwest....*

I. Buffalo Beans

Four hours driving through buffalo beans and six hours digging the truck's tires out of sandy fords had left us itchy and exhausted.

Itchy was putting it mildly. Exhausted meant muscle-weary, sullen in disappointment, past hunger and headachy from the astringent South African wine we'd been swigging for the last three hours as a distraction.

According to the itinerary, we were supposed to be spending the night on the cushy grounds of Chibembe Safari Resort, in Zambia's South Luangwa National Park. Instead, we were trying to pound pegs into the hard grit of a chicken run between the mud huts of the families who guarded the entrance to the park's vast, buffering game reserve.

Nick, our driver, had reasoned to the point of anger with the broad-faced man who'd been summoned into the beam of our headlamps at the Nsefu compound gatehouse. That worthy bore the green shield of the Zambian National Park and Wildlife Service on his khaki sleeve and his Authority to uphold before assembled aides and associates:

Rules were rules. The spindly metal arm across the road would *not* be lifted for anyone until dawn.

So, no hot showers.

No gracious resort-restaurant meal.

No icy beers or gin-and-tonics—the prospects that had consoled us as we'd jounced along the brushy track for mile after mile in the gathering darkness.

Renée, who'd knelt side by side with Nick during the afternoon grubbing under the embedded tires and helping him snake the heavy steel sand-mats beneath the treads, had already passed out. It was she who'd encouraged us, proposed group songs to maintain morale and finally tapped into her store of cooking alcohol and sent bottle after bottle down to me to uncork with my Swiss Army knife.

National rep notwithstanding, Renée wasn't much of a drinker. She lay inert under a blanket on one of the Bedford's vinyl-covered fore-and-aft rear benches while Laura, Jen, Emma and even Mel, the pudgy, pampered princess from Finchley—who could usually be counted on to avoid chores—set about improvising a stew.

They had an appreciative audience. The men who'd gathered at the roadside guard-booth had all ambled over and perched themselves on the low *kraal* rails next to our cooking fire. We were accustomed to spectators wherever we camped, but mostly they were women and children who materialized out of the bush to lurk at a bashful distance. These guys had no qualms about jostling for front-row seats and entertaining one another with jocund running commentary on our curious *mzungu* customs.

Several who were comfortable in their English kept demanding of Jennifer, the prettiest by conventional standards, whether she was married. And of Emma, the Cambridge-bound teenager who'd capped her *wanderjahr* in Africa by having her scalp sheared to a stubble, whether she was a man or a woman.

Melody, who like Jen was in her late twenties and worked in an office in London, had acne and a bulbous nose: She had to suffer the indignity of being generally ignored. When my wife Laura hefted the big teakettle filled with disinfected water toward the fire, a skinny man hunkered forward with his hand extended and offered, "I will help you, *mami?*"

Laura twisted defensively and shook her head in the negative while grunting a perfunctory, "Thanks." Earlier in the day she had found it more amusing to be addressed by middle-aged Africans as "Mommy." But the term of respect reminded her she was pegged as a matriarch, no longer one of the nubile maidens.

I'd noticed the exchange and her reaction while Gerhard and I unstowed the food coolers, the chest of utensils and the folding canvas stools. We'd been on the road for ten days now, so we all had the drill down pat:

Alastair, the dapper, white-mustached bird-watcher/retiree from Sussex, was charged with laying the fire.

Rory, the perpetually good-natured Bristol-Irish second driver, clambered up the ladder into the roof seat over the Bedford's snub cab, delved into the deep bin under the cushion and began flinging down the numbered stuff-sacks that contained our tents, air mattresses and sleeping bags.

Nigel and Ewan, both thirtyish bachelors and accountants, though one in Wembly and one in Glasgow, wrestled the food preparation table from its welded brackets on the truck's right side, unhinged the legs and sloshed Detol-laced water from jerrycans into pots for boiling and into plastic basins for veg and hand washing. Then they went off to put up their tents.

Greta and Reg were the day's designated dishwashers. That freed them to attend to the unfurling of their own bundles of rip-stop nylon, the telescoping and threading of fiberglass poles, the hammering of pegs.

Once I'd finished setting out the stools I collected our stuff-sacks, mine and Laura's, and scouted for a tent-spot that would meet her stringent levelness standards.

Our group was light, nine shy of the safari maximum, so Nick had relaxed the normally rigorous two-to-a-tent policy. Still, everyone except Emma, Alastair, who snored stentorously, and Greta, a sun-dried widow of *un certain âge*— Danish, but living on Mallorca—had dutifully paired: Ewan with Nigel, Reg with Gerhard, Jen with Mel.

It was the latters' turn to spend the night in the truck. So no need for them to pitch a tent. The Bedford's cab and rear door could be locked, but even when rolled down and snugly grommeted, the plexiglass side windows left the passenger compartment vulnerable to pilferage if it was unoccupied.

What with the buffalo bean-dust that no cursory sweeping could clear out—Jen and Mel were working at it, whingeing and leaping out every couple of minutes for a breather to tear at their itches—I didn't envy the girls the convenience of their night's sleeping assignment.

Nick and Renée had crewed together for a year and were the only formal couple on the safari besides Laura and me. In fact, there was a fairly remarkable lack of romantic chemistry in this random grouping of youngish single adults. Only Gerhard, a prematurely balding attaché at the German Embassy in London, seemed at all responsive to Mel's indefatigable coquetry. And certain ambiguities in his conversation had made me wonder if he might not actually be gay.

The otherwise marriageable Brits were homely, quirky men, if adequately amicable. Ewan spoke a barely penetrable Glaswegian dialect, wore a money belt under the waistband of the long pants he favored in spite of the heat and was obsessed with accumulating trinkets to take home as gifts to his coworkers in what he'd called "the Health and Welfare."

Reg, a fortyish auto mechanic in Croyden, seldom uttered more than a half-swallowed phrase he had to be asked to repeat.

Nigel, whose most noteworthy feature was his Adam's apple, affected black ankle socks with skimpy track shorts and acknowledged living with his mum. No wonder Jen had taken a look around and resigned herself to a sisterly alliance with Mel. It turned out the two had gone to the same red-brick university. They politely allowed Emma into their giggly word games and gossip, but her age and more particularly her accent—the only one that might have suited an upstairs lead character on one of those *Masterpiece Theater* manor-house sagas—clearly discomfited them. ("Twits," I'd overheard Jen sneer to Mel about a pair of perfectly personable backpacking Oxford students Emma had chatted with in the pub at Hwange Main Camp.)

Emma was the same age as Laura's daughter Lisa, and her capricious essay in skinheadedness was nothing compared to the mutilations my daughter Megan had inflicted on herself in order to *épater les parents*. I found Emma winning—friendly, unpretentious, no stunner but comely, even without hair. Nick and Rory had already adopted that low-maintenance style; it was Rory who'd egged Emma on and then performed the butchery with his battery-powered clippers after our highlighted boat ride and swim in Lake Kariba. Since that evening, he'd also been quietly slipping into and out of her tent.

There was precious little camaraderie in evidence, however, by the time Laura ladled up our belated supper. It was already past ten. The night had turned chilly. Most of our attention was still focused on restraining the desperate urge to claw at the tiny, fiery fibrils that had infiltrated our clothes and needled themselves into every remote fold of skin.

At the BP station in Petauke, before we'd turned off the tar-sealed highway from Lusaka, Nick had thought to advise us that we'd probably drive through a stand or two of a mysteriously nasty vegetation he'd called "buffalo grass."

"I don't know what it is, but if the stuff gets on y', y'll itch like a bugger. Thing is not to scratch, though," he'd counseled. "If y' can just keep from scratchin', y'll basically be okay. Pretty much goes right away."

The "th" of *thing* came out closer to an "f," and soft glottal stops substituted for his "t"s. He was from Manchester, 26 years old, tall, lithe and strikingly handsome, with full black eyebrows, a ski-jump nose and a strong cleft chin darkened, customarily, by a couple of days' manly growth of beard. With his buzzcut scalp, he looked like one of those voguish male models in magazine fashion spreads. He'd spent four years in the British Army driving heavy trucks similar to our ingeniously modified Bedford, and three years as an assistant or leader on various African expedition routes.

He'd met Renée when she was detailed to be his campmaster/cook on a 23-day "Serengeti-to-Zanzibar Adventure." She was older by a handful of years, recently divorced from a husband with whom she'd been entombed in increasing misery on an isolated sheep station in the Northern Territories. She'd also been the district nurse there—an excellent qualification when, avid to let fresh air into her life, she'd packed it off to Europe and ultimately applied for a job with Mamba Safaris, the expedition company headquartered in London.

It didn't hurt that she was trim, athletic, friendly, competent, dusky blond, with a sprinkling of freckles across her tanned cheeks and the first pale creases I associate with full female sexual maturity visible at the corners of her green eyes.... Frankly, I envied Nick (who treated her in public with typical English aloofness). Envy's too strong a word, I should add, but I did focus all the male charm I could muster, and a good deal of covert attention masked by sunglasses, on Renée. She was somehow both stalwart and succulent. She embodied my stereotypes of broad-shouldered, broad-minded Australian sheilahood. Not that it would have made any difference—my flirting instincts were an evolutionary vestige; I had no actual impulse to stray from monogamy—but I detected no reciprocal interest whatsoever.

As leader, Nick was charged with delivering us, his cargo, undamaged at Lilongwe's Kamuzu International Airport precisely 21 days after greeting us outside the Air Zimbabwe terminal in Victoria Falls. It was also his obligation to assure that in the process we paying passengers experienced each of the dozen advertised "highlights" of this two-thousand-mile overland journey across southwestern Zimbabwe, Zambia and Malawi.

We'd already notched half of them, including a beer-sodden "sundowner cruise on the Zambezi" above the falls; a drenching walk in the awesome rainforest mist and din of *Mosi-oa-tunya*—"the smoke that thunders"—where the broad brown river abruptly widens into many channels that boil over a 350-foot precipice into a narrow gorge; and "gameviewing in Zimbabwe's largest National Park, Hwange."

A first-night, jet-lagged dinner with Rory in a tourist restaurant in Harare (I'd ordered eland steak, rare, Laura chose kudu, medium-rare), and a brief stroll down Cairo Road in shabby downtown Lusaka fulfilled two more "highlights."

Now we were en route to the seventh, a "walking safari in the Luangwa Valley."

In the company of an armed park ranger, the brochure had promised, we'd hike among "some of the greatest concentrations of wildlife in Africa—elephant, buffalo, giraffe, leopard, lion, numerous types of antelope, some four hundred species of birds including Crowned Cranes, Saddlebilled Storks, Goliath Herons... the list is almost endless."

In bush camp the night before, Nick had summoned us with his customary "Listen up!" and carefully unfolded Michelin Carte 955, *Afrique Centre et Sud.*

While we edged around him with our bottles of *Zambezi* Lager or postprandial mugs of tea or instant coffee, conversation attenuated in anticipation of the routine next-day's briefing, he stabbed his forefinger at Chibembe.

It lay at the apex of several wiggly double lines branching off the trans-Zambia highway to the Malawi border. All were dashed in yellow, which according to the legend stood for "*partiellement améliorée*/partially improved."

Only if we continued some four hundred kilometers east on the red motorway to the border town of Chipata, he showed us (red signifying "*revêtue 2 voies ou plus*/2 or more surfaced lanes"), and then doubled back almost two hundred kilometers northwest, could we avoid traversing a stretch of road whose outlines enclosed no color.

"*Sol naturel*/earth" that meant.

Along with "*piste reconnue ou balisée*/recognized track" and "*piste non balisée*/unmarked track," this was a category accompanied by a caution: "*viabilité incertaine par temps de pluie*/liable to be impracticable in bad weather."

(I'd brought along my own map, provisioned at a shop in Berkeley that specialized in travel paraphernalia, and gleaned these details later hunched cross-legged in our tent with my pocket flashlight clamped between my teeth.)

Now midway into June, we had experienced nothing but blue skies and the distinctive long, flat, pearlescent curds of cumulus that were the hallmark of southern Africa's immense horizons. The stifling season of rains had ended in May; we'd entered the balmiest, driest months of subequatorial winter. A pair of khaki shorts, a denim shirt with rolled up sleeves and river-rafting sandals were my daily attire. After nightfall or riding on the shady side of the open truck at highway speed before noon, I kept warm inside a sturdy Norwegian wool fishing sweater.

"Guys who came through with the group before us said this one's gone all to bloody hell," Nick reported, resting the tip of his finger on the first branching road off the main highway, at a town called Petauke. "River took a new course this year."

He scraped his fingernail on the map as if to erase and relocate a blue line that meandered south out of the gray-shaded park boundaries, an unlabeled tributary of the Luangwa.

"Water was still too high for 'em too. Had to go back, all the way round. Took 'em two days to get out."

He circled his finger over a small dot further along the highway. "There's another road, though, not on the map. Just here, before Sinda. Way we went in last year. Very good."

"You and Harry," Rory interjected.

"Yeh," Nick nodded.

Before leading a trip, each driver rode as an assistant to familiarize himself with the route. Rory had traveled through Zambia once before, he'd told us, in the opposite direction.

But when not spelling Nick at the wheel he was often jotting in a notebook. After bidding us goodbye at Lilongwe he was scheduled to deadhead the truck to Nairobi for a major mechanical overhaul, then co-pilot a 15-day circuit of Kenya before returning to lead another Malawi-Zimbabwe run himself. Nick and Renée, meanwhile, would be flying to Dakar, to crew one of Mamba's *pièces de résistance*, the six-month "Great Trans-Africa."

"Dirt most of the way," Nick continued. "Should be all right by now, though. No rain for a couple of months. Have to switch over to four-wheel drive at some point, so that'll slow us a bit. Made it to Chibembe from the turnoff in six hours even so last year, we did. Fastest way in, actually. So up at half-six...."

Mel groaned.

"Petauke's how far?" Renée inquired.

Nick glanced down at the map. "Two hours? Little less, maybe."

"Petrol stop," Rory noted. "Check the tyres and that."

He often filled in details the laconic Nick had neglected to mention.

"I might get a couple of things for lunch if anything looks good in the market," Renée commented. "We'll plan to cook dinner tomorrow night, in case we get into Chibembe too late for the restaurant. If not, I expect some of you will want to eat there."

"Daniel and I do," Laura volunteered.

"I also," announced Greta. "I take a chalet if possible."

"They have nice cottages," Renée nodded. "I don't know how expensive they are. Anybody who wants to is welcome to book one, you know, depending, of course, on vacancies. Our reservation's for the caravan park."

"We'll have dinner in the restaurant tomorrow night," Nick reminded us. "I'll pay for that from the kitty."

At the start of the trip we'd each anted a hundred and fifty dollars in cash—or a hundred pounds—to cover our food supplies en route, fees for camping at formal sites and scheduled hotel and restaurant charges. Nick swapped for local currency as necessary, doled out shopping money to Renée and took care of group bills from the stash, which he kept in a metal lockbox under his seat on the right side of the cab. Whatever was unspent at the end of the trip would be apportioned back to us.

"I'll also pay for your walking safari or a night drive. Your choice, one or the other. Everything else, you're on your own. I'd recommend doing 'em both, actually."

"Let me know by afternoon if you don't want to eat dinner with us," Renée said. "If you do and you're on the night drive, we'll save you something."

"We'll make the dinner reservation for eight tomorrow," Nick said. "That'll give plenty of time to get back. As for tomorrow morning, I reckon seven's okay." He grinned at Mel. "Suit you better, love?"

"Ooh, yeh, brilliant. Need me beauty sleep," she tittered.

"Long as all tents are down by half-seven," he added. "Breakfast and off by eight, then, no later. Gate into the park closes at sundown, so we have some ground to cover." He stood up.

"Questions?" Laura prompted.

"Oh, yeh," Nick grinned. "Questions?"

It was a standing joke between them. Nick's easy authority backed by Renée's regard and Rory's affable sidekick loyalty had won our trust. Even Laura, whose nature and job demanded that she exert control in all situations, had surrendered. I could see her night after night stifling the reflexive urge to argue decisions. Africa, she'd recognized, was not her territory. Of course she had a question, but it was *pro forma*, the mildest assertion of presence:

"Why's the night drive special?"

"Ah. Just see game you don't see in the daylight," Nick replied with a shrug. Elaboration was not his forte.

"Civets, like," Rory amplified. "Rhino, maybe. Or a leopard, if you get lucky. Sittin' in a tree,"

"What's a civet then?" wondered Mel.

We gassed up next morning at a British Petroleum station that would not have looked out of place on the flossiest European autoroute. The cinder-block garage and pumps were new, and dripping oil pans had not yet stained the apron. There was even a low, bordering planter whose wizened tufts were the only greenery in sight at the dusty crossroads except for a big shade tree.

The town itself lay off the highway a short distance. Renée had decided we didn't need to go in, since she'd provisioned pretty amply at the big central market in Lusaka. Women from the countryside had set out tiny piles of vegetables on the ground next to a blocky pastel storefront across from the petrol station. A wizened elder sat outside its door at a treadle sewing machine, a pile of clothing by his feet. Buses stopped there, apparently, though one must have just passed by because only a few people were loitering.

There were several wooden stalls next to the store, whose Indian owners stocked a paltry inventory of "general merchandise." One of the stalls bore a hand-painted sign reading

* Mikate * Bakery *

in painstakingly inexpert fancy lettering.

Renée handed me some *kwacha* out of her fanny pack and told me to go buy a couple of loaves of bread.

I was flattered that she'd favored me with the quest. I strode off manfully, notwithstanding the welling stage-fright I always experience when girding myself for a transaction in a foreign culture. But the rotund man behind the plank counter nodded genially to my English and fished up three fat, golden-crusted cylinders, still warm.

I wondered where the oven was.

He returned a couple of crumpled bills in change as if an American customer were a daily occurrence.

Renée, meanwhile, had acquired a head of cabbage, a bunch of skinny, muddy carrots and a dozen or so brown eggs.

We stowed them in one of the storage bins that lined the interior of the truck's rear. Their lids, behind the seats, formed a high shelf on which I liked to perch, sunning my legs, dangling outside the truck, when we traveled off-highway. (Nick had given us permission to ride that way on the left, the shoulder side, whenever we wanted.)

A small boy had appeared with a basket of hardboiled eggs. He was selling them for a *kwacha* each—a fraction of a cent— along with a tiny hand-twisted tinfoil packet of salt laced with grains of hot red pepper: *periperi*.

Nick dug into his pocket, and when Renée too beckoned at the boy, the rest of us were emboldened.

Gerhard, Nigel, Emma, Jen and I followed Rory's lead and also tried the doughnuts—greasy round balls of slightly sweetened dough—displayed by another young vendor who'd trotted up.

We peeled and dipped our eggs and munched our doughnuts while waiting for Rory to emerge from under the chassis, where he'd wriggled to perform some afterthought of an inspection or mechanical adjustment.

That was when Nick casually mentioned the "buffalo grass."

As advertised, the road was wide and hard for at least the first hour after we'd swung off the asphalt. It wound through rolling country dotted with acacias, mopanis and scraggly brachystegias (cork-barked members of the pea family, according to the Zambia guidebook from the truck's eclectic binful of paperbacks and dog-eared board games, which I'd been pawing through on the highway).

Here and there an elephantine baobab stood in a clearing over a scrawl of shadow cast by its stunted halo of barren branches. Some of the trees we'd learned to identify on our game-drive in Hwange.

The landscape was autumnal, parched like the California foothills in September.

Early on we met a red tractor draped with five animated Africans. On the outskirts of Lusaka we'd stayed at a private campground run as the backyard adjunct to a three-thousand-acre farm owned by an expatriate couple in their forties from New Zealand. (John and Fiona, as they'd introduced themselves over beers by the central barbecue, had originally settled in Zimbabwe, but had relocated to Zambia, the former Northern Rhodesia, in reaction to the former Southern Rhodesia's currency export restrictions; like most expats we met—the codeword for whites—they had nothing but contempt for the two countries' black governments.)

Out here, that tractor was the only hint of anything more complex than subsistence agriculture. We passed two or three modest plots of picked-over cotton, black stubble littered with white tatters, and some small dried-up cornfields near villages. Harvest seemed to be over. I spotted tall sheaves of rust-colored grain—millet, I guessed, or sorghum—carefully bound and stacked upright against a wooden crib on stilts in the center of one of the villages.

Visible habitations were few and far between. Off the track a hundred yards or so you'd see a clutch of mud-walled huts, some decorated with ochre washes or designs. The thatched roofs had generous overhangs that reached to within four or five feet of the ground and were supported by poles to create a shady surrounding loggia. A few chickens and somnolent goats might be visible in the scrupulously swept compound, but seldom people.

Women would occasionally appear at doorways and children dart past their skirts to caper and wave gaily when they heard us rumbling past. I assumed most of the inhabitants were off tending to chores or errands. Women balancing bundles on their heads, men shouldering faggots of spindly firewood or pushing battered bicycles laden with huge burlap sacks regularly plodded along the road margins. A two- or three-day trip on foot to the nearest market town for provisions, clothing or post-primary schooling was routine, Rory had told us. Circles of campfire ash along the roadside, some still smoking, marked the places where travelers had lain for the night.

Except for a short detour around a crew of a dozen men, women and children who were desultorily realigning the grade with handtools (it had the air of a community project, but the stakes and leveling strings had been professionally laid out), we were making good time. Even when the road would suddenly burrow into a tunnel of tall, dessicated grass, Nick kept his foot on the pedal.

Gerhard and Mel had opted to join Greta and Reg—who regularly rode there—on top.

Emma was in the cab keeping Rory and Nick company.

Laura and Renée and I on one side, Nigel and Ewan and Jen on the other had swung up to sit facing outboard. We were braced by a chest-high, fore-and-aft metal reinforcing bar and the framing uprights for the roof, a slab of translucent plastic.

Falling through it, the light in the passenger compartment had a comforting, undersea tint; sitting there like Alastair, you felt as if you were bobbing through Africa in a bathyscaph. But most of the time I preferred full, airy immersion.

It did require that you keep your reflexes toned, however, ready to swing your legs up and inside quickly when a thornbush fwapped by. Those up top had to be equally alert for low-hanging branches. Only if they were substantial did Nick bother to tap the brake.

Just before noon we came to a spot where the road dipped to cross a streambed. Nick downshifted and the truck jolted over the rubble but listed to a sudden whining stop, the rear tires spinning in the ooze between stones.

Nick rocked it in and out of reverse a couple of times, then shut off the engine and flung open his door. We all disembarked to join him in appraisal of the situation.

Laura and the other women immediately unwound handfuls of toilet paper and took turns disappearing into the nearby bush with a trowel.

(There was a button on the front bulkhead of the passenger compartment and another in the roof seat that sounded a buzzer in the cab. We were free to punch it any time we felt an urgent need to relieve ourselves. "2 rings = loo stop," a placard instructed us, "3 rings = photo stop." At either of those signals the driver would start looking for a convenient spot to pull over. Gerhard, who usually cradled a long-lensed 35-millimeter camera in his lap, had been the most likely to leap up and request a halt for picture-taking. "4 rings = emergency," the placard also noted. We'd yet to test it; it was supposed to trigger an instantaneous application of brakes.)

Nick and Rory peeled off their tee-shirts and spent nearly an hour under the front axle grunting through a complicated conversion from two- to four-wheel drive. Meanwhile, Renée handed out "bikkies"—biscuits, or cookies to Americans— from a packaged assortment, our usual midmorning snack. By the time Nick and Rory scrambled to their feet they were drenched in sweat and mud, and streaked with grease.

There was a shallow pool just below the rocky ford. A strikingly beautiful young woman in a striped knit top and a brightly flowered skirt had been squatting there when we'd driven up. She'd watched us quizzically as she'd continued to scour soot off the bottoms of her cooking pots with handfuls of wet sand.

Two other women had come a bit later to rinse out nests of plastic dishes. A fourth—sporting, incongruously, a tee shirt emblazoned with an expensive Italian designer's label—arrived bearing an empty galvanized tub atop her head. She put it down, discussed us briefly with her neighbors, then dipped the tub full of water and ankled away.

Presumably the water she'd collected was for drinking. To be sure, it dribbled among the rocks and looked reasonably clear where it ponded. But I noticed that Nick and Rory were swabbing themselves with rags dampened from one of our jerrycans rather than from the nearby stream.

We'd been cautioned to avoid skin contact with inland waters, especially around the muddy edges. That's where schistosome-infested snails breed. The advice had been reinforced by signs warning of the danger of bilharzia posted prominently along the waterfront in Kariba. Nevertheless, we'd dived and swum and clung to a net in the buffeting wake of a cabin cruiser in the middle of the huge lake created by the damming of the Zambezi at Kariba.

The skipper, a white Rhodesian in his sixties whose sinewy legs were mottled with purple growths—too many years of African sun, I surmised, or could they have been Kaposi's sarcomas?—called that ride in the net "taking a Jacuzzi." We were safe from the snail-spawned bilharziasis flukes, he assured us, far out over the center of the drowned gorge. And upstream two hundred and fifty miles, at Vic Falls, some of us had even slaked our thirst with palmfuls of tepid water dipped right out of the Zambezi. The blond Rhodesian guide who'd taken us canoeing in the current above the falls had promised us it was pure there too, having just percolated over a thousand miles of Kalahari sand.

Once Nick and Rory had the Bedford in four-wheel drive, we negotiated the gentle upgrade out of the streambed handily. But within an hour we were getting our first lesson in the use of the sand-mats.

We'd emerged from thick bush into a wide, level *veld*. Our course was marked by a pair of faint brown tracks worn into a green lane that ran straight for at least a mile between banks of coarse, tasseled grass the color of straw. Obviously there hadn't been much traffic in the month and a half since the rains ended. The fresh green crown and shoulders were the tipoff the road surface was still soggy.

Sure enough, without warning the truck slowed, the pitch of the engine rose and we slewed to another abrupt halt.

Nick and Rory hopped out scowling.

"Lunchtime!" Renée announced.

We dutifully unlimbered the table and the food chests. Various people joined Renée and the day's two duty cooks in washing and slicing tomatoes, cucumbers, avocado and lettuce, grating carrots and cabbage for slaw, sawing up the loaves of bread I'd bought, opening a tin of potted meat, unwrapping a brick of cheese, mixing a container of lemonade and setting out margarine, peanut butter, jam, condiments, bottled salad dressings, bananas, oranges and quartered cantaloupes for dessert.

Renée made sure we ate healthily. Gerhard, Nigel, Reg and I, meanwhile, were on our knees with Nick and Rory, wielding stubby camp shovels and our bare hands to scoop away at the sandy soil in which three of the four big ribbed tires were mired to the hubcaps.

The sky was clotted with tufty cumuli. They drifted steadily across the midday sun, muffling its blaze. The work was hot, though, and most of us—melanoma be damned—were cultivating vacation tans. I'd removed my shirt and slathered sunscreen across my shoulders. I'd also put on the long-billed deepsea fishing cap I'd ordered as part of my trip wardrobe from L.L. Bean. Recently I'd noticed ugly blotches—my doctor called them actinic keratoses—under the thinning hair across my crown. Laura and most of the other women were in tank tops or halters. Emma, Jen and Mel wore swimsuit bras.

Every single one of us by now sported a slender elephant-hair bracelet or, like Laura and me, a tiny carved soapstone amulet dangling from a necklace of waxed string. Laura had bought them—they were called "*nyaminyamis*"—from one of the importunate souvenir-hawkers who thronged Victoria Falls.

When we'd cleared a sort of ramp in front of each tire, Rory unlocked the brackets that clamped the nested steel sand-mats to the truck's sides. There were six of them, each about ten feet long and eighteen inches wide, painted fire-engine red. With three rows of holes running their length, they looked insubstantial, like outsized Erector set pieces. But when I innocently tugged one free, its unexpected weight wrenched it out of my grasp and almost guillotined my unprotected toes.

"Here, have a care, mate!" Nick snapped with a disapproving glare. The mat had clattered to the ground a couple of feet from where he crouched.

Gerhard and Nigel seized it and trundled it over to Rory. Together they levered it under the left front tire. I let Nick and Reg fetch the second mat and joggle it in as flat as possible in front of the left rear tire. I was superfluous, I decided. Anyway, how was I supposed to have known how heavy the goddamn thing was? And besides, I'd developed a tender back.

When the third mat was in place, Nick warned us to stand clear. He climbed in behind the wheel, turned over the engine and gently gave it gas.

The truck gained traction.

He accelerated.

The truck bucked forward the length of the mats.

Suddenly one of them shot out from behind the rear mudflap in a spurt of sand. The truck promptly churned itself to a standstill again.

Nick swung out of the cab and slammed the door hard. "Let's eat," he said.

The inevitable knot of barefoot children in grubby shorts and young women in florid wraparound skirts filtered out of the bush to regard us at our meal. Rory had admonished us in Harare to remember our status as "guests" in the Africans' domain, and to expect and accept what he termed their "unashamed curiosity."

Which we amply rewarded.

When we'd finished eating, Emma went over and distributed the remnant vegetables and bread slices to the children bold enough to step forward with cupped hands. Those bolder still opened their mouths like baby birds, noses wrinkled in leery anticipation, to accept the last spoonfuls of slaw from Laura. Renée bestowed our empty plastic juice bottles on two grateful women. The dishwashers, meanwhile, were sluicing our plates, bowls, cups and utensils in detergent, rinsing them in disinfectant-dosed water and passing them around for "flapping."

Everyone took part in this hygienic ritual. Rather than blotting our kitchen- and tableware dry with towels that could breed and spread bacteria if not properly laundered—hardly possible on the road in backcountry Africa—we all stood around waving them at arm's length in the air until the rinse-water had evaporated.

Devising idiosyncratic arabesques with outstretched handfuls of crockery or kitchen implements felt so silly it always liberated group endorphins. It was good aerobic exercise, too, Renée reminded us. And it certainly provided a boffo finale for the tittering onlookers.

Nick and Rory weren't normally exempted from flapping, but in this instance they'd bowed out to work at repositioning the sand-mats. Once we'd loaded the table and coolers and chests back aboard, Rory instructed Gerhard and me to station ourselves with a mat about eight feet forward of the left rear tire, ready to slap the steel slat down just before the tire had traversed the one it was already on. Then as soon as the rear mat was free, we were to grab it and scamper forward with it to repeat the process. Nigel and Reg would do the same on the other side—two teams shuttling the mats forward, swapping one for the other, fire-brigade-style, until the truck was on firm ground.

With Rory quarterbacking the operation from scouting distance ahead, Nick got behind the wheel. He started the engine and clunked it into gear.

The tires spun up onto the mats.

This time Nick took it slow and easy.

Gerhard and I waited for clearance, flung our mat into place beneath the long-range fuel tanks that occupied the Bedford's tweenwheels space on the left, hopped backwards, eyed the truck's progress, darted in and wrenched the half-buried rear mat out from under the jerrycan rack that was welded abaft the milling rubber.

Across from us, Nigel and Reg were mirroring our actions.

Like two men with a ladder, Gerhard and I trotted forward, gauged our opportunity and slung the new mat down flat under the fuel tanks.

I looked at Rory, who was pacing backwards, squinting at the ground in front of the truck intently while he wiggled his upthrust fingers to beckon Nick ahead... then stabbed the air with cocked forefingers, aimed to the right.

"Okay!" Gerhard barked at me. "*Hop-hop!*"

I stooped and seized the freed mat. The tire at my shoulder abruptly hummed faster and the engine wound upscale. Nick was accelerating. The truck fish-tailed, the treads bit, suddenly all four tires slithered up out of the soft ruts onto the green shoulder and crown. The truck began to labor away from us, gaining speed, faltering, chewing sand and grass, thrusting forward again as one or another of the tires overcame the others' drag.

Rory turned and ran alongside. He waved at us to follow.

I exchanged a glance of coordination with Gerhard and we stumbled into a canter. We almost wrenched the mat out of each other's hands a couple of times until we found our rhythm and skipped into step. Nigel and Reg were at our heels.

Nick kept his sandal pressed to the pedal.

Elated, eager, dogged, the four of us panted after the truck with our sand-mats while Rory bellowed encouragements.

The interval was lengthening and my breath was shortening. I felt a twinge at my tailbone, then a stabbing pain under my shoulder muscle high on the right. The cumbersome sand-mat clattered against my thigh and hipbone. I began to run with a hitch. A sciatic tingle coursed along my right femur. I couldn't stop, though. Behind me, Gerhard was at implacable stride. And the son of a bitch was shoving me along ahead of him.

"Let's slow down!" I gasped over my shoulder.

The ground rushing underfoot was treacherous, rutted sand studded with clumps of grass. I had to watch where I was going, I couldn't swivel my head to shout in his face. And Gerhard was drowning me out anyway.

"Yee-hoo!" he yodeled as Nick powered the truck away from us. "He goes! Brilliant! He goes!"

"Stop!" I begged.

But I was like the tandem wheel of a locomotive tied to a drive-wheel by a steel shaft. I had to pump my knees desperately just to keep my balance. It was nutty, a comedy routine. Only it was serious. If I bailed out on my own, simply let go of my end of the mat, I risked doing Gerhard some serious harm.

"Gerhard! Hey! We gotta stop!" I howled.

Sprinting, if you're out of practice, is vertiginous. Maybe he, balding, soft-bellied, Mittel-European bureaucrat, was beginning to feel it himself. Even if he was close to twenty years younger. Or maybe it had finally penetrated his dense Teutonic nut that Nick was way too far out in front of us now to make trying to catch him worthwhile.

I felt Gerhard's pace slacken.

"Down! Let's put it down," I urged. "'Kay?"

Fifty yards or so ahead of us, the Bedford's brake lights flashed.

I managed to hobble Gerhard to a halt and immediately unburden myself. Gerhard dropped his end too. We both stood bowed over the mat, hands on our knees, sucking for air.

I grimaced at him, then curled the edges of my mouth to transform it into a grin.

"You almost killed me," I wheezed.

"Yes?" he grinned back.

"Uh. Yeah. Whoa. Bizarre. I couldn't stop until *you* did!"

"And I think I'm having to stay along with *you*," he laughed. "You know? *Running* so fast."

Sweat was puddling in my armpits, trickling down my ribs. I took off my cap, blotted my streaming brow with my forearm and pinched the corners of my eyes alongside the bridge of my nose. The brine in my lashes stung when I blinked.

"You're kidding," I said. "It was all I could do to stay upright. Shwhoof. Am *I* out of shape!"

"Not so much, I think."

Reg and Nigel were well to the rear of us. They'd quit the chase a long time ago. They plodded along with their mat just ahead of the rest of the group, who were straggling toward us on their way to reboard the truck.

Laura and Renée and Emma and Ewan were bringing the two mats we'd left behind, I noticed.

At least I hadn't embarrassed myself with a middle-aged pratfall, I congratulated myself, before a bunch of witnesses. The women, especially.

In fact, I thought… for a man on the downside of his fifties, I'd cut a fairly nimble figure.

I straightened my back, squared my shoulders and threw out my chest to flatten my stomach.

"We left *those* guys in the dust, anyway, " I noted.

"You were an athlete?" Gerhard proposed.

"Of sorts, I guess," I acknowledged. "How about you?"

"Football, in school," he shrugged. "Soccer you call it, no? Now just some tennis, maybe."

My question had been a courtesy. He was tall like me—at six-three, I had him by about an inch, I judged—but his breasts and upper arms were soft, the mark of the office-bound. His physique wasn't that different from mine, truth be told, except that I'd had almost two additional decades to melt and redistribute the brawn. While he seemed reasonably coordinated, he didn't strike me as ever having been the jock type.

Then again, neither did the rest of our traveling companions.

Emma and Jen, of course, had the fitness of youth going for them.

Greta was a lean, leathery bird who'd appeared on the cabin cruiser's flying bridge in a high-cut bikini, performed a graceful swan dive into Lake Kariba, swum a mean crawl back to the stern ladder and then matter-of-factly shucked her bra to sunbathe her hard brown nipples on the foredeck, smoking one of the cheroots she favored.

But it was hard to figure out why the others had signed on to this particular expedition, which was geared to "active recreation." Exactly what had attracted Laura.

The role of travel planner had long since devolved on her. Her own first agenda had been to see the flora and fauna of Southern Africa. Laura's grandfather had emigrated from Ireland to the Cape Colony as a young man; her grandmother had been South African of English stock—perhaps, though it had never been mentioned, and had only recently dawned on Laura, Jewish.

Laura's mother had been born in Durban, but bundled off with her parents to Los Angeles before memory formed. Any curious desire Laura had harbored to travel to the land of her maternal forebears had been suppressed out of political considerations during the era of *apartheid*.

Now, finally, in 1993, one could visit South Africa with an unsullied conscience.

But the prospect of taking in so vast a country adequately in the month we could each manage to carve out of our job responsibilities was daunting.

Laura knew I hated canned tours. And she herself wasn't averse to the physical diversions that were my idea of vacation fun. In the nine years we'd been together—seven married—we'd rafted the Salmon and Rogue, climbed the Grand Teton, dived and snorkled the reefs off the Honduran Bay Islands, skied the glacial powder of British Columbia, kayaked the islands off Acadia National Park and backpacked to a variety of remote trout streams so I could trim the bordering brush with dry flies.

We'd begun to moderate our exertions, though. Laura had broken an ankle on Sierra scree a year ago. My pelvic joints were inexorably locking up. So this trip to comparatively less-traveled countries in the south African region, featuring participatory but catered camping and intervals for self-directed adventure, had looked like an ideal combination of interests.

Besides that day of canoeing, Laura and I had spent a morning alongside the upper Zambezi tracking elephants and buffalo on horseback.

We'd wheeled above Victoria Falls in an ultralight.

We'd planned to raft the rapids churning through the gorge below, but the early-June water was still considered too dangerous by the outfitters.

Among entertainments to come would be a night SCUBA dive among the multi-hued fish of Lake Malawi.

Laura was very pleased with her choice, and repeatedly solicited my endorsement.

"You done good," I'd assured her. "Definitely."

Once we'd lugged all the mats back to the truck and everyone had clambered aboard, Gerhard, last in, hauled up the bottom half of the rear Dutch door. It was tethered by a rope and hinged at the base so that, with its two projecting inside shelves, it doubled as a ladder when unlatched and lowered in reverse.

There was a thump on the overhead, one of the riders up top signalling their readiness—Reg, probably. Alastair had joined him and Greta in the roof seat.

"All set?" Renée checked.

We grunted assent. She poked the buzzer: "1 ring = go."

Nick eased us underway again.

We hadn't traveled far before the tall grasses closed in.

The track had become little more than a footpath that essed among hummocks of brush overarched by flat-topped umbrella thorns. The surface was hard and level, and Nick, confidence bolstered by a previous passage, batted along pell-mell.

Yellow dust swirled in our wake. A blizzard of pulverized plant debris—shredded stalks, spikelets, leaves and pods—flurried around us and eddied into the compartment as our front fenders mowed a wider swath.

All of us in back, obviously, had had to snatch our legs inside. Even so, a tendril lashed my right shin and another whipped across my right forearm as I sat sideways on the high shelf. They left scratches punctuated by tiny beads of blood.

I licked my finger, swiped the blood away and slithered down onto the seat, retreating further into the interior of the truck for safety.

On my left, Jen was absorbed in a game of backgammon with Mel. The board rested on the stubby card table that folded into the aisle between them from the front bulkhead. Gerhard snuggled at Mel's side, offering advice on moves in response to her flirtatious wheedling. It was a pretty sickening spectacle.

On my right, Laura had her book open in her lap. She was reading Laurens Van der Post's *Venture to the Interior*, apparently ruminations on life set in motion by a trip to Malawi in the 1940s.

Renée was reading too—the most recent Danielle Steele, handed on to her by Mel.

Ewan was staring heavy-lidded at the blur of tawny undergrowth that passed for scenery.

Nigel, head lolling alarmingly at each jolt, had already drifted off.

I spread my legs wider against the truck's sway, sprang erect, seized the lip of the overhead rack like a subway strap and patted around for my own book—the second of three mysteries I'd grabbed during our layover at Heathrow.

On the plane From San Francisco I'd found myself utterly unable to penetrate Isak Dinesen's *Out of Africa*, which Laura had thoughtfully supplied me. I must admit it felt somewhat perverse, though, to be displacing myself imaginatively to South Florida while bucketing through the wilds of Zambia.

My neck itched at the jawline.

I rubbed my two-day-old stubble absently.

My armpits prickled.

Then my brow at the hairline. I'd taken off my cap.

I became conscious of the webbing between my fingers and toes.

It was as if I were in a jalapeno sweat: a mist of capsaicin suddenly seemed to be oozing through my pores.

I quenched a maddening tingle behind the back of my right knee... did the same on the inside of my right elbow... slapped at my whiskers again, where they rasped the tender skin of my jowl. I insinuated a finger under my belt and massaged the bare, suety bulge trapped by the waistband of my shorts, which suddenly stung.

I turned to Laura. "Uh-oh," I said.

"What."

The monosyllable dripped with uxorial annoyance. She pointedly flipped her book on its spine in her lap, shifted her weight and sighed. The gray wings of her chopped brown hair were pinned up by tortoiseshell barrettes on both sides. She lifted an arm, tanned, plump and firm as a garlic sausage, and delicately scratched behind her ear.

She hadn't had an opportunity to shave under her arms since Kariba, and I noticed the fine hairs reasserting themselves in the pallid triangle above the swell of her breast. She was built like a pulling guard, I'd once kidded her when I was feeling reckless: short, graceful, broad-shouldered and wide-hipped but narrow in the waist, her sturdy thighs and globular buttocks only beginning to be dimpled by cellulite. "Rubenesque" might be a fair descriptive if the subtraction of the "s" hadn't always bothered me. And if the term hadn't been so devalued by its use in personals ads as a euphemism for "grotesquely obese." (I know because I'd discounted it among a string of appealing qualifications and answered one of those ads after the split with my first wife.) Besides, there was certainly a lot more muscle under Laura's flesh than under that of Rubens' doughy nudes.

"This is it, I bet," I said. "Do you feel it?"

"What?"

"Itchy all of a sudden."

"Huh!" she replied.

Her fingers were busy at the vee of her top.

"I think we just got a dose of the buffalo grass."

She screwed up her face dubiously.

I'd been hesitant to voice the proposition. My symptoms were certainly subtle. Invoking the specter aloud risked touching off a hypochondriac reaction. Either in myself or in Laura, by suggestion.

Qualms to which she, typically, was oblivious.

"Renée!" she blurted. "Daniel says he thinks we just went through some buffalo grass."

She paused for authoritative corroboration or denial.

Renée looked up from her book with a small grin. She'd shared my reasoning, apparently. She nodded, expression turning empathetic.

"Really?" Laura exclaimed. "We did?"

Renée shrugged. "Little bit, probably. Best is to try to keep your mind off it."

She was reclining sideways on the bench seat, her back against the rear bin atop which were arrayed our water bottles. I'd noticed her periodically rubbing the tops of her feet and her bare shins with her heels.

"Yeah. I *am*," Laura acknowledged, "kind of...."

She wriggled demonstratively, capping it off with a shudder.

Mel suddenly squealed and leaped in her seat, scattering backgammon disks. She slapped awkwardly at her back, then turned to present it to Gerhard.

"Scratch me!" she urged him. "Under me strap there! In the middle, love? Augh! It's driving me bonkers!"

"Don't scratch!" Renée commanded. "If you can help it," she added more softly. "It only makes it worse."

Within minutes everyone had begun to murmur and squirm.

Because it was another in a series of exotic experiences—the derangements of the quotidian Laura and I had courted across three continents and eleven time zones, after all—I was as much intrigued by the phenomenon as discomforted.

At least for the first half-hour or so.

The irritation was mild at the onset. And my willpower was at full charge. If I studiously ignored each new synaptic alarm as soon as it shrilled, the sensation would gradually subside. Displacement also worked. When the compulsion to tear at a spot on my ankle, say, had become nearly overwhelming, I'd scrub at the palm of my hand or my flank. As much as possible I kept my fingernails out of the action. Fortunately, I'd clipped them to the quick in the ablution block—the washbasin-and-shower facility—at the camper park in Lusaka.

Others were having more difficulty. We'd all soon covered up. I'd put on my shirt and cranked the sleeves down despite the heat. Laura had layered a cotton jersey over her tanktop. Renée had draped a towel across her lap and tucked it under her thighs and calves. The rest of us except Ewan, who was already wearing his customary long pants, emulated her.

We joked and groaned and commiserated, trying to cajole those who were most visibly distressed.

That, of course, included Mel. She jittered and twitched and kept up a continuous reedy plaint in her broad north London accent.

But Laura too was struggling.

She'd gamely insisted on limping another fifteen miles after falling on the ridge north of Yosemite, soaked her ankle for two days in the creek we'd camped alongside and then bushwhacked back out to the car, twenty miles, without a murmur. All on a fractured fibula.

Being swarmed by invisible creepie-crawlies was another matter.

She sat rigid, close-fisted, knuckles white, grinding her molars and occasionally surrendering to a whimper. At one point she threw her head back and started panting breathily.

"Doesn't work any better now than it did when I had Lisa," she declared after a moment. She chuckled bitterly.

"Really?" I said.

I knew she'd used the Lamaze method. We'd never gone into the gory details, though. Like most husbands of my age, place and station, I'd been a participant with Susan, my ex-wife, in the "natural" birth of Megan and Christopher, our own two kids. I'd rubbed Susan's back, swabbed her brow, clocked her contractions, fed her ice cubes and cheered her on when it was time to push.

A few desperate sobbing fits and anguished howls aside, all had gone smoothly. And Susan had hardly let out a peep.

Small joke.

I pictured Laura in full, radiant bloom, pear-bellied, puffing, flushed with pain and panic. There's a poignancy about those images, when she was at the height of her beauty and I wasn't around. Instead, it had been skinny, bespectacled Larry, her mathematician then-husband, at her shoulder. Hopelessly inept if my jaundiced regard for him was any gauge. Self-absorbed, appalled. Maybe he hadn't even been there at all. Holed up in his Berkeley office, timorously anesthetizing himself in the ethers of ring theory.

"Was it tough?" I asked.

"Yep," she nodded.

"Huh!" I sympathized. "Want to tell me about it?"

"God, no!" she exclaimed.

"Didn't expect so," I said. "At least you've got something worse to compare this with, though. Put it in perspective."

"Mm. Great. Such a comfort, you are."

She dug at her upper arm, gray fingernails trailing pink welts.

I grabbed her wrist. "Stop! Don't!" I urged.

"Yaaangh!" she whinnied in theatric frustration.

There'd been an interval after the initial exposure when we'd all agreed the itching had abated. But almost as soon as we'd started to relax, the truck must have plowed through a new cluster. The misery rekindled. Intensified.

I heard four muffled rings through the cab wall. Nick slammed on the brakes, there were shouts and in a moment Reg, Greta and Alastair rattled at the door.

They climbed inside looking disheveled and dispirited. We edged apart to make room. They plopped down.

"Bloody awful," Alastair muttered. He was buttoned to the wattles, as usual, in a suntan safari jacket with a burgundy bandanna knotted jauntily at the collar. Except now it hung like a wadded rag and was nearly black with sweat.

"Won't find it much better down here, I'm afraid," said Jen.

Laura got up and reached across Renée for her water bottle. She glanced at Greta.

"Would you like a drink?" she asked.

Greta, scowling, gave her a dismissive jerk of the head.

"I was thinking maybe you guys were up above it, hopefully," Laura said. "I'd actually considered joining you."

"I don't wish to talk," Greta snarled.

She hunched into the corner across from Renée, hugging herself in misery, her floppy-brimmed khaki bush-hat tilted low over glaring eyes. And she didn't speak again during what certainly has to rank as one of the longest ninety minutes of my life.

But then, nobody had the temper or energy to say much.

Before Gerhard pushed the buzzer to get us underway again, we lowered and grommeted the plastic side windows, hoping to shut out whatever noxious substance was tormenting us. Maybe it was some kind of pollen, I theorized. Maybe the plant released a chemical when lacerated. Some gaseous allergen.

Rory had taken over the driving at the stop. He and Nick and Emma had sealed themselves tight behind the cab windows too, I noticed.

The passage eventually widened. And Rory had a lighter foot than Nick. But there seemed to be no avoiding the horrible itching, which beset us in wave after wave.

What's more, the heat inside the compartment was hellish. We were now slowly fricasseeing.

*F*atigue trumps fear and discomfort, so we'd slept, at least fitfully, that night at Nsefu.

Twice I'd had to creep out into the cold with Laura. She'd squatted by the tent while I'd peered into the shadows around us, on guard to....

...Do what? Ha! I mean... lions!

Once I'd clambered out to piss too. The soft murmurs of the men off by the guttering fire were some reassurance.

Near dawn a loud, feral noise roused us. We listened anxiously to the silence that followed. Not speaking, but both awake.

Next thing I knew light was filtering through the mosquito mesh and the voice of Rory was calling: "Up and off! Rise and shine, you lazy lot! Chibembe beckons. Hot showers. Cold Mosis."

I ached in every joint. But we'd survived our first night of known potential danger.

II. Inambao J. Muchitima, N.P.W.S., Box 15, Mfuwe, Zambia

It was nearly four in the afternoon by my watch when Rory halted. The truck idled at the edge of a broad, sandy riverbed into which the road descended sharply. Through the plexiglass we could see a few skeins of water, meandering among drifts of gravel. The vestigial main channel hugged the wooded far bank, where our route reappeared as a deeply rutted cleft only a little less steep than the flanking clay bluffs.

After a brief contemplation, Rory nosed the truck down the pitch and out onto the flat river-bottom.

We made it about fifteen feet.

In a way, this new setback came as a relief. We piled out into open space. There was no breeze, but the puddles and rivulets and our own instantaneously evaporating sweat gave the air a refreshing piquancy. Especially after we'd stripped off the contaminated outer clothing we'd been dissolving into.

A lush canopy of trees shaded both banks. The late afternoon sun was benign. It shone out of an almost cloudless sky, warming but not superheating the sand, which was soothingly abrasive between the toes. Bilharzia or no—a threat, I'd decided, that was pretty remote, while my itching was immediate and acute—I'd shucked my sandals.

Digging out the tires was hardly going to be a sterile procedure. In fact, rooting on all fours in the coarse, clammy bottom-grit—bare chested, bare legged, using bare hands and forearms to mine toward the buried universal joints—proved a wonderfully satisfying way to scratch large swatches of body without specifically contravening Renée's advice.

Four coltish preteenage boys ambled out of nowhere. As usual. Africans seemed to materialize and dematerialize as if beamed in on sci-fi transporter beams. Two of them carried sticks with nylon line knotted around the tip. The smallest of them toted a plastic bucket with gray water sloshing in its bottom.

"Good morning," smiled one, who looked to be about eleven. He bowed his head respectfully and extended his right hand, forearm propped with his left, to Gerhard, who was closest. The four of them then shuffled among us, carefully offering a palm to each of us as they bade us "good morning." Even Greta and Nick, his eyebrows beetled with worry as he busily assessed our predicament, couldn't begrudge them a smile and a handshake.

"*Jambo*," Nick said in Swahili.

"*Moni, bambo. Mulibwanji*," offered Rory, who'd actually taken the trouble to acquire a number of basic phrases in African languages.

The boys laughed uproariously. (I later learned his Chinyanja meant "good morning, father," as off-kilter as their own anachronistic greeting.)

Having successfully committed English—and pretty much exhausted their fluency, apparently—the four cozied alongside us, somberly considering our labors.

I dug half-heartedly for a while. Wallowing in the sand, as I've noted, at least eased the ceaseless itching temporarily. But my sciatic nerve was inflamed now. And whenever I flexed my back a certain way I'd get a disconcerting tweak deep between the shoulder blades: relic of the sand-mat relay.

I'd done more than my share to extricate us from that last predicament, I reasoned. And frankly, I hadn't paid a couple of thousand dollars to spend my vacation working as a volunteer navvy for Mamba Safaris. Let the hired hands who'd gotten us into this mess get us out.

A young man in his early twenties trudged over on rubber flipflops from the far bank. His shorts were drab and frayed but above them was a crisply pressed forest-green shirt with military creases, flap pockets and some kind of emblem on the sleeve.

"Good day. Hello. *Jambo. Moni,*" he said, echoing each of our acknowledgements pleasantly, dipping his head.

Reg climbed back into the truck and emerged with a handful of hard candies and balloons. He distributed them among the boys, who happily parroted the lead-linguist's "thank you, sir."

Reg had been broadcasting treats like these from the roof seat until Nick had ordered him to stop. None of us except Greta, who'd become his accomplice in the sport, had immediately understood why children on the Matabeleland roadsides seemed to be waving up at us with such frantic glee. And why, glancing back, we'd see them scrambling in our wake, shouting, swooping, converging like seagulls to squabble over scraps of jetsam on the potholed asphalt.

"Just 'avin' a bit of a lark," Reg mumbled defensively when Nick confronted him in camp one night about what he'd finally noticed in the rearview mirror.

"They're not monkeys in a zoo," Nick scowled.

"Little *sweet!*" Reg argued. "Toy *balloons!* No damage in that, innit? Nippers like 'em."

"It's not right, white people, like, feedin' the inmates," Nick explained. "Pitchin' sweets and cheap trinkets to the 'natives.'"

"It's degrading," Renée seconded.

"Sends a wrong message to the kids," Nick went on. "Y' know? Encourages 'em to be, like, beggars."

"We di' it in Tanzania, innit? Whole way through. Two years ago," Reg maintained.

This was his third safari vacation.

"Well, not on my truck we don't," Nick declared.

But this was a different situation. And Nick and the crew were preoccupied.

When the boys started blowing up the balloons, belling their cheeks, trumpeting raspberries, guffawing and weaving dizzily underfoot, the young man in the green shirt stepped forward and admonished them in Chinyanja. He waved them away.

They grumbled formulaically, displaying their independence, but retreated to savor their booty.

"I am sorry," he said in a soft, lilting voice to Laura, who was standing closest to him. She and I were taking a breather. "They are bad boys."

"Oh, not at all," Laura replied. "They've been extremely well behaved, really."

After a moment's silence, he bowed his head at the truck. "Where do you," he asked hesitantly, "come from?"

"Well, we were in Lusaka day before yesterday," she said. "Last night we were bush-camping. We started out in Vic Falls…Victoria Falls. In Zimbabwe? Now we're on our way to Chibembe? If we ever get across here."

He nodded. The blank courtesy in his expression, though, made me wonder how much he'd understood. After a moment's silence he said, "You are from... South Africa?"

"Oh. No," Laura said. "No, actually. Most people here are from England. The company, the truck, is English."

"Ah. English," he repeated thoughtfully. I had the impression his geography was sketchy. Clearly he wasn't adept at distinguishing *mzungu* accents.

"The U.K.," I amplified, thinking that might be a more familiar political term in a former colony.

"But we're Americans," Laura declared, "my husband and I." She indicated me with a bob of the head.

"We also have one person from Australia." She pointed at Renée. "One from Germany, one from Denmark except she lives in Spain. One from Scotland. We're a very cosmopolitan bunch, really. From all over the world."

He stood in silent contemplation. He had a handsome, open face, with high cheekbones and a patrician brow. His hair was cropped uniformly around delicate ears. He reminded me a bit of a young Harry Belafonte, though his features were broader, less Ethiopian, and his complexion was a couple of shades darker. Kind of a cordovan.

I'd always heard that Africans were very black, and in France and Norway I'd seen a few of an ebony, a midnight black, that was arresting. The Zambians and Zimbabweans we'd encountered, however, would have blended unremarkably on any Oakland street corner. Except that you seldom saw a six-footer. This young man was maybe five-nine.

"Americans," he repeated after a moment.

"The United States," I again specified. "U.S.A."

As a sophisticated world traveler, I'm sensitive to the equal continental claims of Canadians and Mexicans, not to mention Guatemalans, Hondurans, Belizeans, Nicaraguans, Costa Ricans, Salvadorans, Panamians… did I miss anybody? And then, of course, there are the *South* Americans.

"You-Ess-Ay. That is very far," he proposed.

"It is very far," I agreed. "Many thousands of miles. Very long trip on a plane. Several planes."

I was reminded of our missed connections, the grueling detour as a result and the desultory waits in Schiphol and

Frankfurt. We'd dined on that woeful tale of international aviation snafu for several days after our arrival.

"We come from California," Laura said.

"California," he nodded. I thought he sounded a bit tentative, though.

"San Francisco," she persisted. "Have you heard of that place? It's a city. In the state of California."

"San Francisco. San Francisco... Forty-Niners!" He beamed and drew his finger across his chest. "On some... singlets, I see."

"Yes. That's where we're from," Laura said, imprecisely.

"What is Forty-Niners? Someone has told me it is a... football side?"

"Yes, a team, a side," I affirmed. "*American* football, though. It's different from... Zambian football. World Cup! In American football, the ball is long."

I tried to indicate the shape with my hands.

"Not round. You throw it?" I mimed a pass. "More like rugby."

"Yes. They are very good, the San Francisco side?"

"Very good," I said. "They are the champions many years. Like Zambia, in your football."

"Yes. Our side has been all killed, however. Now we have new players."

He looked slightly apologetic, for them, or for the situation.

"What's that about?" Laura frowned.

"The whole Zambian national soccer team was killed in a plane crash a while back," I explained. "You weren't aware?"

"I wouldn't have asked if I were," she snipped, "would I?"

"Well, it was big news when it happened," I said. "All but one guy, who missed the trip. I think they were on their way to play in the Africa Cup or something. They were favorites, too. Right up there on a par, supposedly, with the Italys and Argentinas. Brazils. An emerging powerhouse. Very good, very good."

I eyed the young man to see if he could recognize my praise. If my account was reasonably accurate.

"It was a national tragedy," I added.

Laura accorded him a little moan of sympathy.

"That is terrible," she said. "That's sad."

"Yeah," I agreed dutifully.

"Are you a fan?" I asked him. "A football supporter?"

"Yes," he said. But it lacked conviction.

We lapsed into silence.

I watched the muscles play in Renée's back and upper arms as she helped Rory swing the sand-mats down from their brackets on the truck side. She had an ideal figure—square shoulders and nipped waist connected by a vertical dimple of spine that plunged suggestively toward her firm buns. Their cleavage was swaddled under baggy shorts. She never dressed provocatively, only straight-forwardly for the climate in contemporary recreational style. So in fact, her nipples were softly discernible when she turned: she was down to a white jogging bra now. Her bare midriff and flushed upper chest between neckline and collarbone were crusted with sand. Her hair was pulled up into a slatternly topknot. She had a smudge of dirt on one cheek. Sweat accentuated her downy mustache. Sometimes when women sweat they give off a heady estrogenic fragrance. I considered returning to help.

"Why do you come to Zambia?" the young man asked Laura.

"Well, to see it!" Laura replied. "See the animals, the game. The country." She swept the vista of riverbed and forest with her hand. She almost completed a pirouette. "It is very beautiful."

"Although," I offered, "I could do without the buffalo grass."

"Yes!" Laura exclaimed. "Do you know what we're speaking about? 'Buffalo grass?'"

She'd fallen into a formal mode, her enunciation precise, almost British. She had a tendency to do that—subconsciously adopt accents and speech patterns of people she fell into conversation with. I sometimes teased her about it.

"We have all been itching from it, quite like mad, for hours," she frowned.

"I am sorry...," he said.

"Not as sorry as we are," I murmured to Laura. "'Quite like mad.' I like that."

"Oh, it's... shut up!" she chided, nudging me with her elbow. "No, it's just a bit annoying," she assured him. "That's all."

I chuckled. "*You* say that."

"You *are* sorry."

The staccato exchange didn't appear to have registered on the young man. Which we'd intuitively been banking on, I guess, to palliate the *sotto voce* impoliteness.

He shook his head. "...I do not know... this grass," he continued.

"'Buffalo grass?' That's what we were told," Laura insisted. "Very itchy, on the skin."

She earnestly scratched her forearms by way of demonstration.

"Ah. Ah. Buffalo *beans*?"

"They make you itch?"

He nodded vigorously. "Yes! Buffalo beans! '*Itchy* beans!' I have heard some people saying that. Also... 'hell-fire beans.'"

"Really?"

"Boy, that's bang on," I exclaimed.

"Very bad. Very bad feeling." He grinned. He turned it into an exaggerated grimace and sucked air through his teeth.

"But why? What is it about them...?" I wondered.

"What do they look like?" Laura refined the point. "Do you know? So we can avoid them?"

"Yes, yes. I will show you," he said.

He turned and strode to the near bank.

Laura and I and two of the boys followed in train. They'd cheekily edged back into our orbit to eavesdrop.

The undergrowth was thick on either side of the track where it sloped into the riverbed. Our informant paced along the downstream margin, peering into the welter of head-high grasses and waspy brushwood. The patch on his sleeve, I now saw, bore an embroidered tree and the letters "N.P.W.S." After a moment he stopped and reached in gingerly to grasp the woody stalk of a liana. He slowly separated a branch from the tangle and gentled it toward us for inspection.

Laura and I crowded at his shoulder. The plant had small leaves interspersed with clusters of slender green pods. Each pod was about three inches long and covered with a dense sorrel fuzz.

"This is the buffalo bean," he grinned. "Itchy bean."

"Itchy bean! *Inde!*" the boys chorused gaily. "Itchy bean! *Chitedze.*"

"What are they saying?" I asked.

"*Chitedze,*" he repeated. "That is our word for it. In *Chinyanja.* See. Look."

He beckoned to one of the boys and murmured to him. The boy shuffled around us and handed over the crude fishing rod he'd been cradling. Our new friend was holding the liana well away from his body but now he arched his back—we gave way—so that his arm was at full extension. He gently poked the butt of the stick at one of the pods. The air around it instantaneously glinted with tiny, translucent bristles.

The boys squealed. They danced away from us, well out of range, chortling hilariously. "*Chitedze! Cho-ipa!*"

"*Cho-ipa.* Very bad," the young man grinned. "You see?"

He too had flinched at the extraordinary starburst of filaments. He released the stalk, shielding us as he shrank back. More pods fired from within the quivering underbrush.

"That is what...." He stroked the back of his wrist with the pads of his fingers. "... Is feeling bad." He switched to tapping his wrist. "They are... coming in. Into the...."

"Skin," Laura supplied.

"Yes, yes," he nodded. "The skin. Like fire. Like...." He frowned. With thumb and forefinger he pantomimed sewing. "I cannot remember. *Nzingano.* This thing?"

"A needle?" Laura said.

"Yes, yes. Needle. Needles. Very small. Very bad. We say, '*Abwa, nko-kakata ako.*' It is itching quite badly."

"Uh-*huh!*" I nodded. The head plays a large part in halting conversations between foreigners, I've found. "Yes, little needles. Huh!"

I pushed my prescription sunglasses up off my nose and brought the back of my hand as close to my eyes as they'd focus. I squinted at the pocked surface, tilted my wrist to see if I could throw into relief any of the nearly microscopic quills that might be lodged among the sunbleached hairs. I couldn't distinguish any. Even though my flesh was still a hotbed of random galvanic discharges.

"In old days people are eating these beans also, when they are very hungry," the young man said. "But you must cook them many times. In water? And each time you must throw away the water. If you do not, they will make you very sick."

"I wouldn't doubt," I said.

We strolled back toward the truck. The rear axles had now been excavated and Rory and Nick were scrambling about refining the placement of the sand-mats.

"There is a story. Once the *maNgoni* people are coming to a village of the *mChewa*. These are people who are fighting. They are...."

He butted his fists together.

"Enemies," I contributed.

"Yes, enemies," he nodded. "In the old times. And the *maNgoni*, the soldiers, they are finding some of these *chitedze* in a pot. And they are eating them, and they are falling down."

He hunched his shoulders and clutched his belly.

"Their stomachs are hurting, very very bad. They cannot fight. And the *mChewa* are coming back and beating them. They are killing them, I think, maybe." He shrugged. "It is a story I have heard."

"Very interesting," I said.

Through the near cab window I saw Nick's profile joggle into view as he slid behind the steering wheel.

I inclined my head at the young man's sleeve. "En, Pee, Double-ewe, Ess," I read aloud.

"National... Park... and... Wildlife... Service," he translated meticulously, glancing down at the gold embroidery.

I flared my eyebrows. "That's who you work for?"

"Yes."

"Are we in the park, then?" Laura piped up hopefully. She pointed at the sand we stood on.

"Oh no. It is... some kilometres."

"Oh. So how much longer to get to Chibembe, do you think?"

"Ah." He glanced at the truck. "Chibembe. Some hours." He shrugged.

"Hm," Laura responded with a disappointed fall.

Nick started the engine. I realized I should probably lend a hand in shuffling the sand-mats. This time, though, I was not going to get involved in any steeplechases. And I was going to be sure to be the one bringing up the rear. I quickened my pace.

I could've saved myself the effort. By the time I'd circled behind Reg, the safest partner to enlist with, I'd decided, in the sandmat brigade, the truck was once again resting on its U-joints. The rear tires had refused to mount the mats and had simply bulldozed them aslant. The leading edge of the one on the right had tipped upward and jammed against some protuberance on the undercarriage.

"Stop!" Renée had shouted. Those around her on the right side had taken up the cry of alarm.

The steel mat, wedged between the spinning tire and the chassis, had crimped and bent inward at the stress point before Nick relented. He backed off on the revs and let the engine die.

The sudden quiet was, suddenly, disquieting.

Nick swung out of the cab without a word. His unshaven jaw was set so tightly the sinews pulsed all the way up to his temples. He seized one of the folding shovels, glared at the mound of sand churned up around the bent and pinioned sand-mat, then threw himself on his knees and started digging. Renée eyed him for an instant and, just as wordlessly, fell to work beside him.

"Anybody else but me developin' a thirst?" Rory sang out.

He snatched up the entrenching tool he'd discarded, its blade set perpendicular to the shaft. He began hoeing with a will at the sand engulfing the other rear tire.

"There's a beautiful bar at Chibembe," he chanted. "Looks right out on the river. Y' can watch the hippos and the crocs

hippin' and crockin', whilst y' sit and sip a nice cold *Mosi*. That's
the beer round here. *Mosi moa*. Good beer, they say. It is, too. Or
whatever's your pleasure. Gin and tonic? Watchin' the sun go
down? I'm shoutin' the first round! Wouldn't want to miss that
sunset, though, now would we?"

Needless to say, we wouldn't.

But, of course, we did.

The clouds that had begun to puff up low along the horizon
to our left were tinged with lavender and rose before we'd inched
even as far as the river channel. Nick later admitted he'd come
close to despair.

"Couple of times I was on the verge," he said. "Just start
walkin' back. Only thing for it, I reckoned. Leave Rory and
Renée wi' you lot and go find a telephone. Closest one prob'ly in
Petauke. Ring up Mamba and have 'em send out another lorry,
wi' a winch."

That would have meant an unscheduled encampment in this
forlorn reach of bush of at least two days, I figured. The nearest
dispatch point for a rescue vehicle would have to have been
Lilongwe, if not Harare. We'd have been a fairly restive and
unpleasant company, I feared, by the time of our deliverance had
that exigency come to pass. I couldn't see Mel or Laura, for
example, acceding with great grace to the solace to be found in a
wry, "Hey, it's Africa!" (We'd already heard that explanation for
misadventure or incompetence voiced with a sigh, a shrug and a
sardonic eyebrow-wiggle more than once.)

Which lent a certain nervous urgency to our crew's toils.

And indeed, by dint of perseverance, we did finally succeed in
squaring the Bedford atop four sand-mats. A couple of
middle-aged local men had splashed out to us from across the

channel; with Nick's assent, they'd assembled scraps of driftwood to weave into the troughs we were gouging anew for the tires. Nick had pried the bent mat free and Rory had softened the acuity of its angle by turning it over and recruiting several of us to stand on it and flex our knees with him a couple of times, applying our weight. The truck flattened it further as, mat by mat, we began to pontoon across the mushy riverbottom.

This time Nick proceeded at a chary first-gear creep. All of us, including the two volunteers and even the young man in the N.P.W.S. shirt, pitched in with growing jubilance to shunt the mats forward.

The river was only a little above the knees at mid-channel. My knees, a woman's thighs. The final approach was across a spine of gravel lumpy enough to be painful under bare soles. The mats were now at least temporarily unnecessary. I trudged back to retrieve my sandals.

While the truck idled, Nick, Rory and various others waded the ford, carefully toeing the bottom to assess its firmness. The sand was striated with pebbles and seemed compact enough. The biggest problem, it was obvious, was going to be the last obstacle, the bank. It was pure clay: leather-hard near the surface and packed toward the crest but gelatinous at water's edge. Already it was scored by old tire tracks that were a good foot deep. There was no alternative but to climb out over the established roadway, which rose steeply to curve between a thick, badly scarred tree on the left and an even more massive, partially charred stump on the right.

A small crowd—maybe two dozen men, women and children—now congregated at the top of the track, cheerfully watching us.

"Is there a village around here?" I inquired of my newfound friend.

"Oh, yes," he nodded. He waved his hand vaguely at the dense trees off to the right. "Just there."

Except for the road, we appeared to be in untrammeled wilderness—what I would call jungle if I didn't associate that word with palm trees. No clearings or dwellings were in evidence. "And what tribe...?" I asked. The word suddenly struck me as condescending. I wondered if it was an affront to Africans, as, perhaps, was styling their communities "villages" and their deciduous forests "jungles." Westerners don't, after all, talk of the Dutch tribe or the Danish tribe.

"What group?" I amended the question. "Do the people of this... place...belong to? What do they call themselves?"

"We are the Kunda," he said equably. "*mKunda.*"

"Ah." I tried to reproduce his initial nasal hum. "*MKunda?*"

"MKoohndah," he repeated crisply, tightening the slack in my vowel.

"Does that mean you're from here too?"

"Yes. This is my home."

"But you must work in some other place. I presume. If the park is far from here."

"Yes. I am stationed at Mfuwe."

I had no idea where whatever he'd said was. I was impressed, however, by the military verb *stationed.*

"I am on holiday," he explained. "I have come for *maliro* this night. Many people are coming here, from many places."

He lifted his arm and stirred the air with his downturned palm to indicate a broad region.

"What is *maliro?*" I asked.

He shrugged. "That is Chinyanja. I have forgotten how to say in English. A big woman has just died. A crocodile has taken her."

"Really?" I exclaimed in astonishment.

He nodded gravely.

"A crocodile?"

"Yes."

"How does that *happen*? They come in the house?"

"She was washing, I believe. Her clothing? Just there."

He pointed upriver. A woman with her skirt tucked around her knees was even now standing ankle-deep in the water collecting garments that had been draped over bushes on the bank to dry.

"Oh, my gosh!" I glanced down at the turbid current flowing around my calves. Both of us were standing off to the side of the truck, in the river. "Crocodiles are in here, this water?"

"Oh, yes," he said.

I winced theatrically and scanned the opaque surface around us. Blood suddenly thumped behind my eardrums. My toes were invisible eighteen inches down. I restrained the urge to flounder backwards, scramble for dry ground. Rationally, I couldn't imagine a crocodile wriggling into lunging-distance without my seeing it. Not in water this shallow. Anyway, a number of village men were now milling in the river among us unconcernedly. And there was that woman alone upstream, blithely piling laundry into her arms.

Man-eating reptiles were a routine hazard of life here in Africa, I supposed. Like the automobiles that occasionally careen around suburban street corners in California. Every once in while, through ill luck or inattention, someone falls casualty— gets winnowed out of the herd.

"Gee, that's scary," I said. "How old was she?"

"She was... old. Maybe...." He shrugged, giving up on the attempt to estimate. "Old. She was a big woman, like...."

He'd said that before. The image of a stout African crone being dragged screaming down the bank, muttony leg vised in the corrugated maw of a giant lizard, flashed across my mind.

"...A chief, you would say," he amplified.

"But she did her own laundry."

He ignored the comment. "Everyone is very sad," he said.

"I can imagine," I said. I'd begun to edge back toward the gravel bar. "I guess you have to keep your eyes open around here all the time."

I'm not sure he understood the idiom.

"Incidentally," I said, "my name is Daniel." I tapped my breastbone. "Daniel Schuman." I didn't extend my hand but poised it in case he did.

He bowed his head in acknowledgement. "I am James," he reciprocated.

I bowed in turn. "Pleased to meet you, James," I said. "My wife...."

I indicated Laura with my chin. She stood several yards downstream—unknowing crocodile bait—chatting with a big-bellied, middle-aged local in a threadbare khaki shirt-jac. "...Is called Laura."

"Yes," he agreed. Perhaps she'd already introduced herself.

"So," I said. "*Maluri?* That's a ceremony of some sort?"

He stared at me.

"*Maliro!*" he abruptly understood. "Yes, yes."

"Kind of a memorial service," I guessed.

"Yes, I think."

"Did they find her body? Was she eaten?"

"Yes," he said. I wasn't certain which of my questions he was answering.

"Gruesome," I muttered.

"Tell me something, please," he said. "I have heard.... Is it true?" He grinned quizzically. "The... president? Of U.S.A.? Is a film star?"

It took me a couple of beats to figure out the reference. Not only was the *non sequitur* jarring, but I was distracted by the implications. This was the obsolete factoid that had lodged in the mind of a bright young African as the salient feature of my country. Along with a pro football team.

I was trying to compose a comprehensible explanation for the phenomenon of Ronald Reagan, and the march of American constitutional government that had brought... how many comparatively pallid successor Administrations? ...when Nick revved the Bedford's engine.

To my surprise, he started backing slowly away from the channel.

Good grief, I thought, were we giving up? At this late stage?

Renée stood by the sand-mats semaphoring at Nick's face in the rearview mirror. When she flashed her upraised palms, he halted. He shifted gears, gunned the motor, refocussed his attention through the windshield at Rory—who was in midstream waving people out of the way—and bucked forward across the gravel bar, accelerating.

The truck barreled into the water and steamed toward the far bank, a miniature sidewheeler, tires beating a muddy froth. Nick kept his momentum. We all watched intently, rooting....

The cab abruptly surged. Freeboard deepened under the bow. The front treads clawed at the slick embankment.

But the Bedford's pug snout began to yaw. The rear tires, still half submerged, spun faster. Fat bubbles of drowned exhaust boiled at the wallowing stern. The engine sirened to a helpless howl.

All four tires whirred in place.

Shit, shit, shit.

Stuck again.

I flopped my head, compressed my lips and purged my lungs through my nose. I was suddenly aware of the dryness of my mouth and the hollowness of my stomach.

I don't handle that well—anger readily ignites the fumes in my gut-chamber if I let the contents get down too close to empty. Especially at this hour. I eyed my wristwatch grimly: a quarter to six already, dusk looming, and the prospect of dinner— anywhere, let alone in the civilized ambience of the Chibembe resort restaurant, as I pictured it—now indefinitely deferred.

For all my dogging it... or, let's rephrase that, for all my judicious avoidance of excessive exertions, my prudent husbanding of finite physical resources... my back was one hell of a lot sorer now than it had been when Nick and Rory had blundered us into this pit of despond.

I was still tormented by nagging itches from our hapless ramble through the buffalo beans. This was all very colorful—an "African adventure," I supposed, as touted in the Mamba brochures. But the titillation was wearing awfully damn thin.

I noticed the little soapstone amulet resting on my chest: an elongated triangle, like an arrowhead, punctured by two holes to create a stylized serpent's neck and a gaping maw from which projected two curved fangs. Rudimentary eyes, nostrils and the helical coil of a tail had been incised in the soft gray mineral.

I'd been told it represented some powerful water god of the Zambezi. The designation *nyaminyami* was a corruption of the deity's real name in Shona, or Ndebele, or—I couldn't remember exactly—baTonka, maybe. Anyway, the language of one of the riverine tribes flooded out by construction of the Kariba Dam.

Something like fifty Italian workers had been killed in the course of that massive multinational hydroelectric project, I'd read. Their deaths were popularly attributed to the wrath of the discommoded spirit. Wearing the icon, of course, would presumably curry the god's favor. He—she, it—didn't seem to be all that well disposed, however, to our efforts to transit this particular watercourse.

Or maybe I had it backwards. That's the trouble with talismans: bad as things may get, you can never be sure they wouldn't have been all the worse had you not been air-bagged by the charm's aura.

"*Mami*," the fat man observed cordially to Laura, "I think you are spending the night here."

Having delivered himself of that pessimistic assessment, though—which Laura relayed to me a moment later, too beguiled by the honorific to be as appalled as I was by the prospect—he immediately set about contravening it.

Despite his unprepossessing appearance, it turned out, this paunchy guy in need of a shave and some bridgework and a few buttons resewn on his stained shirt was no less a personage than the village headman. Or so Nick would eventually be informed. And by some subtle signal, some cock of grizzled head or purposive hitch of salt-and-pepper-stubbled double chins, he'd soon marshalled nine or ten beefy constituents to shoulder in around the truck.

They injected a vigor we *azungu* had long since been sapped of. By now even Nick and Rory and Renée were flagging. Not that they weren't still groveling gamely in the muck.

You could tell Nick was weary—his air of morose authority had waned into something like benignity. He'd run out of commands to issue. When the village men proposed, he just showed them a resigned, slightly dubious smile and hiked a shoulder in acquiescence.

But our helpers were respectful of protocol. They checked with Nick regularly as they dug and pried, scampered off to retrieve the sand-mats and then began amassing heavy branches from some cache of firewood. That, at least, was where I assumed people had to be getting the sizeable limbs and small logs they were suddenly hauling down the bank. Probably stockpiled for the event I'd been told was in the offing.

I pictured a central bonfire surrounded by dancers. Maybe doing the mazurka. The *mZurka*. (I've always tended to mangle languages in which vowels predominate. Not that I'm any better with languages where consonants predominate. Like Czech or Serbian, for example.)

Maybe there'd be a pyre, on which the remains of the unfortunate crocodile victim would be consumed. There was some consolation in the possibility that if we did have to spend the night here we'd be afforded a peep at an interesting cultural spectacle—presumably a slice of aboriginal African life that Westerners aren't often privy to.

Emma had tweaked our expectation of such serendipity with a story about an impromptu invitation to a Masai wedding she and her safari-mates had received on the second night after her arrival in Africa, while bush-camping in Kenya.

Off they'd all trooped through the dark, led by a pair of tipsy, nearly naked, painted warriors carrying spears, who'd stumbled on their tents in the Masai Mara plain. The tour leader was apprehensive; but it wasn't a ruse, a robbery setup. The welcome was genuine.

Emma and her spunky companions had lingered among the festive tribespeople until dawn, she said, coughing through the dust raised by the intricate nuptial choreography, politely choking

65

down cocktails of blood and milk passed to them in communal goblets hot from the cow, and, if I recalled correctly, getting furry-brained on beer fermented from something like millet and human spit.

I wasn't at all sure I'd have the stomach for such heroic abnegation in avoidance of giving offense. (And why is it always Westerners, I'd wondered, who have to suppress the gag response out of deference to their savage hosts' sensibilities? Why can't we just pinch our nostrils and decline the offered swill with the same righteous snicker of culture-bound disgust and incredulity you knew you'd get if the tables were turned: "Here, have a little of this—it's ground-up pig snouts and sodium nitrite encased in a length of swine bowel." Any doubt you'd be ducking an instantaneous spit-take?)

I was pretty confident, though, that the Kunda wouldn't be challenging us with concoctions as absurdly weird as those favored by the Masai. Who, after all, are nomadic cattle-herders, like Lapps and Touaregs; their disinclination to establish a fixed address helps them cling to eccentric ancient ways.

These folks around us might be living a more or less aboriginal life-style too—mealie-meal *nsima* boiled like grits over a cookfire for breakfast and dinner, no electricity, no indoor (or for that matter, outdoor) plumbing, no phone lines strung to their huts—but they weren't primitives. I wouldn't have been altogether surprised to learn that the headman had a Land Rover or an African Mercedes parked in his breezeway. Almost certainly the local chief did.

Third World they were, impoverished relatives to the First. And rural. But not rustic.

As evidenced by the assurance with which this team of villagers slapped together a serviceable tangle of corduroy road, aligned the sand-mats atop it, scrummaged at the truck's rear to apply added leverage and whooped and whistled Nick up the embankment.

It did take three assaults. But at each stage—ground gained hearteningly toward the crest, then another disheartening skid to a stall—the men hurled themselves into the necessary mud-sculpture and timber-reengineering with undamped ebullience.

There was only so much space around the truck. Like the other passengers, I diddled here and there, showing my willingness to contribute but not really contributing much. Nick, Rory and Renée, of course, had an ownership-stake in the process, as it were. They persisted in the thick of the labor—each carried along as a sort of honorary foreman on the tide of the Samaritans' agenda. Which is what these guys truly were; they'd unstintingly taken on our problem as their problem. And in what at the outset would have seemed miraculous time—less than ninety minutes, I reckoned—they'd conquered it.

The truck slithered uphill the last few yards toward the stump that marked the right flank of the road, crunched against its charred lip, then pivoted on that fulcrum as Nick resolutely feathered the gas-pedal. The tweenwheels storage lockers scraped free.

We all erupted in cheers as the truck topped the hump—a warble of joy and relief from the thirteen frazzled whites who were back in business at last, the watching black women and children whose communal water tap, tub, sink and laundromat was now rid of this hulking contaminant, the mud-caked men who'd dashed toward the rear bumper without regard to peril when the wheel-well threatened to hang up on that last spur, then danced away in self-defense and triumph.

Nick raced down the track about fifty feet, enough to convince himself the level surface was reliable again. Then he braked and swung out of the cab. Subdued as ever, he strode back toward us. Any impulse to celebrate was contained behind a stern mask of responsibility.

"Let's go, then," he snapped. "Rory? See to the sand-mats? Renée! Shovels back aboard, right? Anything else? Give a good look about you, everyone! If you want to go to the loo, now's your chance. Don't plan on stops for a while. We've not much light left, but with luck we might still be able to make it to the gate before it closes."

This time I stuck my hand out to James. Or Inambao, perhaps more authentically. "Inambao J. Muchitima, N.P.W.S., Box 15, Mfuwe, Zambia."

That's what he'd jotted in brisk caps in the little spiral notebook I'd dug out of my shorts pocket a few minutes earlier. He'd shyly asked me if I had something on which to write my name for him. I did, along with Laura's, and our address. After ripping out the damp page, I'd handed him the notebook and pen along with it.

"Please. Would you do the same for me?" I'd requested.

I'd been an indifferent Boy Scout, but I'd learned to travel well equipped. Weighting my left side pocket was a folding stainless steel knife/screwdriver/wirecutter/pliers set—a "survival tool" in outdoor outfitter jargon—that I'd found handy for disassembling clogged backpacking stoves and flattening the barbs on dry flies when local rules specified catch-and-release.

In my right pocket rode a scarlet-handled Swiss Army knife for paring cheese, tweezing splinters, poking loose the gristle lodged between molars, opening tin cans, boring extra holes into leather belts and twisting the corks out of winebottles.

My cargo-style shorts also had four patch pockets with buttoned flaps. Only the left rear was empty. The right held the blue bandanna with which I wiped the teardrop lenses of the prescription sunglasses that hung on an adjustable cord around my neck. In the left front was a butane cigarette lighter, for starting fires without matches, and a folding compass with mirror, for signalling to rescue aircraft and checking the progress of the gray beard I was letting grow. In the right, the pen and notebook. They were obligatory. I considered myself a writer, even though for years all I'd done was edit and approve press releases.

Inambao J. Muchitima—J. for James?—had just supplied its first entry.

Nick, meanwhile, was quietly folding a wad of *kwacha* into the headman's palm. It was a contribution to the community coffers, he specified, in appreciation for the roadside assistance.

The headman was very grateful, Nick reported, since staging the funeral—that's all *maliro* meant, apparently—entailed a lot of expense.

Laura had gone looking for the long-sleeved red jersey she'd peeled off upon our arrival at the river. She'd intended to throw it in the truck but had forgotten. It did not turn up. Universal honesty among people so poor, given such blatant temptation, could hardly have been expected, we rationalized.

"Well, goodbye," I said, squeezing James' slim hand. "It was a pleasure to meet you. I have enjoyed talking with you."

"Thank you for helping us so much," Laura exclaimed. "All of you. You have been wonderful. We couldn't have gotten out without you."

"I will write you a letter," I promised, "from America."

I patted the pocket that held the notebook. I felt the barrel of the pen and realized I'd tucked it away automatically as I'd peered at what he'd printed, searching for sociological insights— scrutinized his penmanship, defter than mine, and the unexpected appearance of a first name that looked almost

Portuguese in place of the prosaic English name by which he'd introduced himself.

I had three boxes of ballpoint pens in my locker under the truck bench. We'd packed them along after having been advised that they were valuable barter items in Africa. Indeed, our *nyaminyamis* had been bought after much haggling for three pens each. Laura had thrown in six pens and the pair of old sandals on her feet to acquire, for fifty Zim dollars (less than ten bucks U.S.), a big, beautifully crocheted tablecloth from one of the women selling their handicrafts at the Kariba Dam scenic overlook.

"Here, you keep this," I said to James, fishing up the pen and extending it to him. "I've got another one."

His eyes glittered and he accepted the gift without even a sham equivocation.

"Thanks for showing us what buffalo beans are," Laura noted.

"How do you say 'thank you' in Chinynanja?" I asked.

"*Zikomo*," he said. He bowed to me. "*Zikomo*."

Jen, Mel and Gerhard filed past us, on their way to the truck.

I thought of giving James a picture of himself as an additional souvenir. Polaroids had proved very popular with the roadside crowds to whom I'd been handing them out—modest reparations, I'd proposed to Laura, for all the images of *them* she and the others were expropriating through the lenses of their thirty-five-millimeter cameras.

But there wasn't time now to rustle up the Polaroid from the depths of the truck-locker. Anyway, James was fairly sophisticated. He probably wouldn't be so dazzled to see his own face slowly assume shape, features and tint out of the blank emulsion.

"You asked me before," I said to him. "Yes, we did have a President in the United States who was a movie star. An actor, in films. But that was when he was younger. Before he became President. His name was Ronald Reagan. And it was... some years ago. We have a different President now...."

"Oh," James said.

I thought I detected disappointment. Probably it was just distraction. The name Ronald Reagan certainly hadn't rung any perceptible bell. Nor had he indicated any interest in learning who the current President might be.

"Maybe," he declared, "I am coming to... United States? That is America."

"Yes, the United States of America."

"Yes. You-Ess-Ay. Yes, someday. I am hoping."

"Well, I hope you can too," I said.

Thinking: yeah, right, lots of luck.

I was also chary of voicing any comment that could be construed, even remotely, as encouraging him to write us for sponsorship, or for accommodations as a houseguest, or some similar inconvenience.

"Daniel! Laura!" Renée summoned us from the rear doorway.

Alistair was poised in arthritic mid-step below her—a preview of the way I'd be moving in ten years. If still moving, fingers crossed. He was the last of the passengers except us to board, apparently. Rory was still fiddling with the padlock on the left sand-mat bracket.

"Goodbye again. We have to go," I said. "What's 'goodbye?'" James regarded me without replying.

"In Chinyanja. How do you say 'goodbye?'"

"Oh. Yes. It is *tsalani*," he said. "*Tsalani*—do not go."

"Yes. Well. Salani," I imitated.

"*Tsalani*." He repeated, snapping his tongue.

"*Tsalani*," I said.

He nodded. He opened his palm, a farewell benediction. "I think you will find much game at Chibembe," he smiled. "It is very good for the wildlife."

"That's what we are looking forward to," Laura agreed.

"*Zikomo! Tsalani!*" I shouted as we jounced away.

Proud of my newly acquired and probably short-lived command of at least a couple of African words.

Dusk had definitely set in. And not five minutes had passed before we'd disturbed another patch of buffalo beans. That's when Renée mercifully broke out the plonk.

For the next several wretched, seemingly interminable hours we itched and fidgeted and moaned and shared one another's saliva as we passed the bottles and listlessly intoned rounds like "Row, Row, Row Your Boat" and "*Frère Jacques*," huddled in our stuffy tube rattling through an Africa that had shrunk to a blurry corridor of onrushing, headlight-lit underbrush.

It was what you couldn't see within that narrow shaft of light when you twisted to scowl dejectedly through the plexiglass—the pods hung like booby-traps primed to detonate when the truck swept by, releasing their insidious clouds of spines—that seemed most threatening en route. Once we'd finally reached the Nsefu entrance, though, it was the danger you couldn't see in the vast darkness *beyond* the light of the campfire and the hissing paraffin gas lanterns that suddenly preyed on your nerves.

We deposited our bowls, cups and silverware in the dry washbasins after downing our stew. We were too tired to deal with them.

The gate would be raised at daybreak, Nick informed us; we should be ready to depart without delay. So up and on the road by six. There'd be no breakfast except coffee or tea for those desperate enough to roust themselves. Alastair, always first out of his tent, volunteered to set the kettle on to boil.

No one, not even Mel, groused about the early rising. The local men who sat on the other side of the fire had readily agreed to feed it throughout the night, Nick told us. We carried our own supply of wood they could use, stowed in a cubby between the truck's rear wheels.

I customarily took off all my clothes before burrowing into my sleeping bag. Even when it's cold—and indeed, wisps of breath curled through my flashlight beam as I crawled into the tent behind Laura—I would very quickly wriggle out of the socks, briefs and tee-shirt I might start with as buffers against the initial nylon chill. Body-heat warms the cocoon more efficiently, I believe, if it's not swathed in insulation.

Laura was of the opposite persuasion. Dismissing my thesis, she usually put on sweatpants, a sweatshirt, thick socks and even a babushka before zipping her bag tight around her.

The bite in the air notwithstanding, she'd slunk behind the vacant hut nearest our tent with her bottle of drinking water while the stew was simmering, and in the darkness stripped and scrubbed her goosebumps with a frigid washcloth, trying to rid herself of the awful remnants of the buffalo beans.

That was before Nick's warning never to venture out of the direct line-of-sight of the group.

Soon after our arrival I'd exchanged the infected underpants, shorts and shirt I'd had on throughout the day for a fresh tee-shirt, a pair of Levis, wool socks and my heavy sweater. Underneath, though, I was still encased in a filthy carapace of dried river mud, sand, sweat-salt and embedded fibrils.

Those fiendish irritants seemed to have sifted into every cranny of the truck, even our lockers; switching into my "fresh" clothes (which I'd worn only once or twice previously) actually set off a new round of itching.

Still, I decided I'd keep the pants, socks and tee-shirt on in my sleeping bag this night. They'd foul it slightly less than direct contact with my naked body, I reasoned. Then too, each additional layer between my skin and the menace lurking on the other side of our flimsy tent-wall helped diminish my sense of vulnerability.

Dressed, even partially, I felt more capable of fight or flight. I was going to have to emerge and struggle out into the intimidating open air at least once anyway, I knew: Laura had made me promise I'd stand watch over her when she had to pee.

"Always take a flashlight with you. And don't go beyond those houses over there," Nick had cautioned. He'd stretched his arm toward the low shapes on the other side of the road.

The faint reflection of our lanterns and our cooking fire on their curved front walls was all that set the huts off from the ragged black forest behind. It was not clear whether people were inside. We'd seen no women or children here.

"We'll keep the lanterns lit tonight," Nick continued. He pointed. "Those trees in the middle of the compound there'll give a bit of privacy." He pronounced *privacy* with a short "i," of course. " If y're in need of it."

By now, in fact, we'd all seen one another at some point standing in the roadside grass with veed legs and squared shoulders, or hunkered behind a sparse bush, in those unmistakeable male and female urinary poses.

"Stay in sight of the fire, basically. Otherwise y' could end up part of the food chain," Nick said. "Mind you, it's all game reserve from here on in. That means the game roams free. These fellows'll be awake right on through the night." He nodded at the men on the kraal rail. "One of 'em's armed with a rifle, y' may've noticed. Any trouble, give a shout...."

"Trouble? Like what?" Laura interrupted.

"Well. Just tryin' t' take reasonable precautions," Nick said. "Few years back, a guy was killed not far from here whilst asleep in his tent. Experienced hunter, he was, too. Lioness clawed her way in and mauled him before he'd had time to react, apparently. Body'd been partially eaten by the time it was recovered."

He looked at Renée, hitched a shoulder and winced, as if acknowledging a cue.

"Probably shouldn't've told you that. Sorry. I'm not sayin' there's much danger, what with our chums keepin' watch. But y' wouldn't want to wander too far afield. Chaps here tell me a pride's definitely been spotted in the neighbourhood. So, I'm just saying, let's all keep our wits about us. We are now officially in lion country."

T hey were surprisingly candid—no attempt to hush up the horror to avoid frightening the guests.

"Must've been a pretty nasty show last night, hey?" prompted Graeme Bosch.

III. The Obligatory Allusions to Joseph Conrad's *Heart of Darkness*

The Chibembe dining room, we'd found when we'd strolled over at about ten to one, consisted of a few large round tables ringing a circular concrete pad under a big conical thatched roof supported by beams on widely spaced posts—mopani trees stripped of bark, stained and varnished.

The space was open to the air. The brochure called the structure a *chitenje*. A massive stone fireplace occupied the center of the floor; its maw was black and empty, of course, at midday, with the shade temperature in the high seventies (or, as I was learning to translate to Celsius, the upper twenties).

Arrayed on a buffet table in front of the cold hearth were platters of *crudités*, assorted salads, onion quiche, cold meats—a sliced ham, roasted chicken, pickled beef—crisp rolls, baguettes, pears, apples, melons, clusters of red and green grapes, and a variety of cheeses. There were also pitchers of milk, juice and water, and elegant silver urns of coffee and boiling water for tea.

Two African waiters in white jackets stood by to serve soup, fill water glasses, fetch orders from the adjacent bar and clear.

Like the bar, which was a separate thatched structure built around a giant, living African ebony known locally as a *muchenja*—it rose through the roofbeams behind the high semicircular counter—the restaurant looked out on a wide bend of the Luangwa River.

The cutbank was slowly nibbling into the flat on which the facility was built—only a few feet of thick, well mowed grass now stood between the simple wooden double-bed cabin we'd checked into and the river's ragged lip. Within a couple more rainy seasons, though, Graeme would later assure us hopefully, the swollen stream would slice through the vestigial neck of the peninsula a mile or so to the west and finally turn this living meander into a dead oxbow lake.

Only the four tables closest to the edge of the bluff had been set for lunch, and only one was occupied when we arrived—by a straight-backed blonde woman with a handsome, horsy face, a tow-headed boy of about ten, an equally fair little sister, and two elderly couples, one of whom I took to be the woman's parents, the children's grandparents.

There was no sign of a husband—perhaps he was out on a game walk, or back at his desk in some high-rise in downtown Jo'burg. They were all dressed in the sort of undistinguished pastel leisure clothing you'd see in the city on a weekend.

We sat at the table next to them, and as I eavesdropped on their guttural chat I realized, by a process of linguistic elimination, that they were speaking Afrikaans. They were the first non-Mamba guests we'd encountered since our arrival just after eight that morning. The lodge, we'd been told when we'd immediately inquired about the availability of a cabin, had opened for the season only two weeks earlier. We were in luck.

We were finishing a starter course of oxtail-barley soup when a youthful, dark-haired man dressed in a crisply creased khaki bush-shirt and cargo pants that looked tailored pulled out the chair next to Laura.

"Excuse me. Mind if I sit here?" he said. "Name's Graeme. Graeme Bosch."

We were slightly taken aback by the intrusion. We'd been enjoying the unaccustomed luxury of a luncheon *à deux*.

Moments after Graeme's appearance we were joined by a second man, also outfitted in safari drill—dust-green multi-pocketed, belted blouse and baggy shorts, tan knee socks, crepe-soled desert boots, broad-brimmed khaki hat with one side pinned up Anzac style. He gave his name as Dennis and immediately spelled it out.

"That's Dee-ee-en-*wye*-ess. Surname's a bit off-beat too. Ace. Spelled Ewe-wye-ess. Do that in case you encounter it in writing somewhere. On a schedule perhaps."

He pronounced the word "shed-yule."

Only when I actually saw his name in print did I register whatever he was talking about. His name was Denys Uys.

"Denys is one of our guides," Graeme explained. "So's Simon here. Simon Nsodzi."

A slim black man dressed much the same as Uys, except for a crushable jungle hat, circled from behind me to proffer a soft hand, bow to Laura and slip into the chair to Uys's left.

No sooner had he placed the hat under his seat, unfolded his napkin and daintily spread it across his lap than one of the waiters leaned over his shoulder and inquired in English if he wanted soup.

"Yes, soup, please," Simon murmured.

Frankly, that startled me. Based on what we'd observed so far, I'd come to assume that a de facto *apartheid* still prevailed in these tourist enclaves. It was gratifying to see a black African in such a setting filling something other than a subservient role. Being accorded equal status at the table. And being waited on by another black African with a remarkable absence of discernible subtext.

"I'm the Eff-Oh," Graeme explained. "Keepin' the books straight, that's my day-job. We always have our lunch family-style here at Chibembe. Boon for us senior staff, of course. Lets us get to know our guests a bit better, answer any questions you might have. Saves a lot of unnecessary work for the waiters as well. No sense making 'em clean and set up extra tables for dinner, hey?"

Both Graeme and Denys were from Cape Town, we learned. That would come out during the course of the meal, part of the rudimentary exchange of *curricula vitae* that humans substitute for canine groin-sniffing.

Graeme had a degree in accounting from the university there, and had been with Arthur Andersen Pty. until taking a full-time position a season earlier with Zambia Trails, the concession operator whose accounts were among those he'd been auditing. (F.O., I realized, meant financial officer.)

Denys, who was in his mid-thirties, had studied biology and wildlife management and had worked in South Africa's Kruger National Park as well as in Kenya. This was his third season at Chibembe.

Simon had been born in a village within the park boundaries, had attended two years of secondary school in Chipata on the Malawi border—a journey of more than two hundred kilometers that he'd made on foot each term, he acknowledged modestly when prompted by Denys.

He'd slept on the floor of a cousin's house until he could no longer afford tuition and books—and had then distinguished himself as a *fundi*, or armed scout, sufficiently to earn promotion to driving-safari guide two years earlier. Last season he'd passed his Grade-One license to lead walking safaris.

Through Graeme and Denys, we learned that Simon had a wife, two small children and his own house in his natal village. "Quite a nice *new* house y've built for y'rself, hey, Simon?" Denys had winked. For us he'd added: "Concrete block, it is, with a bright green fibreglass roof! Very lekker."

Simon smiled with shy pride. His might have been one of those incongruous structures we'd passed driving from Nsefu through the early morning smoke and mist. Flanked by traditional mud-brick dwellings, a depressingly raw exemplar of lowest-end urban residential construction technique would suddenly appear in a forest-ringed compound.

I'd noticed one with a mahogany-veneer six-panel front door, the sort of cheap *luxe* you'd find in the States at a discount warehouse depot. Several of them were punctuated by aluminum—aluminium—sliding windows. No doubt they attested to the owners' affluence and modernity.

The little settlements were almost all scrupulously neat, the ground swept bare within a pale of straw. If those cinderblock-and-fiberglass houses were esthetic sore thumbs, sadly retrograde in my eyes compared to the elegant simplicity of earth and thatch, they at least appeared to be painstakingly maintained. There were jobs in the area, obviously. But above all, there seemed to be a pastoral dignity absent in the teeming, ramshackle cities.

From which Graeme had just flown back this morning, he said. He'd spent two days in Lusaka arranging provisions and attending to paperwork at the resort's headquarters, he explained.

Most guests, in fact, traveled to and from South Luangwa National Park by air, he added, either in private planes or on one of four weekly Air Zambia flights in and out of a small strip at Mfuwe. Only the overland safari parties like ours braved the full stretch of patchy track, the unreliable fords and the buffalo beans.

The suspicion was dawning on me, in fact, that Nick, as part of Mamba's plan, had deliberately courted the rigors we'd experienced along that particular route in order to satisfy our Livingstonian exploration fantasies. (Rory had joked during our first orientation talk in Harare that Mamba was an acronym for "Many Anxious Moments in Bleedin' Africa.")

"Here's an item of local colour for you," Graeme said brightly. "Met one of the guys who takes care of Mpamvu, our little elephant, on the road coming in this morning. Clingin' to the upper branches of a big *msikisi* tree, he was."

He paused for effect.

"Saw his bicycle first, just leanin' there. Thought someone'd abandoned it. Bit curious. Looked up and there he was, hanging on for dear life. Told me he was coming in to work when he'd happened on a pride of lions with a fresh kill. Nine of 'em, he'd counted. Well, they'd finished their breakfast and sloped off for a morning lie-down long before we appeared, but the guy'd still been afraid to come to earth. Spooked to begin with, don't wonder. From all of what he told us, actually."

That's when Graeme mentioned the previous night's "nasty show."

"Yeh," said Denys. "Shot the bugger, at least, Simon did. Eh, Simon?"

Needless to say, we pricked up our ears at what seemed a familiar subject among the three guides.

"And we got the body back for 'em," he added. "Most of it anyway."

"A good thing," Simon said. "If we had not, the men would be killing many crocodiles."

"Precaution much as revenge," Denys nodded. He glanced at Laura uneasily, lifted his napkin to his ruddy face and dabbed his lips as if to wipe away the indelicate subject matter. "Tryin' t' make sure they'd got the one that took the boy."

"Would've been a big headache for us, all right," Graeme commented, his eyes flicking to us. "Government requires us to fill out a report whenever anyone kills something in our sector."

"Rangers patrol for poachers," Denys chimed in, "and hunting's completely *verboden*, of course. Like last night, though, you don't want 'em on the loose once they've acquired a taste for human flesh. Or if they charge, attack a party on walking safari, as an example... self-defense, you can shoot."

"We have to spell out all the extenuating circumstances, though," Graeme said. "In excruciating detail. Otherwise we could lose our permit to operate. So we'd've had to try to stop 'em from butchering crocs wholesale."

"Not much bloody hope," Denys muttered.

"Ironic, isn't it?" Graeme smiled. "More bureaucratic hoo-haw if an animal's killed than if a human's taken."

"What Simon and I have been at this morning," Denys added. "Doing the paperwork."

"Wait a minute," Laura interjected, wide eyed. "What are you saying? Happened!"

Denys stared at her for a moment. "Oh. Thought you'd have heard by now," he said.

"Croc," Graeme informed her in an offhand tone. "Took a boy last night."

Laura gasped softly. I hadn't yet told her about the old woman. This news shook me too—I hadn't realized these incidents were so commonplace.

"They fish, village boys, in the river," Denys explained. "Crocs or no. May seem foolhardy to us, but it's their way. Tradition. Use nets, which they simply drag through the water, hey? Meaning one of 'em has to wade out and hold one end."

He swirled his spoon in his soup.

"So what he does, he carries a pole, a long pole...."

He lifted his outstretched arm to the side.

"...And he probes with it. This way and that. In front of him, along the bottom."

He pumped his fist up and down as if divining for lumps in the thick dark broth in his bowl.

"Crocs lie there doggo, slink up close and submerge, waitin' for an impala or a zebra or a wildebeest or some such likely prey to come down for a drink."

He pronounced *zebra* with a short *e*, and *beest* as two syllables.

"Idea, of course, is that the guy with the net doesn't want to step on one by accident...."

"My God! What if he *does* stir up a crocodile with his stick?" Laura exclaimed. "Wouldn't that be just as bad?"

"Well, see, there's a rope tied round his waist. His mates have the other end. They're supposed to haul him in the instant he gives the cry. Croc'll usually just swim away, though. Don't like it when they're bothered, mostly."

"Wow," I muttered, "that's a system."

"Truly," Graeme agreed.

"It is how they catch the fish," Simon observed quietly. He hitched his shoulders. "The old way. Quite dangerous, no doubt. But what else are the people to do if they wish to eat fish? It is not easy. The crocodile is in the river, and a man cannot see. However, he must be very hungry, the crocodile, a very big one, to take a man."

"Yeh, you and I have certainly done our share of wadin' in that river, hey?" Denys smiled wryly at Simon. "Poor guy last night, stroke of bad luck. He scares up a croc, yells for his mates to yank him back in. No problem, ordin'rily. This time, though, for some reason they couldn't... or didn't... do it fast enough."

"Ugh," Laura shuddered.

"First we heard the screamin'. Those of us over in the bar. General commotion. Then some of the boys ran up from the river. '*Mangu-mangu! Ng'ona! Katenge mfuti!*' And so on."

He looked at Simon, as if for confirmation of the scene and his dialogue.

"Bloody to-do. 'Quick! *Upesi!* Bring gun! Crocodile!' All that sort of business."

He swung back to face Laura and me. "Steve and I were in the bar having a lager...."

"Another guide," Graeme murmured. "Guy from New Zealand, originally." He shook his head at his own digression. "Not important."

"Simon and Steve had been out on a night drive," Denys continued. "Party there, next to us, actually."

He cocked his head toward the neighboring Afrikaners, who were just rising from their table.

"Simon was still checkin' over the HiLux. Steve yelled for ' im to grab the big Brno...."

"The what?" Laura interrupted.

"Ah, rifle. Anyway, it was too late, sorry to say. By the time we got there, croc'd dragged the poor bugger under. Made pretty short work of him."

He milled his forearm in the air.

"How they do it. Can't get a purchase in the water, just tumble over and over, workin' their jaws, teeth, till they tear their prey to pieces."

"What a horrible way to die," Laura breathed.

"Not how I'd choose to go," Denys nodded, "I must say."

"But you shot it eventually," I prompted.

"Yeh...."

"Downstream," Simon said, "Six hundred metres, perhaps. There is a small island. We were searching with the torch...."

"Sharp eyes, he has," Denys declared. "Spotted blood in the water, near some logs where the crocs make their burrows. What they don't eat immediately they bring home to store away for more leisurely consumption. This one was about to shove his snack into the larder. Simon saw a flick of the tail, put a couple of three-seventy-five rounds in the bugger's brain. Brilliant marksmanship, night and all, only a torch to light the target. Scouts went over in a punt and fetched the carcass. Gave it to the village blokes, along with the boy's remains. Most important of all, I suppose, get those back, hey, Simon?"

"Yes," he agreed.

"So, they'll be having a...." I paused to recall accurately. "A... *maliro*?" I ducked my head modestly, watching Simon to see if I'd said it right.

"Yes," he allowed.

"One of the few words I know," I smiled. "Chinyanja, right? I learned it on our way in, when we got stuck crossing a stream. Where exactly the same thing happened. An old woman had gotten snatched by a crocodile a few days ago, they told me. Washing her clothes."

"Where'd you hear that?" Laura challenged.

"James. The guy we were talking to back at the river."

"Really? You didn't tell me!" she objected.

"Just hadn't come up yet. Opportunity. Sorry."

"Does happen once in a way," Denys acknowledged. "Not altogether a rare occurrence."

"Why it's hard to change the African mentality about wildlife conservation," Graeme observed. "Eh, Simon? People in the compounds not as enamored as we are of elephants, lions, crocs. All threats in one way or another. Like the guy this morning. Cape Town or San Francisco, you're commuting to work, you might find yourself stuck on the flyover. Or crawling from robot to robot. Our chap's late to work because of an encounter with lions. Starting to learn though. Game brings in tourists, who bring in money. Government understands."

"And as well," said Denys, "where they've poached off the crocs...."

"Why would people do that," Laura interrupted.

"Do....?

"Poach crocodiles. What value...?"

"Skins," Graeme answered. "Shoes? Handbags?"

"Ah. Obviously," Laura nodded.

"Lot of demand for the leather," Graeme went on. "In the developed world. Big payoff. What keeps the illegal market thrivin'."

"Trouble is," Denys resumed, "when the crocs're gone, catfish come in. Drive out the native species. Kinds of fishes the people eat traditionally. Happened in many parts of the continent. Crocs are opportunists when it comes to predation. Mainstay of their diet is fish."

"Which are what, in this river?" I asked. "What kinds? The native fish."

Although the guidebooks had mentioned burbling trout streams on Malawi's Zomba Plateau, I'd seen no watercourses so far in Zimbabwe or Zambia that looked fast or clear enough to suggest a fly-cast could be fruitful. And the rivers were brown and clotted.

"Barbel, mostly," Denys said. "Anyway, point is, crocs fulfill a function. Bloody buggers. Balance of nature and all that. Price of a boy, a woman here and there."

"Well." Graeme shoved his chair back. "Not exactly an appetizing subject. Sorry about that. Sad event. Ag, shame. Way it is, though, sometimes, here. Beauty of Africa. Stark contrasts. Life and death."

He eyed Laura's plate. "Quiche today, hey? Recommend it?"

"Oh. Yes. Very good," Laura said.

"Hope we haven't put you off your feed. Excuse me."

He rose and headed for the buffet table. Denys and Simon excused themselves and got up to follow him.

"Guy doesn't sound like what I'd think of as a South African, does he?" I commented in a subdued voice. "I'd've said he was English."

"Maybe they have a different accent in Cape Town," Laura suggested.

"Maybe. There's a typical way of turning some vowels into diphthongs and elongating others that I can usually pick up on, though. As South African. Hard to tell from Australian or New Zealand, but.... Anyway, neither of these guys has it, as far as I can tell."

"You're not thinking of Mandela....?"

"No, no. But maybe it *is* more people who speak Afrikaans as their first language. I don't know. You'd think with a name like Uys...."

I looked around and beckoned at a waiter.

"I'll have another bottle of *Mosi*, please," I said, pointing at the bottle. "How about you? Want anything?" I asked Laura.

"How is that?" she asked.

"Good!"

Like someone in a TV commercial, I turned the blue label toward her. It bore a picture of Victoria Falls, slightly out-of-register.

"Good beer, as Rory said. Although I think I liked *Zambezi* better."

I'd bought myself a souvenir tee-shirt, in fact, at a shop in Victoria Falls with the latter's green label (also depicting the falls, more expertly) reproduced on the front and the legend "*Zimbabwe's Finest Export Lager*" on the back.

"I think I'll just stick with gee-and-tee," Laura said.

She handed the waiter her glass, empty now except for a crumpled lime rind, the ice cube long since having melted.

"Gin and tonic," she reminded him. "May as well indulge," she said to me. "All I plan to do this afternoon is sleep."

"Sleep is all?"

She mugged. "I was awake all night last night! Weren't you? Between the itching and the scratching and the listening for lions? I could've sworn I heard something rustling around the tent outside. I think I was holding my breath for most of an hour. I was about to make you get up and go out and investigate."

"Yeah, thanks," I said.

"Can't I count on you as my protector?"

"Oh, sure. No problem. 'Shoo, cat!' Drive off a slavering lion with my bare hands."

"I'm sure I heard one roar, actually!"

"Yeah! I heard that too!" I concurred. "Something, anyway. Toward morning?"

"And it wasn't that far away, either."

"I know. Didn't sound like it. Although they say a lion's growl, or that weird kind of coughing grunt, really carries."

"And now when I take my nap I can dream about getting eaten by crocodiles! A new worry. Good reason to get totally plotzed. Pretty graphic, huh? What they were saying? I'm not sure I needed all the gory detail."

"Maybe you're not so hot any more to take that walk on the wild side."

"What? The walking safari?"

"Mm-hm. Maybe we should just stick to the night drive. Presumably more protected, in a car."

"We're doing that tonight."

"I know. We could cancel the walking safari tomorrow, though, if you wanted. Is all I'm saying. All that talk about animals charging. Shooting in self-defense. What if they miss?"

"Doesn't sound like they miss, from what they were telling us about Simon's exploit, last night."

"Yeah, but what if Simon isn't the one who's with us?"

"I'm sure," she comforted me, "they wouldn't offer it if it were really dangerous."

"No, that's probably true. It's just that an alternative would be to hang out here... take advantage of this break from roughing it. Make real use of that nice, soft double bed. Aren't you in the mood for a little hanky-panky? A little prolonged hanky-panky?"

I gave her a leering grin. I immediately regretted its goopishness. Not likely to ignite desire.

"Get up every so often for a sunbath maybe," I went on. "Soak in the pool, cocktails in the bar, sumptuous repast to replenish our energy. Then back to the sack for yet another bout of mad, passionate love-making."

"Shhh!" she remonstrated. "They'll hear you. They're coming back."

"Yeah. We certainly wouldn't want anybody to suspect a husband and wife might dream of doing such a thing, would we?"

"We certainly wouldn't," she said.

The remainder of our lunch-table conversation was devoted to more benign topics. Although, if you thought about it, there was always a slightly problematic underlying motif: In response to our questions, Denys encouraged us to take the walking safari. It offers "the real feeling of Africa," he assured us.

"We haven't lost a guest yet," he winked.

Graeme and Simon gently kidded each other about an upcoming soccer match—this year's debut of a series of intramural contests, Graeme explained, that pitted the "Chibembe Lions," a team of black employees, against the "Wazungu Warriors," all white, of course.

And they recounted what Graeme styled "the saga of Mpamvu," a crocodile-scarred baby elephant that was being bottle-fed here on the grounds and taught to forage for itself in hopes it could someday be weaned back to the wild.

The managing director of the resort company, Zambia Trails—who otherwise spent most of his time in Lusaka—had happened on the orphan while on a foray into the bush during the pre-opening, post-rainy-season renovations and preparations some four weeks earlier, Denys said. The mother had either been killed or, for unknown reasons, had shunned the infant, as occasionally happens. Rather than allow it to starve, the guides had coaxed the little elephant—perfectly content to attach itself to them—back to a straw-strewn nursery in a hut behind the commissary.

That journey itself had almost ended in tragedy, however. Too cumbersome for any boat, the youngster had been nudged into the river, to swim across beside its newfound human herd, who were in an escorting boat.

In mid-river, a crocodile attacked.

Mpamvu sustained a deep wound in his hind leg, but struggled on bravely, bleating and kicking as the guides shot the predator and succeeded in driving off others.

Christened after that incident with a name meaning "strong" in Chinyanja, Mpamvu was now recovering nicely under the round-the-clock care of two shifts of attendants. They even slept beside him on the straw—baby elephants thrive only with constant companionship, which they're accustomed to in the herd, Denys explained. The men suckled their ward with long-necked plastic jugs of milk jiggered to resemble elephant formula, and took him for daily mud-baths in a nearby hole.

There was reason to be optimistic about Mpamvu's survival prospects, Graeme said; he was gaining in size and had trumpeted greetings to other elephants he'd glimpsed at a distance on his training walks. On the other hand, a baby elephant adopted by the Chibembe staff several years earlier under similar circumstances had eventually languished and died.

Simon was the first to push away from the table.

Laura and I sipped coffee and nibbled grapes while Graeme and Denys polished off pears with wedges of Stilton.

Heading back to our cabin, we passed Rory and Reg, who were smoking and nursing *Mosi*s at a table in the bar.

Gerhard, Mel and Jen, oiled and recumbent on lounge chairs, sunned beside the pool. We exchanged comradely waves. I felt a certain sheepishness, though, as if Laura and I were defectors who'd broken the group bond by using our comparative wealth to opt out of the character-testing communal tenting ground.

Not that we were alone by any means. Greta was installed in the "chalet" next to ours, as she'd announced as her intention, and Jen and Mel had decided to splurge on one too.

Nick and Renée had already told us they'd be staying apart from us in a room at every fixed lodging on our itinerary—a perk Mamba offered its road-weary drivers and, in this case, campmaster/consorts.

Rory had to maintain guard over the Bedford. He'd be sleeping for the duration in its roof-seat.

As I was plumbing the pocket of the clean white tennis shorts I'd put on for the restaurant, digging for our door key, Laura spotted Mpamvu. He was lumbering along the trail from his mudhole, swathed in refreshing black slime and flanked by his two custodians, both in high rubber boots. They carried what looked like gallon containers of bleach.

Those, we learned, were Mpamvu's bottles.

One of the men happily demonstrated its use for us when we hastened over to make closer acquaintance with the little elephant. Mpamvu curled his trunk out of the way, lifted his head and took the proffered neck of the jug in his pursed, pink-lined lips. He guzzled placidly.

"May I pet him?" Laura asked.

She extended her hand. The man nodded.

I wondered which of the two guys had spent the morning in the tree.

Laura stepped forward and tentatively tapped Mpamvu's horny hide just forward of the big leathery flaps of ears. I did too. It was one of the few places that wasn't slathered with nasty mud.

Mpamvu's shoulders reached to my waist. His eyelids ended in glamorous black lashes that looked as if they were made of sailmaker's twine. Even as a toddler, his gray skin was dry and crazed, loosely puckered over six or seven hundred pounds of immature pachyderm bulk. Docile, trusting, dependent, Mpamvu was, no question, cute.

"Oh, you're a doll," cooed Laura.

Mpamvu twitched his bony tail and emitted a borborygmic fart.

When Laura went in to lie down I said I'd follow in a few minutes. I knew she'd rebuff any advances before she'd napped.

There were two metal chairs on the low front porch; I sat in one and immersed myself in the scene before me.

To the east, where the river first looped into view against the jagged, vertical mudbank on our side, I counted... two, three... four... five... six, seven! Seven hippopotami lolling in the stream.

Hippopotamoi, I always remembered that from my classical Jesuit education. The true Greek plural. River-horses. Their mounded silhouettes might have been flotsam or islands of silt except for their sporadic stirring.

Now and then the enormous silence of the sun-stunned African afternoon would be broken by a faint snuffle, a languid yawn, a sudden bubbly hiss like a whale spouting as a subaqueous slumber was interrupted for breath. Or somehippo would jostle somehippo else, or step on somehippo's toe or something. That would provoke an angry, blubbery bellow, a brief flurry of weight redistribution, an assertion of territory or dominance.

One of the rotund beasts splattered ashore in a huff, revealing an underbelly pink as a pig's.

The far bank was a broad mud-flat on which I made out two widely separated Nile crocodiles basking. Here and there a dirt-encrusted log had washed up. It was difficult to distinguish the reptiles except that they were tapered fore and aft. They lay inert as logs.

Between them, at what appeared to be a very safe distance, three impala had come down to the water to drink. While two sipped with bent necks, the third stood wary, its antelope nose lifted to sample the neighborhood aromas.

Earlier in the day, when we'd first checked into our cabin, there'd been more action at the river's edge. We'd seen several waterbucks, a couple of eland and, most entertaining, a pair of giraffes. They'd almost had to do the splits with their forelegs to crank their ridiculously overspecialized necks down to drinking level.

Lines of hoofprints in the mud showed where ungulates had crossed the open strand in file from the low mud cliff carved by the river when it had been full. Trees crowded its edge. I noticed a trio of zebras sheltered in the shadow-striped grass, either contemplating or just finished slaking their thirst.

The one most in the open was uncharacteristically fat. After a moment's scrutiny, I realized it must be pregnant—a mare that would soon drop a spindly-legged, black-on-white foal. Or was it white-on-black?

To the southwest, the river curved out of sight again beyond the tall *msikisi*s—a type of mahogany, I was later told—

that ringed the resort grounds. The only clouds in the sky floated low against the horizon there. A bird circled lazily above the break in the treetops that marked the river's course. It was a raptor of some sort, coasting on a thermal zephyr... probably a fish eagle.

That's what it was, all right, I decided when it banked low enough for a white head and rusty belly to flash against the backdrop of dark foliage.

Made sense. The African fish eagle is Zambia's emblematic national bird.

In fact, I'd been surprised to find, birds featured as prominently as animals on our game drive through Hwange National Park.

In part that was because the latter were scarcer. Except for a couple of warthogs irately snorkeling for roots, our sightings of mammals had been pretty much confined to the mud pans.

From roadside viewing platforms or the back seat of an open Land Rover, we'd peered out at congregations of Cape buffalo, impala, kudu, elephants, zebras, giraffes and baboons, emerged from the forest to wet their whistles in the water that collected in the shimmering basins. But birds were ubiquitous—far more numerous—not to mention a pretty flamboyantly noteworthy lot in their own right.

Our teenaged guide and driver at Hwange, Malcolm, pointed out snowy sacred ibis whose black heads, curved black bills and black-tipped wings were immediately familiar from a thousand reproductions of the hieroglyphs in pharaohs' tombs... and ugly, bald-headed marabou storks with shriveled pouches... and Egyptian geese waddling around on long pink legs... and a regiment of helmeted guinea fowl in panicky rout across our track, their horny yellow casques bobbing atop blue-and-red caps.

The sparrow-like birds with brilliant lavender throats and blue tails that rocked and dipped through the camelthorn were lilac-breasted rollers, Malcolm informed us—"rollers" for their eccentric flight patterns. We'd also seen purple rollers—and, of course, a pair of African fish eagles. Which is why I could identify this one.

"The gull-like cry of the fish eagle," I'd read in Alastair's field guide, which he'd shared with us across the Land Rover's seatback along with his binoculars, "is one of the characteristic sounds of the African wilds."

Now I listened. I heard nothing but the dense forest silence.

Suddenly broken by the muffled clatter of the diving board and a splash from over behind the pool enclosure.

I pictured Gerhard doing an ungainly half-gainer.

The impala were departing in file.

The zebras had already vanished.

The crocodiles lay petrified.

The hippos dozed.

It was the hottest part of the day.

In Africa.

I was in Africa.

As a child I'd been a voracious escapist into the stirring foreign worlds depicted in comic books; I can still recall my rapt absorption in the panel illustrations of the Andes as Donald Duck searched serially for Inca chickens that laid square eggs.

I was an avid reader of books as well: *Robinson Crusoe*, *Treasure Island* and *Kidnapped*, of course, later Nordhoff and Hall's *Bounty* trilogy... then the Balkan spy novels of Eric Ambler....

It was the settings that engaged me more than the plots or narratives: the brilliant South Pacific under the plunging *kamikaze* in *Life's Picture History of World War II*, the canyons and mesas in the *Arizona Highways* on my grandmother's coffee table, the Klondike of Jack London, Kipling's Afghan frontier, Maugham's sweaty spice islands and Malay rubber plantations... and, eventually, Conrad's *Heart of Darkness*.

I had a visceral yearning to experience such places, yet hadn't the least expectation I ever would.

My father's only significant sortie from Louisville had been three years at Yale Law School, after which he'd returned to keep his widowed mother company in a shotgun house in Phoenix Hill while practicing as a junior associate at Ogden, Newell & Welch. He went to work patriotically for a New Deal agency during World War II, then he and three partners opened their own struggling firm. His father, my grandfather, had been a concert master at a failing *biergarten* established by his immigrant father's father's father beside the New World's Rhine, downstream from another German enclave, Cincinnati.

My mother was a placid onetime belle from South Carolina, permanently estranged by her family's loss of fortune in the Depression and her irreconcilably liberal views on race.

She never seemed to be bothered by her fall in station. When I was born my parents were still living with my grandmother, my father's mother. Family vacations throughout my childhood consisted of a week of nature walks and group sings across the river at an Indiana state park. From my upstairs bedroom window in Indian Hills, where we'd moved after my little brother's birth, I could see the arc of limestone knolls I had no reason to think wouldn't define—confine—my life as it had every other male in the Schuman line since 1848.

My awe was almost palpable, then, when I'd stood at the promenade-deck rail of the M/S *Stavangerfjord* soaking in the sight of the little white Norwegian houses flying their red-blue-and-white Norwegian flags on the rocky islets dotting the choppy blue Oslofjord. A junior-to-be in college—the University of Louisville, naturally—I'd been told by a professor about the availability of scholarships to a six-week international summer school at the University of Oslo. My father hadn't seriously objected when I'd applied—and been awarded one. I was the first Schuman to set foot outside the United States in four generations.

This was Europe, I kept reminding myself.

Europe! The greater world! I'd actually managed to make my way to it!

Funny, though. I'd still felt distanced. It was as if I were permanently encapsulated in the everyday, the commonplace. I'd brought it with me. My very presence dimmed the power of the exotic.

And that sense of disconnection, of vague disappointment in what should be strange and glamorous, persisted even as I increased the dosages—went to graduate school in Manhattan, signed aboard a Norwegian freighter on a whim, caroused in waterfront dives and explored guilty commercial sex in places like Manila, Kaohsiung, Yokohama, Bangkok, Balikpapan, Djakarta, Singapore, Cochin, Aden and Genoa, then followed by joining the Navy and serving as a destroyer officer throughout Southeast Asia on the eve of the Vietnam War.

No matter how fantastic the circumstances I found myself in—and there were more than a few that were pretty colorful—the fact that I was in the picture reduced it to the ordinary.

I still had that sense. But the world *has* been leached of much of its exoticism, hasn't it?

From Oakland, in just a couple of hops, you can fly into Mfuwe. David Livingstone was slogging laboriously toward it through Zambia's Bangweulu swamps when he died in the 1870s—at a village called Chitambo, no further from here than our bush-camp beside the highway the night before last.

Felled by hemorrhoids, no less, the poor bugger. Can you believe it?

I'd always been struck by the hardships unfamiliar climates seemed to present to the Victorians. In the old *Illustrated Weekly* engravings, the sepia photographs of intrepid travelers posed with their mule trains, their camel caravans, their strings of loinclothed bearers, they're always buttoned properly to the necks in suits and ties or high-collared blouses with muttonchop sleeves—full-skirted, sturdily booted, carefully veiled, topeed, parasoled. Even in places as salubrious as California or Hawaii.

The sun was their bitter nemesis. The wind. The dust. The snakes. The insects. The bacteria. The native peoples.... All nemeses.

And here I was, larking about Africa in sandals and shorts. Legs bare, head bare, shirt open or off, my body freely exposed to the elements. As easily and casually adapted to this alien environment as any native.

What had changed?

Well, of course, medical science for one thing. Laura had made us both appointments with the doctor for recommended polio boosters, diphtheria/tetanus, yellow fever and gamma globulin shots. Typhoid immunization had been suggested too, but we'd finalized our trip plans too late for its protection to take. Iffy, apparently, anyway.

Every Thursday since the week before our departure we'd been dutifully popping a mefloquine tablet to ward off malaria. At dusk every evening we religiously anointed our foreheads and necks and arms and the backs of our hands and any other exposed patch of skin with pungent bug juice.

Still, every white person we'd met so far who'd spent any significant length of time in Africa—even Nick and Rory—had quaked through a bout of malaria, precautions notwithstanding.

There'd been some question whether Malcolm, our 17-year-old Rhodesia-born driver-guide in Hwange, could make it with us into the afternoon; when he'd pulled up in his open Rover to load us aboard after breakfast he was ashen-faced and numb with headache from a malarial relapse that, he reluctantly admitted, had drenched him in fever-sweats the night before.

So this modern Africa wasn't altogether benign. The protozoal parasites that the anopheles mosquitoes inject when they bite are increasingly drug-resistant. Twice we'd been stopped at public health roadblocks where our truck had been cursorily examined and sprayed for tse-tse flies.

And, of course, AIDS was rampant. Not that it was likely to pose much risk to travelers like Laura and me, practitioners of marital fidelity at this passage in our lives. Speaking for myself, at least. And relatively confident about her.

But there were, in fact, reminders that a terrible darkness still loomed over the continent.

At the pub in Hwange we'd fallen into conversation with a Scottish doctor and his wife, medical missionaries on brief caravan holiday from their clinic in rural Mashonaland. The incidence of HIV-infection among the patients he saw was frightening, he said. But the gravest devastation, he predicted, was soon to be suffered by the middle class because of the sexual mores of the men of that social stratum, abetted by their mobility and means.

Within a decade, he feared, AIDS would have scoured Africa of its entire cadre of managers and leaders. (Still to come: viral hemorrhagic fevers like Ebola.)

Really, I reflected, I was fooling myself if I thought I represented some evolutionary advance over Livingstone and his contemporaries.

True, with the diving board whumping in the background and grapes and brie in the commissary cold-locker, this didn't feel much like the Heart of Darkness. The black people we'd met—James, and that village headman, and Simon—certainly they weren't savages. There were no skulls impaled on stakes around village compounds.

You didn't have to go very far, though—south across the Zambezi into bordering Mozambique, north to Conrad's Congo, and, of course, beyond—to find horrible civil unrest, endemic disease, violent death.

The glowering soldiers who'd strutted in front of us at a highway checkpoint outside Lusaka, circled the truck staring at us until we averted our eyes, then wordlessly scrutinized the passports Nick handed over before waving us on our way... those guys didn't exactly foster confidence in our security.

Two young European hitchhikers, a boy and a girl, had watched us morosely from the shoulder—apparently in the soldiers' custody. Africa was still a troubled, uncertain place. But so is almost everywhere.

Maybe in a weird way, I theorized, my comparative comfort here stemmed from the fact that by the end of the twentieth century we've all become Kurtz. Like Conrad's mysterious Belgian ivory trader unstrung in the fastnesses of the Congo, modern Westerners have "gone native."

Some of it is American influence: We Americans, acknowledge it or not, are fundamentally African. (With liberal splashes from the aboriginal and Hispanic gene pools.)

I'm talking about us European Americans—descendants of the British colonists, the mid-19th century French, German and Scandinavian immigrants and the Southern and Eastern European "wretched refuse" funneled through Ellis Island. But even the newest arrivals who trace their ancestry to Asian enclaves soon absorb, as they enrich the hue of, Americanness. Which is infused to its core with black.

The real "horror" Kurtz relived as he lay on his deathbed wasn't his embrace of black license, after all. It was his dissolution into *white* barbarism.

Compare whatever's going on in Africa to what goes on in the Caucasus, our racial eponym. Rwanda-Burundi, meet Armenia-Azerbaijan. (Or whatever are the latest loci of senseless carnage.)

More probably my ease was just a product of naiveté. And of that invincible, bourgeois, middle-American provincialism that swaddles me as thoroughly as the Victorians' starched collars, dusters and pith helmets.

Aware or not, sockless, pantless, shirtless, hatless, I remained blithely insulated from the full electric charge of this "prehistoric earth"—to use Conrad's lurid description.

My musings were interrupted by the sudden stirring of one of the crocodiles. It rocked up on its stubby legs and scuttled into the water.

They're said to be the closest things left on earth to dinosaurs. (Well, discounting the tweety little birds.)

I got to my own feet and stretched. My mind was churning but the pressure of fatigue and the two beers at lunch had built behind my eyes. I hadn't, in fact, slept well the night before.

My neck was stiff; yesterday's pain was evoked when I lifted my elbows and pinched my shoulder blades together. I was still troubled by the dull sciatic twinges someone had likened aptly to a "toothache in the leg."

Despite the cushioning inch of air in my inflatable mattress, I was finding the hard ground tough on my aging bones and joints.

The soft bed inside beckoned.

I lay down on my back beside the snoozing Laura and molded the pillow over my eyes. I'd dozed soundly for nearly an hour when I woke up because my body temperature had dropped. I slid my shorts off, sat up to untangle my polo shirt over my head, flicked loose the stainless steel band of my wristwatch, put it on the bedside table and snuggled under the coarse sheet and thin wool blanket, next to Laura's warm rump. She was in panties and bra.

Nearly another hour had passed when my slumber again wore off. Laura was still snoring lightly. I went into the compact bathroom, relieved myself and brushed my teeth, combed my fingers through my hair, assessed my nascent beard, my tan, my musculature and the little *nyaminyami* on its string between my pecs in the mirror. Then I padded back to the bed with the paperback mystery I'd been reading on the truck, plucked in passing from my canvas suitcase. I doubled the pillow against the headboard, switched on the gooseneck lamp on the little bedside table next to the plank wall and climbed back under the sheet. I rested my right hand on Laura's hip.

Her breathing had quieted. After a few minutes she rolled onto her back. I began to caress the insides of her thighs absently, occasionally walking my fingers across her pantied crotch. Soon she spread her legs wider, telegraphing interest. I started suggestively tracing the warm concavity below her mons. I ran my hand up over her belly button, and then slowly down under the waistband of her panties. I fingered the grain of her flattened pubic hair. My penis had begun to distend my own underpants.

"I should brush my teeth," she murmured.

"So you *are* awake," I said.

"Mm. That was wonderful. I slept like a log. I needed that." She lifted her knee. I could sense her gathering herself to rise.

"Don't go unless you have to. Your breath's fine," I said. I laid my book aside.

"How would you know?" she challenged.

"I'm sure. But let's test." I braced myself on my elbow and leaned over her face. The scent she exhaled was musty but not unpleasant. Her lips looked slightly swollen from sleep. I pressed mine softly against them. Our mouths gradually widened. We found each other's tongues. I placed my left hand on her full right breast in the lace bra.

"You smell sweet as a lily," I murmured.

"You brushed your teeth."

"I did," I agreed.

I worked my hand inside the bra cup, mindful of my fingernails. I flinched as her hand found my scrotum in turn. My balls are always tender at first touch.

"Sorry," she winced sympathetically.

"'S okay, " I assured her.

She fondled the hard lump at my groin. My penis was still constrained.

"What have we here?" she teased.

"Just something I'd like to get straight between us."

The dialogue wasn't original, but neither was it rote.

I kissed her again. Her nipple firmed and the areola wrinkled beneath my circling thumb and forefinger. She slipped her index finger under the legband of my briefs and suddenly touched my bare penis. I twitched, allowing her to free it to stretch up hard against my taut abdomen. I fumbled at the front clasp of her bra. The lace cups parted and fell aside. I wriggled lower and nuzzled her breasts. I gently nibbled each pap in turn. With my left hand I stroked and parted her labia. Her breath caught when I touched her clitoris. Then mine did too as she closed her fist tightly around my erection.

At fifty-one, she needed a little help with lubrication. I interrupted our protracted kiss to work up saliva, put the pads of my fingers to my mouth and then transferred the viscid liquid to the portals of her vagina. She gasped softly, with pleasure. Slowly I massaged her, alternately agitating the little, growing bump of clitoris, then working my finger down and ever deeper into the widening vaginal passage.

"Let's get rid of these," I said. I stretched the impeding undergarment with my wrist.

She lifted her hips accommodatingly so I could drag the panties down over her thighs and knees. She bicycled her legs to get free of them, kicked them aside. I hurriedly jettisoned my own briefs. She sat up to shrug off the open bra.

"Would you like me to suck you?" she said. She looked into my eyes with a blurry intimacy I saw only in these moments.

"If you want to," I said huskily.

She rolled onto her knees, bent over me, white breasts and *nyaminyami* dangling, daintily brushed away the hair that fell around her face, pinched the pendant out of the way against her chest and tentatively licked the rubescent crown of my straining penis. I groaned and lay back limp as I saw her fit her lips around it, and gradually, up, down, up, down, up, down, swallow more and more of the shaft.

I'm always vexed by the lack of simultaneous reciprocity in oral sex, even when you curl into the 69 position, which I find ultimately unsatisfactory. After a moment I reached out toward the brown bush of hair visible below her belly and, as she squirmed to facilitate, inserted my finger into her vagina. I thumbed her clitoris.

"Careful," I gasped after enjoying as much as I dared of the lubricious sensation she was slurpily giving me.

She brushed her hair aside, met my eyes again and lay back. I rolled atop her, kissed her, pressing hard against her spongy flesh. I lowered my lips to her earlobe. Then the hollow under her chin. I worked my way down, a reverent kiss for her neck, each breast, her inny navel, the furry, tousled mons, the fine brown strands trailing around her pink, parted labia. I licked her clitoris. The faintly uric fragrance intensified when I flicked my tongue into the salty folds of her wet vulva. I began a steady back-and-forth stimulation with my tongue and lips.

"Aaahhh," she purred. "Use your finger too."

I did.

After a few moments I felt her hands cup my ears. She was lifting me away.

"Come up here, beside me," she invited. "But I want you to keep on rubbing."

I spat into my cupped fingertips as before. Her hand went to her mouth at the same time. Tenderly we moistened each other. She began to pump my penis in slow rhythm with my palpations of her clitoris.

She came very quickly. We'd made love only once since our arrival in Africa, in our tent in the campground at Lake Kariba. Because of the cramped setting, the insubstantial privacy and the hard underlayment, she'd been distracted from achieving orgasm. I've always felt that to be a failure on my part. Not that it happened often. And she always reassured me that it was a question of her state of mind, not of my inadequate technique or unwillingness to persist. This time, though, I could feel her tensing, see her cheeks raddle and a flush spread across her chest, hear the low gurgle start in her throat.

"Okay. Yes," she grimaced. Her back arched. Her grip on my penis clenched. "Okay. Oh. Yes. Oh! Ah!"

She shuddered and began to thrash as my finger slithered back and forth over the fibrous clitoris and darted deep into the socket of her vagina. I shared her excitement as if it were mine.

Her orgasm continued in several waves. Then, urgently, she coaxed me on top of her. She guided my penis inside her syrupy sheath and began to rock with me as I pumped, subtly at first, my arms wrapped around her, supported by my elbows, then with accelerating intensity. Sometimes I could feel her cervix if I drove in too fiercely, so I restrained myself. Her knees were pulled up high, her thighs tight against my hips, her pelvis tipped to accept my full penetration.

"I love to fuck you," I whispered.

She smiled, a bit shyly. "I love being fucked by you," she said. Her green-flecked irises were misty.

I stopped thrusting and relaxed slightly, transferring some of my weight off my elbows to her torso. Her breasts pillowed me, nipples on nipples. For a moment I simply relished the miraculous pleasure of being entwined and engulfed by this plush woman's body. Laura's body. My wife's body. To be hilted within her. Warmed by her genitive juices. About to spew mine.

There was an unmistakeable physiological lurch. No need to hold back. She'd had her orgasm.

I pushed myself up, supported on stiff arms, and bent my neck to watch the glistening root of my penis slide in and out beneath the two tufts of damp hair between our groins. Looked up to watch her breasts surge and sway as I rammed into her. She spread her arms wide, armpits white and naked, shaved before lunch. There was a sheen of sweat at her hairline and on her upper lip. Her tongue peeked from the dry corner of her mouth. She stared into my eyes and nodded.

I thrust, thrust, began to lose focus on all sensation except one, the pressure surging now irreversibly in my loins.

"Uungh!" I announced. "I'm coming."

Her irises rolled up behind her lids and she flung her arms around my neck, fingernails raking my shoulders.

"Unh! Unh! Unh!" I grunted as I jetted my semen into her. At each spasmodic spurt she shuddered with me.

"Give it to me!" she hissed. "Give it to me!"

I heard her as if on tape delay. At the orgasmic instant I was in what's said to be ecstasy. A vertiginous oblivion to everything but the release.

"Oh, yes," I said, cognition returning. "Oh, yes. You have it."

I continued the metronomic motion, part reflex, part intent, long after I was spent. Then I again released most of the weight of my upper body onto her. We lay in each other's embrace, cheek glued to cheek, the excited thump of our hearts resonating in each other's ribcages. Every so often I'd play a reminiscent little pelvic riff.

"I love you," I whispered, my lips brushing the fine-china intricacies of her ear. Having years ago read the repeated criticism that American men are reluctant to express that sentiment, and determined to conform to no stereotypes, I'd become very free with "I love you"'s. It was a modest favor, an ego-boost a man ought to be willing to accord a woman, I'd reasoned, and I almost always believed it when I said it, depending on definitions. Especially in these moments of post-coital gratitude. If sticking around for nine years meant anything, my declarations to Laura came with a minimum of qualifications.

She gave me a vaginal squeeze. "I love *you*," she echoed.

What with jobs and daily stresses, our love-making was now down to about once a week on average—usually a Friday night after a vinous restaurant meal or a quiet Saturday or Sunday morning on languid first waking, rather like this afternoon. Sometimes the periods of distracted abstinence stretched longer and sometimes—especially vacations—we shared randy patches and repaired to bed a couple of times a day, or almost daily for a week. I'd say our sex life was still pretty satisfactory overall, even if the fervor with which we'd clawed at each other when we'd first met—made love standing up in elevators, huddled behind the car-door at rest stops on interstates, awkwardly seated on the can in the lavatory of a 747 *en route* to London on our first major trip together (claiming our membership in the Mile-High Club), shoulder-deep with swimsuit bottoms pulled down in the Mediterranean off the crowded beach at Cap d'Ail (her bravely uncovered breasts *a la mode* had had me in a state of perpetual hormonal *qui vive*)— was certainly a thing of the past. Age played a part. Menopause loomed for her, though she hadn't yet reported any major symptoms. And my erections tended not to last as long as they once had. Though they were still reliable and lasted long enough.

This one wasn't altogether typical. I must have been really horny. As she'd been too, thankfully.

"That was a good one," I sighed.

"Mm. Definitely."

"You want me to come out?"

"Not yet, if you don't want to."

We clung together, silent, blissful, cradled on each other's placid breathing. The current of air between the two open, gauze-curtained cabin side windows caressed my back, my buttocks, my thighs and calves, the soles of my feet. I replayed the sensations I'd just experienced—still languished in—and chuckled at the marvel. Sixteen years of prurient Catholic education in the repressive Midwest of midcentury had left me, paradoxically, with sex as my only sacrament.

Laura squirmed beneath me and tapped my back. She coughed demonstratively. "You're getting too heavy."

"Sorry," I said. I raised myself off her using my elbows again. As I shifted I felt a gout of clammy semen trickle from her. I'd begun to wilt.

"I'm going to come out now," I said.

"Okay."

I bowed and gently kissed her lips. I kissed each softening nipple as I slowly withdrew. Then I crouched and kissed the pungent tangle on her mons.

"I love all your parts," I said. "Thank you, parts. Thank you, Laura. *Zikomo.* Salami."

"I think you mean *sala-NI*," she said.

I rolled onto my back beside her. "*Tsalani*," I whispered in agreement.

My penis was still semi-erect and glazed with its exudate. I reached over to touch the oozing wetness between the lips of her vulva.

"Too bad we never used this stuff to make a baby," I said.

She laid her hand over mine, interlaced our fingers, as if helping to hold my semen in. "I know. The timing was just off. I was too old by the time we got together."

"Not really," I said.

"Forty-four? When we were married, anyway. And I don't remember you pushing me to get pregnant back then."

"Well. Women have been known to have babies at that age."

"Yeah. Not this woman."

"Even now, it's possible. Through the miracles of modern science."

"Yuck! Can you imagine us in our seventies still trying to cope with a teenager? Assuming there weren't any problems with Down's, or multiple fetuses, or any of that other horrible stuff that can happen when your eggs are old."

"Rich guys do it. With their trophy wives."

"Better get yourself a trophy wife, then, bud. This one's through with child-bearing, thank you. Having Lisa wasn't exactly a picnic at thirty-one. Anyway, I don't recall our having had this conversation when it counted, strangely enough."

"Of course we did. Subliminally."

She snorted. "Possibly if we'd've gotten married right off the bat...."

"More than subliminally!" I persisted. "We talked! We both knew how each other felt. You were really into career, for one thing."

"I did used to think about it," she admitted. "When we'd first started making love? I was so smitten? I'd just secretly stop taking the pill and conceive your love-child. Throw it all away. Wouldn't that have been romantic? Wouldn't you have just been tickled pink?"

"Absolutely."

"Uh-huh. The detectives would've still been on your trail, trying to track you down."

"I'd be in Africa."

"I don't think so. The only reason you're here is because of me."

"True. The only reason I'm anywhere, my dearest, is because of you."

"Got that right."

"I'm not saying we *should've* had a child of our own," I retracked. "I'm just saying that sometimes I think it's kind of too bad circumstances didn't work out that we did. We'd've made a good one."

"Good looking," she agreed wistfully, "I don't doubt. One thing both of us have is very good-looking children."

"No thanks to their other parent."

"Absolutely not. It'd be interesting to see what a child of ours would've looked like."

"Would it have been short and squat like you? Or tall and lithe like me?"

"Yeah, with your beady little eyes and big hook nose...?"

"You know what a large nose is a sign of," I said archly.

"...Or my eyes...?"

"Your big beautiful orbs and your high cheekbones and your elegant features," I proposed.

"Mm," she murmured, disarmed. "Something like that."

We both lay silent for a moment.

"Anyway," she said, "then we'd've just screwed the kid up like the rest of 'em."

"That's *all* the fault of the other parent," I said.

"Or so it's tempting to think."

"Anyway they're not so screwed up. Merely teenagers, for the most part..."

"Megan and Chris are far from teenagers."

"Yep. I keep forgetting. Okay. Young adults. With all the attendant tribulations."

"I know. You're right."

"And I think Lisa's doing great," I declared. "Seems to've been a good year for her. Once the homesickness wore off."

"Passed her courses, anyway, apparently. Since I haven't heard anything except that she's going back in the fall. Have you? Of course, we have no idea what her grades were, except the one A. That still gets me, that they're not allowed to tell you any more."

"She'll do fine. She'll have her ups and downs."

"Oh, really, doctor?"

"*Ja, mein frau.* Life *ist* vewy divigult. Vee must press onvarts ass best vee *kann*."

"I certainly appreciate your wise counsel. If not your atrocious accent."

"Eet ees free, ze counsel. *Und* vorth every *pfennig*."

"Indeed. I now understand why your own children are such healthy specimens."

"Are they not?" I bristled, suddenly concerned and defensive.

"No, no, I just mean they're... normal too. Still working out their own... agendas."

"Read 'problems.' 'Hang-ups.'"

"Read what you will."

"Yeah, well, it's true. They've got... issues they're still trying to resolve. They aren't there yet. Where I'd like to see 'em, anyway—happy, fulfilled people."

"They'll get there," she said. It was her turn to be reassuring. "Chris called right before we left...."

"You didn't tell me."

"Well. You wouldn't've remembered anyway. You were at the office still?"

"What'd he say?"

"Nothing special...."

"Not asking for money," I inquired suspiciously. "Or wanting to stay in the house while we're gone."

"No, no. He was just saying goodbye, before we left. Wanted to wish us *bon voyage*. Hoped we'd have a good trip."

"Mm. That was nice of him."

"It was."

"How'd he sound?"

"Perfectly fine."

"I'm assuming he's still working."

"I'm assuming too. I didn't ask."

"I just don't like the idea of his living off his girlfriends. That seems to me to be unfair. That's what bothers me sometimes. I wish my kids had set better precedents."

"For Lisa."

"Yeah. And...."

"Actually, she and Megan talk a lot these days. Did you know that? She says Megan tells her 'Don't make the same mistakes I did....'"

"Make different mistakes."

"Mm. Something like that, I guess. 'At least make your own mistakes,' is the implication. She's become a real confidante and counselor to Lisa. Which is great. Megan's maturing, I think."

"She's worrying me less. She seems to've calmed down considerably."

"She has. If that's the word for it."

"Nothing left to pierce, anyway."

Laura chuckled. I felt a fresh dribble of semen against my fingers.

"But I've always been a with-it father of the Nineties, haven't I? Whatever turns her on, I said. Now that it isn't guaranteed to freak Susan out, I think it's lost a lot of its allure."

"You had things much easier, though, you know that. Since they weren't living with you, with us. That made it that much easier to stay calm and detached and tolerant. I sympathize with Susan on that. I was scared to death Lisa was going to emulate Megan and come home one day with a nose ring. Or a safety pin through her navel."

"She does have five holes in her ears."

"Ah, well. That's just the style."

"As aren't clitoris rings?" I pointed out. I immediately regretted the ill-chosen anatomical reference. We were, after all, talking about our daughters. "Or, um. Whatever. Piercings."

"I guess," she agreed. "Some of it, though, like that, seems to me to be more of a statement. A cry for attention. Help. I don't know. I mean, really. More than just a style thing. Self-mutilation. Which is when it makes me uncomfortable. Thank God Megan never went that far anyway. So I have no trouble with pierced ears."

"Actually, what it is is kind of African," I proposed. "You know? Ubangi lips. Bones through the nose. Long, distended earlobes. Western women are beginning to share the beauty standards of primitive people. Or maybe I should say... tribal? Aboriginal?"

"Not that I've noticed too many plates in lips. Or purposely distended earlobes."

"Well, I have. A few ears, anyway. Even on guys. Always astounds me. But okay, so don't take me too literally. Just wait, though, you know, maybe? I mean, even something like having five or six jewels or posts or danglies in your ears, like Lisa—in the cartilege, and all around the outside. Or a ruby in the flange of your nostril. A ring in your eyebrow. Megan. Think how the grandmothers react!"

"Not to mention the mothers."

"Exactly. It's so *unpuritan*! So... *unwhite*!"

"Well...."

"*Tattoos*!"

"Mm," Laura muttered.

"Full arms! All over the back. In colors."

"Yes. I fully expect Lisa 'll come home with a tatoo somewhere before the four years are up, if that's what you mean. If nothing else than to spite me. I've reconciled myself to that."

"Used to be only low-lifes had 'em. A woman with a tattoo was a hooker, or a biker babe—moll, mama, whatever the term of art is, or was."

"Just so it's tasteful. Not too conspicuous. That's all I hope."

"Now all kinds of people are tattooed. George Schultz, supposedly. Princeton tiger on his ass. You'd think that'd squash the fad right there."

"I need a towel," Laura suddenly declared. "See what a mess you've made of me, you pig? With your disgusting male demands?"

"You were a mess long before I ever got hold of you," I said.

I swung my legs to the floor and circled the foot of the bed to the bathroom. I grabbed one of the two fresh white terrycloth handtowels off the bar beside the washbasin and blotted my own genitals before returning to slip it in gently below Laura's pubic triangle. She lolled there with one hand behind her head, bare as a peach except for the towel pinched between her thighs, her *nyaminyami* and her braided elephant-hair bracelet—a sexy touch. My corpulent Maja, my steamily satiated, middle-aged odalisque.

"You're still in great shape, Daniel," she abruptly volunteered, "you know that?"

She was appraising my nakedness as frankly as I was appraising hers.

"Well! Thank you," I replied. I inflated my lungs and subtly tightened my pecs and abs. "Actually, I was just thinking the same thing about you."

"No, I'm too fat," she demurred. "You said it yourself. 'Squat....'"

"But squat in a *good* way!"

"Ah. Yeah. I'd forgotten there was that aspect."

"You're round and firm and fully packed," I offered. Once voiced, the catchwords insisted on completion. "Free and easy on the draw."

She cocked an eyebrow.

"That's a slogan from an ancient cigarette commercial," I explained. "You're too young to remember, I guess. Actually, I am too." I was startled by the abrupt surfacing of that shard from some midden of antedeluvian memory.

"'Round?' Thanks a lot. There's a description I find really flattering."

"Firm. Fully packed," I emphasized.

She patted her slack abdomen. "I need to lose twenty pounds."

"You'd be a wraith. We're both wearing the padding God intended us to put on at this stage in life. Tide us through the vicissitudes. Famine...." I couldn't think of anything else appropriate for a list. "Famine especially."

"We should skip dinner tonight."

"It's with the group. That wouldn't be friendly."

"So we'll just have to order lightly."

"Fine with me," I said. I sucked in my stomach and tapped the flesh around my navel, testing its resilience, feeling its blubbery thickness. I could still evoke a faint shadow of vertical definition between the muscle groups. "Gotta try to get back a six-pack. That's Chris' thing, huh? Why he works out all the time? Wow the babes."

"He's a hunk all right."

"So what am I, chopped liver?" I objected. "Where'd he inherit that bod!" I grinned, cocked my arms, elbows forward, fingertips on hipbones, held my breath and, short of flexing, subtly tensed every muscle that would tense. "What d'you think? Still a six-pack in there, hey?"

"More like a keg," she said. "And you're dripping."

I exhaled sharply, looked down to see the dangling strand. "Oops," I apologized. I snatched the towel from between her legs and caught the bead before it fell to the plank floor. I started to wad the towel back when she pivoted on her buttocks and sat up.

"Never mind," she said. She took the towel from me, rose and waddled to the bathroom clutching it in place. "Let's go for a quick dip in the pool." She swung the door shut behind her. "If there's time," she added, voice now slightly muffled. I heard the muted sizzle of pee striking water.

I went around the bed and checked my watch, then slipped it over my wrist.

"Ten of four," I called. "We'll have to make it fairly fast."

"Get your suit on, then," she instructed me. The toilet flushed. Tap water started running.

"Yes, ma'am," I obliged. I went to my suitcase and pawed through it for the blue nylon shorts-with-liner I'd packed to double as swimming trunks. I would let the chlorinated water cleanse me.

The bathroom door opened and Laura jiggled out. Her suitcase was on the folding luggage stand next to mine. When she sidled near I reached out and steered her into my arms. I clasped her tightly to me, breasts mashed against ribs, flank against flank, skin once again squeaking against skin. I bent my neck and kissed her upturned mouth. Sometimes I loved Laura, felt her presence as my fated soulmate, with such goopy intensity it was almost scary. Probably to her even more than to me. Without anticipating it, I started to get aroused again.

She pulled away from my lips with a playfully definitive "mwaa!" and danced backwards, shielding her crotch.

"Oh, no you don't, buster!" she chided, grinning. "No more of that. Maybe later tonight. We've only got till five, you know. Game drive leaves right on the dot, they said."

I drew a deep breath. "Promises, promises," I grumbled. I picked up my trunks. "Hey," I said, stepping into a leghole and regarding the obstacle of my horizontal penis. "I just realized something. We've only got two continents left to make love on."

She thought for a split second. "South America. And Antarctica."

"Yep!"

"I somehow think we may never complete the course."

"The circumscrewigation of the earth. Who knows? We're pretty adventuresome. We've done it underwater. We've done it a mile high. Now we've done it in the Heart of Darkness...."

"Poor Africa, always to have that label attached."

"Yeah. It's the law. You're not allowed to think about Africa without making the connection. The obligatory metaphor. I think it's a requirement of the UN Stereotype Commission. Like always linking the Amazon with headhunters and poison darts and piranhas. Buenos Aires with Carnival...."

"Carnival's in Rio."

"Rio, I mean, right. I always get 'em confused. Buenos Aires is the tango. Huh? *Evita*. The South Pole is penguins and polar bears."

"What are we talking about?"

"You figure it. Our next two trips."

"I don't think I'm all that into the game, really."

"You wouldn't want to see penguins and polar bears? The Ross Ice Shelf?"

"Just so long as I don't have to make love on an ice shelf. In the missionary position, anyway."

"You can be on top."

She shimmied as she worked her black one-piece up over her hips. "I'll go anywhere you want, as long as you're the one who makes the arrangements. And I'll be just as appreciative as you've been, of all my efforts that got us here."

She hunched her shoulders and dropped her breasts into the under-wired cups of the bra. Then she straightened and held her decolletage in place while she poked her arms through the straps.

"Hey, I've been *very* appreciative!" I declared.

"No you haven't," she pouted.

"I have so! Okay, then. I'll say it again. Are you listening carefully this time? It's a *great* trip! A *great* trip!"

"It is pretty neat, isn't it?"

"It certainly is. Probably the most interesting we've taken so far."

"And we're only halfway through it," she noted.

*T*hey were no more than fifty feet from us, ears pricked forward, faces turned to watch us, but otherwise sprawled unmoving.

Four of them cozied together on a grassy hummock in the crook of a tiny stream that zigzagged across this barren stretch of veld. Two others lolled a bit apart, on the lip of the trough cut into the laterite subsoil by the spring-fed trickle. One posed in regal library-steps attitude—forepaws out, haunches folded, head high. The other was partially hidden below it.

All six were males, Steve said.

That surprised me, since none of them had a mane. Still too young, he explained. And some males never sprout them. They were fully grown, though. Even I could see that

IV. Night Drive

Steve, at the wheel of the open HiLux, spotted the tawny shapes among the tawny swales of the broad plain from well over a mile away.

"Lions," he announced curtly, pointing.

"Ooh, brilliant!" Mel yelped, bouncing with excitement behind us. "Where?"

"Ah, yes," Graeme murmured, having immediately pulled himself to his feet by the door's window-frame and braced himself to train his binoculars in the direction indicated.

The HiLux was a stock Japanese four-by-four pickup with the cab roof and windshield removed. Graeme was riding shotgun, supposedly as Steve's spotter. Laura and I sat on the first bank of seats bolted to the bed behind the roll-bar welded at the driver's back. Mel, Jen and Gerhard were on a second triple bench, to the rear and stepped above our heads.

"Off to the left. About ten o'clock," Steve replied.

Deftly he swung the HiLux in a quick quarter-circle and nosed toward them, maneuvering at a steady twenty miles an hour or so among the spongy depressions and angular creeklets that scarred what otherwise appeared to be a level brown savannah.

The rills were like crevasses on a glacier, disguised in the thickening amber light until just before you bucketed into them. But Steve knew the terrain. He kept to the salt-whitened hardpan and steered us to the brink of the tiny stream beside which the lions reposed.

We were halfway there before I could distinguish them from the background.

We sat with the motor idling and studied them as they regarded us. We spoke in low voices, but they looked pretty unflappable.

"Had a good feed this morning," Steve commented. "Big alpha male with a black mane in the pride too, as well as several females, according to what the boy said. Off having a look-see somewhere, those are. No sign of 'em at the carcass."

"Did we go by it?" I asked.

He nodded. I guess he hadn't wanted to call our attention to a pile of gnawed ribs and carmine shreds.

"If the females are in oestrus," he continued, "the alpha male could be busy on the job. A lioness is quite demanding when she's in heat. But the male is fully up to it, so to speak. There's a record of a single male lion having accommodated half a dozen of the ladies in his pride no fewer than one hundred and fifty-seven times within a period of fifty-five hours. Nonstop copulation. Once every twenty-one minutes on average."

I glanced at Laura and raised my eyebrows. She grinned and lifted hers.

"That's a factlet I bet you never miss an opportunity to throw out," she said to Steve with a laugh.

"*Is* the sort of thing people tend to find memorable," he acknowledged. "Though reactions seem to differ, men's to women's."

"Pretty intimidating," I agreed.

"One hundred and fifty, tops, for me, I think," Gerhard nodded.

"Oh, too *right!*" Mel hooted. She hit him on the arm with the back of her hand.

I had a sense that they had not, in fact, slept together.

The lions' ears flicked at the sharp movement.

"Whoops. Sorry," Mel murmured, sliding low in her seat. After a moment she added, "They're lovely, aren't they? Loungin' about like big tabbies."

Without manes the young lions did resemble housecats, housecats pumped up on steroids. Sleek, heavily muscled, with larger heads in proportion to more compact bodies than domestic cats. Their brindle backs, shoulders and ears, I could see from this proximity, were actually darker than the tufts of coarse grass on which they rested. And their underjaws, chests and bellies were paler, glowing golden in the waning light.

Somehow the combination made for perfect long-range camouflage. Their muzzles appeared to be framed by blond Van Dyke beards.

It wasn't hard, though, to imagine the terror Mpamvu's attendant had experienced pedaling up suddenly upon these guys. No wonder he'd bolted for the tree. Not that they couldn't have scampered up and clawed him out of it if they'd been of a mind to.

There were a couple of scrawny, flat-topped thornbushes growing where a greener tint to the grass indicated a fork in the rivulet, off beyond the furthest lion. No refuge for a fleeing man there.

The horizons were an unbroken ring of olive-gray scrub sparsely dotted with uprights—solitary acacias or whatever. At least half were dead. The smooth gray trunks rising to skeletal vees of bare branch looked like bone—too pallid, I thought, to have been killed by fire. Thirst, perhaps? In any case, the closest tree one could run for was a good thousand yards away.

"They don't seem to be bothered by us, by our being here," Laura observed.

"They're interested. You can see they're paying close attention," Steve assured her. "So long as we're inside the truck, though, we aren't in danger."

"What if we got out?" she proposed. "What if somebody were to start walking toward them?"

"Yeh, give 'em a pet. Tickle 'em behind the ears," Mel giggled. "They look all cuddly enough now, they do."

"Make it about two steps," Steve said. "You'd be amazed at how fast these guys can cover ground. Shape of the lorry's no threat to 'em, but once you were away from it, afoot, you'd look to be prey."

There was a certain exhilaration about loitering so close to these huge, feral carnivores. In the open HiLux, even though our seats were well above the ground, we'd be utterly vulnerable should they decide to leap at us. Which is why, no doubt, Steve had kept the motor running.

Imagine if it were to suddenly cough, sputter and seize. Or the tires were to spin themselves into the dubious turf when Steve started to accelerate away.

Been there, done that. This time I doubted any of us would be dismounting to dig and push. I was reminded of a cartoon, an old Gary Larsen "Far Side," about lions swarming over a Land Rover full of tourists, and one telling another, "I actually prefer the canned to the fresh."

I also recalled a similarly *a propos* punchline, though the cartoon involved polar bears pawing at an igloo: "These are my favorites: crunchy on the outside, soft and chewy on the inside."

Whether by design or simply as dictated by the topography, Steve had positioned us so that the narrow stream separated us from the lions. It served as a psychological moat, if nothing else. Nothing else, indeed.

"I don't suppose the creek'd be much of a deterrence to 'em," I mused aloud.

Steve responded with a dry chuckle.

"So are they a threat to humans generally around here?" I wondered. "Like crocodiles?"

Steve accorded me a glance over his shoulder. His expression was quizzical, but I think it was just because of his position, neck twisted, near eyebrow raised.

"Not really," Graeme interjected. He was anxious to come off as knowledgeable too. Riding as Steve's spotter was an apprenticeship; within a few weeks, he'd given us to understand, he'd be taking the exam that would allow him to drive guests around the park by himself in search of game. For now, though, he was still just a Cape Town accountant eager to pose in the khaki mantle of White Hunter.

"Steer clear of people for the most part, they do," he continued. "Wary of us as we are of them. Only attack if they feel threatened. Or some poor chappie finds himself in the wrong place at the wrong time."

"Twelve-year-old girl in a village down near Chichele was taken by a lion about a month ago," Steve observed. "Doesn't happen often."

"'Taken,'" Laura murmured. She caught my eye. "They always say somebody was 'taken.' Have you noticed?" She shuddered.

"We were told a camper was killed in his tent by a lioness not long ago. Near Nsefu," I said.

"Can't say I know about that one," Graeme mused.

"Nor I, and I would," Denys said. "Perhaps they were talking about Roger van Wyk. Famous hunter, safari leader. One of the founders of Zambia Trails. But that was nearly twenty years ago. And it was up on the Mupamadzi River."

"Mm." I raised an eyebrow. "Still...," I said.

Gerhard had been busily snapping photos, checking light settings, exchanging lenses. The rest of us had memorialized our encounter with the lions on film too. Mel, Jen and Laura had brought along standard consumer-grade 35-millimeter single-lens reflexes. At Laura's prompting, I'd dutifully produced the little autofocus micro-35 I'd tucked into my shirt-pocket—the only camera I still owned besides the novelty Polaroid. (I'd bought that so Christopher could keep a step-by-step record of where all the parts went when, at 18, he'd set about dismantling the engine on my old Fiat Spyder. A midlife-crisis present to myself on my forty-fifth birthday, the sixties-vintage car was his, I'd promised, if he could make it run again. And he had, for a while.)

My role, Laura had made clear, was to be her documentary backup, for the slide show she would inevitably compile for the edification of family and friends when we got back home. And I guess it really would have been perverse of me to have visited Africa in this day and age and not to have come back with any pictures. Although at best the lions were going to show up as unimpressive middle-distance blobs, like the rest of the wildlife I'd been shooting without the benefit of a zoom lens.

At various stages in my life I'd been a serious photographer, starting in high school when I'd patrolled the sidelines at football games with a cumbersome, then state-of-the-art Speed Graphic. I even loaded and developed its film plates in the darkroom-closet next to the third-floor chapel.

Being sports photographer for the yearbook was a mildly shameful alternative to wearing pads on the muddy field myself. But the clattery, grunt-accentuated collisions I was freezing with my flashbulbs truly frightened me. Anyway, having entered kindergarten almost a full year younger than my classmates, I was too short, thin and timorous for varsity sports in high school. And when I belatedly beanpoled to six-three (and about a hundred and sixty pounds) between the fall of my senior year and my sophomore year in college, it was too late for major conference basketball or competitive swimming.

The former had been the passion I'd nurtured in friends' backyards and playground courts throughout my childhood. Basketball was a finesse game back then. And I'd never stopped honing my skills—dribble, pass, float the jumper, post up, launch and score from deep... and yes, more recently, box out ferociously, bang the boards, strain for the put-back tip—with four- or five-day-a-week YMCA gym fervor until only a couple of years ago. My battered joints had finally begun to betray me.

Swimming had been something my mother had encouraged; swimmers, she'd frequently explained, have the best male physiques. (An intriguing observation in retrospect, since my father generally shunned water. His physique had always seemed ideal to me, though, toned successively by baseball, basketball, volleyball, tennis, golf and bowling.)

As a freshman in high school, however, I'd shrunk from the pool as I had from the basketball tryouts. They'd meant revealing in the locker-room that I hadn't yet sprouted pubic hair. By my junior year that technicality had been taken care of, but the ensuing growth spurt somehow spoiled my hydrodynamic profile as it slowed my footspeed. Still, I'd swum intramurals and continued to grind out fitness laps sporadically for most of my life. Recently I'd even been considering joining a master's swim club, on the theory that coaching and real training and attrition among the competition might by now be sufficient to give me a geriatric shot at medaling in competition. Not to mention, of course, that the non-weight-bearing exercise would be easy on arthritic joints, good for the heart and helpful in transmuting that incipient abdominal keg back into a six-pack.

As to photography, I'd often been sent out with a camera as a general assignment reporter for the small suburban Bay Area daily that gave me my first job after the Navy. Later, in a variety of PR jobs, I'd found it useful to take my own pictures at times rather than try to instruct a hired photographer in the angle or composition I thought I wanted.

I'd published a couple of text-and-photo essays in local Sunday magazines as a journalistic sidelight, but as the years went by my pictures got lousier and lousier. I think it was the smiling heads that did it—those ritual left-to-right lineups of the bush-league personages in attendance at ribbon-cuttings or civic luncheons we were promoting. Slightly tilted, posed clumsily, just a hair out of focus, my frames gradually became too poor even to send out to the throwaway rags that would run anything.

It was a subconscious rebellion, I guess, an expression of contempt, or self-contempt. And fortunately I'd soon risen in rank sufficiently to be able to assign such scutwork to lesser minions. My engagement with photography had never revived.

I'd always had a subversive sense anyway that the apparatus interposed between me and the subject was not an orderer and focuser of experience, but rather an obscurer and narrower. Maybe that's why I preferred wide-angle lenses. I was a big believer—evidenced, I suppose, by these digressions—in peripheral vision.

So I took my perfunctory, but well composed, two quick shots of the lions for Laura. And when Gerhard had finished diddling with the array of lenses and camera bodies in the leather bag between his feet, we all agreed we'd sufficiently contemplated the lions contemplating us.

Steve crammed the HiLux into gear and drove us away.

Curious, isn't it? You fly ten thousand miles to see wild animals, gawp with excitement at first sighting, stare for five minutes, and then, bored and restless, depart in search of the next ephemeral stimulus. Kind of a metaphor for life, I guess. (We'd probably have stayed a few minutes longer if the lions had been fighting, fucking or feeding.)

The next stop on our itinerary was a hot spring that bubbled up out of the turf to create a shallow pond from which radiated most of the slender streams that crisscrossed this band of open land.

I'd noticed odd white splotches along the rim of the brook beside which the lions lay—mineral salts, I now realized, crystalized around the pond.

This whole *veld* was parched. The earth was gray and alkaline-looking where it shone through the clumpy stubble, like patches of mange on the coat of an ailing lion. The rocks appeared lichenous, and the subsoil visible in cracks was oxide-red.

There was an arctic quality to the land; it called to mind tundra. Maybe the reason the grasses were so stunted and so many of the surrounding trees were dead was that they'd been poisoned by the harsh groundwater that funneled up here.

Steve shut off the engine and he and Graeme got out. We all climbed down too as they dragged out a copious ice-chest of bottled beer and sodas.

"Cocktail hour," Steve declared. "We'll take a break here till dark."

I'd heard the muffled rattling of the bottles in the space behind Steve's seat and I'd been anticipating this stop. Free-flowing beer was one of the highlights of each of our safari "highlights," I'd found. We'd toasted our canoe excursion above Vic Falls with *Zambezi*s plucked dripping from a shallow cache at the haulout; we'd uncapped endless bottles from the boats' cold-lockers on our river and Lake Kariba cruises; we'd washed down a delicious picnic lunch of cold roast chicken in Hwange and that barbecued lamb in Lusaka with beer plentifully provided.

A civilized appreciation of alcoholic refreshment was a trait I'd always admired in the Brits and their colonial cousins—stoked in the Navy when an invitation to the wardroom of a ship flying a white ensign promised convivial rounds of the grog forbidden us American officers aboard our own puritanical vessels.

With the setting of the sun, Laura and I were metabolically primed for drinks anyway. We'd packed into our luggage plastic water bottles filled with gin, vermouth and stuffed olives, and it was our custom to mix ourselves martinis to sip before dinner in camp, as we did every night at home. In fact, we'd treated ourselves to an early one already—enticed by the luxuries of real glasses and a bucket of ice from the bar—while dressing for this drive after our hurried swim.

Everyone except Mel opted for a beer. We lounged against the fenders or perched on the hood of the HiLux, chatting desultorily. One by one we strolled over to dip a finger into the riffle in the pond. The water was tepid in the outflow arms, warmer but no more than lukewarm as far as I could reach in the central pool. The differential, however, suggested that the temperature might be quite hot at the source. Probably not scalding, though. There was no discernible odor.

"Anybody ever come here to soak in this for pleasure?" I asked Steve. "Like a natural hot tub?"

"I've never done," he replied. "You're certainly welcome to give it a go."

That set Mel and Gerhard and Jen off on a round of teasing. "Shall we?"

"Sounds a brilliant idea."

"I will if you will, Jen."

"I think not, actually."

"You're a prude, you are. Gerhard's always game. Right, Gerhard?"

"Of course."

"You can go first, love. Tell us how it feels."

"Yes. Thank you. But always ladies first."

"No, no. Don't worry. If you say it's delicious, we'll follow right behind."

"Speak for yourself, Mel."

"I go only with company," said Gerhard.

"You're just keen to see us to drop our knickers, aren't you, you dirty man?"

"Oh, we'll all drop knickers, of course. Who'd go in with clothing on?"

Et cetera. Ad nauseam.

Jen, whose charms I would not at all have minded assessing unclad, was really quite prim. Swimming in Lake Kariba and at the Chibembe pool she'd worn a constructed one-piece black suit that was relatively unrevealing except for the modish high cut of its legs. She had a shapely figure, shoulder-length auburn hair that fluffed out full when it wasn't damp or too long unwashed, and porcelain English skin she was trying carefully to darken in the sun. A faint rash where she'd razored herself to accommodate the narrow crotch of the bathing suit had been visible in the milky flesh at her groins.

For all the superficial vivacity she displayed with Mel, Jen was as essentially private as the rest of the Brits. None of us had been so impolite as to have plied her for more than the most basic occupational and biographical outlines, at least within my hearing. Laura, though, had caught an allusion in a conversation between

Jen and Mel that suggested Jen was newly divorced. She seemed young for that. But it would certainly explain her solo travel.

Melanie, less favored in the looks department, was readily acceptable as unattached. But if Jen had been hoping for romantic distraction when she'd signed on for this safari, she'd struck out badly. The unfailing good grace with which she was responding was admirable.

Steve and Graeme, no surprise, were playing to her. All the male guides had. (There'd been only one female guide we'd encountered, a pert, twentyish blond with a ponytail and a killer Rhodesian accent—the refined, strawberries-and-cream version that went with a hyphenated last name—who'd provided the horses and squired us on our canter through the bush above Victoria Falls. Philippa Hampton-Smith had not, I must admit, played to me.)

Steve and Graeme, like the others, were sufficiently professional to keep it within bounds. They were at least trying to distribute eye contact and banter to everyone in the group. Nor did I see or foresee any sparks being struck by either of them in Jen's heart.

Steve, the Kiwi, was gruff by nature, stocky and knobby-kneed in his butt-hugging, abbreviated Down-Under-style khaki shorts. He was in his mid-thirties, I'd judge, with a stripe of glistening mahogany scalp running from brow to crown and a bushy brown beard worn as counterpoint to the close-clipped residuum of early male-pattern baldness.

The younger, gangling Graeme, meanwhile, was too loose-strung physically and too tightly wound psychically—affable in a way that seemed counter to basic character, earnest in a way that did not inspire confidence—to appeal to the self-possessed Jen, I thought. I could imagine my son

Christopher—at least in the jargon of his teen years—dismissing Graeme as a "wannabe."

In Jen's vocabulary, I suspected, he was a South African version of a "twit."

With the fading of the light, the sky in the west flared a brilliant scarlet. A soft breeze soughed around us, still balmy with the heat off the land. That was one marked difference between the climates of equatorial Africa and coastal California: Here, sundown, shadow or overcast did not bring an immediate drop in temperature.

A strong scent of burning vegetation laced the warm gusts. I realized I'd been smelling it subliminally throughout the day.

Driving toward Chibembe in the early morning we'd seen swaths of charred grass and had coughed through a drift of acrid smoke slanting across the road off a line of live flames that were almost invisible in the daylight. Now the wispy pall hanging over the land showed clearly against the band of deepening color in the sky. And all along the western and southern horizons, fire pulsed behind distant silhouettes of trees and bush.

It was unsettling, this guttering glow. Especially to a Californian who'd nearly lost two houses to wildfire.

The first time, a midweek September morning in the nineteen-seventies, I'd been heading out the door to work when I'd noticed a black plume and then a spurt of flames on the ridge to the west of the wooded cul-de-sac in the Oakland hills where Susan and I had bought a tiny bungalow, our first venture in home ownership.

"Hey, come look! There's a fire!" I'd exclaimed—and almost in the same breath amended it to "Uh-oh. A *big* fire!"

We'd watched in awe as the blaze, with astonishing rapidity, widened and spilled down the hillside toward us. Soon I was on the roof flooding the aged asphalt shingles with a garden hose while Susan tossed the family photo albums and four-month-old Megan into our VW bug. ("Did you take your silverware?" her mother asked. Susan snorted in derision.)

I'd sent them off to safety and prepared manfully to defend our mortgage—until the eucalyptus tops started exploding at the end of the block.

The main fire was still on the far side of the canyon, a mile away to the east. But the hot, eerie wind was flinging deadly outrider sparks across the gap.

My naive valor yielded belatedly to discretion; I scrambled down the ladder and screeched off in our remaining car.

As it happened, we were not among the dozen residents of the neighborhood who had to rebuild on scorched foundations. And that luck held twenty years later, when most of the city's northeastern ridgelands were again swept by wildfire and I anxiously sniffed the sky for the southerly wind-change that would doom the Montclair Tudor Laura and I shared.

The Santa Ana-ish easterlies and the firefighters' lines held steady. I and mine were twice spared. That poor old first house, though, was reduced to a puddle of molten bathroom tiles the second time around. Not even the concrete piers and footings survived. It was near the epicenter of the later conflagration, and the extent of my previous good fortune was driven home with grim clarity: A family of four, my erstwhile neighbors, were overtaken in flight and cremated just past the foot of my former driveway.

So the sight of flames flickering unchecked across the landscape had my hackles bristling.

It was obvious we weren't in any danger; Steve and Graeme showed nothing but nonchalance, and only broad, spare savannah surrounded us. The smoke certainly made for a magnificent sunset. The spring, reflecting the ruby streak above the horizon, glistered like a puddle of red-hot lava on the darkling plain. Beyond, the rim of the earth crackled with fire. It was as if we were on a sightseeing tour to the threshold of hell, sipping cold beer and listening at our smug ease to the far-off hiss and pop of the inferno.

In the airy nightfall silence, the progress of the flames through the distant bush did seem to be audible. But it was a synesthetic phenomenon, I decided, a trick on the ears caused by the ebb and rush of the breeze and the fluctuating intensity of the glimmer.

"You don't try to fight wildfires out here, I guess, obviously," I said to Steve.

"Not much we could do," he replied, "even if we wanted to."

"No borate bombers stationed at Mfuwe."

He chuckled. "Not much bloody hope."

"You don't worry about the resort?"

"Well, we're well away from it, aren't we? Actually, this soon after the rainy season there's little real risk to the woodlands. Grass and thornscrub goes up first. The occasional leadwood. Might smolder for days, even weeks. Those are the skeletal remains you'll see out here for the most part, incidentally. Leadwood, killed by fire, often years ago. Type of combretum."

"What's the cause? Of the fires?" I asked. "Lightning? We passed a couple this morning, too, in fact, grassfires."

"People, rather more like it. Not very careful around here, actually. Build a little cookfire for the night... don't want to be on the road after dark, you don't, might walk under a tree with a leopard in it.... Heat their little pot of mealy-meal, throw on a few more sticks to hold the lions at bay, have a doss, next morning they're away. Leave the ashes smoldering. Grass all around. Or the wind comes up." He shrugged. "Poof. No worries. Just a bit of *veld*. Sometimes it's clearing the fields, burning off the stubble.

Set it, go home for a toes-up. Grass'll come back. Good for the puku, even."

"I guess they can outrun these sorts of fires, the animals. Doesn't seem to be any shortage of puku around here, that's for sure."

The slender little antelopes probably made up eighty percent of the game we'd seen since our entry into the park. Thanks to Steve, I could now distinguish the puku from the impala I'd originally thought they were. The keys, he'd explained when he'd heard me misidentify a grazing scatter to Laura shortly after we'd set out this evening, were the impalas' larger size, longer, lyre-shaped horns and black stripe down the rear of each white haunch.

"Yeh. Whistle y' to sleep at night out in the bush camp, puku will. Way they call to each other. Breed like bloody jackrabbits."

"We call 'em the jackrabbits of the Luangwa Valley," Graeme echoed.

With the sighting of the lions, Laura and I had now bagged three of the "big five" African mammals. That list had originated with hunters, who prized ferocity and size, preferably in combination. So it did not include spotted hyenas or warthogs, both very nasty pieces of comparatively small business; nor zebras, nor giraffes, notwithstanding their flamboyant exoticism; nor any of the antelopes, even the kudu or eland, notwithstanding their bulk and extravagance of horn; nor *declassé* wrigglers or fatties like crocodiles or hippopotamuses—notwithstanding the fact that those are perhaps the two most dangerous animals in Africa, according to Steve.

"Don't want to get between a hippo and water," he'd warned en route from the lodge.

He'd accelerated sharply to cross a heavily wooded stream in which a hippopotamus and calf wallowed knee-deep a few yards from the road.

"Or between a mother and her calf," he added. "Kill a lot of people who understimate how fast they can move. Hippo'll come at you like a rhino, and just as bad-tempered when it comes to protecting its territ'ry. No hesitation about taking on a lorry. Bloody well imagine the kind of damage that can do."

Technically, Laura and I had notched our first elephant and our first African buffalo on horseback outside Vic Falls. In both instances our jodhpured guide—the aforementioned, magnificently monickered Philippa Hampton-Smith—had raised her hand suddenly and we'd reined up behind her, silent in obedience to the finger at her lips.

Her Ndebele assistant, riding as if to the saddle born though in sandals and a frayed gray mechanic's jumpsuit, with a rifle slung barrel-down across his back, had jockeyed up quietly alongside us from the rear to direct our attention to something deep in the tangled undergrowth.

I caught a glimpse of the elephant's head looming momentarily above the scrubby tops of the red bushwillows. It blinked an annoyed little eye at us and crunched off in search of privacy.

But I'd had to take Philippa's word for it that the dark shapes in the high, shadow-flecked grass 15 minutes or so further on were buffalo. And she was intent on keeping us downwind, well away.

Fortunately, we'd been able to observe whole herds of both species to our hearts' content at Hwange's pans. So of the big five, only leopard and rhinoceros remained to be scored.

According to Steve and Graeme, nighttime offered the best hope of crossing paths with either of them.

The transition from dusk to darkness was fast on the winter *veld*. By the time I'd drained my second bottle of *Mosi*, the Southern Cross was clearly visible.

I always sought it out in the night sky here, and I always felt a curious, reminiscent tic of pleasure when I found it—proof that I was clinging upside down like a bat to the bottom half of the Earth.

Navigational stars—big, bright, first-magnitude stars, anyway—are scarce in the heavens of the Southern Hemisphere. *Crux Australis* has two of them. Although, of course, you'd have to choose between them if you were trying to locate yourself inside a triangle of LOPs—celestial lines of position.

That much I remembered from the Navy—along with the absurd girth of the triangles the quartermaster and I had often come up with, hunched over the chart table comparing our scribbled sextant readings against the columns in *H.O. 214* and the *Nautical Almanac*.

We'd stab a finger somewhere in the middle of the three LOPs, as close as conscientiously possible to our dead reckoning track, and hope our next morning's twilight and noon sun observations would correct the imprecision.

Which I in no way acknowledged, needless to say, in my evening position report to the captain.

(I remembered exchanging grins of self-mocking relief with the QM when the radarmen announced they'd picked up the dot of Wake Island in lonely mid-Pacific. We were on our way to Pearl from Yokosuka. Solo. Of course, we'd had Loran to back us up. These days ships can rely on satellites and the Global Positioning Network and digital readouts on liquid crystal displays. Do ensigns and j.g.s, I wonder, still turn slow pirouettes on bridge wings at dawn and dusk, frowning down at clumsily oriented star finders and then gawking up in search of *Altair, Vega, Deneb…?*)

Ideally you wanted three stars, each about halfway between the horizon and the zenith, 120 degrees apart.

Aim your sextant, adjust the index arm until you locate the star, bring the center of the pinprick of light down to the faint line in the horizon mirror, brace yourself against the roll and pitch of the ship, squint through the telescope lens and try to center the tiny image of the star on that bobbing hairline of aqueous horizon. No easy trick. Especially with night fast erasing the demarcation between sea and sky.

Then, satisfied or resigned—"close enough for government work"—you read off the sextant altitude of the star in degrees on the instrument's graduated limb. Noted it quickly, along with the time, so you could shoot another before it got too dark.

No wonder you were grateful to have an enlisted man, a petty officer who'd done this thousands of times to earn his crow, at your shoulder duplicating the process and checking the esoteric math from which is fashioned a celestial fix.

Somewhere on a bookshelf at home I still had a yellowed edition of *Dutton's Navigation and Piloting* (picked up cheap in Kaohsiung; Taiwan didn't honor copyright laws). Thirty years in disuse, that abstruse competence hard-won at O.C.S. and honed in the charthouse of the USS *Huckaby*—DD-803, a vintage 1944 Gearing-class destroyer—had long since evaporated.

I wasn't even sure any more which of the stars in the cross was *Acrux* and which *Gacrux*. We'd only dipped below the equator once during my time as navigator.

(Already initiated as a shellback aboard the Norwegian freighter but unable to prove it, I'd had to undergo the same good-natured humiliations as the *Huckaby*'s other Pollywogs when we'd crossed the line. That trivial injustice lingered more clearly in memory than the stars by which we'd steered from Subic to Singapore.)

Most of those skymarks, of course, would have been in constellations common to both hemispheres. Like the only one that I could identify tonight aside from the Southern Cross. It reared above the horizon to the east, stinger curled and pincers flung high: Scorpio, my favorite.

Too bad it wasn't my birth sign. Of all the zodiacal configurations, Scorpio is the most vividly representational, the most animated. And it's as easy to spot as Orion, or the Big Dipper, or Casseopoeia's Chair.

All of which, of course, lay below the horizon, visible only from the other side of the globe.

The eye of Scorpio is *Antares*. That was at least one navigational star I could pick out with certainty in this sky. The rest of it was an anonymous scatterplot—the Milky Way the modal distribution.

The Greeks certainly had graphic imaginations. Somewhere up there, I knew, undulating amid all that galactic turbidity, was Hydra, the water serpent. And somewhere else was smaller Hydrus—her male counterpart, the particular scourge of crocodiles, I'd read.

Hydra was nine-headed in Greek mythology. One of Hercules' labors was to slay it, but each time he lopped off a head it grew back. Finally he had to cauterize the roots by plunging a firebrand into the bloody neck-stump as soon as he swung his sword.

Grisly too, those Greek imaginations.

A little sea serpent dangled against my chest, come to think of it. Under my shirt. My little amulet. My *nyaminyami*. To what extent, I wondered, do you have to believe to make an amulet effective?

Magic lies in taking the avatar *for* that which it represents— that which is fearsome and more powerful than you.

Like the wafer in Holy Communion—it *is* God, the Son. Once you don't believe that, you're... well, some kind of Protestant.

And what about modern Western science? Innoculation: That involves ingesting a protective dose of the toxin. Not all that different in rationale, when you get right down to it, from eating the heart or liver of the beast you've just hunted and slain with your bow or your spear. Hope you can appropriate to yourself some of the noble prey's strength and courage.

Cannibals in New Guinea tap their enemies' intelligence and virtues by supping on their brains. Absorb a deadly vector in the process that drives 'em crazy, unfortunately. Turns their own brains to mush. Creuzfeld-Jacob syndrome, mad-cow disease. Proving something about the reliability of human constructs.

Steve and Graeme collected our bottles as we emptied them, then stowed the cooler. We all climbed back aboard the HiLux.

Jen, Mel and Gerhard occupied the forward seats this time. Laura had offered to switch and they'd taken her up on it. An offhandedly gracious gesture—although of course it hadn't taken into account my preference.

Or maybe it had, unconsciously.

With a last name whose initial letter is in the rearguard of the alphabet, I was accustomed as a child to being assigned to the tail section of lines and to the back rows of classrooms. Coupled with a natural diffidence, that distancing became comfortable to me.

In college, where seating was freeform, I'd invariably pick a desk in the furthest corner from the greenboard.

As a reporter covering trials and political assemblies and public sessions of various civic boards, I'd always found it advantageous to perch somewhere unobtrusive, blend into the woodwork.

In meetings throughout my subsequent business career, unless I was supposed to be in charge, I'd gravitate to a chair along the wall or to the lowest end of the conference table. It wasn't self-deprecatory, it was a subtle declaration of detachment. Organizational life was something I was taking under advisement.

On backpacking trips you'd find me either shepherding the stragglers, Tail-End Charlie, or slogging along on some parallel trail within eyesight but not within the footsteps of the main party.

When Susan and I skied, I always followed her down the slope. Ostensibly it was to come to her aid if she fell. I was still doing that with Laura—although more often than not it meant she was getting in two runs for every one of mine. She'd wave at me from the lift chair on her way back up as I sat brushing snow out of my ears and gathering breath after my latest wipeout among the moguls.

And in fact, she was the kind of person who'd charge down a hill first, take a seat in the front-row-center at a lecture, sidle forward to hover at the elbow of the docent on a guided tour. To accord with my theory of childhood habituation, her maiden name should have begun with a letter from the vanguard of the alphabet. Instead it was Jensen. So go figure.

Actually, I *was* happier in the rearmost seat of the HiLux. We looked out over everybody. And it *was* generous of Laura to have yielded the position closest to our guides.

Steve headed away from the fire, veering confidently across *veld* that was nearly pitch black now except for the weak cast of our headlights. With nothing in front of us to deflect the air streaming against our faces and upper bodies, Laura and I were suddenly chilly. We pulled on the sweaters we'd brought.

How we were supposed to be able to see anything in this darkness I wasn't sure. But then, as I was turning back from a glance over my shoulder—a pink haze low on the ragged western skyline was the only visible indication now that fire was sputtering across the Luangwa Valley—I caught a sharp glint at the edge of my shifting field of vision.

It was like the wink of a lightning bug, only brighter. And briefer. More like the flash off a jewel's facet.

I tried to focus on the spot where I thought it must have been—assuming I wasn't having a small stroke. Somewhere just to the right of our headlights' beam....

It repeated. Only this time the sparks were twinned.

And abruptly that pair was surrounded by others, maybe half a dozen, all in pairs, and with ruby tints like little lasers blinking on and off in the night.

"Puku," Steve said, easing back on the gas pedal.

As if cued, Graeme leaped to his feet, shook loose a coil of electrical cord and plugged a powerful flashlight into the HiLux's dash. He aimed the flashlight ahead and immediately lit up a cardboard antelope.

Or so it appeared—motionless and flat in the two-dimensional glare, a primitive painted cutout devoid of modeling, the color washed out, matted on its black velvet shadow.

Graeme swung the beam and picked out the rest of the herd. A little knot stood quivering on dainty legs on either side of our headlights' throw. More of them clustered further ahead.

Indeed, hundreds, we could now see, lurked in this transition zone between *veld* and woodland—a vast field of ruminant statuary posed in the darkness among columns of pale, dead trees. Everywhere Graeme swept his spotlight the night twinkled back at us.

Eyes.

But not very interesting eyes.

Puku eyes.

What we wanted were leopard eyes.

Or, less likely but maybe even a greater prize, black rhinoceros eyes. North and South Luangwa national parks were among the last refuges of the dwindling species in southern Africa, according to our brochures and Nick's and Rory's teasers.

Steve had pretty much damped our hopes of sighting a rhino, though. In fact, he'd told us, less than a handful were known still to be roaming the Chibembe sector, and one of those few had recently been found dead, killed by poachers.

"Try as we do, and the government does, we can't watch over the whole bleedin' valley," he'd lamented.

"Is it mainly the horns they're after?" Laura inquired.

He nodded. "Leave the rest of the carcass to rot. Even kill off a calf for its little stubby horns. More precious than gold."

"I've read that a kilo sells for upward of a hundred and seventy-five thousand Rand on the Asian black market," piped up Graeme. "That's, what? Almost thirty-five thousand pounds? More than fifty thousand dollars U.S., per kilo! Makes it about the most valuable stuff on earth, I reckon, rhino horn."

"Makes it obvious why guys'd take the risk," Steve said. "And it *is* a risk. N.P.S. has squads of armed trackers out patrolling the bush, on the lookout for rhino poachers. Pretty nasty firefights every now and again. Brought in a couple of the buggers slung on poles over at Mfuwe last season, shot dead. Made the mistake of returning fire when the scouts flushed 'em, up on the Mwaleshi River. Carrying AK-forty-sevens, they were."

"We're losing the war, though, all over Africa," Graeme declared. "Facing extinction, the rhinos, I'm afraid."

"It's an aphrodisiac, what they use it for, innit?" Mel said. "Chinese people and them. Help get it up?"

"No position to give any testimonials, but yeh. So they say," Steve replied drily.

"You find many remedies of this sort," Gerhard volunteered, "in Hong Kong, Taiwan, China, at the chemists'. If your eye hurts, you must buy a cream that is made with the eye of an animal that sees very well. If you are sick in your bones, you need a plaster from an animal with strong bones, like a tiger. Ancient Chinese medicine."

"I see, so to get in the mood, t' get yourself really horny, thing for it is to swallow a pinch of the biggest horn you can find, eh?" Mel tittered. "Makes sense, innit?"

"Yes, and there are med'cines of elk horn," Gerhard noted. "Deer horn. Antelope horn. For that purpose too."

"Not puku horn, I wouldn't think," Jen murmured.

"Why don't they just grind up the rhinoceros's penis?" Laura proposed. Rather daringly for her, I thought.

"Brilliant!" Mel exclaimed. "Didn't they do that with whales in the olden times? Certainly put a rhino dick to shame!"

"When you think about it," Laura said, "lions eat puku, but they don't eat rhinoceruses. Do they?"

"Certainly don't," Denys replied.

"And look at how potent the lion is!" Laura declared.

"It is also for relieving pain," Gerhard added quietly. "The rhino horn. For the rheumatismus."

"Maybe that's what I need for my hips and back, huh?" I muttered to Laura. "If we do see one, I'll jump out and try to rub against its horn."

"Well, that shouldn't be a problem," she replied.

"Actually," Graeme was pontificating, "there is, apparently, some slight medicinal value. About what you'd get with an aspirin. Hardly enough to warrant killing a magnificent three-or-four-tonne beast for, however."

"And it's outlawed, embargoed," I put in, "right? For international trade? Like ivory?"

"We saw a notice about that in the giftshop at the Victoria Falls Hotel," Jen recalled. "Illegal to take carved ivory out of the country. They had some quite beautiful pieces there, too...!"

"Didn't they!" Laura agreed. "Exquisite."

"Not that any of it was within my budget, I must say," Jen laughed.

"Really," Laura seconded.

"Yeh, rhino horn's covered by an international convention against trade in engangered species," Steve said. "For all the good it's done. You've been through Wankie, right? Usual Mamba route?"

Steve was referring to Hwange National Park by its old colonial Rhodesian name.

"Last week," we nodded.

"See any rhino, did you?"

We responded in the negative.

"Wouldn't wonder. There were more than three thousand black rhino in Wankie only a couple of years ago. Now they're down to three hundred. If that. Perhaps in all of Zimbabwe."

"Shocking decimation in so brief a span of time," Graeme nodded.

"Actually, *worse* than decimation," I observed. "That's *nine* out of ten!"

Graeme looked at me blankly.

"Situation's so bad they've taken to dehorning the ones that are left," Steve went on. "Track 'em down and tranquillise 'em and remove the horns with a chainsaw. Hope is that'll destroy their value. Make 'em worthless to poachers, so they'll spare 'em. Too late for that sort of programme here, even if the government had the resources."

"Isn't it terribly painful, though, to the animal?" Jen winced.

Steve shook his head. "No more so than when a farmer clips a bull's horns. They're all just made out of protein. Keratin. Same stuff as our hair, fingernails. So except for the dart, the tranquilliser, it's no more stressful to the rhino, really, than gettin' a haircut would be to us. Or when we clip our fingernails."

"And I could certainly do with a tranquilliser when *I* get me hair cut," Mel laughed.

"Sad part is, it doesn't seem to be doing much good," Graeme said. "Poachers'll shoot a dehorned rhino just for the little bit that's left in the sockets. And it grows back in a year or two anyway. At Wankie what they've been doing is affixing a transmitter, radio transmitter, round the rhino's neck, whilst it's out cold. Way to track 'em down again next time they have to do the job."

"If y' should happen to see a rhino in Wankie, chances are it'll look more like an oversize bull terrier," Steve said. He snorted bitterly. "What it's come down to."

"Are they, like, really black?" Mel asked.

"Ah. Nah. Just the name, the species," Steve said. "*Diceros bicornis.* Latin for 'two-horned.' They're all more grey-like, mostly. Even the whites. Which you won't find here. Zululand, Zaire, still a few white rhinos left in reserves. Bigger, they are. *Ceratotherium simum.* Eh? Impressed? Just by way of showing off. We do make it our business to know a bit of formal zoology and botany."

"What's your background?" I asked.

"Well. Sciences, in point of fact. Did mining and metallurgy, at Otago. What brought me out here, originally. First job in the Copperbelt, through an uncle. Outfit Zambianised, though, eventually. You know, this is an incredibly rich country! Incredibly rich! Ought to be, at any rate. Has fully an eighth of the world's known copper reserves! Cobalt, the cream of it. Coal, lead, zinc... iron ore... limestone, cement. Power enough from Kafue and Kariba to have phased out all the thermal plants. Quite a flourishing new fishery at Kariba...."

"We saw the boats going out at night," I told him. "From the Zimbabwe side. Very picturesque, with their nets and lights."

"Mm. And no lack of land for cultivation. Timber. Amethysts...."

"Emeralds!" Laura interjected.

"Ah, of course! Major source of emeralds," Steve agreed.

"Which you can't even buy in Lusaka, for some reason, " Laura interjected. "I happen to know that, because we spent a lot of time looking. In vain. It's my favorite gem."

"Oh, yeh! No. No, the government keeps 'em all! Who knows what they do with 'em? Officials lining their pockets, no doubt. Steady level of theft. And apart from that, half the country's treasury's been siphoned off to finance wars of liberation in this region. Mugabe, Nkomo, the A.N.C. Perhaps not an entirely wicked rip-off, but nevertheless.... I mean, this bleedin' country could be the jewel of southern Africa! All the potential in the world! There's the shame of it! Government ballocksed up the economy all to hell after independence. Not a clue, Kaunda and his people. And the price of copper, world market...."

He lifted his right hand from the steering wheel, jerked his thumb downward and blew a razzberry with his tongue and lips. "May be cause for encouragement today, though, I suppose. Price on the climb once again. New government's set out a programme to privatise the Zed-Cee-Cee-Em. State mining monopoly, that is. There'll be more redundancies among workers in the north, but also a big increase in international investment. Talk is perhaps two billion dollars, over the next five or six years? Not going to affect me, however. Directly, at least. Changed *my* line of work years ago. Much more fun, I must tell you. Ecotourism. Figgered there's a better future in it."

"That could be an advertising slogan," I said.

"Ha. Good on y'. Suppose it could be," he smiled.

"And you never know," Graeme chimed in brightly. "It *is* possible we could see rhino tonight. No way to predict what one might stumble upon from moment to moment here. That's what makes every game drive different, exciting!"

"Right enough," Steve dutifully attested.

And I will hand it to Graeme, grudgingly; the hour and a half we spent cruising the African night did pretty much live up to his billing, for all its banality. And even though our principal quarry eluded us.

Graeme was on his feet most of the way, busily playing the spotlight from side to side, into the surrounding underbrush, the treetops, the savannah grass. Intent behind him, we scanned the darkness for the responsive gleam of eyes.

To be sure, riding in an open car envisioning a sable leopard suddenly plummeting out of an overhanging branch—hissing and slavering, shredding your scalp with its claws and ripping at your jugular with its fangs while you, its unlucky selected victim, shrieked and flailed—kept participation in the exercise keen.

There was no question from Steve's scowl, and his occasional terse directions to Graeme who'd immediately beam the light at a particular place in the tangled canopy ahead, that caution was called for. But I also soon understood that Steve had a better sense than Graeme of nocturnal habitat.

So no leopard. No rhino. But two tiny bush babies perched high on a limb, goggling at us through bug-eyes so enormous they looked like kitsch renditions of "cute as a monkey."

Mel, Jen and Laura, of course, all keened with delight— apparently an involuntary manifestation of maternal wiring. The common name for the jug-eared little creatures probably contributed to the feminine "oooh"s.

"Also called galagos," Steve instructed us. "Primates. Right. That's enough."

Graeme promptly flicked the light away.

"Don't want to blind 'em, any more'n we already have," Steve explained, driving on. "Wouldn't be fair play, would it? Render 'em defenseless against predators in admiring 'em."

Then there was a ratel, or honey badger, which turned tail to scuttle back into the elephant grass like a fat, oversized skunk. And a sleek genet, dog-nosed, spotted, ring-tailed.

"Carnivore," Steve declared. "Out looking for mice or snakes."

"Is that the same as a... what'd y' call it... a civet?" Mel asked.

"Well, no, but they are cousins, yeh," Steve replied. "Same family. *Viverridae*."

A few miles further along, in a stand of forest, another pair of beady eyes glittered out of the darkness; Graeme immediately reversed the slow arc he'd been traversing with his spotlight and methodically raked the thicket at the back of a small clearing.

Something mottled, beigeish—color was hard to judge in the artificial blaze of the flashlight, as was distance and therefore size—leaped for a low branch and disappeared in a rattle of twigs and foliage.

"Leopard!" I exclaimed. "No?"

Instantly I was doubtful. It had definitely had spots and a striped feline tail. I thought.

"No, no!" Steve snapped.

"Cheetah?" Gerhard was proposing at almost the same instant.

"Seldom if ever find cheetah round here," Steve said, shaking his head in dismissal. "Too small, it was, anyway. That was a serval."

"Ooh, yeh?" Mel trilled.

"Yeh. Pretty sure. Little serval...."

"Oh. I thought you said 'civet,'" Mel complained.

"Nah, civets have short legs. Entirely different conformation. I didn't get a real good look, but it was a serval, I'd warrant."

"I believe you're right," Graeme nodded. His manner and tone managed to combine sycophancy with an assertion of equivalent expertise. I instantly doubted he's ever seen a serval. Even so I couldn't actively dislike him. There was something naive and guileless about his unctuousness—he was just a chap who desperately wanted approbation.

So that was the extent of the *rara fauna* we could add to our catalogue of African game sightings thanks to the night drive. We turned up a plethora of puku and impala, not surprisingly. We also saw the hippopotamus family again. And a small herd of zebra—a word, I found, I'd now become reluctant to speak aloud. Like everyone else we'd met here, Steve and Graeme invariably said "zebra." But to abandon the long "e" of my lifetime habit and my own national accent seemed inauthentic.

Pretentious. I was not, interestingly—I guess because the distinction was subtler—as conflicted about adhering to my customary "jur-aff" (instead of "djir-off") and "willduh-beast" (instead of
"villduh-bay-est").

As to excitement, we had a moment of that, too.

We were headed home, only a couple of miles from the lodge, when a small elephant ambled out of the reeds along the boggy roadside, into our headlights.

Steve braked quickly.

As we idled, an adult nosed out of the reeds behind the calf.

They have elegant profiles, African elephants. The narrow skull tapers to a limber proboscis that is somehow patrician for all its exaggeration. And they move with a fluid if heavy-footed, floppy-kneed grace.

Calf and mother, as Steve identified the larger elephant, plodded across the road diagonally toward us from the left. Neither seemed to pay us any particular heed. Heads bobbing and ears rippling in stately rhythm, they marched to the right shoulder and bustled into the bush on that side.

Graeme was following them with his light, illuminating the female's swaying rump and limply whisking tail.

"Why does the elephant cross the road?" Mel piped, chirruping at her own joke.

Suddenly there was a violent stir among the reeds abreast of us to the left. It was accompanied by a sharp, piercingly resonant shrill, like a treble blast from an alpenhorn.

We all jumped in alarm.

"Bloody hell!" Steve swore. He wrenched the gearshift lever forward, stamped on the gas pedal and jolted ahead.

Our necks snapped and Graeme dropped heavily sideways, the beam of his light probing the sky wildly as he floundered and folded onto his hip in his seat.

Steve sped down the road a few hundred yards.

"Big bull!" he called over his shoulder.

We rounded a curve and he slowed to a stop.

"Sorry about that. Everyone all right?" He swiveled to appraise us. "Didn't mean to throw y' about that way."

He glanced at Graeme. "Y' okay, mate?"

"No damage," Graeme assured him. He tugged at the wrinkles in his twisted khakis and rearranged himself in a normal sitting position.

"Big bull, that was," Steve explained, "trumpeting. Only a warning, fortunately. Can't afford to take chances, though. Got ourselves between him and his family. Not a position you want to be in if you value your long-term health. My fault, didn't hear 'im trampling about out there. Sure everyone's all right?"

Nobody whimpered or claimed whiplash.

"Right. Good on y'. My shout, when we get back to the bar."

"Which reminds me," I said to Laura, loudly enough for the others to hear. "Rory owes us one too. Remember? He said he was buying. Back when we were digging the truck out, at the river."

"So he did," Jen agreed, turning to show me her pretty smile.

And we all collected.

Rory, a fresh packet of fags propped invitingly open on its lid on the low table alongside the latest in a day-long succession of *Mosi*s, was only too happy to honor his promise once Steve had made good on his. Rory had spent the afternoon in the bar with Reg, and both were jolly and red-eyed.

To Laura's disgust, I even smoked one of the cigarettes Rory slyly tapped my way. He did it to tease her, ostentatiously covert, having seen how she'd chided me the first time I'd bummed one from him at the game restaurant in Harare. And to tease me as well, a test of how low I'd bow as henpecked husband.

When everyone had assembled and we'd sufficiently lubricated our appetites—Emma, Greta, Nigel and Ewan were the last to arrive, having been on a night drive too, with Denys and Simon—we rose and roistered over to the dining pavilion for our scheduled group dinner.

Spirits were high as we commanded bottles of red and white wine, consulted the neatly hand-inked menus in leather folders the waiters had placed before us, and dithered among ourselves about choices of appetizers and entrees.

"What's *chambo*?" Laura asked Renée, using a broad American "a."

"*Chombo*," Renée replied, refining the pronunciation. "It's a fish. Very tasty. Rather like... I dunno, catfish, I suppose. If I can find some good fresh ones we'll try to have it for dinner one night, in camp, at Cape Maclear or Senga Bay. They catch 'em there, in the lake."

"Lake Malawi."

"Mm."

"Is it bony?"

"Not terribly, I shouldn't say."

"'Fillets of *chambo* with a light herb sauce, garnished with peas, Vichy carrots and Duchesse potatoes,'" Laura read aloud from the menu as if no one else had one.

"Delightful," Renée nodded. "Although I think I'm leaning to the breast of chicken Marsala, myself."

"That sounds good too. 'Vegetable saffron rice,'" Laura noted, her chin uptilted, eyebrows raised and eyelids lowered as she read through a pair of half-rimmed dime-store magnifiers perched school-marmishly on the tip of her nose. She carried them in her fanny-pack for such exigencies.

After my afternoon's exertions, I was in the mood for red meat. I vacillated between a "fillet steak with tapenade butter" and the mixed grill—"baby sirloin, lamb chop and ostrich banger." That last piqued my interest; I'm always inclined to sample the most idiosyncratic local fare. Which would have commended *chambo* to my consideration too if I hadn't been spared by Renée's notice of intention to serve it on a later occasion.

Neither Laura nor I, for all the sophistication that should have rubbed off on us as avid consumers of upscale restaurant cuisine wherever we traveled, could remember with certainty what "tapenade" meant. Nor, for that matter, were we clear on the significations of "Vichy" and "Duchesse."

Our Australian camp cook wasn't much help when we confessed our ignorance to her. The dubious suggestions the three of us began to bandy were a source of much self-deprecatory amusement.

Laura and I usually found ourselves sitting with Nick and Renée. Although more aligned by age with Greta and Reg—Alistair was in his own generational category—Laura and I never really connected with either of those two unattached and introverted contemporaries. The span of years between us and Nick and Renée was more than twice the separation between them and the youngest person in the group, Emma; nevertheless, we seemed to be on a similar plane of maturity and experience based on our mutual engagement in a sustained relationship.

Even Nick, over drinks and unbuttoned, was capable of surprisingly sensitive discussion of the joys and sticky points of couplehood. In a way, I thought, they regarded us as a reference resource; they were curious about how we'd come together, and how we stayed together—the dynamics of marriage.

Laura and I were too discreet to broach the subject, but we couldn't help speculating about their future, whether they'd end up going through a wedding as we had.

Renée did say she still hoped to have children. Nick, looking anything but the reliable mate with his punkish shaved head, five o'clock shadow and roguish Errol Flynn features, asserted his concurrence in that aspiration. But he wasn't sure what sort of career options would be open to him upon his return to England.

They both vigorously rejected the notion of staying on in Africa in some capacity after Mamba. The routine disdain of the white expat minority for the indigenous black majority was utterly repugnant to them, they explained. And the chasmic economic and social inequities between the races too troubling to try to adjust to.

Their plan was to remain with Mamba for a couple more years, then, probably, see what Australia had to offer. They'd spent a three-month leave recently driving and camping across Renée's continent—literally a busman's holiday, I thought—and Nick had found the people and the ethos sympathetic.

Conversation around the dinner table consisted mostly of a raucous rehash of reactions to the buffalo beans—full of sportive finger-pointing, jeering, confession and mimicry.

Rory as usual served as *de facto* master of ceremonies. His droll *bons mots*, puns and gibes always startled me for their acuity. I'd long since come to expect verbal facility in Brits—the guys, after all, who'd invented rhyming slang. (Not all Brits, of course: Nick, Nigel and Reg represented the low end of the continuum, from taciturn to inarticulate; Alistair was given to Blimpish maunderings; and though Ewan gave indications of harboring a sly wit, it was basically inaccessible under its dense Glaswegian furze. In all but the most routine exchanges, he might as well have been burbling in Russian.)

Among Americans, in my experience, love of wordplay is most often a Southern trait. Maybe I'd inherited mine from my mother. Louisville had never really felt like the South to me. My father—although he was loved puns and sesquipedalian words ("the Ohio River," he taught me to recite at the age of about five, "is formed by the confluence of the Allegheny and Monongahela Rivers")—identified his heritage as German-American and had come home from Yale with an Eastern sensibility.

My closest friends in OCS, Navy schools and the *Huckaby*'s wardroom always turned out to be guys from Sewanee, Duke or Auburn—the sort who in their twenties still unabashedly referred to their fathers as "Daddy" and proudly expressed intention as "fixin' t'."

Shooting the breeze with them was a kind of American-style Monty Python Show. We might veer from riffs on one anothers' tics of speech to the concoction of our own shipboard Japanese pidgin to long conversations consisting entirely of acronymns in the International Phonetic Alphabet. ("Hotel, Tango!" for "Hey, Tim!" To which the response was "Yankee, Delta?" for "Yeah, Dan?" And so on in lengthening skeins decipherable only to ourselves by *tours de force* of inference from context and voice inflection. "Whiskey Delta Yankee Whiskey Tango Delta Tango—for "What do you want to do tonight?" "India Delta Kilo. Whiskey Delta *Yankee* Whiskey Tango Delta...?" Hey, a lot of Navy life is boring.)

The theory, I'd heard, was that an ear for the music of language develops most keenly in class-conscious societies. And a lot of Southerners, at least until recently, were as attuned as the English to the rank and regional credentials one opened along with one's mouth.

It's an ironic twist that the accents of the South are for the most part regarded as *infra dig* by educated middle Americans—an exception, perhaps, the patrician drawl of the planter classes, the softenings and vocalizations affected by Northern actors in Tennessee Williams plays, for example, although never quite gotten right.

At the same time, homogenized Americans are only too quick to buy into the English caste system. So Rory's skinhead guise, his lorry-driver career status and his distinctly non-U accent initially led me to underestimate him. I initially imputed to him only a coarse, street intelligence. Nothing could have been further from the truth. Among other things, he read constantly and widely— trekking the roads of Africa with cosmopolitan groups of tourists who arrive packing paperbacks and depart with souvenirs they need to make space for in their luggage affords plenty of opportunity and motive to burnish a liberal literary education.

In the campground in Vic Falls I'd seen Rory immersed in a thick, garishly bound spy thriller. At Kariba he'd sprawled in the truck with a novel emblazoned "Booker Prize Winner." And at Lusaka he'd walked by me with a beer in one hand and the forefinger of the other sandwiched in a bulky paperback copy of Levi-Strauss's *Tristes Tropiques*.

"You read French?" I'd exclaimed in astonishment.

"Bi' of it," he'd nodded nonchalantly, as if that were all it took to get through Levi-Strauss. "Comes in handy, y' know, if y're in the Francophone countries. Côte d'Ivoire, Congo, them...."

Like most of the Brits on the truck except Ewan, Rory spoke a variant of what one of my current friends—himself a transplanted London School of Economics product—calls "estuary English." Rory's was quite broad and had a lilt I surmised to be Irish-influenced, though he'd grown up in Bristol.

To one degree or another they all swallowed their "l"s—Mel's were actually Ws, which occasionally conveyed the effect of a lisp. And they favored glottal stops over "t"s and "k"s in words like "righ"' and "te'nical."

Their vowels were diphthongized too, closer sometimes to Cockney than to BBC "received pronunciation." Even Emma fell into it when she was in a playful mood.

The estuary voice, rooted in London, has widespread appeal and is gaining currency throughout England, my friend explains, precisely because it blurs class distinctions.

On phonetic grounds, I had to admit, I preferred the Queen's English. I was disappointed at the absence of an accent among our company that had the undiluted, plummy *cachet* we Americans have always envied while resenting.

Over the appetizers of "assorted *crudités*," those of us who'd been on the night drive compared experiences.

We in Steve's group were the lucky ones, for having seen the lions. The others had missed them, as well as the genet and the serval. None of us had seen a leopard. They'd sighted hyenas and a jackal, though.

As we worked our way through cold cucumber soup and the main course, our wine goblets were continuously replenished from bottles of excellent chardonnay—South African, from Stellenbosch, according to the label—or merlot, from Paarl.

Laura ended up choosing the steak; I had my mixed grill. The ostrich banger proved dry and indistinguishable from a sausage of any other meat.

I went for the very English-sounding bread-and-butter pudding for dessert; Laura passed, but as usual sampled about half of mine.

We all ordered tea or coffee, and liqueurs—a cognac for Laura and me. Then we had a nightcap single-malt Scotch in the *chitenje* bar, where Mel, Gerhard, Jen, Emma and Rory were settling in for another long, high-pitched evening.

Our guides, Steve and Graeme, convivial but subdued by comparison, had pulled up chairs with them by the time Laura and I excused ourselves. Nick and Renée announced their intention to leave in a moment too. Alistair, Reg, Greta, Ewan and Nigel had drifted off earlier one by one.

The night was cool as Laura and I walked to our cabin along the bank above the river. There'd been a fire going in the big stone fireplace in the dining room, and the smell of woodsmoke was strong in the air. I wondered if its source was the chimney that jutted through the thatched rondavel roof behind us or the wildfires licking across the *veld*.

I could still see the black tubular silhouettes of crocodiles, I thought, on the far shore. Faintly lit by the incandescent glow from our side.

No other animal shapes were discernible. Laura held my hand.

At Hwange, we'd met a wildebeest in the darkness when we were returning to our tent from the pub. No sooner had we realized the ungainly, possibly dangerous creature was out there, snuffling toward us in hulking silhouette along the same path, than it pricked up at our footfalls and, after what seemed an instant's panicky confusion of its own, leaped a rail fence and galloped off.

The encounter was too short for fright to fully register. Still, you didn't know what might slink out of this remote bush. Our cabin here was at the furthest end of the compound, too.

But we arrived without incident. We threw the doorlatch behind us, undressed, brushed our teeth, *et cetera*. First Laura, then I flopped wearily, a bit blearily, onto the bed.

"And we were going to eat light," I mused, fingering the taut mound of my midsection.

She sighed. "You only live once," she murmured.

"So they say. And this is the way to do it. Eh?"

"This is the life," she concurred. "You're not going to read, are you?"

Without waiting for an answer, she tugged the pillow out from under her head and blindfolded herself with it.

The lamp on the bedside table next to me was still on. In fact, by habit I probably would have picked up the paperback splayed spine-up beneath it. Even in a tent, in a sleeping bag, head propped on my folded clothes piled under my inflatable pillow, book pinched open awkwardly in one hand above my face and fading penlight aimed unsteadily at the page with the other, or jutting from between my teeth, I'm accustomed to reading myself to sleep. But I was sufficiently wiped out tonight to defer to her.

"Not if you don't want me to," I said.

I struggled up on an elbow, twisted and planted a kiss on her lips. That too was a bedtime ritual.

She grunted in Scotch-and-toothpaste-scented, already slightly groggy surprise at the touch of my lips and sprouting beard.

"'Night," she muttered. "Love you."

"Goodnight. I.... oh, my gosh!" I exclaimed as I started to roll away from her. "My *nyaminyami*! It's gone!"

"What?"

"I just noticed! I've lost my *nyaminyami*! The string must have broken!"

Haplessly I slapped my chest, shoulders and the back of my neck for the thin waxed twine that had held the little soapstone carving, whose absence I'd just remarked.

"Or else the knot came undone."

Laura peeked out from under her pillow and blinked at me. "Really? Gee! *That's* too bad. Are you sure?"

I pawed the sheets beside my hips, checked under my buttocks and pillow.

"Well, it's certainly not around my neck anymore."

She eyed my chest.

"Nope," she confirmed, "it's not."

She wriggled up into a sitting position and glanced at the table by the headboard on her side of the bed. Her own *nyaminyami* lay there amid its loop of string, her rings, her elephant-hair bracelet and her wristwatch.

"I don't remember anything particular happening, though, that could've caused it to break," I said.

"Wouldn't it have fallen inside your shirt? If it had come loose?"

"You'd think so," I agreed. "Except I didn't always have it tucked in. Maybe when I got undressed...."

I hopped out of bed and sorted through the clothes I'd draped over a chair. I checked the polo-shirt especially carefully, in case the *nyaminyami* had come off with it when I'd unwrapped it over my head. I investigated the chairseat and the floor beneath. I padded around the room scowling at the varnished planking and the knotted-rag throw rugs. I looked in the bathroom. I even crouched on my hands and knees and peered under the bed.

"Maybe you'll find it in the morning, when it's lighter," Laura said. "You can check in the bar and the restaurant."

"Maybe it dropped on the path. I don't think it'd be much use to go out there and try and look for it with my little flashlight in the dark, though."

"Do you remember the last time you noticed you were wearing it?"

"Well.... I had it on at the pool this afternoon. Right?"

"Yeah...," she nodded. "I believe so. Pretty sure you did."

"And I had it on... or at least I was thinking about it.... When we were at the hot spring. Cocktail hour. I just assumed it was still on then. I didn't actually check to see."

"Can't you feel it?"

"Not really. You get used to it. Are you aware of yours all the time? And when I've got my sunglasses off too...."

I wore a cord affixed to the earpieces so my aviator-style sunglasses hung around my neck, jostling against my chest below my collar, when not on my nose. Even though night had fallen and I'd been gazing up at Hydra through my *clear* glasses, I hadn't yet folded the sunglasses away into their leather case.

I didn't think I had, anyway. Possibly it could've come off with them.

"Well. That's a real shame," Laura said.

She reached around and plumped her pillow.

"I hope you'll find it in the morning."

"Yeah, me too," I said. "I was growing attached to the idea of wearing an amulet. I had a scapular medal when I was a kid, a couple of 'em, actually. Little silver discs on silver chains? I thought they looked cool. I wasn't real big on the religious significance. Matter of fact, I always lost those too. But a *nyaminyami*. From Zimbabwe. *Way* cooler."

"It did give you a certain *je ne sais quoi*," Laura nodded. "I thought it would. Especially fitting for a Pisces, seemed to me, huh? Why I bought it for you."

"Yeah, and that's why I'm especially upset if it's really gone for good, that it was a gift from you."

"Well, we'll hope it's not for good," she said. She collapsed supine again.

"Now I think I will read," I said as I settled back too. "Just for a bit."

She grasped the sheet at her shoulder and rolled decisively away from me, exposing my outboard leg and foot. She jerked her pillow out from under her lower ear and slapped it down on top of the upper, covering her eyes.

"Suit yourself," she muttered. "You'll regret it if you stay up too late, though."

"Why?"

"We have the walking safari tomorrow."

"Yeah, but not till afternoon. We can sleep in for a change."

"Great. We'll need to if you're gonna keep on talking all night."

"Blah-blah-blah. Okay, there, I'm finished. Good night, sweetie darling. I love you," I said.

"Mp," she allowed.

*I*t was so stupid! Such an utterly brainless thing to do! I've had nightmares about it. Awakened to my own anguished groan—a cry that began on the Luangwa of sleep—and lay there sweating... the dream-scene as vivid, as awful, as the memory that formed it, and that I now had to mull.

V. Walking Safari

Denys met us at two o'clock sharp in front of the office. We'd spent a leisurely morning—English-style breakfast of scrambled egg curds, limp bacon and fried tomatoes, nutritionally enhanced by tall glasses of orange and grapefruit juice and a bowl of diced-fruit salad from the buffet, which also offered a variety of packaged American cereals and freshly baked bread, brioches or dry toast.

That was followed by reading in the shade of the cabin porch while watching the morning's stately parade of four-legged drinkers approaching and departing the river's far edge.

Then an hour or so of pre-zenith sun beside the pool. I made a half-hearted overture to Laura when we were back at the cabin, but the timing wasn't propitious. It was already well past noon and we both wanted showers before a fairly early seating for lunch. We were still scrubbing off the dermal memory of the buffalo beans.

In the dining *chitenje* we sat with Marguerite and a French businessman from Clermont-Ferrand who was decompressing between Lusaka and Harare. It would be his penultimate stop on a six-month tour through Africa selling industrial machinery. His English bore only the faintest accent—he even pronounced Chibembe and Chicago differently, with a "Tchee" for the former, *mirabile dictu*, and a proper French "Shee" for the latter—and he was full of knowing commentary about the political and economic climate of virtually every major country on the continent.

When Laura and I returned to the cabin to digest and gird ourselves for our walking safari, we found our bed made and our

173

folded clothes back from the laundry. Both clean and dirty, quill-infested regardless, we'd emptied almost everything out of our bags to be washed when we'd figured out how inexpensive the convenience would be. Now it seemed we'd finally put the itchy-bean episode behind us, consigned it to amusing anecdote.

Unlike the previous day when he'd shown up at our lunch table in the ubiquitous khaki uniform of safariland, Denys was outfitted for our game walk in surprisingly touristy kit: a gray nylon baseball cap, a buff-colored short-sleeved sportshirt, white shorts, salt-and-pepper ragg-wool ankle socks and chukka boots. The only equipment he carried was a pair of binoculars in hand.

Although I hadn't really considered it, we were not, we saw, the sole participants on the walk. Nigel and Ewan were already present, smiling at us shyly in greeting.

Nigel wore a red tee-shirt that had faded to pink, his skimpy white nylon track shorts, dark dress socks and a pair of suede leisure shoes like American Hush Puppies. A well-stuffed red-and-black canvas daypack was strapped to his back.

Ewan was in bleached denim cut-offs, the frayed, slightly uneven ends revealing knobby knees and hairy white shanks that ended in gray nylon running shoes—"trainers," in his parlance. He was sockless and shirtless as well. He had not, obviously, been out of his teeshirt or long pants often—his skinny, freckled chest was sallow in contrast to the raddled tan above his neckline and on his arms below the biceps.

He was wearing a *nyaminyami* on a woolly black-and-red braided cord, I noticed. Ironic, in a way, on him—or maybe not. Maybe it made perfect precautionary sense. Ewan had been the only one in the group who'd declined the day's boat cruise on Lake Kariba; he was a non-swimmer and uncomfortable on water, he'd been frank to admit. We'd found him at the truck when we'd returned—quite content, he'd declared himself, at having spent the hours alone strolling the shore, encountering a pod of hippos and shooting off a roll of film at them.

He had his camera with him now, too, slung bandolier-style across his chickenbreast. He'd apparently left his money-belt behind.

"I hope you put on sunscreen, Ewan," Laura immediately twitted.

His grin broadened sheepishly and he wagged his head. "Naw, Ah didnay," he admitted.

"Well, you're making a mistake," she chided. "With your fair skin, you'll be burnt to a crisp in no time. You have a shirt, at least."

"Aw, aye," he humored her. He shrugged in the direction of Nigel. "Yin's in 'is sack."

Laura unzipped the fanny-pack she was wearing turned to the front. She fished out a small tube. "Here. You want some of this? It's only SPF fifteen."

"Naw, 's okay, really, Laura. Ta."

She shrugged, the tube still proffered. "I think you'll be very sorry."

He caved. "Och, aye. Thanks, then," he said, accepting it with a dubious smile. "Just a wee dod."

A few feet away, I'd noted, a blade-thin, thirtyish black man in an olive-drab military-style uniform lounged in a pool of tree-shade, one hand on his hip, the other on the muzzle of a formidable rifle at parade rest. His shirt had epaulets but no insignia, his pants were tucked into dusty, well broken-in black lace-up boots, and he wore a khaki web belt.

"This is George," Denys said, gesturing toward him, "our *fundi* this afternoon. George Mkombwe."

The man bowed his head and smiled at us in acknowledgement of the introduction. His round cheeks and underslung chin were tufted with nubby whiskers, almost a beard but too patchy and short to fully qualify. Black men often find it difficult to shave daily, I'd heard—their stubble tends to curl back in on itself, burrow under the skin and become irritatingly ingrown.

"George is an excellent tracker and a dead shot in the unlikely event we need 'im to be," Denys continued. "Fixed up, then, hey? We all know each other. Let's be off."

Nurturing my own beard had heightened my awareness of others'. Falling into step beside Laura, I ran the fingertips of my off hand along my jawbone, first with, then against the grain. I lifted the bristles with my thumb and pinched them to gauge their length. I could do that now. I had a real beard, all right: intention fully evident and the effect beyond slovenliness.

It was important to cross that divide before we reached the Malawi border. Although things had loosened up recently, Nick and Rory had cautioned us about the country's reputation for enforcing strict dress and grooming codes.

Under the rule of the straitlaced former president, Dr. Hastings Banda, and the pressures of a significant Muslim population, Malawi officials had been insisting that women wear over-the-knee skirts at all times and that men have short hair. Tourists who ignored those dictates, who were judged to fall within the parameters of "hippie," had been turned away at the border, harrassed, even arrested, fined, jailed or deported, according to Nick, Renée and Rory.

Forewarned by Mamba's pre-departure literature, Laura—like all the women on the truck—had packed a prim skirt for Malawi. And I was prepared to cloak myself indignantly in my estate as a grizzled patriarch if any whippersnapper of a border guard tried to give me grief about my beard. Or the hair I combed proudly over my eartops.

With George in the lead, we took a path that curved past the rear of the office/kitchen/commissary, past the one-story senior staff housing block—the posts of its verandah twined with thickly blooming scarlet poinsettias—and past the open-fronted, thatched manger in which Mpamvu and his two attendants were lazing out the heat of the day.

The men lifted limp hands to us as we trudged by. Mpamvu was sorting idly through the straw on the ground with his trunk.

We entered the mopani grove.

There was just enough shade to cut the actinic sting of the sun, but the air was still close and hot. Sweat started to dribble down my ribs under my khaki shirt. I unfastened the last two buttons above my belt, worked my shoulders and tugged at the yoke to loosen and open the collar wider. I was wearing cargo shorts, freshly cleaned; my feet, though, were swathed in two pairs of socks—thin cotton under ribbed wool to prevent blisters—and ankle-high hiking boots of Gore-Tex-and-leather.

I'd had to sit on the toilet four times this morning. Blame it on the previous night's wine and the six or seven cups of coffee I'd injudiciously sipped along with breakfast. They were teacups, after all. And I have trouble practicing moderation when morning coffee is conveniently at hand.

Nevertheless, I was now aware of the uneasy peristaltic shifting of my bowels as I walked.

It was like hiking through a California oak woodland in the fall. The biggest trees were well spaced, many with multiple trunks that veed apart to let in light like live oaks, their foliage feathery, small-leaved and pale, the underbrush thin, dun, crackly.

Flycatchers darted through the stripes of yellow sunlight.

A couple of vervets suddenly skittered higher among the branches above us, hissing and chattering imprecations at each other.

The lanky little monkeys—black-faced, long-tailed, quadrupedal—roamed Chibembe's grounds, though not as thickly or as mischievously as at the municipal caravan park where we'd camped in Victoria Falls.

Twice, there, one of the resident troop of sneaky marauders had managed to hop up on our food table and steal something from under our noses. The most memorable heist was our whole loaf of packaged bread for lunch, which the simian perp bore off under its arm into the nearest tree.

There it crouched, smugly aware that it was safely out of human reach, clawing the plastic wrapping to shreds and defiantly slapping slice after stolen slice into its monkey maw. Until forced to flee to preserve the swag—unsuccessfully, of course—from a converging pack of gibbering mates.

Denys identified the flycatchers and the vervets in response to Laura's questions. She, of course, had stationed herself at his shoulder. The rest of us bunched close around them as we walked.

"We have several species of guenons here in the park," Denys noted. "There are these, the green monkeys, fairly numerous, and we have a few blue monkeys. All the same genus, just slightly different distinguishing characteristics. Mostly a question of the sort of sheen given off by their fur. Green monkeys actually have a blue scrotum, males do...."

He slid a quick glance at Laura, not quite embarrassed but fazed enough to check to see if there was reason to consider being.

"I'll try to point 'em out to you...." He realized that too was a double *entendre*. "...The, uh, the different types. When opportunity arises."

His voice had fallen to a mumble. He quickened his stride.

"What was it you just called 'em?" I asked him.

"Vervets?"

"No, the other word. 'Guh... known?'"

"Oh, right, French, I suppose. 'Gueh-nonh' more, hey? Gee-ewe-ee. En-oh-en. Type of monkey. Guenons. *Cercopithecus*. See 'em in zoos overseas quite often. Very popular. Very cheeky. This tree?"

He suddenly pointed and veered to the side of the path, where he halted to slap a thick trunk. "This is wild teak."

"Teak!" Laura repeated, lifting her eyebrows.

We all cocked our heads back to appraise the intertwined limbs above us, which were midwinter bare but studded with what appeared to be delicate, fluted flowers. On closer inspection of those on the lower branches, however, we saw they were fibrous—flat pods, almost pink, with a furry brown center that looked like a bristly tuft of stamens.

"*Mulombe*. Type of teak," Denys said. "Heartwood's a beautiful dark brown, almost black."

"Used for woodworking here too?" Laura asked.

"Oh, yeh. Fine cabinetry. Paneling. Great stuff. Export it. Piano keys."

"The black keys."

"Precisely," Denys nodded. "Also used in traditional carving. Masks, figgers. Knife-handles. Main hardwood milled in this country, actually. Another name's bloodwood, for the sap. Bright red. When y' cut into it, the sap oozes out, makes you think it's bleedin'."

"Pleasant image," Laura murmured.

"What," I asked, "was the name you originally said? The other, the native name, I guess."

"*Mulombe*," George offered in a soft baritone. He was standing a couple of paces from Denys, waiting attentively. "This one we say is *mulombe*."

Denys nodded equably. George's participation was obviously no encroachment.

"*Mulombe*," I repeated, hoping the syllables would stick. I looked at George. "Is that, uh, *mKunda*?"

"Yes. Chikunda," he said. "Chinyanja." He waggled his hand. "Same."

"But they're different languages," I asked.

"Basically they're just different dialects," Denys broke in. "They all understand one another. Y' know, y'd be surprised, but this valley wasn't even settled until the seventeenth, eighteenth century. I mean, there were whites, Portuguese traders swapping beads for ivory, down along the Zambezi... Dutchmen raising cattle, the Boers, on the Cape... long, long before George's ancestors wandered this way out of the north. Zaire, they were from, originally. Congo. The Kunda, the Chewa, the Nsenga. Three original tribes here in the Eastern province. And it wasn't 'til about twenty years before Livingstone saw Vic Falls... which was eighteen-fifty-five... only a couple of decades before that when the Ngoni armies tramped up here out of Zululand. Conquered 'em all. Fierce warriors, the Ngoni. Rebels against Shaka. I guess you've heard of *him*."

"Shaka... Zulu, eh?" Nigel said.

"Aye. On the telly," Ewan added.

"Despot, but bloody brilliant general," Denys continued. "Anyway. They all talk the same lingo now. Chewa... official language over in Malawi, call it Chichewa, but it's really no different... Kunda, Ngoni. All been sort of blended together as

Nyanja, which is the national language here in Zambia. Newspapers, army, police, government. Kids in school all learn Nyanja. Right, George? *Chabwino?*"

"*Inde nduthi*," George nodded.

"Why have I heard it called Chinyanja?" I wondered.

"Ah. *Chi* just means it's the language," Denys explained, "language of the Nyanja people? Like they say '*Chingelezi*' for English. *Chifaransa* for French. Et cetera. Same principle turns it into *Kiswahili*, which is really what you should call the language. *Ki-* same function as *Chi-*. Nyanja, incidentally, means 'lake.'"

"Lake?" Laura inquired. "Where's the lake?"

"Malawi. Where you've just been. Or you're headed, rather."

"Yeh, going there from here," Nigel said.

"Really! Lake Malawi?" Laura exclaimed.

"Used to be called Lake Nyasa," Denys added.

"I'm reading a book about that. Nyasaland," Laura said. "*Venture to the Interior*. Laurens Van der Post. Have you read it?"

"Afraid I've not," Denys said. "When we get back, perhaps you can write that title down for me. I'll try to find it. Any event, Lake Nyasa rather infelicitously works out to 'Lake Lake.' Another form of the same word."

"So that's the lake that Zambians are speaking the language of, though," Laura mused. "Huh! It seems so far away! A whole 'nother country."

Denys shrugged. "Well. 'Countries' here are rather the legacy of the *Mangelezi*. British Protectorate. Northern Rhodesia. Nyasaland." He stirred his finger around horizontally. "Really just split 'em up for mod cons."

"Mod cons?" she puzzled.

Denys chuckled apologetically. "Oh, sorry. From the adverts. Modern conveniences. In the geopolitical sense."

"A lot of people speak English as well in this part of Africa, I guess," I interjected.

George nodded. "Yes. All people in Zambia are learning to speak English. In their studies, at school," he said.

"How about Swahili?" I asked. "Or Kiswahili."

"Hear a bit of it," Denys affirmed, "but not as much as in East Africa. Traders, mostly. Used with whites and that, occasionally, round here, since many of us tend to know more of it than Nyanja. Those of us who aren't resident expats. Both're Bantu languages, in fact, though, so many of the words aren't actually that far off. *Wazungu*'s what whites are called in Swahili. *Wazungu*. It's *azungu* in Nyanja. Elephant's *ndovu* in Swahili, *njovu* in Nyanja."

"So you speak Swahili," I inferred.

"Picked up a bit in Kenya. Not much Nyanja yet, I must admit. Phrase here and there. I'm working on it, though, with George and his mates. Eh, George? *Ndimayankhula pang'ono*," he said haltingly, "*Chinyanja?*"

"*E*," George allowed with a nod and a diffident smile. "*Kaya*."

"Not bloody easy, the lingo," Denys muttered. "Thing about it, syllables are always open. Always end with the vowel. Say '*Chee-nya-nja*,' not '*Cheen-yan*-ja.' Eh? Want to say 'quick!' it's '*msa-nga*,' not 'em-*sanga*.' So on. Same with all the Bantu languages, actually. Fairly unnatural for us *Ma-nge-le-zi*, though. *Ma-nge-le-zi*," he repeated, having stumbled slightly the first time.

He set off again. George hefted his rifle—he carried it at his side; it had no strap—and forged to the point. We clustered along.

"You'll notice there isn't a great deal of shade in here in the *bushveld*," Denys observed after a moment. "When the sun hits 'em full on, the mopani's leaves fold together, hang down limp like. Y' can always recognise mopanis by the leaves, see?"

He pointed at a clump of foliage on a bough that angled over the path ahead of us. "They're paired, like butterfly wings. That's why this is also known as the butterfly tree."

"Now that *is* a nice image," Laura approved. "They *are* kind of the same shape as a butterfly's wings."

"Mm. See the pods? Paired as well," Denys pointed out, waggling two fingers.

As we approached the bough I gauged the height of the lowest clump of leaves, judged it to be less than ten feet and reachable without unseemly exertion. I lagged. No need to call undue attention to my childish impulses. Nor to display my ineptitude or my clumsiness should I flail and come down without having snatched what I was grabbing for. Nor to shower everyone else with the debris I'd probably bring down if I succeeded.

Which I did.

Breaking stride only enough to plant both feet simultaneously, swing my arms to the rear and sink on my knees to tense thighs and calves, I sprang off my toes.

I plucked loose a spray of leaves.

The recoiling twig lashed the surrounding foliage as I thumped to earth on my waffled bootsoles. A mild pain flashed up my right leg.

I bounced back into stride just as everyone whirled, startled by the sudden sharp rustle.

I'd felt a light rain of dust and chaff on my cap in the instant before I'd ducked clear. I grinned and nonchalantly displayed my little green posy.

Denys gave me an inscrutable glance before lifting an eyebrow—whether in dismissal or tolerant fellowship I couldn't determine. He resumed his pace. George, I noticed, had clapped his free hand to the barrel of his rifle as he'd swung around.

Nobody commented. Crazy American, they were probably all thinking.

No skin off my nose. Christopher would have been appreciative—he too was a basketball junkie who couldn't resist testing himself against street signs, theater marquees, overhead banners, high ceilings. And although three inches shorter, he could dunk as easily as the Old Man. What's this crap about "White Man's Disease?" All Schumans got hops.

Or did, in my case, until a half-century of rebellion against Earth's gravitational oppression took its toll.

I caught up with Laura and presented the gift to her. I'd managed to rip the main stem off cleanly at its base. The leaves were undamaged.

"For closer inspection," I told her. "I didn't figure picking just a couple would count as despoiling the environment."

She examined the three little pairs of soft, triangular, lime-green leaves—the shape reminded me of elephant ears—then zipped open the pack at her waist and tucked them inside.

"Too bad you didn't get me any seedpods," she said.

"Want me to?"

"I don't want you to make another production of it. If you can reach them easily."

Laura had been squirreling away seeds and plant specimens since our arrival. She was thinking of trying to propagate an African corner in our garden, she'd said. She had no qualms about attempting to smuggle her agricultural booty past the customs inspectors at the airport.

"That's how the South got overrun with kudzu," I'd clucked. "That's why swarms of killer bees are slavering at our borders. *Africanized* bees. That's why feral rabbits hold Australia in thrall."

She'd laughed—*at* me, not with me.

"Don't worry. I'm going to take it all up to the Botanical Garden," she'd assuaged me. "I won't put anything in the ground till it's checked out."

As a university administrator, she was quick to take advantage of her access to varieties of academic expertise. "Everything'll be all dried up and useless by the time I get it home anyway," she added.

"Maybe not," I'd said. "African flora has to be able to survive long periods of drought. We could end up recreating the Heart of Darkness in our own back yard."

"'The horror!'" she'd mimicked. "That's what I already think to myself every time I walk out there, since I don't have enough time to work in it. And I don't have anybody willing to help."

My impulse was to object. But I let it ride. She wasn't wrong. Gardening isn't my thing. Not when the alternative is basketball. Or was.

I started looking for mopani seedpods. Within easy reach.

"Is *mopani* a Nyanja word?" I asked Denys.

"Mm," he replied. "Though it's in general use. Eh, George? *Mopani?* Chinyanja?"

George swiveled his head and nodded. "*E, mupani.*" After a moment he added, "Kunda people are saying *chanya.*"

"Traditionally, mopani thicket is where you'll find the biggest game," Denys noted. "Of course, we're a bit too close to the lodge in here. Other side of the river's where we're heading. Not too hot today, really. Cooling off as we go. Should be a fine afternoon."

My back was itchy. Some of the chaff I'd brought down with my little jeté had sifted down my collar. So far, nothing had bitten or stung me, at least. And I couldn't feel anything crawling around in there.

I figured dignity would no longer be compromised, though, if I pulled out my shirt-tail and gave it a flap, which I did. I reached up inside and swiped my sweaty shoulderblades and spine with the back of my hand. I took off my cap, swatted it against my shorts and put it back on, bill squared and level on my brow. I started cramming my shirttail under my belt again.

Denys had dropped back abreast of me. "Want to watch it, mate," he said in a conversational voice without turning his head. "Gave me a bit of a skrik back there. Shakin' stuff out of trees. Might get an unpleasant surprise."

"Oh, I looked," I assured him. "Before I leaped."

"Yeh, well. Pretty hard sometimes to pick out what might be up there. Sunnin' itself, maybe. Stretched out on another limb altogether. Very well adapted...."

"What. Snakes? Is that what you're talking about?"

"Mm. Word to the wise."

"Geez." I scanned the branches and foliage we were passing beneath. "What kinds of snakes *are* there? That you'd find in these trees, possibly?"

Denys expelled a chuckle. My question had been overheard. Ewan and Nigel and Laura quickly closed ranks on us.

"Eh, name it," Denys said. "Mopani snake, for starters, hey? Least of your worries, though. Not a biter, as a rule. And the venom's pretty mild."

"So there's even a specialized mopani *snake?*" I marveled.

"Oh yeh. One name for it. Also bark snake."

"What's it look like?"

"Ag. Like bark, I s'pose. Speckly. Grey, grey-brown, black spots. Black head. Sort of pinkish round the eyes. Tail, sometimes, too. I've also seen 'em a yellowish-orange, the tail."

"That sounds pretty garish," I said. "Don't they stand out?"

"Be surprised. Blends right in. Sun and shadow. *Sol y sombra.*"

"Is it big"?

"Nah. Little bugger." He held his hands apart in front of his chest. "Maybe this long. Thirty, forty centimetres. Boomslang's a bit larger."

"Boomslang?" I repeated.

"Oh, yeh. Also arboreal. *'Boom'*'s Afrikaans for 'tree.' *Very* poisonous, the boomslang. Want size, though, think of mambas. Black mamba'll go three, four metres. That'll make y' take notice, hey? Green mamba's a little shorter. You've heard of the mamba, no doubt."

"Och, aye," Ewan exclaimed on our behalf.

"Very fond of climbin' trees. Find yourself wearin' a mamba necklace...." He jabbed his thumb playfully at Ewan's *nyaminyami*. "...Might as well start sayin' your prayers. Good as done for. Bite's very nearly one-hundred-percent fatal."

"It's interesting," I said, "that the word *mamba* means 'crocodile' too. Right?"

"Yeh, Swahili," Denys corroborated.

"That's what the Mamba people keep telling us," Laura added, "'Not the snake! The crocodile!' I always thought it was kind of an offputting thing, to call a safari company, even so."

"No exactly the clincher, eh?" Ewan laughed. "When y're tryin' t' decide amongst the lot."

"Yeh. Word for the snake's the same in Nyanja as in English," Denys agreed. "Crocodile's called *ng'ona* in Nyanja. *Mamba*'s from the Zulus, the Ngonis...."

"So *their* name, the tribe, actually has to do with 'crocodiles,'" I declared, making the connection.

"No, no. You may not be able to hear the difference off my thick *mzungu* tongue, but 'Ngo-ni' has a hard gee."

He said the word again twice, experimentally, a nasalized hum followed by a sharply emphasized second consonant. "Like the en-gee in 'lingo,'" he added. "Altogether different syllable, *ngo* to *ng'o*. Can you make it out? '*Ng'ona*,' now, 'crocodile...' there the sound's much harder for us, at the beginning of a word. It's supposed to be soft, as in 'singing,' hey? They spell it with an inverted comma after the gee, an apostrophe, in the written language. To make the distinction. *Ng'ona*."

"*Ng'ona*," George echoed, nodding, providing the standard.

"Anyway, getting back, Latin name for mamba is *dendraspis*. 'Tree snake.' Which pretty much tells the tale. Cobra family, in fact, they are. Plenty of those in the park too. Egyptian cobra, spittin' cobra, black-and-white-lipped forest cobra.... Most likely find 'em on the ground, livin' in a termite mound or something. Cobra'll climb a tree once in a way, though."

"Maybe we should go back," I said, not altogether jokingly. "I think I'd just like to lie down by the pool. George can sit next to me with his rifle."

"Nah, nah," Denys said. "Don't take me wrong. Snakes aren't a problem. No worries, long as y' don't do something foolish. Watch where y're walking. Keep your hand out of holes. Common sense. More afraid of you than you are of them...."

"That's certainly what they always say," I muttered.

"There is one bit of vital information I have to give y', though, before we continue."

He stopped. The four of us drew to an expectant halt around him.

"Now, there is a snake I haven't mentioned that we also have here in the Luangwa Valley. Python. African python."

"Ah, yeh," Nigel said. "Like to see one of *'em*."

"Now," Denys said, his voice very sober, "you might find a python in a tree, or you might find one in the grass. Could find one in the river, too, matter of fact, but. Thing is, they're very quick. They can outrun y', out-slither y', no matter how fast you are. So. Here's what you have to do."

He drew a breath.

"If, by some chance, we should come upon a python," he continued, "and if it happens you're the closest one to it, best thing is to immediately lie flat on the ground. On your back, feet together, arms at your sides, head well back...."

He braced himself at attention, demonstrating with a stiff-backed, chin-high posture. "...And just stay there, maintain that pose, without so much as a wiggle, until help arrives."

He paused. We gaped at him.

"Now," he resumed, "meanwhile, what the python is gonna try to do, see, is t' get y' in its clutches. That's how it kills its prey. Wraps itself round...."

He circled his hips with his right hand, then brought it up to his chest.

"...Squeezes the air right out of the victim and strangles it. Waterbuck, for example. Though it could be a human. Anything looks appetising."

He stroked his chin.

"That's what you want to avoid, then, hey? Once the prey's been snuffed, like, suffocated, python starts in swallowing. Jaw unhinges, as you may know. And they can stretch their ribs to bloody amazing proportions."

He spread his cupped hands outward.

"Full-grown waterbuck, wildebeest's no problem for a python to get down. Horns and all."

He paused again. We shifted nervously.

"So. What you *don't* want to do under any circumstance is let the bugger work its head under your body. 'Cause that'll be what it'll be tryin' to do. Tryin' every possible place. Nosin' all around you, curious like, seein' if it can slide its head under your ankles, under your knees, under your shoulders, under your neck."

He lowered his voice.

"But the thing is, y' can't let that happen. See? Y've gotta just lie there, calm and quiet. Legs, arms, back, head all pressed good and tight and firm to the ground, way I showed you. Calm and quiet, that's the ticket. One little frightened twitch...!'"

He snapped his fingers. I flinched. I was not the only one.

"...And the python'll have y' in its grip! Snake its coils right round y' and crush y' to death."

"But how could anybody *manage* that?" Laura piped incredulously. "For God's sake! Oh, yeah, I'm sure! 'Stay calm.'" She snorted. There was a kind of plaintive indignation in her voice.

"Won't they bite or what?" Nigel asked.

"Only if provoked," Denys said. "Teeth're very nasty indeed. But they're not venomous. Won't strike anyway, a python, if you do what I've been telling y'? Bit more to it, though."

"So, what, they'll just crawl away after a while?" Laura said.

"No. No, that's the point. That's the next part. Very important, see. What's going to happen is, is if you can manage to stay all still, according to these instructions, then the python'll eventually get frustrated, get tired of pokin' its ugly snout at you and figger it's time to get on with the business, skip the customary preliminaries. Just start in gulpin' you down. Like as not he'll begin with one of your feet."

"What!" Laura yelped.

"Och, man!" Ewan protested.

"I know, sounds bad, but it doesn't hurt. And it takes a long time. See, that's the thing, you've got to just keep cool. You lie there the way you were, not moving a muscle, and let the python do what a python's got to do, as they say. Quite painless, apparently. Tickles, like, especially if you're wearing shorts."

He glanced around, scowling, lips compressed, silently reminding everyone of us except Laura and George of the bareness of our legs.

"Teeth fold back. Can't digest anything 'til it reaches the stomach, so no worries there. If you do start thrashin' about, though... keep in mind, if y' panic, lose your head, python'll whip its tail right round y', whup, whup, whup, and you'll be a goner for certain."

"This is some kind of joke," Laura challenged. "What, are we supposed to give him fatal indigestion?"

"Ah, nah, nah. Quite serious," Denys insisted. "This is advice for missionaries I'm passing along. When they were settin' out for the wilds of Darkest Africa. Back in the nineteenth century. How to cope with a python."

"Seriously?" I murmured.

Denys nodded somberly.

"Idea of it is, see, you just lie there patiently while the python slowly works its way up to your knees. Then you ve-ry, ve-ry carefully...." He pantomimed. "...Slip out your knife. And, quite gentle, you slide it down along your leg and inside the python's mouth, down the side, where it's distended. Then... fwip!"

I flinched again, probably we all did, when he made the sound and simultaneously jerked his fist away from his thigh. "With a quick motion you just slit the bugger right open!"

"Och, aye!" Ewan reacted.

"Cripes!" Nigel exclaimed.

"Neatly done, hey?" Denys grinned. He broke into hearty laughter.

A lot of the seriousness of his mien as he'd regaled us with this "advice," I realized, had been due to the dogged tightening of the facial muscles necessary to tamp the mirth beneath.

George was smiling patiently—at our reactions, I supposed, not the story, which he'd probably had to listen to repeatedly.

"That *is* a joke. Right?" Laura demanded earnestly.

"Oh, yeh! Yeh. Shaggy python story, you might say. Please. Don't take any of what I just said literally. Though the way it came down to me, that was set forth in all seriousness originally. Nah, never fear. Haven't lost a guest to a python yet. Never had to put that little scheme to the test, either, fortunately. Interesting notion, though, hey? I thought you might enjoy it."

"Especially those of us who don't have a knife with us," Laura murmured wryly.

"Och, aye." Ewan said, patting his pockets and waggling his eyebrows. "But y' mean t' say y' havenay got a wee knife in there wi' the sunscreen and aw that, Laura?" He cocked his head at her waist-pack.

"Actually," Laura said thoughtfully. "I do, in fact. Tiny one. Thanks, Ewan, for reminding me. For all the good it'd do me."

I had a momentary vision of myself wearing a python stocking. Left leg up to the knee in its viscid throat—my left side, for some reason, having been in my mind's eye throughout Denys's scenario. Trying to insinuate my hand surreptitiously into one of the front pockets of my shorts, finger out and tweeze open the stubby blade on either the Swiss Army knife or the multi-pronged "survival tool" I had in an opposite pocket.

Which would be better for the job? Sharper?

Actually, I guess the snake would be pretty preoccupied at that point. Although there'd still be plenty of tail free to lash, as Denys had warned. Not very inspiriting, the prospect. At least I had the satisfaction of knowing I was rudimentarily armed for such an eventuality.

"What *should* we do then, eh, if we see a python?" Nigel asked.

Denys shrugged. "Ag, run like bloody hell, I'd recommend!"

"But you told us...," Nigel objected.

"Nah, nah." He drew a breath and assumed a more serious expression and tone.

"First of all, that's why we've got George here with us, hey? Secondly, if y' *were* to stumble on a python face to face, so to speak, in the track, chances are he'd be off the mark and away...."

Denys scrawled sharp esses in the air with his forefinger.

"...Before y'd have time to react and bolt y'rself. Back into his hole he'd go. Snake's first instinct is to escape, not attack."

"As is mine," I muttered.

Denys gave a signal to George.

"Better be on our way," he rallied us. He about-faced and we followed in a loose vee, like migrating geese.

Although not hurried, the pace George set was brisker now. It felt more purposive.

The alley we were threading among the mopanis began to descend. To our right I caught a glimpse of the sunny open corridor cut by the river. Then I saw the water itself glinting through a break in the brush beyond a group of smooth-barked trees that Denys told us were sycamore figs—ficus, he added.

Ahead, to the left, there was a level, shady clearing... and there were men in it. Five of them, Africans, heads all turned, impassively watching our approach. Two lay stretched out on their sides, taking their ease. One was sitting, one was squatting over a pile of smoky sticks he'd apparently just set alight. One stood slightly apart with an automatic rifle dangling at his hip from a loose shoulder sling. There were a couple of dented aluminum pots and canisters arrayed beside the smoking kindling—which, in keeping with Steve's commentary yesterday, was, I noticed, laid without apparent regard for the dry leaves and grass under and around it.

The men wore either khaki or military green shirts unbuttoned over bare chests, or dirty white tee-shirts, and gray pants or fatigues. The one hunkered at the fire was in rubber sandals. One of the reclining pair was barefoot, his pink soles thickly callused and cracked. The rest had on the kind of World War II combat boots that buckle around the ankle. There was also a pair of battered boots—the barefoot guy's, I guess—that had been shed beside a nest of rifles stacked upright against the huge tree behind them, a sycamore fig with a complexly fluted bole.

The rifles looked like what George was carrying, handsome weapons, bolt-action, more rich brown wood than anodized steel. The one slung from the shoulder of the guy who was standing was a different matter: It was stubbier, cruder and uglier, with a pistol grip and a magazine, which were inverted since he carried it casually, hanging upside down, barrel slanted toward the ground. His was a contemporary military weapon, no question. An AK-47? A Galil? Some kind of Commonwealth version of the M-16?

I knew almost nothing about guns. At OCS we potential officers and gentlemen of the seagoing service had fumbled our way perfunctorily through the manual of arms with dummy M1s. They could as well have given us muskets, or sticks. And the only trigger I'd ever pulled was on a Colt .45 automatic. Our Exec had arranged an afternoon training outing for the wardroom to a Marine pistol range in Pearl Harbor during one of the *Huckaby*'s layovers there, typical soft duty for a ship's visit to Oahu.

The Colt .45 is the officer's traditional sidearm when standing watch on the quarterdeck, but those at the range had been jiggered to fire .22-caliber ammunition. Even so, and despite earplugs, I couldn't suppress a huge flinch at the noise every time I squeezed off a round. To my chagrin, I hadn't punctured the paper target even once. I'd always assumed I'd be a crack shot.

"*Moni,*" George acknowledged the men in a low voice as we passed.

"*Moni,*" Denys said equably. Laura and Ewan and Nigel and I bobbed our heads.

A couple of the men nodded back. None offered a smile. The one on his feet, who was closest to our path, responded with a grunted "*moni*" and edged away. If they'd been in conversation, it had lapsed until we were out of earshot. There was an almost pointed lack of warmth in their stares, although not exactly overt hostility, either. Everything about them radiated: tough characters.

From George's and Denys's demeanor, I figured they must belong here, must be some kind of friends, not enemies. But the profundity of their indifference was scary. Particularly since they were armed.

We walked by in silence, feigning nonchalance, sneaking a glance at them now and then as if it were part of our intense, generalized appreciation of the ecosphere.

Okay, speaking for myself. But no one, as far as I could tell, challenged their stony gaze for any appreciable span. And I noticed that no one, not even George or Denys, muttered a word again until, a few moments later, we veered downslope into a stand of tall grass that parted to reveal the broad brown river flowing almost at our feet.

More surprising, there was a muddy shelf below the lip of the embankment from which jutted a crude dock. A battered boat floated beside it.

Broad in the beam, with low sides and a blunt stem and stern, it was what we called in the Navy a punt.

Two black men on the dock cranked themselves up off their haunches at our arrival.

"*Moni, kapitau,*" Denys greeted them. "*Mulibwanji.*"

"*Moni, bwana,*" one of them replied with a smile, stepping forward. "*Ife tili bwino. Mulibwanji?*"

"*Ndili bwino,*" Denys nodded.

"We are waiting for you," the man said to us.

Both were in shorts. The one in the rear was shoeless and had on a threadbare tanktop. The other, who had spoken and seemed to be in charge, boasted a pair of battered, laceless hightop leather basketball sneakers and a maroon tee-shirt with a trademark blue swoosh on the breast. The back, I saw when he turned, bore the motto in blue letters "Just Do It."

If he'd ever actually played basketball, he must have been a point guard. He was about five-five.

We scrambled down a steep staircase of roots and slumps in the mud-bank to crowd behind Denys onto the rickety dock—weathered planks laid on mushy stringers spiked to a pair of log posts jutting more or less vertically from the water. The whole structure swayed ominously with our weight.

I scanned the margins of the river and its opaque shallows, upstream, downstream.

I saw no animals.

No crocodiles.

"Right," Denys said. "As I said, we'll be crossing the river for our walking safari today. Hopefully there'll be a fair amount of game about, so we should be able to do some interesting tracking.

Now, when we reach the other side, I want you to step out of the boat and move on up the bank smartly. But wait till everyone's ashore, don't wander off on your own. That's important. I'll have a few more words of wisdom to impart once we're across. Right, then. Laura? Why don't you be first in? Take that broadest thwart there, in the middle, the forward one."

"Which way should I sit?" she asked.

Ewan and I, who were shoulder to shoulder, made eye contact. From a twitch of his lips I recognized that he, like me, had been visited by the urge to supply the obvious joke answer.

For an instant I thought we might squat in tandem: "Like this."

We sublimated in an exchange of tiny grins.

"Bow points into the stream," Denys replied. "Might as well face in that direction."

He offered her his left hand and indicated with his right.

The two crewmen had knelt, and were holding the craft close to the dock. I shifted my feet to sidle around Nigel, who was in front of me, to assist Laura too. But it would have been awkward, a disturbance on this narrow, precarious platform. Anyway, my help wasn't necessary.

Laura seized Denys's wrist, marshalled her equilibrium at the dock's edge and stepped down into the waist of the boat, which rocked deeply under her off-center weight despite the crewmen's efforts to damp the motion.

With a vocalized exhalation, still clutching at him, she plopped onto the bench, twisting at the knees to bring her rump down more or less amidships.

Ripples purled downstream as the punt's flat bottom spanked the current.

Denys turned. "Nigel, it is, hey? Seem to be next in line. Laura? You slide outboard a bit now. That's it. Make room for Nigel."

Laura had nodded and wriggled to her left.

"Nigel? You sit beside Laura there, then, okay? Hand here if you need it."

Nigel stepped forward, shuffled in a half circle, bent at the knees and reached up for Denys' handclasp as he poked his Hush Puppy off the dock and probed backwards for the punt's floorboards.

It tilted under him as soon as he transferred his weight. He adjusted nervously, clinging to Denys until he felt secure, then pushed off and ricocheted heavily against Laura as he slid into sitting position. She braced herself by grabbing for the pocked toprail that ran around the boat's sides, at her hip. They both laughed at the clumsiness.

Denys looked to me. I glanced at Ewan.

Ewan, the hydrophobe, tilted his head, flared his eyes, twisted his lips and bared his teeth in a parodic grimace of disquiet and reluctance.

"No what I'd call walkin', then," he muttered. "Must've misunderstood. Ben the lodge, thought they said *'walkin'* safari!'"

"It's not that far across, actually," I suggested.

I appraised the opposite bank through my sunglasses.

The river was about as wide as a six-lane freeway. Its shrinkage from flood-level now that the rains had ended had exposed a narrow mud-terrace on the other shore too. A rampart overgrown with tall grass rose behind it, slightly less sheer than the cutbank on this side. Several defiles led up from the terrace into a thicket of large trees.

Our dock was on the outside of a gentle bend, so what I was facing, the inside bank of the meander, appeared to be a promontory. Its shape was doubled by an inverted wedge of umber shadow on the river's syrupy tan surface.

White-haloed whiffets of high blue cloud were also mirrored, nearer, and if I looked downstream, past snags and eddies and a fairly large bar or finger heaped with driftwood and tufted with brush, the ball of silver sun blazed out of its glare on the water, the reflection resolved by my polarized lenses.

"Who's next then? Daniel!" Denys said, urging the show on the road. "Tell you what. You can get in behind them, hey?"

He gestured at the after of the two central thwarts. "Stay in the middle for now. Help steady matters."

I nodded, strode to the edge and stepped off with only the briefest of hesitations to aim the foot I'd alight on—the left—squarely amidships on the bench. Old blue-water sailor, I needed no help getting into a boat; I spurned any reliance on Denys.

It was like hopping down a couple of steps on a staircase. I landed, immediately bent and snatched at Laura's shoulder from behind for support as I completed the stride by planting my right boot in the well below.

The punt tipped and swayed under my stagger-step; the fluid in my bowels lurched with it. It was as if I were a level, and that was where the bubble was.

I let go of Laura and rode out the surge for a second or two loose-kneed, to demonstrate my sealegs, my small-boat aplomb. Then I lowered myself onto the thwart.

"Ewan," Denys said. "Want you beside Nigel. Three abreast. Laura? Edge over a bit? Right. In you go, Ewan."

"Och, aye! Set a mind at rest! 'In y' go,' man. I cannay swim, eh?"

"Not to worry," Denys soothed him curtly. "River isn't all that deep. Y'd touch bottom most of the way."

"Touchin' bottom's no really the question, is it?" Ewan grumbled.

He angled himself—with a nimbleness one wouldn't have anticipated from his gangly physique—down into the punt alongside Nigel.

Denys followed. He settled on the two-person thwart forward of Laura, Nigel and Ewan, but with his knees toward theirs, his back to the prow, positioned to watch over us during the voyage. George assumed the forward lookout post, crouched over his rifle in the space behind the narrow wedge of thwart in the squared bow. He gazed vigilantly ahead.

The boatman in the tanktop leaped onto the thwart beside me; I wormed left to give him room to sit.

I was immediately enveloped by his body odor. Which was pungent, complexly human—meaning, in fact, animal, musky, but not what I'd consider foul.

He held onto the dock stringer while "Just Do It" clambered into the stern, unfastened the frayed rope that served as a mooring line and withdrew the working end of a long, slender pole from under the thwart at my feet. He said something, and the guy at my elbow gave us a shove off.

Leaning into his pole, Just Do It slowly propelled us out into the sluggish current.

*T*he riverine air was refreshing. You couldn't say there was a breeze, but the movement of the turbid water was accompanied by a cooling molecular rustle of the atmosphere floating atop it.

We spoke little, and kept our voices low when we did. The arrhythmic plup... plup... of the skipper's pole breaking the river's viscous skin was the dominant sound. There was an afternoon placidity, a somnolence, to the moment—no monkey chatter, no carnivorous roars, and only thin, sporadic avian twitter audible from the trees on either side.

VI. Seeing the Elephant

Nor, in fact, was there any animal life at all visible along this stretch of the river, at least from our vantage. That didn't bode particularly well for our upcoming excursion—although who could say what feral eyes might be scouting our approach from the thick bush we were gliding towards?

Once we'd reached midchannel and could see around the point of what I'd thought was a finger of land but now showed itself to be a slender island, we discovered three hippos taking footbaths in its lee. They clustered near the downstream end, where the river began a reverse meander and the true bank behind them was sharply undercut.

Hippos are pretty nearsighted, apparently. Or perhaps we were simply inconsequential to them. They gave no sign of noticing us.

In front of me, Laura dug her camera out of her waistpack and raised it to her eye.

"Too far to look like much," she murmured, "even with the zoom."

Her lens only went to seventy millimeters. That wasn't nearly powerful enough to get the kind of fly-on-the-nose, tickbird-on-the-shoulder closeup detail you see in professional wildlife photography.

"Beautiful, though, the scene," she said, "isn't it?"

I leaned forward and rested my hand on her back with casual affection, confirming her assumption that I'd be listening.

"You're shooting into the sun," I reminded her.

She didn't reply. After a moment for composition and f-stop setting, she clacked the shutter.

"You should put the strap around your neck, you know," I murmured into her ear. "Whenever you have that thing out in a boat?"

"Mm," she agreed with a grudging bob of her head.

She ducked into the embroidered loop.

It was a small win for me: the point made that people of intelligence and good will can forget the precaution.

Two summers earlier, kayaking out of Bar Harbor, I'd asked Laura to share the binoculars she was wearing so I too could get a closeup look at a bald eagle we'd spotted circling a towering white spruce on one of the outcrop islets we were drifting past. She'd unstrapped the glasses and carefully handed them back to me from her position in the front cockpit; I'd adjusted the focus and studied the rough assemblage of sticks that appeared to be the eagle's nest. I wondered if a chick might reveal its head.

Without thinking I'd set the binoculars aside on the shelf of deck behind my cockpit so I could pivot the kayak for a more comfortable observation of the aerie.

No sooner had I dipped my paddle blade than I heard a splash and swiveled to watch helplessly as the two-hundred-dollar binoculars slowly spiraled out of sight below me into the blue-grey depths of Frenchman Bay.

Talk about feeling like an idiot. And Laura's scorn still burned— her disbelief and disgust so acute at that moment she'd hardly wasted breath on rebuke.

One hates to diminish oneself in the estimation of one's spouse: begin to layer on the persona of The Bumbler, The Chronic Fuckup. It seems to be a ready dynamic for a couple to fall into. And now I'd lost my *nyaminyami*. Still, I wasn't rooting for her to lose her camera overboard to square accounts.

Our boatman had angled his course to compensate for the river's set; we were only a bit downstream of the dock we'd left when, with a last strong lunge against his pole, Just Do It drove the punt's bow firmly aground on the Luangwa's northwestern shore.

George and the guy next to me sprang over the side a split second before the landing, and together they maintained the punt's momentum, running us up the slope of the terrace so far we didn't even have to get our feet wet when we stepped over the side to disembark.

Ewan, then Nigel, then Laura, then I joined George at the base of a faint trail that climbed the shoulder of the floodbank into the tall grass on its crest.

Last out, Denys arrived to provide the promised marching orders.

"From here on," he announced, "we'll walk single-file, with George in the lead. I want you to keep close enough together so you always have the person in front of you and the person behind you within eyesight. Clear enough? Especially important for the last in line: don't fall too far behind. Second to the rear, keep a watch for your mate at the back, hey? In some patches the kasensi grass grows very thick, perhaps even over our heads. So we'll close up in those spots, right? Anyone has a problem, wants to stop for a breather, has a bit of gear to fiddle with, sees something you'd like to photograph, whatever it may be, just pass the word and we'll all halt and wait together. Right enough? No need to be bashful. Others'll probably have much the same idea as well.

"Now, as soon we begin tracking," he continued, "we'll want to keep our voices down. No unnecessary chat, hey? And once we get close, we'll switch to hand signals."

He raised his arm above his head.

"That's to get your attention. 'Look at me. Watch me.' Maybe I've spotted something but I don't want to spook it by singin' out. I'll point."

He jabbed his finger in several directions by way of illustration. Then he put it to his lips.

"Quiet, that means, hey? Silence. Simple enough."

He wiggled his hand up and down, parallel to the ground. "Slow."

He cocked his wrist and held his palm up, fingers rigid: the universal sign for "Stop."

He flapped the hand away from himself vigorously. "Go back. Or...."

Again he jabbed his forefinger at various quadrants. "I might point in the direction I want you to move. Or...."

He switched his hand to the "stop" position and then lowered it slowly toward the ground. "Get down. That means, like crouch. No need to lie flat. Whatever it is," he concluded, "whatever signal I give, the person behind me 'll pass it along. And so on, hey? All down the line. Shouldn't be too difficult."

We nodded our comprehension.

"Right, then. Any other questions before we head out?"

There were none.

Denys nodded at George, and the two trudged up the bank. Laura followed Denys. I fell in behind her. Nigel trailed me. Ewan brought up the rear.

We maintained that order at various intervals as, for the next fifteen minutes or so, George led us inland through stands of mopani and what Denys distinguished as winter thorn, knob thorn and false thorn.

"Always find ants under the false thorns," Denys noted. "Not a good shade tree to choose for a picnic."

We crossed a belt of stunted grassland dotted with huge crenelated pink termite mounds, into stalky, armpit-high dry brush islanded by clumps of dwarf acacia.

We saw no game.

Denys tried to point out elements of interest, like the hulking, bottle-shaped stele that was a dead baobab.

"This was a flourishing tree when Jesus Christ walked the earth," Denys said after a pause for Nigel and Ewan to catch up. "Live for two thousand years or more, they do, baobabs. Fruit bats pollinate 'em at night when the flowers open—which is only a single day in the year. Another curious thing—they never fall when they die. Just slowly decay, crumble in on themselves. Eventually all that'll be left here is a heap of black fibers."

"Eh, what's he say?" Ewan hissed at Nigel, who'd arrived first.

"Baobab," Nigel reported. "Dead. Two thousand years old. Never fall down."

"Aw, aye," Ewan nodded and dutifully snapped a picture.

We set off again.

Laura and I were still close behind Denys. After a moment, I asked him: "Who were those guys back there? That we saw just before we crossed the river?"

"Ah. Anti-poaching patrol," he replied. "Looked to be on recce."

"Guess they hadn't caught anybody," I commented.

"No prisoners to be seen, hey?" he agreed. "Do the best they can. What with more than a million hectares of parklands to cover...."

"That's how many acres," I wondered.

"Mm. Not quite sure, actually. Several millions, I reckon. Entire Luangwa Valley game management area's more than five thousand square miles. So they're spread bloody thin, anti-poaching guys, you can imagine."

"Yeah. Steve was telling us that yesterday," I said, "on the night drive."

"Went out with Steve, did you?"

"Uh-huh. And Graeme."

I thought I detected a dry chuckle, although only a sliver of his face was visible from the rear.

"Spot a good lot of game?"

"We saw lions," Laura declared triumphantly. "Saw a pair of bush babies."

"Ah," Denys commented. "Fair treat."

"A genet and a serval cat," I noted. "Puku."

"News there."

"Elephants," Laura added. "One of them charged us, in the car."

"Really," Denys said.

"Well. Actually, I guess he only... trumpeted," she admitted. "Threatened to charge. Steve drove us out of there fast."

"Right thinking," Denys approved.

"I noticed," I said, returning to the original subject, "one of those guys back there had what looked like an AK-Forty-Seven."

"Eh?" Denys inquired.

"The patrol. The rangers or whatever."

"Ah. Did rather appear to be, didn't it?" he agreed after a beat.

"I wonder if those weren't the guys who killed a couple of poachers last year?" I concluded. "Steve was telling us about it. Fierce gunbattle, he said. Said the poachers were armed with AK-Forty-Sevens...."

"Yes," George confirmed over his shoulder. "It is those men, yes. One of them is the cousin of my wife."

"Really! They didn't seem exactly friendly," I observed. "I mean to you! Considering."

"It is very hard sometimes, this work they do, I think," George said. "They are very tired."

"Far better to be on staff at Chibembe, hey, George?" Denys teased. "Get to take a nice little promenade in the bush on a beautiful afternoon like this. Then back to the lodge for some tasty tucker and home to the *mkazi* and the *ana*."

"Yes. It is better, quite," George allowed.

We were approaching a line of trees.

"Let's keep it down now, for a minute," Denys said.

He'd turned, glancing at me first. His gaze immediately flicked past, checking on Nigel, maybe fifteen feet back, then Ewan, doggedly clutching his camera to his bare ribs as he slogged along in our zigzag wake another twenty feet or so behind. When he saw we were looking at him, Ewan gave a quick, cheerful wave.

The plane of the brush, the ragged brown twig-tops and tassels we were wading though, came to about Laura's chin. So all of us were clearly visible to one another—if nothing else, as bobbing heads and shoulders.

The undergrowth was complexly layered, but for the most part the small leaves on the plants below knee-level were furry and the long-stemmed grasses were pliant and yielded readily to our strokes as we swam in the short-lived swath cleaved by George and Denys.

Like three of the four of us in his charge, Denys was wearing shorts, which was some consolation: my shins and calves were now crisscrossed with tiny white hatchmarks, and I kept reaching down to slap at incipient itches.

I noticed that an older scratch on my right shin was inflamed around the scab. I hoped it wouldn't get torn open again. I was beginning to wonder just how inappropriate, how regrettable my wardrobe selection might prove to be.

George seemed to be carefully skirting the tallest, thickest, spiniest patches, at any rate. Presumably he was also on the alert to avoid buffalo beans. Nonetheless, I kept my eyes peeled for anything that might harbor pods like those James had showed us back at our first river crossing.

It occurred to me to ask Denys whether buffalo beans were a scourge around here too. I was mindful of his admonition, though. We tramped in silence for a few moments. Then George, up ahead, murmured something over his shoulder to Denys.

Denys nodded and slowed to allow Laura to close on him.

"Elephant," he said in a low voice. "In behind those trees."

He extended his arm, pointing slightly to the left. "We'll try to circle a bit nearer. Can't really see yet, too much bush between us."

Laura squinted in the direction he'd indicated, then looked around at me.

"I heard," I nodded.

She wheeled excitedly after Denys. I tarried for Nigel.

"They've spotted an elephant," I informed him as soon as he'd trudged to within a few yards. Keeping my voice to a surreptitious undertone did impart a certain spice to the situation.

Nigel's eyes widened and he swallowed in anticipation, his Adam's apple riding up and down in his scrawny neck like a hotel elevator.

"Still too far to get a good look at, apparently," I added. "Other side of the trees somewhere. We're trying to work our way closer."

"Ah... hah," he nodded.

I turned in pursuit of Laura, Denys and George.

"Elephant!" I heard Nigel stage whisper to Ewan. "On the trail of an elephant now!"

George set a course that approached the treeline diagonally. We walked at about the same pace as we had been, making just as much noise crunching through the brittle grass as before, so neither haste nor stealth seemed to be considerations.

Lanes opened in the thicket as we worked our way south along its front. I peered down them, searching for the purported elephant somewhere in the tawny clearings and branching alleys that were revealed.

Eager, on the hunt, we were pressing on one another's heels now.

"I still don't see anything," Laura muttered.

"They're there, no worries," Denys replied out of the side of his mouth.

"More than one?"

"May be. We'll see soon enough."

I was breathing harder, not panting but sucking in more air more deeply to feed my heart as it pumped in serious accommodation of the steady tramp and the atavistic dribble of adrenalin that attended the stalking of a mammoth.

George slowed. He was carrying his rifle at port arms now.

Denys raised his hand and we all scrambled to a stop behind him. He swung his fist and leveled his index finger at George, or rather, I realized, a few degrees to the right of George's ear.

I squinted into the bush along the bearing suggested—middle distance... on a little further....

And caught movement, all right! The grass suddenly shimmied far off.

A dark, rounded shape shook free, winked in and out of the sunlight falling through the tops of a ring of trees, then disappeared into a brown brake beyond.

The hump of an elephant, I'd have been prepared to depose. Maybe the batwing flutter of an ear.

I had the impression of a creature on the stroll, not the run.

Denys had trained his binoculars at the spot. Now he swept them slowly to the right. He steadied and pointed again.

"Two more. And a baby, just there. About a thousand metres? Okay. Baby just went behind a thorn. Adults still in the open. Probably females. Head on to us, hey? Can you see?"

The backdrop, the horizon, was a solid wall of forest—low, bulbous treetops mottled by shadow, their deep green darkened by the thickening afternoon light and the cast of my sunglasses. Hummocks of shrub, tangled lianas and solitary trees hung with huge pods like smoked sausages dotted the amber *grassveld*. Its surface was streaked too, bands of vivid straw-gold alternating with strips that were coppery brown, and here and there a dull grey-green scrawl where some lingering moisture was still available to be sucked out of the earth, which was hard as pink stucco underfoot.

I tried to judge a thousand meters. Ten football fields laid goalpost to goalpost. That's a long way.

What would the world's burliest fullback, plunging over center, look like at that remove? Number 44, Jumbo Elephantovski.

I wondered if trees, like the goalposts that would clutter my imaginary perspective, were blocking the line of sight.

"Yeah! I see 'em!" Laura exclaimed.

"There they are, right enough," Nigel nodded.

I was annoyed. I was one of the better spotters on the truck. More often than not I'd been the first to call others' attention to interesting game *en passant.*

"Where are you looking?" I frowned, side-stepping toward Laura's shoulder.

She pointed.

I stared. I wagged my head in the negative.

"Okay. See that dead tree?" she said. "The tall one with just the bare branches?"

Its silhouette was distinctive, a good landmark. But it was much closer than a thousand meters.

"Yeah...," I said.

"Okay, now go out from there. Look straight on out.... You see there's kind of a triangular patch of green to the right a little bit? And two trees off to the left of that, but back still, with leaning trunks?"

"Mmm." Hard to be sure what she meant. "I guess...."

"Okay, between 'em."

"Okay! Right!"

Two knobby elephant pates jutted out of the savannah like rocks off a distant wooded coast!

"Sure! Right!" I declared.

I narrowed my eyes by myopic instinct, trying to tighten the focus—you could easily miss them, dusty grey-brown blobs on a vast, motley sea of yellows, browns, dead greys and blackish greens.

Although now that I'd pinpointed them they were unmistakeable. Unmistakeably two large elephants. The wrinkled tops of their trunks were visible but not the lobes of their flared ears. Their tusks if any were hidden too. They stood more or less motionless, not apparently alarmed if even aware of our remote presence.

And now that you concentrated you could see their ears begin to ripple faintly, spread and go limp, their backs sway, their shoulders pulse sporadically. You could sense the movement of their forelegs as they shuffled languidly toward us, or really toward an island of thorny shrubs that presumably now hid the baby Denys had announced.

"See 'em, do you, Ewan?" he queried.

"Aye," Ewan said.

"Anybody want a peek, through the binocs?" he offered.

"Yes, please," Laura responded immediately.

We each took a turn after her. Nobody hogged the glasses, out of consideration for the others, especially Ewan; the elephants would soon be obscured by the patch of thornbush.

"What do they eat mostly around here?" I asked Denys as I placed the binoculars in Nigel's hand.

"Very fond of the young mopani leaves," he said. "Also strip the bark off trees of various sorts."

He turned to George and they exchanged a couple of quick, *sotto voce* words. I couldn't make out the language because Laura at that instant muttered, "Too bad we didn't have binoculars to bring of our own."

She gave me a wry sidelong eye.

"Maybe that's what I should get you for your next birthday," I said. "What'll it be...? Sixtieth, is it?"

She pulled out her camera.

"Every year around you is like a dog year, all right," she snorted. She poked me in the ribs with an elbow. "You take a picture too, okay?"

I patted my pocket, then thought better of it. "Nah. They're way too far," I said.

"That's okay," she insisted. "Just this whole scene. I still don't trust mine entirely to come out."

"Tell you what," I said. "How about if I take a picture of you taking a picture?"

"Don't," she said.

I backed away a couple of steps and off-centered her in the viewfinder from the waist up, with Denys and George behind her shoulder. I flipped the camera vertically and knocked the bill of my cap askew—I reached up and righted it—then sidled left to get both of the latter into the picture from head to toe. That gave me more of Laura, as well as the complete context: the sere grass we were awash in, the exotically pod-decorated crowns of the trees around us, the forest horizon, the distinctive cloudlets, blue-bellied but snow-white on top, riding low in the cerulean sky.

Only the minuscule elephants were missing.

I hesitated until Laura grew uncomfortable and lowered her own camera to stick out her tongue at me. Had I been mean... but I knew it was not an expression she'd really want memorialized. I waited another couple of beats, and in the fleeting instant when she relaxed her face—self-possessed, slightly quizzical—and before she'd had a chance to harden it again into a posed smile, I pressed the button.

In this full sun, with ASA-400 film, the shutter opened and closed behind the pinprick aperture in probably 1/200th of a second. Too quickly for the moment to blur:

Laura in Africa.

Beautiful, at peace, happy.

"Right. We'll follow the other one for a bit," Denys said, "try t' see what he's up to. There's a *dambo*, a clearing, off in there with a nice little pond in it. Fair bet he's headed that way. Perhaps off to his afternoon wallow."

We resumed our trek.

Nigel, who'd fumbled his camera out of his rucksack belatedly, had been slow to take his snaps. I hung back as well, gesturing to Ewan to skirt on around me.

Even if Denys hadn't mentioned it, I'd always felt a visceral responsibility for the stragglers on a hike. I saw myself as some self-appointed equivalent of a ski patrolman, charged with herding the last hapless snowbunnies down the icy slopes after the lifts have closed.

That analogy came readily to mind because it's exactly the role I'd played with Susan and the kids when they were little and stretching their skills at Squaw and Alpine. So maybe my impulse to shepherd strangers was testimony to my laudable belief in the family of man. Or maybe it was a residue of having been a naval officer, obligated for the welfare of subordinates.

Was *that* how I really regarded other people? As subordinates? Inferiors? Was I trying to exert psychological power over them, claim the *noblesse* I'd once been entitled to—a gentleman by Act of Congress—through voluntary displays of poise and vigor and vigilance? Feed my illusions of manly mastery?

Whatever, just as Ewan's sun-pinkened shoulder blades winked out of sight among the trees to our left, Nigel exclaimed, "Eh! There's the little one now too!"

And I peered and spotted the diminutive head for myself. Maybe a third as big as the adults', inching out of the mound of thornbush.

My immediate thought, of course, was to call to Laura and the others; as quickly I decided against it as a violation of the mood and the setting. Not to mention of stalking principles.

So Nigel and I lingered briefly to take in the sight we'd been privately accorded: the partial figure of a wild baby elephant foraging the green-and-gold Zambian *veld*.

"We'd better get going," I finally suggested, "don't you think?"

"Ah, yeh, indeed," Nigel agreed. But it took him another moment to tuck away the camera and shrug into the straps of his daypack.

I set off tentatively, glancing over my shoulder to make sure he was really in train.

You had to hand it to these guys, these bachelor accountants, I thought. These unlikely African adventurers with their indoor complexions and birdlegs and clueless safari outfits and affable diffidence—both Nigel and Ewan were proving themselves game. Stolid, hard to ruffle.

And I had no difficulty, fortunately, tracing the trough the others had trampled in the grass. Although I was a little piqued at Ewan's irreponsibility. For all he could know, we were still back there where he'd last seen us—desperately flailing for our lives against a pack of slavering lions or hyenas who'd jumped us from ambush.

I thought of the old Mad Magazine cartoon captioned something like "Alfred E. Neuman and the Buddy System": all the kids standing in pairs in the camp pool, each with an upthrust arm, each conscientiously clasping his partner's hand... and Alfred just as cheerfully holding up the limp arm of his own partner floating face-down beside him.

Some buddy. As another cartoonist always had it, "unclear on the concept."

But we did catch up after a minute or two of determined striding. And there was maybe apology and relief in the look Ewan threw over his shoulder when I made a hard left around an acacia and saw his skinny figure finally looming ahead.

As soon as our eyes met he twisted away, nodding to himself in guilty satisfaction. It occurred to me that there was actually some resemblance between Ewan and Alfred E. Neuman, that jug-eared, apple-cheeked signature "Mad" character.

Ewan, Neuman... a near rhyme, even.

But Ewan was no cretin. He'd let a lot of space open between himself and Laura. I took that as another sign he'd been aware of duty—no doubt he'd have sung out and summoned everyone back for us if we'd failed to turn up when we did.

We'd tramped on a fair distance, in fact, before I actually caught sight of my wife's ample rump.

A very Victorian figure, hers was, I mused— square-shouldered, nipped at the waist, then flaring generously to complete the hourglass. And all without the aid of puffed sleeves, corsets or bustles.

(She'd taken off the denim shirt she'd been wearing over a white knit tanktop, and knotted its sleeves at the belt of her khaki pants. The effect from the rear was that she had on a short, flaring overskirt.)

Born a century too late to be fully appreciated, poor Laura. Or to appreciate herself.

If she knew I was assessing her so intently from behind she'd be extremely uneasy. Even ashamed—of her failure to conform more closely to the willowy, media-mediated, late-20th-century ideal.

And in all honesty, would I have preferred her slimmer?

I certainly responded to Renée's narrower lines. And to the youthful wispiness of Jen and Emma. Mel was shorter and fleshier, more like Laura in construction, but there was absolutely nothing wrong with her young body either.

Fact was, I was just wired to react to the female physique. The real thing, not the anorexic, amuscular, spaghetti-armed version seen so frequently in tony magazine ads. To me, those skeletal waifs were turn-offs.

Still, yes, since we were talking brutal candor, I guessed I would have preferred a slightly less opulent Laura. A younger, saucier Laura, too, while we were at it, who'd glory again in bikinis and the flouncy microminis that were back in style and that she'd worn in the sixties, no doubt, before I'd met her.

Just as I'd have preferred being a better-buffed, washboard-stomached, more youthful looking specimen myself. But not enough to do anything about it.

I'd have preferred to own a full head of distinguished iron-gray hair, for that matter. And perfect white teeth. And, hey, to be a critically acclaimed novelist rather than a PR-flack. With the royalty income to summer at my villa in Juan-les-Pins... waterski over to my anchored yacht each morning, to tap out prize-winning prose under an awning on the quarterdeck, like Jack London aboard the *Snark*... buzz the Moyenne Corniche in a Ferrari Testarossa or whatever the tony hell. Which in my fantasy reincarnation I'd actually be able to shoehorn myself into.

Sure. But those "preferences" were only the vaporiest of intellectual exercise. I had absolutely no complaints about things-as-they-were.

Nor should I have had, for God's sake. Leading the material life of the most fortunate fraction of a percentage of the world's human beings, able to traipse the planet at the waft of a credit card, free as far as I knew of carcinomatous nuggets or coronary occlusions or cerebral aneurysms or any other major, imminent threats to middle-aged health. Progenitor of two sturdy, self-sustaining children and step-father of a third. Blessed with the loving companionship of a scintillating if, okay, slightly overweight woman.

Whoa. No. No. It was she herself who'd conditioned me to think of her with that qualification. Laura kicked ass. As Christopher would've had it.

Watching her march along, confidently swatting aside protruding stalks and low-hanging branches, Gap-trousered, Land's End-topped, grey-streaked Empress of the *Veld*—*She*, all right, every bit the avatar of Rider Haggard's African Amazon—American, fifty-something, indomitable... I was flooded with satisfaction.

It was moments like this, the emotive highlights of travel, that a camera can't capture.

And they were what I traveled for, really, scrupulously reminded myself to fix in memory—instants when, like a rodeo cowboy at the top of the bronco's buck, I felt myself riding right out there on the absolute apex of the arc of mortality.

We were entering a band of thicker woodland. The pod-laden trees were interspersed with banks of ground-hugging thorn.

I pressed on Ewan's heels and he duly shortened the interval behind Laura. She was keeping fairly close to Denys, whose bright cap, shirt and shorts occulted reassuringly in the bush ahead.

George was harder to keep track of. His olive-drab drill and dark skin were distinguishable primarily as brief flickers of movement between pools of afternoon shadow.

And then, abruptly, we all caught up to them. They'd stopped at the last rank of trees which, we could now see, bordered a broad clearing—a *dambo*, Denys had called it.

He flapped his hand at us for quiet.

There was a reflective sheen in the middle of the open expanse, a sizeable oblong of brown water. The groundcover before us was thinner and greener, twiggy plants topped by small leaves at about knee height, all underlain by a straw-colored mulch that sloped to the rim of a muddy pond that was as large as some of the pans at Hwange. In contrast to those busy oases, though, no wildlife congregated here.

Which made the sight all the more dramatic and somehow poignant:

On the far side of the sump stood a lone elephant.

We couldn't have been more than two hundred yards away now. Still, it was difficult to judge how big he really was.

But big. And "he" because that was Denys's pronouncement.

"Young male," he said very softly. "You can tell straight off from the shape of the forehead. More rounded than a cow's. Cow's belly is curved, as well, whilst the bull's slopes straight down from the chest."

He put the binoculars to his eyes.

But magnification wasn't necessary to appreciate the nobly distinctive form on display: muscular proboscis dangling like a supple fifth limb between blunted, not yet mature nicotine-yellow tusks; heroic ears; barrel torso; underbelly drooping indeed toward the loose-fleshed, lithely articulated haunches, which hid the penis.

The sun was declining over tasseled waves of dry grass behind him. He stood out against the flaxen background with the clarity of one of those plane-spotters' flash-card silhouettes: *Elephant, African, Mark 1 (Side View)*.

"This is who we've been following?" I whispered.

Denys nodded.

If the young bull elephant had had any intention of wading deeper into the muck for a soothing loll—the spectacle Denys had suggested we might be treated to—our materialization at the *dambo*'s edge had probably put him off the project. Although he certainly didn't act startled or frightened. In fact, there was no overt sign he'd even seen or scented us. He simply set off again on his inscrutable cross-country march.

In the deep quiet you could hear the faint sucking sounds as the massive beast plucked one umbrella-stand foot after the other out of the mud along the pond's margin.

Further along, again on solider ground, the weight of his footfalls was visible—puffs of dust and chaff.

He thumped away toward the trees, his gait unhurried but methodical. He was bound more or less southeast.

That, if I hadn't gotten hopelessly turned around, was the direction in which lay the river.

All of us had brought our cameras to our eyes and managed to click off a shot or two before he was screened from us.

"That should've been a pretty good one," I muttered to Laura.

"Yeah. I was having trouble with the focus again, though, for some reason," she said.

"Gee." I shrugged. "You just put it on 'Infinity.'"

"I know."

She frowned at her camera, turning it this way and that as she squinted at the gradations etched on the barrel of the lens.

"But when I do, it still looks blurred," she complained. "It seems like I have to back it off slightly. Right? Isn't it blurry?"

She held the camera up for me to examine over her shoulder. "I have a hard time telling without my other glasses."

I bent and lifted my sunglasses off my nose so I could peer under them, looking for the little lazy-eight on the knurled lens cylinder. My vision problem was the opposite of hers.

"It isn't quite lined up with the mark," I confirmed. "If the setting's supposed to be 'Infinity.'"

"Hn!" she snorted. "That's what worries me. When I crank it all the way out it goes blurry right at the last. I have to come back in a tiny bit to make the edges match up in the crosshairs."

George and Denys had already moved out into the open; Ewan and Nigel, after a pause, sidled around us.

"Maybe it got dingged somewhere along the way," I said. "But I'd just go with the optics. You're focusing through the lens anyway. Doesn't matter what it reads on the outside."

"I know," she nodded. "That's all I *can* do, isn't it?"

"Come on," I nudged her. We followed the others.

"Anyway," I reassured her, "when you're stopped down for this bright light, it gives you more depth of field, so it's more forgiving. What were you at?"

"What, eff-stop?"

"Yeah."

She glanced down at the camera again. "I don't know. Five-point-six, I think."

"Gee. What shutter speed?"

"Two-hundredth?"

"Huh. What-speed film are you using?"

She checked the camera back, where a frame held the yellow cardboard top she'd torn, as I'd taught her, from the film box. "One-twenty-five."

"Is that what you were using for the lions?"

"Yeah."

"At sunset. Well.... Okay, you might try some of my four-hundred stuff the next roll. Then you could use a smaller eff-stop. I'll bet it's fine, though."

"I sure hope so. I'd hate to think I'd go back and find out everything I'd taken in Africa was completely out of focus or way underexposed or something."

"Wouldn't be sure *what* you'd experienced, would you?"

"An absolute blank," she nodded. "Hey, if you haven't got pictures, it didn't happen!"

"Socrates, I believe it was, said the unphotographed life is not worth living. No way to tell if your focus is correct, I guess."

She snorted. "At least," she said, "our problem won't be underexposure."

The sparse growth along the perimeter of the *dambo* made for easy travel. We all gradually fanned out.

When I glanced down at one point to pick my passage between tussocks, I saw a jagged track of coagulated blood on my right shin. Raised like maroon embossing, it had dribbled from the old scratch, whose scab had indeed been dislodged and clung by only a few strands.

I reached down and plucked it off. The exposed crater looked larger now. The surrounding skin was flushed and the core pale with pus. So it was probably just as well that it was getting an airing.

I thought of the Hemingway story, *The Snows of Kilimanjaro*, in which the writer-hero dies on safari from a thornbush scratch. Exactly the same negligible mishap as mine—only in the story bad infection sets in, then gangrene, then feverish, poignantly evocative flashback sketches from earlier life and love, finally the striking titular hallucination.

Individual symptomatology may vary. Let's hope, I reflected.

When I was a child my mother had painted my cuts with iodine or mercurochrome. Somewhere along the way those quaint antiseptics had fallen into disrepute. As a sophisticated adult I relied on nature to heal punctures and lacerations—the initial gush of blood, maybe an extra pinch to encourage the cleansing ooze to wash away pathogens, soap and water, my immune system. (Bolstered, of course, by an up-to-date tetanus inoculation.)

Typically, I'd done nothing whatsoever to treat either of the two casual wounds I'd suffered on the way to Nsefu. ("Wounds" and "suffered" I considered laughable exaggerations.) And, as a matter of fact, I'd weltered in filth and buffalo-bean residue for almost twenty-four hours before I'd had a chance to shower clean.

The scratch on my forearm did seem to be healing on its own. No redness around the thin scab that was already peeling off at the ends.

When we got back to Chibembe this evening, I thought, I'd better be sure to squeeze some antibiotic ointment into the pallid quick of the ulcer on my shin. I'd brought along my compact backpacker's first-aid kit. Nurse Renée had a much more advanced armamentarium of dressings, medical instruments and pharmaceuticals at her disposal in a cartridge box on the Bedford. Remind me to ask her advice, I told myself.

To avoid the furthest boggy reach of the pond, George turned into the trees. And once more we arranged ourselves in file.

This time I fell in behind Laura. Predictably, she'd reasserted her place after Denys. She hadn't had to jostle for it, either; Ewan and Nigel seemed to have no objections to playing caboose, one or the other. That had come to feel like the standard order of march, in fact.

I checked my watch. It was only a little after three-thirty. So there'd be plenty of time for polite variations before this walking safari was over. Wouldn't want anyone's nose to get out of joint.

I wasn't altogether sure we were still tailing the elephant. George's pace was about the same as it had been since he'd announced the initial sighting. Or whatever sensory stimulus had alerted him. We were tromping along vigorously but with no fatiguing urgency. And I certainly couldn't see any clues that an animal had preceded us along the route we were traveling. No broken branches, flattened grass, big circular footprints, steaming turds—the sort of glaringly obvious spoor my tracking abilities would require.

One thing I did know: We'd taken a different tack out of the *dambo* than the young bull.

But within a couple of minutes Denys stretched his arm above his head and started stabbing the air with his leveled index finger.

Unsure what he was trying to convey, what we were supposed to do, I frowned in the direction he was indicating... off to the right where the growth was densest....

Again a tumult in the brush preceded the first glimpse. Then there it was. Momentarily visible, breasting the grass and lianas, forging its wild way among the trees. And closer still!

Credit George. His course had put us on the quarry's quarter, gaining ground.

Now we were really keyed into the thrill of the hunt.

The elephant's presence was audible. Denys gave the silence-signal.

Periodically, as if telepathically hooked to George in front, he'd throw up his hand and the four of us would skitter to a stop behind him and we'd all listen for the telltale bustle of low branches, look for riffles in the undergrowth behind the scrim of intervening trees. And in a moment we'd hear our pachyderm pal chuddering along through the acacia thorn, then see his grey ears, dun body and mud-brown haunches briefly appear above the plane of the grass....

Even if the weapons we were fingering were only cameras and the trophies we'd bring back only color transparencies—perhaps enlarged as prints, the most beautiful, the most National Geographic-like shots, to frame and hang on our walls at home like heads or horns—we were as hyped by the proximity of our prey as any party of pot-hunters or poachers or blood-sportsmen.

George and Denys themselves seemed vivified, though this sort of pursuit must have been their daily fare. I supposed it was professional pride in their ability to give their guests dramatic experiences. And I suspected it wasn't in fact every outing that turned up an opportunity like this, to play hide-and-seek with a ranging elephant, test just how up-close-and-personal you might get before he spooked....

The afternoon was still breezeless. A major advantage. Whether by luck or design—and I'd bet on the latter—the track George had picked seemed to be keeping us downwind of our quarry no matter what faint air currents might prevail.

I broke stride for a moment to swivel my face experimentally, trying to discern a differential tingling of the damp flesh on my cheeks or the sweaty hair at my temples....

I could detect no ambient vectors at all.

We were now in a grassy corridor that ran between two ranks of trees. Their foliage hung dead still. For the first time I noticed the absence of the sausagy pods. We were in mopanis. They all had the delicate butterfly leaves.

Nigel had almost caught up with me. We exchanged grins of comradely high spirit.

I skipped off again, momentarily lengthening my strides, upping my pace to restore the proper intervals.

My bowels gurgled loosely. I had to consciously clench my sphincter.

At some more convenient moment, I thought, I was going to have to nip into the bush and relieve the pressure.

The trees to the left ended just ahead. And in a moment I realized why.

Though it had appeared we were approaching another *dambo*, what I was looking at was actually the grassy fringe of the Luangwa. Both its flat shoulders, in fact. The far one was visible across the still only narrowly perceptible channel.

As we trudged further I saw that we were nearing a bend that cut sharply toward us through the *veld*. The corridor we were threading would skirt its apex.

George and Denys suddenly froze in mid-stride.

Denys threw up his hand.

Laura, then I, aped the gesture.

The footsteps behind me stilled. No one moved.

On the other side of the trees to the right, still partially obscured by clusters of brush, the elephant had paused too.

We waited motionless as the animal slowly lowered its massive head and fluttered its ears. I expected him to look toward us at any moment, but he didn't. He swung and curled his flexile trunk from side to side, absorbed momentarily, it seemed, in sniffing the history of this particular patch of bush from the complex of aromas it held.

Then, satisfied, the bull ambled on.

I took a couple of careful steps closer to Laura and Denys.

"Think he knows we're here?" I whispered over her shoulder.

George replied. "He has not seen us."

His mellow baritone was even more mellifluous when subdued. "He cannot smell the scent of us just now, I think. But he is hearing, as we walk."

He looked at Denys. "*Njovu mva bwino m'tengo.*"

"Elephant has good ears," Denys nodded.

"Is he headed for the river?" I asked.

"Yes, the river is there," George agreed obliquely.

"We'll try t' give y' one more really good photo op," Denys said.

He glanced at Laura, apparently having overheard our earlier exchange. Conscientious guide, he was alert to the satisfaction of his customers' needs.

"Then we'll break it off. Idea is to tread softly on the land, hey? Don't want to harry the game needlessly. Quiet as possible, then. '*Ta-tini chete*', as they say here."

"*Ta-tini chete*," I repeated under my breath.

George nodded approval.

Tautly erect, cradling his rifle in both hands, followed by Denys, who was nonchalantly dandling his binoculars (the officer is always too absorbed in leadership and strategy to deign to carry any but symbolic arms) and their four tenderfoot charges—gripping cameras in readiness—our *fundi* resumed the stalk.

We were still partially masked from the elephant by the brattice of small mopanis on our right. They grew to within thirty or so feet of the abrupt drop to the river.

But the elephant's path was converging on ours. And indeed, moments later he emerged from the trees into the open swath in front of us, no more than fifty yards away.

Again he paused, just as George and Denys halted and the latter flung his forearm up.

Instantaneously Laura and I repeated the gesture.

At my back, Nigel scuttled to a stop in the tall grass. Presumably he signalled Ewan.

The river flowed between almost vertical banks here—only now were we close enough to see down into the channel and glimpse moving water.

The elephant seemed to be contemplating the cleft before him. He belled and relaxed his ears in lazy, syncopated waves. His tail switched limply. We were looking at him mostly rump-on.

Out of the side of his mouth, Denys hissed at Laura: "Better take your pics."

Laura raised her camera and looked around at me. I nodded, displaying my little camera in turn in both hands to indicate I'd understood. I twisted at the waist and repeated the pantomime for Nigel's benefit, pointing with my right hand at the camera in my left, and then back at the elephant. He rocked his chin to show he'd caught my meaning.

All I'd seen of Ewan was his shock of dark hair and his round red face occasionally rearing above the tan surface, like a man treading for life in a sea of grass. It occurred to me that only Laura and I, and perhaps Nigel, were in position for good shots.

Which explained, of course, why Ewan continued to plod closer.

I'd squinted my left eye shut—a bad habit I'd never succeeded in completely breaking—and was studying the elephant through my viewfinder when I became conscious of the persistent rustling from the rear. I heard Laura's and Nigel's shutters clop.

The elephant too had become conscious of the sounds or the movement. His head swung around and he loured over his shoulder, for the first time eyeing us directly. Both spatulate ears fanned out full; each was larger than his narrow wedge of face, which tapered sharply from osseous brow to trunk and protruding ivory fangs.

I pressed the button on my camera. Then I blinked open my left eye.

Denys was glowering and punching his hand at me urgently.

I flushed with guilty confusion, wondering what I'd done wrong. Immediately I realized it was not me but Ewan the gestures were intended for.

Only Ewan couldn't see them, apparently.

Denys was trying to be as surreptitious and yet as imperative as possible, trying to screen the jabs from the elephant's line of sight with his torso. Obviously he didn't want to call out.

Ewan came on doggedly for several more steps before he caught the signal. He halted, close behind Nigel now, who'd started fluttering his own hand ambiguously.

Ewan stared at Denys, attentive for further instructions. Suddenly his eyebrows went up and his head jerked backwards with astonishment. He'd only at that instant, I realized, actually seen the elephant.

He grimaced and nodded. Then he jammed his camera to his nose.

I swiveled back to the subject myself. My hands hadn't moved; my camera was still poised as I'd learned to do it while covering the anti-Vietnam War marches in Oakland in the '60s: ready to fire by reflex if the action I was aiming at warranted it, but keeping a weather eye on the wider scene. You could always crop to compensate for lapsed composition, but you couldn't always see a police billy club or a teargas canister coming at you if you were concentrated only on what was framed in your camera's tiny porthole on the world. And you might miss a better picture off to the side somewhere.

The elephant was still there. Still almost centered when I ducked to peek again through the viewfinder. No point clicking off another shot, though, unless I wanted two of the same pose.

He continued to ponder us over his left shoulder. Then, warily, he shuffled his feet and began to turn....

I pressed the button. The shutter tripped and the little servo-motor that automatically advanced the film emitted its brief high-pitched whine.

Around me shutters were clopping and gears softly ratcheting as Laura and Nigel and Ewan spooled mechanically through their film rolls. I also heard a more substantial metallic clatter as I recorded another aspect of the elephant's maneuver.

"Enough," Denys snapped.

The young bull now faced us squarely.

"'S enough, then," Denys breathed. He showed us his palm. "Ewan? Start backing away. Slowly. Everyone! Back, now."

He kept his voice low, calm. But their clipped edge made the words galvanic.

Ewan obediantly began to shamble backwards in retreat. Nigel shrank along after him. As did I. And Laura. And Denys himself.

Only George stood where he was. Feet apart, elbows out, rifle angled in front of his chest—the same Minute-Man posture he'd assumed when the elephant had hesitated in front of us.

George hadn't remained immobile, though, I realized. That clockwork, oiled-steel click-clunk I'd heard had been the bolt of his rifle.

George had chambered a round.

"Steady on," Denys encouraged us. "Watch your step."

He was alternately eyeing the elephant and our herky-jerky, now backpedaling, now side-stepping withdrawal along the same winding furrow we'd trodden in the grass. "Let's all just stroll on over to those mopanis. Eh, Ewan? Lead the way?"

Denys gestured at a tangle of trunks in the *veld* grass nearest the trough cut by the river, maybe one tree, maybe several. The coppice stood slightly apart like the dot to the exclamation point formed by the irregular line of mopanis we'd had on our left as we'd trailed the young bull here. Punctuation to the concept *refuge!*

Not that I was frightened. On the contrary, I felt excited and engaged, but in a detached, oxymoronic way. I had absolutely no sense that I might be in any serious personal danger. I was full of unrealistic confidence. I'd inhaled Laura's thesis utterly: If I was here, if she and I were here, our guides must have the situation well in hand.

When I tossed a glance over my shoulder, Laura met my eyes and offered a lop-sided smile that reflected something of the same provisionally ebullient assurance. She wiggled her eyebrows. I knew immediately what she was thinking, and if we weren't keeping mum would have spoken—one of our standard ironic quips when the recreation turns harrowing, when the rental car's *en panne* at dusk on a foggy sheeptrack off a deserted road that does not appear on the Carte Michelin for the Hautes Pyrenées, when the mainsheet has just fouled in a fresh gale off the Potato Patch with an outbound containership looming through the Gate, when you're both clinging to the side of the raft coughing up nosefuls of river and you hear more Class-4 whitewater boiling ahead:

"Are we having fun yet?"

Oh, we were indeed. *That* fun, same fun one courts running before the bulls down the cobbled alleys of Pamplona... too factitious a thrill, by the way, ever to have merited even my callowest consideration. But the parallel became exact in the next eyeblink:

Beyond Laura, beyond Denys, beyond George—both of whom were now showing us their backs, on rearguard alert—I saw an ominous sine wave suddenly course the elephant's stout trunk, saw his ears twitch, saw him stamp a foreleg irritably....

"Run!" Denys said.

His voice was so level and so curt I didn't register it immediately as a command. I was distracted by the sight of George jerking the rifle to his shoulder, tilting his head over the stock, sighting along the blued steel barrel, muzzle now trained at the huge animal....

But Laura, who was closer to Denys, reacted instantly. She sprang at me.

"Run!" Denys repeated, more forcefully.

Hey, my synapses weren't *that* sluggish. I'd spun already. Lunged away. Adrenalin spurting, the "Oh-my-God-gotta-save-my-skin" flight syndrome pumping my arms and legs and numbing my brain.

In front of me, Nigel had flashed an expression one associates with a horse in a burning stable. He might even have whinnied. He certainly kicked up his heels.

No need for me to echo Denys's order: Nigel was out of the gate at a gangly gallop, hissing at Ewan, "Run, mate!"

To which his Glaswegian compatriot responded like Groucho Marx in a Roadrunner cartoon.

Once again on this trip I found myself forced into a lock-step sprint. As I had been with the sand-mat, pressed from behind by Laura and perhaps by Denys behind her—not the time to check—or if nothing else, by his peremptory instruction... following Nigel, who was pounding after Ewan, who was just a dark head and bright pink shoulder blades zigzagging with mad determination toward the island of trees.

But within a very few yards my reflexive panic ebbed. The immediate crick in my hip and the sciatic twang down my leg with each thud of bootheel certainly contributed to circumspection. Which translated physically as a hitch in my git-along—a limp— and mentally as the resurgence of gallantry:

Laura ought not to be back there at the first mercy of the elephant, I realized. That was the wrong way around. Shameful. I was supposed to be protecting *her!*

I throttled back to a nominal, gimpy trot to let her catch up. I looked over my shoulder to negotiate the exchange of places, usher her by me. Obviously, I was still comfortably dissociated. You'd have to wonder how readily I'd have honored such an impulse if I'd truly believed a bull elephant might thunder down on me, that I ran real risk of ending up spitted on an ivory tusk or mushed under 5,000 pounds of flailing pachyderm toenails and sole-leather.

And that's when Denys called out: "It's okay! No need to keep running! 'It's okay. Y' can slow down now!'"

Agile, Laura was breathing down my neck—had been all the way.

I stopped, and she windmilled to a halt, a grin breaking across her face. She really was a natural athlete despite her girlish hitches and self-deprecation at unfamiliar acts like pitching a baseball or dribbling a basketball—a smooth swimmer, a graceful ice skater, a cynosure when she boogied-down on the dancefloor, the kind of white woman whose body undulates so loosely, at such perfect rhythmic pitch, she has black men fifteen years younger crowding to partner her. (She'd had an affair with one during her first marriage, I'd learned. An endocrinologist.)

At thirteen, she boasted, she'd taken an older Billy Jean Moffett to three sets and only lost eleven-nine; she was still a potential tennis club age-group champion if she ever got serious. And she was deceptively fleet of foot—just like one of those pulling guards I'd teased her about resembling, one of those sturdy stalwarts you realize is invariably out in front of the scatback leading the blocking almost stride for stride.

I extended my arm. She accepted the embrace and nestled against me, curling her own arm around my waist and grabbing a handful of shirt. I staggered slightly as she sagged into my hip, panting. We looked back along the vee we'd just sliced through the grass.

Denys was there, trailing after us at a saunter. No sign of George. Neither was the elephant visible. We were in a slight swale, I saw now, and the tassels and bush acacias crested above even my elevated line of sight in all directions.

"Bit dicey there for an instant," Denys offered lightly as he approached. "Thought it best to put some space between us in case the bleeder should decide to have a go."

"In which case George would've shot?" I said.

"Oh yeh. If all else failed."

"Like what else?"

"Well. A shout, perhaps. We do try very hard not to shoot 'em. I'd be in deep soup if an elephant were killed on my watch. Show of dreadful judgment."

Laura let go of my shirt and eased out of my arm. She wasn't comfortable looking too lovey-dovey in public.

"Can you aim over their heads? Fire into the ground or something," I wondered, "to make 'em turn?"

"Well, elephants *will* mock-charge. So there's a chance there. Problem is, y' don't have a great deal of time to make the decision. Rifle's crack isn't going to mean much to an elephant once it's up to speed. And we were quite close. Besides, only three rounds in the magazine. First duty's to see to it no harm befalls any of our clients. Fortunately, all quite hypothetical, hey?"

Nigel was staring at us from where he'd pulled up, about thirty feet on. He'd almost overhauled Ewan, who'd himself nearly made it to the trees when he'd registered the signal to relax.

"What kind of a rifle is it, that George has?" I asked as Denys paused beside Laura.

"Four-fifty-eight. Parker-Hale," Denys replied. "Not altogether sure how he came by such a weapon, actually. Packs a hell of a wallop. More than enough to drop a bull much larger than our friend back there, with a single shot. Provided it's properly placed, of course."

"Which is where?"

"Wherever," he smiled. "Does the trick. Properly placed if the bugger drops, I should say."

"How close do you think he was to charging us?"

"Ah." Denys shrugged. "Never know for certain, of course. Till they do. Expect we let ourselves get a bit carried away with the picture business." He turned his smile on Laura. "Happy, are you? Got what you wanted, I hope?"

"So do I," she agreed.

"About as near as you'll ever want to find yourself to a bull like that," he said. "Under the circumstances. Smell him, did you?"

"Gee, no," I said. I was disappointed. Apparently I'd failed to register a unique sensation, some distinct, funky essence of wild elephant.

Laura shook her head too. No doubt an odor would enter our recollections of the experience, though.

"We'll all have sharp appetites tonight," Denys grinned. "And speak of the devil."

George's thin, green-uniformed figure loomed into sight. He was walking easily, his piece at port-arms again. He was swinging the butt and barrel loosely from side to side to brush away stalks of grass in his path.

"*Njovu* content again, now we're off?" Denys said to him when he neared.

George nodded. "*Chabwino nditu,*" he grunted. It was clear from the matter-of-fact fall of his voice that all danger was past.

"Join the chaps, shall we?" Denys bade us, indicating Nigel and Ewan. "See what new adventures lie in store."

He strode off. I glanced at Laura, waiting for her to take her usual place behind him. But instead she cinched her shirt tighter around her waist and then knelt on one knee; the laces trailed loose on one of her boots, I now noticed. She quickly reknotted them.

When George saw me hesitate, he edged around us—a sure sign, I thought, that there was no danger the elephant would crash into view in pursuit.

Laura gave the bow a final tug of adjustment and held out her hand to me. I clasped it, braced and hoisted her to her feet. To my surprise, she kept coming, leaned into me, still gripping my hand, coquettishly applying her soft breasts to my arm. She smiled up at me.

"Were you scared?" she murmured.

"Strangely, not really," I said. "Were you?"

"A little, maybe," she said.

And then, to my astonishment, she cupped her free hand around the nape of my neck—the unexpected, intimate touch of her fingers as jolting as a caress with live wires—invited my face down toward hers and pressed her lips against mine.

"I love you, you know," she whispered into my teeth. She winked and skipped away, pulling me along with her for a couple of steps before wrenching her hand free.

"What brought that on?" I asked as I trailed after her.

"Nothing at all," she answered gaily. "Are we having fun yet?"

*M*uch as I hated to reveal any chink in my physiological armor, especially in the company of men, I was risking real embarrassment if I didn't tend pretty immediately to my importunate bowels.

You're reluctant to intimate that you're a wuss who can't hold his water. That would be the assumption—possibly suffering from a ballooning prostate. Distinctly masculine as that trait might be. More distinctly geezerly, though.

I was proud of my sturdy bladder. And I didn't feel like announcing my actual need. Denys might think it was a function of fright.

VII. The Point of the Exercise

As we regrouped under the mopanis, I asked Laura: "You want to make a loo stop, maybe?"

I turned to Denys. "This a reasonable place for it?"

There was at least the suggestion that I had my wife's interest foremost at heart, I figured. And I thought it probable she'd rise to the cast. We'd been walking for nearly three hours.

"Actually, that's a good idea," Laura nodded.

"Sure," Denys assented. "Just don't wander too far."

I sidled close to Laura, my back to the others. "Can I borrow some of your toilet paper?" I asked. I kept my voice low; not a whisper, though. I was trying to be discreet but nonchalant. After all, we were only talking about natural bodily functions.

"What's the matter?" she inquired.

"Nothing!" I muttered. "Gotta go, that's all."

"Go? Number Two?"

"Mm."

"Gee. Are you feeling okay?"

"Yes! I just had too much coffee this morning. I thought I'd pissed it out. Something else going on. Could we not make a production, please?"

She opened her fanny pack, unwound a couple of turns from the small, flattened roll she always carried and handed it to me. Then, just as we did when the Mamba truck pulled to the berm and the women took one side of the road and the men the other, we waded off into the grass in opposite directions.

Nigel and Ewan moseyed along with me, each of us diverging toward a private patch of his own.

I circled behind a treelet of a type Denys had identified as scented thorn—a dense tangle of viciously spiked branches mounded close to the ground.

Hiking in the Sierra, I would always try to find a boulder or a fallen log to dig my shit-hole next to, so I could rest my tailbone on it when I squatted, for comfort and three-point balance low to the ground. No such amenity was available in this vicinity.

I checked among the clumps of grass at my feet for snakes or biting insects. Satisfied, I took out my Swiss Army knife, crouched and stabbed the dry, friable pink earth with the blade, scooped away what I'd loosened until I'd hollowed a rudimentary catchbasin a few inches across and a couple of inches deep.

It was the best I could do—or anyway intended to do, without a better tool. Hardly necessary to be fanatical in the wilds of Africa, I assuaged my conscience. Anyway, a trove of human shit, Euroamerican shit, ought to be an olfactory bonanza for any animal here that happened upon it, I reasoned.

I turned, unbuckled my web belt, unbuttoned and unzipped my shorts, stepped out of them because it was easy—no point hobbling myself or chancing an accident from an errant involuntary squirt, as I'd learned from sad outdoor experience— and laid them aside over a tussock after taking the toilet paper out of the pocket. Then I tugged my blue cotton briefs down to my knees, hunkered precariously, tucked my shirttail up and clutched it against my thighs, splayed my boots as far apart as possible, frowned between my legs to adjust the bombsight, looked up, took a breath, composed my mind and relaxed my sphincter.

Nigel, although he was staring down rather than around, suddenly edged into my sight-line and stopped twenty or thirty yards away.

I didn't have a lot actually to void. It was more a question of diarrhetic discomfort to vent. Which entailed a certain amount of humbling noise.

Vain hope that it wouldn't carry.

I'd cast only a few furtive glances at Nigel, on the well established grounds that if you beam your consciousness directly at someone it'll eventually make itself felt. But I couldn't help looking his way to see if he was hearing me.

Apparently so. He returned my sheepish peek with a sympathetic, apologetic wince of his own and swung his shoulders to accord me illusory solitude—as well, I suppose, as to block any view I might have of him at his simpler business. All he could see of me, I was sure, was my head. Still, mine was a low posture that instantly keys a vivid mental picture.

Nigel finished and retreated.

Rocked back on my heels, thigh muscles quivering with strain, I couldn't have lasted much longer. I straightened and wiped myself. To my chagrin, I saw that my aim hadn't been very good.

Dabbing fastidiously with the toilet paper, disgusted at my own ineptitude, I tidied around the edge of the hole, shoving in what had missed and tamping it down lightly with wadded tissue. Although I was careful, it was the sort of thing that really made you wish you had soap and water to wash your hands with afterwards.

I couldn't sniff anything on my fingertips. I rubbed them in the dirt anyway and scrubbed my palms with the coarse dust and tiny clods I sprinkled over my deposit before touching my briefs or shorts.

When I was once again zipped and buckled up, I gouged loose some more dirt with the edge of my bootheel and kicked it over the mound until the last wink of white tissue was thoroughly buried. Then I packed everything down lightly with my sole, tore out a couple of handfuls of dry grass and strewed them over the spot to finish things off. The camouflage looked excellent to me.

We covered a remarkably varied range of country during the next hour and a half.

George led us along the river's course for a while, away from the elephant. At one point we heard strange wails, almost like a nurseryful of crying babies, and came on a flock of trumpeter hornbills fluttering in the wide, flat crown of a tallish tree.

"Feeding on the seeds, in the pods," Denys exclaimed. "Love 'em, the hornbills do. That's a pod mahogany. When they're in flower you'll see 'em covered with butterflies. Quite a sight."

We stopped for a few moments to watch the white-bellied birds with their exaggerated yellow beaks, flapping and swooping and squabbling as they pecked at the long, curly pods in the topmost branches of the mahogany. Laura, Nigel and Ewan took pictures but I doubted the hornbills would look like much at this distance.

"Young tree, this one," Denys said. "They can grow a lot bigger. Boles up to a metre in diameter. Locals hollow 'em out for canoes."

A bit further along Denys pointed to a stand of trees whose dense foliage was a green so rich it was almost black.

"Now those over there are Natal mahogany. Or so they're called down in Ess Ay, in Kruger," he said. "Different family entirely from the pod mahogany. Both used for furniture, but these are said to be especially good for tool handles, because of the flexibility of the wood."

"For the assagai, this one," George commented over his shoulder. "*Ngamo.*" With his free fist clenched above his shoulder,

George mimed the thrust of a spear. "Very good for the assagai, also."

"Add to my store of knowledge," Denys acknowledged.

In the temporary absence of game, and because we'd shown an interest, Denys continued to identify trees for us as we walked.

"Said to be as many as two hundred species in the Luangwa Valley alone," he observed. "Really an amazing variety found in this sector. Must admit I have a hard time distinguishing among some of the acacias. Question of the shape of the thorn, for the most part. Over there, now, we have a marula. Very interesting species. Elephants've been at it."

A tree whose long, curved trunk rose to an elaborate eruption of gnarled branches topped by a thick thatch stood out from the spindlier neighboring acacias. It reminded me of something you'd see on the Monterey coast. The scaly grey bark on the near side of the tree had been peeled away, leaving a raw, reddish patch of exposed cambium.

"Kill a tree that way," Denys noted. "Bit ironic, since they fancy the marula's fruit even more than they do the bark. See an elephant come up and curl his trunk around one and give it a good shaking to bring down the ripe fruit."

He held out his thumb and forefinger. "About the size of a plum. Locals known to make a pretty potent brew of it. Eh, George? *Moa* from that one?"

"*Kachasu*," George said.

"Ah, yeh, more like wine. Amazing source of vitamin C, actually, the fruit," Denys continued. He pronounced it "vittamin," I noted. "Four times as much as in an orange, they say. And if you break open the stone, you'll find two or three nuts inside that're also regarded as a delicacy. People like to chew 'em or eat 'em as a relish with their mealy-meal."

We'd turned inland on what seemed to be the bed of an old meander. Tall grass and trees lined both sides, but the broad stripe we were in might almost have been mown and raked. The only vegetation underfoot was dry stubble and some kind of sparse, clumpy green groundcover.

After a bit I noticed a slender crevice that crooked down the left side of the corridor. I veered nearer and saw there was muddy water at its bottom. This residual creek, I realized, must swell to the proportions of a small river at the zenith of the rainy season. In flood it had drowned the grasses between the banks and deposited the thick, now dry sediment the green creepers were sprouting through.

Ahead of us there were other forks branching through the *veld*. Vestigial flood channels flanked by bush outlined the tiny living streams. Narrow as lightning bolts, only a few feet across and a few feet deep, the jagged minicanyons held rivulets to which game came to drink.

We began to raise scatters of impala and zebra—they seemed to mingle freely.

"Hey, I saw those guys before!" I exclaimed.

We'd come on three zebras nibbling at a stand of green brush in the middle of an intersection of several broad-banded streambeds. Two had their hindquarters to us but the third stood side-on—its stripe pattern paler than the others', fading into white on the legs and on the underside of a massively distended belly.

"See the one on the right?" I said. "It's pregnant!"

"Really?" Laura replied.

"Yeah! They were at the river, at Chibembe, yesterday. I saw 'em from our porch. I recognize all three of 'em from her. At least I assume the other two are the same ones."

"Gee, it does look odd," Laura agreed.

She lifted her camera to her eye and broke stride for a moment to study the zebra through her lens. She snapped a picture.

"I was wondering what was the matter with it," she said. "You're sure it's not just fat or sick or something?"

"Am I right?" I asked, seeking confirmation from Denys.

"Mare in foal," Denys nodded, "indeed."

"That's neat," Laura said.

"Of course," I allowed, "I suppose there might be more than one pregnant...." The pronunciation issue flitted briefly through my mind. "...Zee-bra in South Luangwa National Park. Stripe pattern looks familiar, though."

"I was wondering. Is every one of them really different? Their stripes?" Laura asked Denys.

"No two the same," he assured her.

"Like snowflakes," she mused.

"One might also make a comparison to fingerprints," Denys said.

"Need a zebra registry...," I free-associated.

"Be very useful," Laura agreed. "I'd sure be hard pressed to distinguish one from another."

"So I shouldn't depend on you as my witness if I fall a victim to zebra crime," I said.

"Haven't had much of that around here, glad to say," Denys observed dryly. I liked him for responding to my humor in kind. "Terrible thing indeed, when a zebbra goes bad."

I chuckled. "Sounds like a Larsen cartoon," I observed to Laura. "Probably was one."

"No doubt," she nodded.

"Are those males or females," she asked Denys, "the ones that're with her? Can you tell?"

We were still striding along. George was out front, Laura was at Denys's right shoulder and I at hers, Nigel and Ewan trailed close behind us, walking abreast.

"One in the centre's male," Denys said. He put his binoculars to his eyes and nodded after a moment. It was the tallest of the three animals, I noticed, and the mane that bristled along its graceful neck—stiff and uniform as a shoebrush—was blacker than those of the other two.

"Each stallion usually mates with two or three mares," Denys continued. "His little harem there. Form the basic family group. Burchell's zebbras, these. Most common species in southern Africa."

"What others are there?" Laura asked.

"Well, to the north, up in Kenya, y' can still find some Grevy's zebra. Further south and west, Namibia, there's the mountain zebra. Smaller, bit different in the striping. Both are endangered, actually."

"What about... what is it?" Laura asked. "Burchell's, you said these are?"

"Mm. Down in numbers too, all right. Not yet threatened as severely, however. Good habitat for 'em in places like this, the national parks."

Here and there, spaced widely around the zebras, an impala stood on alert.

Suddenly another one popped up out of the cleft running between us and the game.

It must have spied us over the rim, when it looked up from lapping at the stream.

The abrupt movement—the impala pogoed away in panic toward the boundary trees—seemed to startle the others, who immediately broke and fled in five different directions.

We were closing on them anyway. The pregnant mare's companions had been staring at us nervously over their withers. Now they too wheeled and cantered for the forest.

"See the shadow stripes?" Denys said. "Y'll notice they all have a fainter stripe between the main ones. Probaby most apparent on the flanks. Very characteristic of our local breed."

"Her condition sure doesn't seem to have slowed her down," Laura noted.

The pregnant mare, despite the ponderous cargo she was laden with, ran easily alongside her partners. They plunged through a gap in the bank of thornbushes lining the higher ground at the edge of the floodbed and disappeared into the trees, followed closely by a female impala.

The zebras' hoofbeats and horsy gait—necks canted forward—contrasted with the pronking bounds of the smaller antelope, which carried its neck at an elegantly vigilant ninety degrees to its gracile body.

"How soon do you think she'll give birth?" Laura wondered.

"Quite soon, I should think," replied Denys. After a pause he added: "Foal'll be up and on its feet within minutes. Mother'll lick it whilst keeping the other mare at bay. And the rest in the herd as well, so the baby'll bond with her. Continue that for several days. A newborn foal'll follow anything that moves. Not too many hours and mother and infant'll be trotting along happily side by side."

"I suppose a baby zebra has to be pretty nimble pretty quick," I said, "or they'd be completely vulnerable to predators."

"Precisely," Denys acknowledged. "Precocial. That's the biological term, when the young undergo most of their motor development inside the womb. Find the same thing amongst much of the game of the African plains. Wildebeest calf, for example, stands almost as soon as it's shucked the placenta and runs as fast as an adult within twenty-four hours. Baby elephant'll be walking about only hours after birth...."

"I've forgotten. How long's their gestation period?" I asked.

"Elephant? Mm... twenty-one months."

"Whoa," Laura murmured. She shuddered. "Imagine having morning sickness... walking around on swollen ankles... for nearly two years."

Beyond the complex of streams we entered an open grassland studded with mouldering termite castles. Some of their towers and battlements rose six or eight feet high. They and a few widely spaced baobabs cast long, tapering, fantastically shaped shadows.

The sun was on our necks, declining toward the forested horizon. Hot still, though.

George and Denys paused to give us a break in the thick shade under a tall tree that was not a baobab. Its gnarled roots gripped the base of a decayed termite mound.

Laura and Nigel took water bottles out of their packs. Laura and I shared; Nigel was also carrying Ewan's. George leaned on his rifle slightly apart from us.

The water was tepid but refreshing gurgling down the throat, sopping into my mustache and beard, trickling into my shirtcollar.

Denys and George both declined a drink when offered.

"You have a Band-Aid in there by any chance?" I asked Laura as she was screwing the lid onto the plastic bottle, about to tuck it away again.

Flecks of dry grassflower had adhered to the lymph in the wound on my shin, I'd noticed. It was still draining. I'd started to wipe it with my fingers but decided that would be unsanitary.

"I do, as a matter of fact," Laura said. She dug around and produced a small perforated bandage.

I stooped and applied it. I put the wrapping and the stickum protectors in my shirtpocket to be disposed of later.

"Call this a jackal-berry in Kruger," Denys was saying in the meantime. He was staring up at the glossy canopy of the tree we were sheltering under.

"*Muchenja* locally. *Diospyros mespiliformis*. African ebony. Same tree the bar's built around at Chibembe. Should be setting fruit in a month or so."

He circled his thumb and forefinger, indicating the size, about an inch in diameter. "Very tasty to the birds, monkeys, jackals, of course, supposedly. Natives grind up the muchenja berries, make med'cines. Treat everything with it, from dysentery to leprosy. Notice how it's growing from an old anthill? Underground chambers provide air and retain moisture. Tamarind's another that always seems to favor anthills. Termitaria, they are, officially."

"Are they still active?" Laura asked. "Are there termites actually inside?"

"Well, not this one, of course," Denys said. "But others, quite so." He swept an open hand at the landscape around us.

"Very good, to eat them," George commented, "the *inswa*. When they are coming out." He flapped his hand. "They are flying up, many, many. After the first rains."

"The winged, alate stage," Denys explained. "Future ant-kings and queens, off to mate and build new colonies. When they swarm, the local folk build a grass roof over the exit hole, so that as they emerge they'll strike it and tumble to the ground."

"The *inswa* are coming into the hole, in the *mbiya*. The pot," George nodded, wiggling his fingers as if they were the legs of a crawling insect. Then he hammered his fist up and down. "*Na-te-nga inswa zeni-zeni za tunta na-kobvola*," he addressed Denys, who looked puzzled but nodded tentatively.

"We are...." George gestured with his fist again.

"Ah, pounding. Mashing," Denys supplied the word as he mirrored the pantomime. "Yeh, they mash 'em and dry 'em in the sun and sprinkle 'em on their mealy-meal. I've tried it, the white ants, actually. Quite palatable. If you can forget what it is you're eating."

"Take your word on that yin," Ewan spoke up with a grin.

"Ah. From someone who considers haggis a delicacy," Denys riposted.

Ewan grimaced and laughed. "No me. I'd as soon try the wee buggies, ta."

Denys chuckled. "Well. Shall we?" he said. "Push onwards?"

The terrain we'd been traversing had been flat, or at least had felt relatively flat. And the encompassing sea of forest leveled the horizons.

Certainly there were no koppies jutting anywhere—*kopjes* the Afrikaans word Rory had taught us for the region's humpy little hills. But apparently we'd been striding up a long slow rise, and had now reached some sort of relative eminence.

Mindlessly following where Denys and George led, I'd completely lost track of the many twists in direction we'd taken. Interestingly, they'd followed no paths and consulted no maps.

The sun was heating my right cheek when we departed the shade of the big ebony, so we were heading for the trees that fringed this open plateau at a new angle—more southerly.

Was that right? At sea, I always had to stop and think whether winds that were "southerly" were blowing to or from the south. The mnemonic for me was the "ly," translated to "lee." If you were in the lee of something, I reasoned, you were sheltered— you were behind it. So a southerly wind didn't blow *toward* the south, which would put the south in front of it, it came *out* of the south. That was where you'd head to get behind it.

On the other hand—but by extension of the same analogy—a southerly course meant you were seeking a lee *in* the south. You were *headed* that way. Which is exactly backwards from the usage for wind direction. Pretty confusing, this language we muddle through, isn't it?

Up ahead I saw movement. Tawny shapes that blended almost perfectly with the short, dry grass were stirring beneath the trees.

Adrenaline fizzed into my brain. My first thought was lions.

I squinted, slightly dizzy, and recognized that the shapes were smaller—monkeys—just as George noted under his breath, "*Anyani.*"

"Baboons," Denys echoed simultaneously.

Heartbeat abating, I counted off six—three scuttling about fitfully, halting, sitting for a moment, then pacing on all fours with rumps high and tails crooked awkwardly as if broken in the middle. Framed by sidewhiskers, their long doggy faces seemed to be set in perpetual scowls.

I made out several more reposing motionless, backs erect, knees akimbo, watching us through narrow-set eyes.

Clusters of the huge gray bockwurst-like appendages I'd noted earlier dangled on long cords from the branches overhead. As we drew nearer I saw a large baboon clutching the remnant half of one of these pods in the toes of its right foot. Its left hand was poised at its mouth; it was munching solemnly on a handful of the pod's pale inside fiber. Chewed scraps littered the dirt beside it.

"They're eating those gourds or whatever," I suggested to Denys.

"Mm. Sausage fruit," he nodded. "Not a favorite, usually. Probably after the seeds, they are. Outer skin starts to peel away after the fruit's lain on the ground a few days. Marula, tamarind much more to the baboons' liking, actually. In season, of course.

Figs'll be fruiting out soon. Last July we had a troop that passed an entire week in the top of a big *ficus Capensis* not far from here, fattening on the ripe figs whilst elephants congregated below cleaning up what the baboons dropped. Brought guests out every day to see it. Made a lovely tableau of the African bush."

"You called it sausage fruit?" I said.

Denys tilted his head. "Sausage trees. Is what those are."

"Obviously!" Laura exclaimed with delight. "How could they be anything else?"

As we closed on the baboons, the nervous ones let out a few low barks that seemed to be commentary on our presence. It became apparent that the grassy terrace we were crossing fell away sharply beyond the rank of sausage trees, and as the slope itself gradually came into view we saw and heard more of the troop below the rim. They'd been taking their leisure in the late afternoon sun, apparently.

Mothers nimbly jockied by their babies padded about. Pairs and trios sat grooming one another. Youngsters grubbed idly or cavorted as the elders contemplated the scene or perhaps pondered the greater sweep of the baboon comedy.

Our encroachment on their territory was a disruption. The colony began to pullulate with excitement, and in another moment, though I heard no shrills or "bok-kums" of alarm— Malcolm had described them for us at Hwange—the baboons suddenly erupted in a mass scamper down the hill.

At first I thought we'd put the troop to flight. But it seemed to be just a short relocation, albeit probably triggered by our appearance. Because even though we followed close on their tails, digging in our heels as we skittered, loose-kneed, down the steep pitch behind them, the baboons didn't show any particular fear or intent to elude us. I saw no mothers loping away with their babies tucked under their stomachs, another indicator of grave baboon concern, according to Malcolm.

At the base of the slope there was a mature sycamore fig. About half the troop bounded up into its lower boughs while others fanned out around the fluted yellow bole.

And there they immediately resumed their routine baboon business. Those in the upper stories clambered from limb to limb; those below scratched in the dry underlayment of old fallen leaves or resumed their previous desultory activities of daily living. The neighborhood was full of bustle and chatter.

"Rather expect it's their sleeping site for the night," Denys said. "Generally head for it about this time of day."

He squinted into the crown of the tree as we descended toward it. "Looks to 've been pretty well picked over by now. Sycamores bear about a month earlier than the Cape figs. Ah!"

His arm shot up and his finger tracked the shimmering flight of a bird, an extraordinary rainbow of blues, greens, yellows and blushing reds, that had suddenly burst out of the high foliage and beaten away toward a new refuge, dislodged by the foraging baboons. In its dark beak I'd glimpsed a yellow fig.

"Purplecrested lourie!" Denys declared. He put his binoculars to his eyes briefly, but the lourie dipped almost immediately out of sight among other trees.

"Do baboons ever attack humans?" Laura inquired as we continued our downhill scramble. "They look pretty fearsome, really."

"Oh, yeh, fierce! Chacma baboon's canines are actually longer and sharper than a lion's. And they're very strong. You wouldn't want to square off hand to hand against one of those boys, I can tell you. They'll come to each other's aid, too. Saw a group once almost kill a big croc that had managed to sieze the leg of one of their mates, trying to drag 'im down into the water. Would've been finis for the unfortunate victim. Very impressive, way the baboons teamed to effect the rescue. Gave the croc a hell of a go. But they'll generally make way for us, for humans. As we've seen."

Below the slope was a parkland of widely spaced trees. As George led us out onto the flat, Denys continued to offer nuggets of lore about the receding baboons.

"Wouldn't recommend staring an old alpha male straight in the eye, though," he said. "Might take it as a challenge to his authority. Certainly would if you were another male baboon. And especially if you belonged to the lower ranks. Very hierarchical, baboon society. The subordinate males always have to show deference to superiors. Lower their gaze. Step aside politely. Otherwise they'll get a good thrashing and have to kowtow and display their bums to the master every time he comes near."

"No all that different from us, then, eh?" Ewan observed.

"Don't think I'd want to be in your line of work, from the sound of it, mate," Denys replied.

Ewan's smile turned defensive, uncertain.

"Nah, I catch your meaning, indeed," Denys added quickly. "Baboon behaviour's just more, what... literal, I s'pose you could say. Fascinating study. Dominant males make all the decisions for the troop, and in return they always get first choice of tasty morsels. Get to sleep in the best perches up in the tree at night— nearest the trunk, those are, usually. Get first go at the most desirable females...."

Denys glanced at Laura, either uneasy at his choice of words, I thought, or once again assessing how graphically it would be politic to continue discussion of baboon sexuality. The moment was pregnant, though, it seemed to me, with the inferences for Nigel and Ewan, two manifestly low-ranking human males by this calculus.

"When a female comes into oestrus," Denys continued, "the sexual skin on her rump swells up and turns a brilliant red. She'll flaunt it in front of the males to entice 'em. And even the lowliest bugger may mount her early in the cycle. But later, when conception's most likely, only the leader is allowed on the job."

"Where did you learn all this?" Laura asked. "From actual observation?"

"Well, largely, yeh. Seen my fair share of baboon interactions. But one does amplify one's own necessarily limited experience through studies, of course. Ranger training. Reading, palaver by the campfire, over drinks, swapping tales. Especially with the older hands. It's my business, after all. Have to be able to answer guests' questions, offer at least a few insights into some of the truly remarkable things one observes whilst making one's way about this extraordinary patch of the planet. Hey? Rather the point of the exercise, I should say."

"It's wonderful," Laura assured him. "We really appreciate it."

I wondered to what extent Laura was showing her rump. Denys was unquestionably the dominant male in this circumstance. Safari literature's rife with trysts between the stalwart white hunter and the smitten wife of the hapless client, out of his element, diminished by comparison.

The Short Happy Life of Francis Macomber, e.g. World-weary guide accepting the nightgowned visitor into his double cot with the same detached contempt for her husband, too weak to hold onto his wife, that I'd felt at twenty-five during my one fleeting affair with a married woman. Not on safari, of course. Unlikely concatenation of events during a five-day ship's visit in Singapore.

Ten years later I'd been the husband, role reversed, when Susan had started working late into the night at the magazine where she was art director. When I'd finally surmised, in shock, that she was sleeping with the hotshot new managing editor, that the three-day conference she'd gone to in Aspen had been spent sharing a rumpled hotel bed with the bastard—happy couple gazing into each other's eyes against the sawtooth mountains while I was feeding the kids pizza and supervising their homework—I'd slammed away in anguished rage. Demanded a divorce.

Got one. Fifty-fifty split, no alimony, shared custody (though in practice, Christopher and Megan lived with Susan almost all the time in the house I let her keep by not demanding my share of the equity).

Subordinating my shame and resentment to the good of the kids—and mollified, of course, by my lubriciously developing relationship with Laura—I'd lost the edge of grievance.

Susan, of course, had her own take on the situation: It was my lack of pizzazz, my self-absorption (or absorption in things like earning a living and Monday Night Football) that had been the catalyst. *I* was why *she'd* succumbed; my neglect had spurred her to seek elsewhere for intimacy. Yada ya… da da.

But eight years together, a couple of genetic coproductions and a habit of mutual well-wishing is not chopped liver. As partners in maintaining the infrastructure of our children's lives, Susan and I strove to negotiate amicably.

We became confidants. We became friends.

We even made reminiscent, hedgy love in her (formerly our) king-size bed one tipsy night when she'd invited me over to discuss upcoming school arrangements when Laura was away on business (I had strong suspicions that time too) and Susan was between men (the editor a distant memory). Her handing me a rubber had really felt bizarre. Had almost squelched it. And she'd kicked me out at one a.m. so there'd be no chance confrontations, no awkward questions from the children in the morning.

We were both as rueful afterwards as teenagers who've gone all the way—titillated by the experience but terrified of any commitment that might be inferred. Our relations were scrupulously platonic thereafter.

Laura could be a very effective flirt. And she'd never had any compunctions about demonstrating it in my presence. At one level, I thought, she couldn't help herself—evolutionary biology had equipped her with an autoswitch that tripped whenever she breathed in a certain concentration of male pheromones. But there was also a performance element, a knowingness to the exercise: It was a way of demonstrating to herself and to me that she was attractive, that she remained, as a primatologist might have it, sexually viable.

As for me, of course, I had to subsume my jealousy in tolerant understanding. Human mind over monkey instinct. No striding across the room and slapping her sharply but affectionately on the cheek to remind her of what was what, no seizing the windpipe of the smarmy asshole who was encouraging my cuckoldry, no flattening his nose for him—avenues of action I had come several times within a furious pulse or two of pursuing.

Masculine puissance (which is an uncomfortable choice of words with that sissy French "pw" sound, but an attempt to convey at once muscular strength, masterful character and aggressiveness) is celebrated—a good—in traditional Western culture. Ordinary experience tells us women respond to it. Consider the bodice-ripping heroes in romance novels.

On the other hand, it's pretty obvious women don't want to be dragged around by the hair. They don't want to be brow- (or otherwise) beaten. And if you make a habit of punching guys' lights out in fits of Neanderthal possessiveness you're likely to find yourself, in this litigious age, fighting off civil suits if not criminal charges.

I used to lament the demise of the duel. Nice ritualized resolution to the hopeless dilemma we modern husbands find ourselves in—caught in the bind between domain, dominion and domineering.

Simpler, certainly, to be a baboon. Dine on sausage and figs, fuck promiscuously, bite the shit out of any interloper who tries to usurp your prerogatives.

Big, athletic, smart, good looking, seasoned—I hadn't a doubt in the world, needless to say, that in baboon society I'd be a dominant male.

As I was, in all modesty, modestly, in human society. No, not a magnate, not a politician, not a CEO, not an admiral, not a professional athlete or movie star.... But powerful in that I was in general command of the terms of my life.

I might be fired, sure, but I was confident I could survive by my wits if it came to that.

My allegiance was to my *métier*—manipulating language, putting it to paper convincingly, spinning, establishing a climate of favorable opinion through honest accentuation of the positive—rather than to an employer, though I was loyal.

I'd prospered at my *métier* because I was good at it. I'd never lied, I'd always counseled frank admission of infrequent corporate error with a promise of correction, and no one had ever suggested I compromise those scruples. If they had, I'd have resigned.

The CEO and board of the large regional utility district where I'd worked for the past decade as Director of Public Relations valued my advice and my contributions, I thought. Providing energy to power the homes and workplaces of several tens of millions of people is an honorable activity. Not like selling people cancer sticks or gewgaws. The advertising and publications I oversaw to tout these benefits were clever and won awards regularly. It was likely I'd serve out my career in the organization, retire with honor and a testimonial lunch at sixty-five and belly up to the novel about Seventh Fleet life I'd been gestating for thirty years.

But, in this business, nothing's guaranteed. I could also fly home from my Mamba Safari to find a request for my resignation on my desk. It had happened to a counterpart. While on vacation, charges had festered that he'd been guilty of insensitive language and discriminatory behavior to the minorities on his staff. He was summoned to a hearing immediately upon his return, and boom.

For all I knew, it was true, he'd deserved it. As far as that goes, I got along swimmingly, I believed, with everyone who worked for me in my own department. I tried to be proactive in hiring. My art director was African-American, my assistant a woman in her 50s, the editor of the employee magazine Asian and the office manager a Latina. Pretty well covers the bases, no? All I needed....

Well, I just resisted a politically incorrect and, it must be stressed, personally offensive strain of humor. Trying to make the point, though. You do your best; life is replete with vicissitudes.

I could take Denys. Sizing him up out of the corner of my eye, I accorded him an edge in agility and stamina. But I had bulk and malice.

Having played as much disorganized basketball as I had, you got accustomed to altercations. The woofing escalates, maybe you're in a bad mood because your shot isn't falling, somebody aims a clearly vicious elbow at your ribs or jaw, deliberately tries to undercut you when you're going up for the jam on a breakaway—you've got to retaliate. Or lose face.

And I did go off when those situations arose. Saw red, as the cliché accurately paints it. I became slightly crazy, spouted slur for slur, returned shove for shove, swing for swing... stupidly disregardful of the peril to my natural teeth, the handsome scaffolding of small bones below my brow, the skin over my knuckles, the brittle metatarsals, especially the fifth, which I'd in fact broken on each hand with a punch (a left that had glanced off a forehead, a right that had been directed injudiciously at a gym wall after a loss in which I'd played particularly poorly).

Hang up my suit and tie in a locker and I was transformed. Like Clark Kent... only into something more like Subparman—a bundle of primal synapses ready to fire on provocation. A baboon who had to be wrestled out of trouble by his teammates so he could cool down and the game tensely resume.

I was always aghast, in retrospect, at my immaturity.

So Denys might outpoint me with fancy footwork and cute jabs in the initial rounds, but I'd parry and keep coming. I've always had fast hands. Eventually, I was sure, I'd land a flush blow, snap his head back definitively.

I wondered if George might enter the equation. Turn his elephant rifle on me:

Blam!

Rogue male. *Bwana* went rabid. Had to be put down.

Wasn't this a scenario to make Laura proud? Object of manly combat, every woman's dream? The two of us strolling back to Chibembe hand in smitten hand, Denys slung unconscious over my shoulder because *noblesse oblige*, she and George gazing up in rapt admiration at my square, bearded jaw, eyes aflash and figure aglow in a fine-mist halo of testosterone.

Uh-huh. About as ridiculous as it gets, considering that Denys was conducting himself with meticulous rectitude. And Laura was not in fact flirting.

I'd seen Laura flirting; she was not flirting.

A few minutes later we struck the river.

George and Denys, I concluded in retrospect, had taken us on some kind of double loop. The place where we'd been chased by the elephant had been the midpoint.

I recognized it as we hiked back upstream along the bank.

Denys confirmed my observation. Off to the left were the two ranks of mopanis and the distinctive tuft toward which we'd fled when the elephant had threatened to charge. We'd walked right over its tracks. Right past the spot where he'd wheeled and flexed his ears and trunk at us.

No sign of him now, of course. He'd long since ambled away.

We passed several shallow reaches where hippos waded belly-deep near shore. Once, when we paused to look down on them, we saw a big bull suddenly flutter its tail and broadcast a noisy fan of dung that peppered the water and the muddy bank behind him—startling all of us into scatological laughter. Even George and Denys chuckled at our reaction.

"Territorial marking," Denys explained. A rich injection of nutrients into the aquatic biosphere in the bargain.

"Now we know why Kipling called it the Great Grey-Green Greasy Limpopo River," I said to Laura. "Remind me not to go swimming in waters where hippos have been."

"Really," she nodded, nose wrinkled.

We got a closer look at the mudbank/island we'd poled past when we'd crossed to this side. Sparse brush grew on its crest through a clutter of driftwood. There were more hippos cooling themselves in the narrow inshore riffle now than when we'd come over.

A couple of crocodiles lay loosely curled near the upstream point.

Then we spied our waiting boat. It rested on the muddy slope of shore where it had been dragged up close under the bank. Just

Do It and his deckhand idled with their backs against the gunwale, attending our return.

Across the river the rickety dock broke the brown current. My watch said five-thirty-five. Almost precisely four hours that we'd been afoot here on the west bank of the Luangwa.

Just Do It spotted us winding in column through the kasensi grass; he grinned and raised his pink palm in greeting.

Five minutes later Denys was handing around bottles of *Mosi*.

There's nothing like that first pull when you're lathered. Bittersweet bite of hops, malt, toasted barley. The slick, cool kiss of glass on parched lips, the expectant headtilt to unkink the gullet, a quick acrid swish to melt the mucilaginous coating on tongue and gums... then look out stomach, as the doggerel skoals, here it comes.

Ah.

And another.

Always the beer afterwards. So thoughtful. So worldly. Maybe the best part.

"I think," I said, settling beside Laura on the bench created by a root that elbowed out of the bank, and leaning my shoulders into the bare red earth rising behind us, "I think this may be the best part. My favorite part, anyway."

"Of what?" she said. "Which?"

"The beer. Of the whole African shtick."

"Shtick," she noted.

We both raised our bottles to our mouths and drank.

Denys, Ewan and Nigel were standing by the boat, *Mosi*s in hand, chatting over the cooler, which Just Do It and his mate must have gone back to fetch from the bar after ferrying us across. George, I noticed, still positioned himself slightly apart.

He'd exchanged a few pleasantries in Chikunda or Chinyanja with his fellow Africans but wasn't hobnobbing with them. He hadn't taken a beer, either. Just as well, I thought, a man with a rifle. He, at least, was still on duty.

"So what do you think?" Laura said. "Was it worth it?"

"What! Getting chased by an elephant? In exchange for this, the inevitable post-safari beer?"

"Yeah."

"Absolutely."

"Good. So do I. I'm *really* glad we decided to do this."

"Yep."

"See? You were so worried. But we survived."

"A bonus indeed. And I was not 'so worried.'"

"Look at all we saw and learned."

"Just ask me about the trees of Southern Africa," I nodded. "I'll bore your ears off. Or the toilet habits of the hippo. Or the sex life of the baboon. Especially the *bimboon*. Shaking her bootie...."

"The...? Ah, I get it. Bimbo. Bimbo bamboon," she understood. "I mean bam... no, *ba*boon. Bimbo *ba*boon. That's hard to say. "

"Fortunately, few do," I observed.

"Very fortunate," she agreed. "A boon. A boon few... broon...."

"Bruit," I suggested.

"Bruit the brimbo bram... brooms. Braboons. *Bab*oons! The bimboons. Boogy-ing in the bamboo. Shaking their boobies...."

"Two sips," I said, wagging my head, "and the girl's gone. Completely out. Ga-ga."

"Bet you can't say that," she challenged.

"You'd win. Bet you couldn't again either."

"A boon when blingo blagoons... blaboons... play with baloons.... You're right. It was clever, though, wasn't it?"

"It was very clever," I said.

"What do you think? We must have covered... five miles? Ten, maybe? I'm tired. My legs. I'll admit it." She sighed and rested her shoulder against mine.

I swallowed the mouthful I'd just tipped in from the long-necked bottle.

"It was a nice hike," I said. "But you know? It's interesting. Except for having to run for our lives... which I'm not sure we ever really did have to do, you know. I mean, that elephant never actually came after us...."

"Sure it did."

"No it didn't. Did you see it?"

"Okay, that's true, apparently it didn't. But it might have. It looked to Denys and George like it might. What! You think they just cooked the whole thing up?"

"No," I said, "I'm not saying that. Maybe there was just a little heightening of the drama, though."

"I don't know. I think it was more a question of better safe than sorry."

"Yeah. Be that as it may... it was exciting and all. But when you get right down to it, we could have gotten almost the same thing out of a day at the zoo."

"Oh come on," she protested.

"No. A good zoo. With a good docent."

"It's not the same thing at all!" She removed her shoulder, sidled away indignantly.

"Sure isn't. For one thing, we'd have spent about five thousand dollars less."

"More like six," she corrected me. "And this is the cheapest tour I could find."

"So we come all this way," I continued, "we see elephants and zebras... zebbras... and giroffes and hippopotamoi and baboons.... And bimboons."

"And wildebeests, and impala, and puku, and bush babies. Wart hogs."

"Vervets...."

"Water buffalo...."

"A ratel...."

"Lions! All *kinds* of fantastic birds! So what's your point?"

"Quite a laundry list, isn't it?"

"You have such a romantic soul," she sighed. "A true poet."

"Anyway, the point is... what *is* the point? That's my point. What's different about being here from just going to a zoo? What's the essence, the nub of this experience?"

"Oh. You're a philosopher."

"Yep. What I'm trying to figure out, to get to, is why we really came all this way. Just for some fleeting glimpses of a few exotic animals? Which...."

"In their natural habitat."

"...Which are not even so exotic anymore, or *at all* exotic, given the shrunken nature of our modern world. Who hasn't seen a ratel by now?"

"Right."

"No, but an elephant or a crocodile? I read somewhere that more people in the United States and Canada go to zoos each year than attend all sporting events combined."

"I'm glad to hear it."

"So, is just observing African creatures in their natural habitat for a few minutes at a time reason enough to make the effort to come here? Are we any better for it? A National Geographic Special'd tell you far more about the actual behavior of lions, say, or hyenas, or you name it, compared with what we're getting."

"No," she announced, "you know what it is we're getting? Well, I'm getting back to my roots, in a way. That's part of the attraction for me. But there's also, what we're getting, more specifically... is a sense of being up close and personal....Agh! Pardon the cliché. They're so insidious. But, I don't know... *connecting!*"

"'Only connect,'" I muttered. "E. M. Forster."

"...With something that's really fundamental. We're reliving a genetic memory. It's a visceral... re-experiencing of what it was like at the dawn of time. When our ancestors were hunters. When human beings first roamed these plains...."

"The Mother Continent."

"Exactly! Tracking these animals for their supper. And when it was implanted in us to be awed and fascinated by, and of course to be terrified by, all these huge predators that were all around us. Unlike in modern times. Leopards, lions, whatever! Who might leap on us at any moment! We were at their mercy.... And still are, here."

"That's deep," I said.

"It is! It's embedded in our genes."

"Sounds uncomfortable. Sounds like buffalo beans. Glad I'm wearing my shorts instead of my jeans."

"Mm-hm."

"No, it's sort of conventional wisdom, what you're saying, I'll agree."

"Why do people go to France, for that matter?" she challenged. "Why do they go to Mexico, or anywhere?"

"It's embedded in their jeans?"

"Probably. Probably is, in fact. Some nomadic instinct."

"So I guess here I'm just confused because I'm focusing in on the question of the game-viewing."

"I suppose," she said. "I mean, in France people look at cathedrals and go to the Louvre. It's what's there. Even though they could find plenty of pictures and detailed descriptions in books if that's all they wanted. It's getting back to your cultural heritage. Here in Africa the game is what's here... and might *not* be for much longer, either, you know. That was one of the things *I* thought about! How much longer would we have an opportunity to *see* the animals of Africa outside a zoo? See the world my grandparents lived in."

"They lived in Cape Town. Durban. Big cities," I said.

"I'm not sure where they lived," she acknowledged. "But they saw... these clouds!"

She was looking up at the sky.

"It *is* different," she insisted. "Actually being here, no matter *what* you say! I'll always think of these unique clouds when I think of Africa. And the mopanis. And the sausage trees. And...."

She held out her beer bottle and swept it in front of her.

"...And everything! This incredible, stark, primordial beauty!"

"Not to mention the shanty towns," I noted. "Grinding Third World poverty. Hutus cutting up Tutsis. And vice versa. Ebola virus. AIDS...."

"Those kinds of things are everywhere," she said dismissively. "At least by coming here as tourists we feed something into the economy."

"I'd like to hope so," I said.

"But that's what makes this particular experience we've just had so exceptional," she continued. "It's *incredible*, isn't it? I'm *so* glad we did this! Not like in Hwange, or even worse, from what I hear, in Ngorongoro. Or Serengeti. Up there they have these big traffic jams of Land Rovers and buses filled with tourists around every lion. But here we're... just on foot. Wandering exactly where and in the same way *homo habilis* once did."

"You read that too, about Zambia."

"Yes! Isn't it neat? I mean, for all we know a couple of our dim ancestors...."

"You think they were dim?"

"Yours, I suspect. No, our *remote* ancestors. To be more precise. As in 'the human race....'"

"Our mitochondrial mama. Our Pleistocene papa."

"Uh-huh. They could very well have been sitting in practically this very same spot two million years ago, just the way we are now. Watching the river go by, listening to the quiet...."

"Sipping brewskis."

"Having second thoughts. About ever getting together, the woman, anyway. Because look what it would ultimately come down to. You, the dead end of the human line."

"Ooh. That's cold," I said.

I took a sip of beer.

"Your explanation is what's called the biophilia hypothesis," I told her after I'd swallowed. "Did you know that?"

"Not in so many words."

"People come to Africa to fulfill their biophilia. Which is this built-in affinity for animals and nature that we're all hard-wired with at the cellular level. We respond strongly to other life forms since we're all related through evolution."

"Don't tell that to the creationists."

"It's why people keep cats and dogs, pets of all kinds."

"Lisa. With her cockatiel, her white rat. Her turtle. Her goldfish...."

"An extreme case. The ultimate biophiliac, Lisa is. But that's what keeps Pee-Bee-Ess in business."

"And the Discovery Channel."

"Mm. But there's also an instinctive hatred involved, as well as love. Or fear, more. Like with snakes, which is the usual example

270

given. Whether it's the serpent in the Bible, tempting Eve, or whatever, there are all kinds of cultural icons in which the snake is a symbol of evil. And even kids in the city who've never seen or probably even ever thought about a snake will go 'eek!' and shiver and cringe away the first time they're shown a live one."

"Because it's in their genes. That's what you're suggesting, right? *Exactly* what I said. Isn't it?"

"Yep. You're a natural genius. You've intuited, I guess, what this guy at Harvard spent years and years of scientific study coming to a conclusion about. Wilson. I think was his name. His real field was ants."

"Speaking of basic human dislikes. Insects. Of any kind."

"Yeah! And you know why?"

"Sure! They crawl up your legs. And they bite you."

"They wiggle and they swarm! It's the movement. That's what's associated at some gut level with the danger. Which is the biting, yeah. Many insects are poisonous. So a valuable survival trait for early humans to pass on genetically and that we've inherited is an immediate fear of things that wiggle. Or beat their little wings in flight. An instinctive wariness. Same goes for snakes. Many also venomous. It's their motion, their wriggling, the side-winder slithering and coiling, like pythons.... *That's* really what turns people off about snakes. Studies have shown."

"Not that they look like penises."

"Ah. Well, and that. Although certain people I've known actually find penises attractive."

"I doubt it. Useful, maybe. Weirdly fascinating."

"Some people even lick 'em."

"Ooh. I can't imagine such a thing."

"Anyway, that's what I have to say about that. Now I'm gonna go get another beer."

"So you ended up agreeing with me?"

"I think so. I kind of lost track."

"You can bring me another one too, please," she said, extending me her empty.

Denys took it, and mine, and uncapped two cold bottles in exchange. He followed me over to where Laura was sitting at the base of the bluff.

"Cheers," he saluted her. "Well. How did the walking safari square with our adverts at table yesterday?"

"It was great," she said emphatically, accepting the *Mosi* I was handing her and tipping its neck to him in return. "It was wonderful! Thank you. A really interesting, informative... exciting experience."

"Hope there wasn't too *much* excitement there for you," he said. "For a moment or two. Although I can assure you you were in no serious danger at any time."

"No, no," she said. "It was very memorable. To be able to be in such close quarters with an elephant in the bush."

"We do our best," he said. "We like to think that at the end of the day our guests have had a taste of Africa unavailable in any other venue."

I'd been nodding my head and smiling in endorsement of Laura's praise. "That's just what we've been talking about," I said.

Denys drank. He wiped his lips with the back of his hand. "I apologise if I laid it on too thick at times. That python business...."

"Oh no, it was very funny," Laura smiled. "You really had us going there for a minute."

"Bit out of the way. Accurate enough on behavioural characteristics, at any rate, I hope. African python...."

"Missionaries in the nineteenth century?" I proposed.

Denys smiled. "Yeh. Or so one's been led to believe."

"We were just talking about fear of snakes," I said. "How it's instinctive in humans. Fortunately, that was an instinct we didn't have to plumb for ourselves today."

"Mm. Didn't expect we would do, actually. Pretty shy and retiring, most of our snakes round here." He looked me in the eye and grinned. "Unless *you'd* happened to have batted one down out of a tree for us."

"No worries," I said.

I was pleased at the Britishism I'd spoken spontaneously. "You cured me of that very quickly. What with that catalogue you listed off, of the local viperous denizens."

"'Viperous denizens,'" Denys chuckled. "Rather fancy that. Have to incorporate it."

"Don't encourage him," Laura said. "He's going to be insufferable enough when we get back home, what with all we've seen and learned this afternoon."

"Well. I hope it was interesting to you, my long-winded narrative. We have a philosophy here that one must always look about with wonder. Look about with wonder, hey? Drink in the smallest detail. No aspect of this amazingly complex world...."

He extended his arm in an expansive gesture.

"...No phenomenon or... whatever... no detail so insignificant as to merit dismissal. Why I tend to go on at the length I do whilst we walk. Whether it's about the type of tree and the uses of its fruit, or the nesting habits of a particular bird, or the behaviour of a white ant colony.... See each bit as the true warp and woof of the whole great fabric. Life."

He batted his eyelids and canted his head in embarrassment. "One might say."

He put his bottle to his mouth and drank. Both Laura and I followed suit. We were all silent for a moment.

"I was interested in your last name," I said.

"Ah. Odd spelling, I suppose, hey?" Denys replied. "Not uncommon, actually, in Ess Ay."

"I was thinking I'd heard it before, and...."

"Pieter-Dirk. The comedian," he nodded. "Or satirist, or whatever. On the television."

"I guess," I said uncertainly.

"Dresses like a woman? Visits with the politicians?"

"Did he also...?"

"Ah! No. The film maker! Of course. Jamie Uys!"

"Yeah. *The Gods Must Be Crazy*, right? Wasn't he the one that made that?"

Denys nodded with vigor. "Did indeed. Very good. Became famous round the world for those movies, I s'pose. No relation that I'm aware of, unfortunately. Either chap."

"So it *is* the same name. I'd always wondered how you pronounced it."

"'Ace,' yeh. Dutch, originally. Some *voortrekker*, I reckon."

"Do you speak Afrikaans, then, too?" Laura asked.

"Actually, I don't, except for a few basic expressions. Got away from it a long time ago in our line. Men tended to marry women of English extraction down the years. Name about the only Afrikaner remnant. Mother was Australian, as it happens. I grew up in Kenya and the U.K. before coming back for university. Makes me rather a Commonwealth mongrel."

"My grandmother was from South Africa," Laura declared. "My grandparents lived there before they came to America. My mother was actually born in Durban."

"Yeh?" Denys responded with that rising inflection of voice and eyebrows that indicates special interest in a discovered fellowship.

"My grandfather was from Ireland originally. Came out in his early twenties, apparently, to seek his fortune in the gold mines. Ended up a printer apparently. In Cape Town and Durban. Fitzpatrick. Francis Miles Fitzpatrick, was his name. Hers was Samuels. Elizabeth Samuels."

"Find those surnames readily enough in Ess-Ay," Denys acknowledged.

"Really?" Laura said. "I've always wondered if I might have relatives there. Cousins, whatever. Someday I'd like to try to trace it back."

"Interesting undertaking," Denys said.

"Unfortunately, my mother has no memory of anything. And her parents were very reluctant to speak about personal matters or their own family backgrounds when she was growing up. Extremely close-mouthed people. She was an only-child. They died before I was born."

"It's always sounded to me," I commented, "like your grandfather left South Africa under some kind of a cloud. On the run. Maybe from creditors. Bankruptcy. If not the police. Witness protection program."

"Who knows? Could be," Laura agreed readily. "Mother doesn't even know if either of them had brothers or sisters. Can you imagine that? Ladysmith. Is where her mother was from, is all I've heard. I'm not even sure where that is."

"Ah, Natal," Denys said. "Coalfields. Long way from the Rand, though. Where most of the gold was. Can't say I've ever been to Ladysmith. Picturesque country, I believe. Mountains, rising toward the High*veld*. Not far from Durbs. Durban."

"Boy. It'd be fascinating to me to go and see those places," Laura mused.

"You should, then," Denys shrugged.

"Yes, well. The travel's so expensive, from California," she said. "And once you've come that far, you want to see as much else as you can. This is going to be our Africa trip for a while, I'm afraid. We've thought about it. To be perfectly frank, though, we haven't wanted to have anything to do with South Africa until very recently, because of the racial situation."

"Not alone," Denys nodded, peering into his bottle.

I was surprised by Laura's candor and slightly embarrassed. This didn't seem like the setting to allude to so prickly a topic. But Denys's reply had piqued my curiosity. Was he making a general observation about the world's boycott of the white regime, or expressing a shared revulsion?

I was reminded of the German couple I'd met on the *Stavangerfjord* crossing the Atlantic in the late nineteen-fifties, a fortyish doctor and his *soignée* wife. They'd scribbled their telephone number on a cocktail napkin one convivial night in the first-class bar—which my cabinmate Tom and I, sauntering through the door in our suits behind two other couples, had managed to crash—and invited us to visit their Black Forest home when our summer school session ended.

Over my protestations that it had merely been polite, slightly tipsy convention, Tom called them from Stuttgart as we were hitchhiking our way south from Blindern Studenterhjem in hopes of seeing Brigitte Bardot sunning topless on the beach in Saint Tropez. They insisted we come, gave directions, welcomed us warmly, showed us to a cozy upstairs room with twin beds and feather bolsters where we could spend the night, asked over a couple of friends their own age for drinks and a *gemütlich* supper with the two adventurous American youths. During which Tom mentioned the difficulties we'd experienced getting rides until we'd bought miniature flags, stars and stripes, to display on our backpacks.

Hitchhiking students in Europe in those years were assumed to be Germans. Jolly, robust, they filled the hostels and rose at dawn to clock as many miles as possible before dusk. But virtually every driver who'd braked for Tom and me in Denmark, Holland and Belgium (and later Switzerland, France and Italy) had told us explicitly we'd still be languishing on the roadside if he (or she, once) hadn't glimpsed those flags propped prominently at our feet.

Indeed, after pumping our thumbs in the European *auto-stop* manner at the Norwegian-Swedish border for six hours, to no avail, we'd finally surrendered and bought train tickets straight through to Copenhagen. We'd fallen into conversation with an attractive blonde on the compartment's facing seat, unfortunately a few years older, it turned out, a teacher in Kristiansand. When we'd noted our problem, she'd explained the situation and suggested the flag. She'd also recalled a game she'd played as a little child—smiling sweetly at German soldiers as they strode by, then spitting on their boots and running away.

To me the war was ancient history. To Europeans, it became clear, memories were still fresh and bitter.

Oh yes, the middle-class Germans in that comfortably appointed Schwartzwald household agreed, their occupying armies had no doubt done terrible, shameful things during World War II; the enmity of neighbors was understandable. Personally, though, they assured us to a man and to a woman, they had detested Hitler and everything the Nazis had stood for. ("But it is very hard to wish that your country should lose a war," the wife had added.) Moreover, they volunteered, they'd had no idea whatsoever of what was being done to the Jews during that period.

Later I learned that the Württemberg region had been studded with concentration camps. Hard also to have preserved such innocent ignorance from 1933 to 1945.

Was that Denys's squalid story? Had he endorsed, or merely acquiesced in, a heinous system that had provided him so many comforts and benefits but which he would now claim to have opposed all along? Had he been tacitly complicit like those hospitable couples in the upscale village outside Schwenningen, like so many white South Africans, from what I'd read? Had he done his compulsory Defense Force service? Fought in Angola, maybe, viciously rooted ANC organizers out of Soweto, fired into crowds of black demonstrators...? Just following orders.

Perhaps in fact it had been the opposite. Perhaps he'd been like our own Vietnam-era students, a draft avoider, an active protester (the University of Cape Town had been a center of anti-*apartheid* activism, I'd read too). But this was no can of worms to probe into with polite small-talk over refreshments after a pleasant game walk.

Anyhow, I'd always had trouble staying in the saddle of the moral high horse. My mother's forebears had fought for the Confederacy, after all. Above the mantel in my maternal grandmother's home near Abbeville, which I'd visited only once, as a child, hung portraits of her two uncles in their high-collared cavalry officers' grays. ("They were loved by their slaves. They treated them very well!" she always insisted in her patrician drawl.)

For years I'd felt a fondness for the stars and bars and the Lost Cause. My own Navy service had come to an end, luckily, before I'd had to make a choice between duty and principle when it came to the Vietnam War. From neutral to sympathizer to protest marcher, my allegiance had lurched very quickly to the left after the Gulf of Tonkin incident. (A typical shipboard snafu that

I could picture vividly: general quarters, all hands at battle stations, fatigued and on edge in stormy seas, sonarman reports odd noise, radarman sees ghostly blips, jumpy captain concludes he's under torpedo-boat attack... hysterical messages soon have the two destroyers whanging away at each other.)

U.S. intervention in Vietnam was badly wrong, I believed, its scorched-earth pursuit increasingly difficult to conscience. Getting a deferment was only rational. Heading to Canada was an act of courage, probably greater than submitting to induction. But I didn't have to worry about either one. Nor did I have to take deadly fire on patrol in the Mekong Delta, which I'd almost surely have been doing if I'd accepted the billet they'd offered me as an inducement to prolong my hitch—skipper of a PT boat homeported in the Philippines.

As to the state of interracial relations in the United States... well, in my estimation, it still couldn't be said to be much more than *apartheid* with a human face.

Ewan and Nigel had shambled into our orbit. Each was wearing the vacuous grin one assumes when trying unobtrusively to infiltrate a foreign conversation. Their presence, of course, effectively insured this one didn't go any further.

"Oh, my God, Ewan," Laura exclaimed. "Have you looked at yourself? Your shoulders!"

"Aye," he acknowledged.

"You're gonna *blister!*" she declared. "Why don't you have your shirt on?"

"No much point, the now, eh?" he smiled. He seemed almost proud of his perverse accomplishment. Not Alfred E. Neuman: It was Howdy Doody, I thought, he really resembled.

Laura tilted her head, squinted and clicked the side of her tongue in a "tsk" that was both empathetic and disapproving. She sighed—a repression, I knew, of the urge to tell him she'd told him so. With her left hand she unzipped her waist-pack.

"Better put some more of this sunscreen on, anyway," she said. "Just to keep the skin moist if nothing else. It's all I have. Does it hurt?"

Ewan wrinkled his nose and shook his head, an unconvincing denial.

"It will," she nodded. "Let's see your back."

Ewan dutifully pivoted. He'd been behind us for most of the last several hours. Or at least had not been a subject of our undistracted regard. In that time, I now saw, his narrow back had cooked to a solid, radiant pink except for a sharp diagonal stripe of white flesh where his camera strap had ridden. The base of his neck was also pallid under the woven cord that held his *nyaminyami*; otherwise, the nape and the sharply crested tops of his shoulders were almost scarlet. The sunburn spilled down his chest in splotches, the brightest smear in the concavity between his collarbone and sternum, below the triangular talisman. There was another angry, irregular belt just above the waist of his cutoffs where the flesh was puffy even though he was otherwise quite skinny. There was a bright dot of color above each bony knee, too.

"Well, you'll know you were in the sun," Laura said.

"Couldnay say y'd been on proper holiday in Africa if y' didnay come back broun," Ewan rationalized.

"You'll be coming back peeled, is what you'll be doing," she countered. She set her beer bottle on the muddy ground by her boots.

"Aw. Knew I'd be skint one way or another before it was ower, eh?"

"Here," Laura said, producing her tube of sunblock and unscrewing the top. She glanced at the label. "This says it has aloe in it. That'll help. Get Renée to give you something medicated to put on it when we get back."

"Want to see to that, you do," Denys echoed, nodding somberly. "Open skin can turn septic fast in Africa."

Laura squirted a fat, oleaginous worm of white lotion across the fingers of her cupped hand and rose, beckoning.

Ewan took a swift step backwards.

"Naw, really, Laura. There's nay need." He worked his shoulders one at a time, experimentally, and grimaced when the skin bunched. "I'd prefer y' no to."

"I'll be real gentle," she assured him. "I'm sure it's probably sore. This should make it sting less. But...." She shrugged. "It's totally up to you."

Ewan was not the man to resist a woman in mothering mode.

"Och, aye, then," he said. "If it's nay bother. Ta. Just go easy, eh, Laura?"

He scrunched his round face in leery anticipation, bowed his head submissively and presented her his back.

When Laura first anointed his shoulders he sucked air through his gritted teeth, but then he relaxed. It was soothing just watching Laura's slow, circular strokes as she carefully spread the blobs of cool, scented unguent she squeezed from the tube onto Ewan's inflamed skin.

He was an easy traveling companion, a bit of a dip but an estimable human being to the extent I had grounds to judge, whose receipt of my wife's ministrations under painful circumstances I didn't in the least begrudge him. Ewan was at least one adult male who didn't excite even a twinge of jealousy.

I lost interest and squinted into the red sun, scanning the forested banks of the river downstream. I wondered if the fires were still burning on the *veld*, far beyond the trees to the southwest.

I drained my *Mosi*.

"Soon as y've all drunk up, we'll cross over," Denys said. "No hurry. Take your time." He eyed his wristwatch.

I strolled to the plastic ice-chest beside the punt and nested my empty among the others inside it. There were still two unopened bottles of beer, I noticed, along with a few sodas. It crossed my mind to pop a third, guzzle it quickly. I'd missed my chance, though, unless I wanted to look like a hog, and an alky. Probably just as well anyway. The hair of the dog seemed to have settled my innards once and for all. We'd have martinis when we got back to our room. Nice clear glasses, ice cubes. Wine or beer with dinner. No point in pushing it.

I glanced up at George and our eyes met. I smiled and nodded, unable to think of anything to say to him on the spur of the moment. He nodded back pleasantly.

"That's quite a beautiful rifle," I finally observed.

"Yes," he agreed.

"It must cost very much, to buy a rifle like that. Lot of *kwacha*." I rubbed my thumb and forefinger together tritely.

"Yes," he said. He volunteered no more.

We stood there awkwardly, each managing to look somewhere else as soon as the other uncertainly broached eye contact.

I was upset with myself. Why had I mentioned the rifle's pricetag?

Answer: because of Denys's comment about not knowing where he'd gotten it.

But that was pretty damn impolite. Only a boor compliments someone on a possession by alluding to its cost—not that there aren't a plethora of boors in circulation. I'd rather not be among them.

Had I condescended so thoughtlessly to George because he was black? A poor African? Even the fact that I always thought of him by that single first name seemed to relegate him to the class of servant, inferior. Which was a telling thought in itself, since what but a first-name basis characterized my relations with Denys and the other white guides? And I certainly couldn't remember the last name Denys had—give him his due—supplied for George.

What—was I going to call him "Mr. Mtango" or whatever? One of those double-consonant Nyanja names? Or Kunda names. Why was it harder to get a mental grasp on something like Mpamvu—which I'd asked to have spelled out—than a double-vowelled Dutch name, as in *U-y-s*? But I'd encountered the latter in print before.

I'd always been good at languages, at least for an American: quick to acquire a basic vocabulary, habile enough at grammar, fairly labile at contortions like purifying vowels and swallowing or trilling "*r*"s. With one proviso: I had to see the strange foreign words written down somewhere before I could retain them. I needed a visual underpinning to the oral and aural.

In Oslo I'd pored over the day's *Dagbladet* and *Aftenposten* with my *ordbok* in hand, then practiced by chatting up the few little children who played in the courtyard at Blindern—the only Norwegians who couldn't yet switch to fluent English when their impatience with my halting *norsk* got the better of them.

With Latin and Greek under my belt from high school, I'd taken accelerated conversational French and French lit courses at Uof L. I'd expected that to have enabled me to stare undistracted at B.B. undulant in *Et Dieu Créa La Femme*, which I saw during a weekend side trip to Stockholm. But in fact I ended up having to puzzle out the Swedish subtitles, which were mostly just Norwegian oddly spelled. Weird.

Street signs and billboards were reinforcement when I traveled in Europe or Hispanic America, so I'd picked up smatterings of German and Spanish. Conversely, the year the *Huckaby* had spent operating out of Yokosuka had been a great frustration: I could repeat a few necessary phrases like *"mo ip-pun bir-ru"* taught me by bargirls and phonetic transcriptions like *"oyasumi nasai"* contained in my *Pocket Guide to Spoken Japanese*. But the *kanji* and *hiragana* through which the language lived in the day-to-day environment were inaccessible to me.

Ultimately I memorized the *katakana* syllabary because then I could at least decipher the foreign words like *Su-kot-to-ran-do-no u-i-su-ki* (literally whiskey of Scotland) or *A-me-ri-ka-no ta-ba-ko* (American tobacco) flashing in neon outside the interurban train windows as I shuttled to and from Yokohama or Asak'sa.

I wondered how quickly I'd be able to banter with George if, like Denys, I were to linger here in Zambia. Within no more than a few weeks, I'd bet—as long as I could get my hands on a good English-Chinyanja dictionary.

"Zikomo," I could already say. *"Tsalani." "Morn..."* no, that's Norwegian. *"Moni!" "Moni"* is the Chinyanja. Kind of a curious similarity there, though, isn't there? For an African and a Teutonic tongue....

With relief I heard Denys say behind me, "All set, then?"

I turned to see the others following him toward me.

Denys policed the empty bottles and set the cooler in the boat, shoved under the thwart I'd sat in coming over.

Just Do It and his mate had sprung to their feet.

Nigel retrieved the rucksack he'd taken off, dug into it and handed Ewan a balled-up green tee-shirt, which Ewan very warily pulled on over his greased shoulders. It was his own, bought at the souvenir shop in Vic Falls: "Zimbabwe," it read across the chest, the letters made up of stylized birds and animals. He slipped his camera strap over his head, then immediately winced and ducked out of it.

Laura stood beside me as we awaited boarding instructions.

The three Zambians—George using his free hand, the rifle held out high as counterbalance in the other—dragged the boat down the muddy slope until its bow was well afloat. The two crewmen stood in the river not quite knee-deep, steadying the craft by its handrail as Denys directed us in one by one from the stern. It was still aground, so our feet stayed dry, essentially.

George went first. He clambered into the bow, followed by Denys, and then Laura, who took the same outboard midships seat on the port side she'd occupied earlier. Ewan followed and sat beside her, sandwiched by Nigel to his right. Then I climbed in and settled behind Laura.

Just Do It sloshed out of the river, retrieved his long pole, and as the mate hauled at the bow, bent his back over the transom, grunting and shoving until the newly weighted tail of the flat keel bobbed free.

The two boatmen walked us out a few more feet, and then they both vaulted aboard, the mate plopping wet and redolent beside me.

We nosed out into the Luangwa, headed home.

*I*f the water had been clear—a mountain river, the Caribbean off Roatán, a lake like Kariba where our cabin cruiser had floated toward the Zambian shore above the ghostly branches of a petrified submarine forest.... If this water had offered even a few feet of murky visibility below its surface—the slightest hope of being able to see what skulked about, to anticipate what might be coming at you, to somehow defend yourself....

VIII. Hippos and Crocs

L ooking downstream into the sun and the sparse flocking of backlit cumulus to the west, you saw a river aglow with deceptive color.

The salmon flush that was just becoming visible on the horizon where the channel meandered toward the south, the china-blue sky dotted with clouds translucent as skim milk, the jet-black edging of silhouetted forest—all were mirrored in the river's skin to suggest water of limpid purity. The hippos standing in their own reflections between the island and the shore might have waded into a crystalline lagoon. You could map the riffles, shoals and snags in the channel by the intense sparkles off its luminous veneer.

Looking upstream where the late sunlight diffused, softer and no longer requiring that you narrow your eyes behind your sunglasses, you saw a different picture. The Luangwa now resembled something like cocoa, mixed with 10W30 motor oil—wanly brown with a sebacious sheen, oozing at you around a bend walled by exposed mud and dusty foliage.

Looking straight down into the water that sluiced under the gunwales you saw a thin, umber fluid that went opaque with solute within the span of a dipped hand. When you reached experimentally over the side to take the temperature of the tepid river, your fingers disappeared. (Not that you'd want to do that further out in the stream, lest your fingers literally disappear.)

As we had for most of the first crossing, we all slouched silent, subdued by our long hike, the beer and the respite from gravity's normal grasp. We lolled to the gentle rockabye roll of the cradling punt each time Just Do It in the stern thrust his pole.

Obviously the river wasn't very deep. How long was that pole? Maybe ten feet?

If so, the bottom couldn't be much more than four, five feet down, judging from the length he was wielding when I checked over my shoulder. No reason for Ewan to be hydrophobic here.

A loud, watery snort broke the quiet. It came from downstream, where the hippos basked. We all swung our heads.

A very large hippopotamus was heaving itself upright, breaching ponderously from a hole in which it had lain immersed. It began to grunt—the rasp of animal irritation unmistakeable.

A second hippo of about the same size stood facing it on shallower footing. Only a calf and what I assumed to be the mother, idling on a shoal at the mouth of the side channel, were between the bigger pair and us.

The point of the mudbar was, what, maybe two hundred yards away?

Streaming water, the offshore hippo thrashed to its feet. The other sloshed backwards a couple of steps. Then it opened its porcine chops and lowed.

"What's going on?" Laura asked Denys.

The hippo that had surfaced had its rump toward us. Over its glistening gray-brown yoke we saw the bulbous muzzle lift. Vapor smoked from its nostrils.

We heard an answering roar that dwindled into a spate of hoarse barks. They echoed eerily.

"Bit of a dust-up, appears," Denys said. "Two bulls. One on the left is making it known it's his territ'ry. Y' can hear the other hippos all up and down the river, hey? Call and response."

"Do hippos fight?" Laura asked.

"Oh, yeh!" Denys said. "Quite nasty, these disputes can be. Losers been known to die of their wounds."

"Wounds from what?" Laura asked. "Oh my gosh! Look! He's yawning!"

The inshore hippo had tipped its head back and stretched its massive lips wide. Now it stood that way motionless, as if expressing defiant boredom, a pardon-me-if-I-don't-give-a-damn bravado.

We had a view almost straight down its gullet. The inner lips, tongue and gums were a pink so pale they appeared white at this distance and in this light—a vast cavern coated with guano and guarded at the portal by a faintly discernible snaggle of stalactites and stalagmites....

"Teeth!" Denys said. "Powerful weapons, those lower tusks especially. 'S what he's about right now, showing off the damage he can do."

He raised his voice slightly and looked beyond me at Just Do It.

"Here, *kapitau*...." He held up his open palm. "*Sia*. 'Kay?"

He turned to George, who knelt behind Denys on one knee at the prow. "We'll have a look-see for a moment at the *ampangwe*."

George glanced over his shoulder and nodded. "*E*," he said. Then he too spoke to the skipper: "*Dibwa, kapitau. Pang'ono pang'ono*." He wigwagged a hand horizontally.

"*Pang'ono pang'ono*," Denys repeated to the boatman.

Just Do It grunted an acknowledgement and reversed the angle on his pole. He leaned into it: All Stop.

Instantly we lost forward momentum and began to bob slackly.

The hippo with its tail to us was returning the dental exhibit. The two antagonists remained in that strange pose for several long seconds.

On my nape, now that we were out in the channel and lying dead in the water, I felt the first faint puff of the warm wind that kicks up at sunset. In front of me, Laura unzipped and fumbled at her waistpack.

"I've gotta get a picture," she murmured.

"Our Luangwa hippos seem to be particularly contentious," Denys noted. "Constantly sorting out these differences. Function of population density. Did a survey of the river a while back, found an average of almost fifty hippos per kilometre."

He fell silent. We peered at the two massive animals.

"Call a hippo *mvu* in general, in Nyanja, but a bull's *mpangwe,*" Denys noted. "Add an 'ah' for the plural—*ampangwe.* Female and calf probably belong to that old fellow out there in the centre. This is his group's feeding territ'ry. Other one seems to be a younger bull who's wandered in to test the waters, so to speak."

Laura was having trouble disentangling the camera strap from the shirt she'd rolled tight and managed to stuff into her waistpack, I noticed.

I was aware momentarily of another feathery gust on my left cheek when I glanced toward the sway-beamed dock on the opposite bank. Our bow had begun to swing downstream.

A flurry of splashes erupted from hippowards. The wallowing bull had lunged toward the interloper, and was now ducking its snout and pushing forward gouts of water like a kid tormenting another in a pool.

"Oh, wow," I declared.

"They look like they're playing!" Laura exclaimed. She'd finally gotten her camera to her eye.

"No, no...," Denys said.

They were remarkably nimble, these rotund porkers: the yawner had clapped its mug shut and danced backwards a couple of startled steps under the water attack.

"Damn!" Laura grumbled. "I wanted a shot of him yawning."

Although the hippos were the focus of my attention, I caught a brief movement on the mud-island's point.

A crocodile.

No doubt annoyed by the disturbance of the neighborhood peace, it uncurled and slithered into the river.

"He may do, again," Denys soothed her. "Whole ritual they go through before they actually come to grips. Should things in fact develop so far. Often it's just posturing. They'll engage in an elaborate exchange of roars, tusk displays, scoop water at each other...."

"So it *is* a form of taunting," I said.

"Mm. Perhaps as much a demonstration of manoeuvrability," Denys replied. "Warn the other, 'I'm too fast and too agile for you, mate. Bugger off.'"

Just then the interloper countered with its own mock charge. It tossed its head, raising reciprocal waves and spray.

"My God, that's fascinating," I declared.

I put my left hand on Laura's back as I unbuttoned my shirt-pocket and pulled out my own little camera.

"Are you getting this?" I asked her?

"No!" she said. "I'm having the same trouble...."

"Infinity," I whispered.

"I know that!" she snapped.

"And strap around the neck."

"Aangh!" she snarled in frustration and resentful concession that my reminder was warranted. "I know that too!"

She flipped the camera strap over her hair. No hypocrite, I wriggled my wrist inside the loop of cord that dangled off my own little point-and-shoot.

"There! He's got his mouth open again!" I said.

I tipped my cap-bill higher on my forehead to accommodate the camera and winked my left eye shut to examine the scene with my right, peeping into the tiny rectangular keyhole. With my index finger I located the button that caused the cover to flip aside—to a tiny battery-powered sigh—exposing the inset lens. I crooked my fingertip along the top of the body and felt for the dome of the trigger button. I exerted pressure.

A fuzzy green dot of light winked at the blackened edge of my vision, just to the right of the four hippos dwarfed in the panorama of river and forest framed by my viewfinder.

The shutter flopped and the film automatically spooled forward with another electro-mechanical hum.

I'd heard the trio in front of me clicking off pictures as well. The boatman next to me had exchanged brief commentary with Just Do It.

"Still really too far to be able to tell in the picture that they're actually splooping water at each other, probably," I said into Laura's right ear. "Did you get him yawning?"

"Mm-hm. Presumably," she said.

"You know what we really ought to have for a situation like this? A video camera."

"I know!" she exclaimed. "I'm surprised not a single person in our whole group has one."

She raised her voice.

"Denys? Can we get any closer?"

He'd been watching the hippos through his binoculars. He lowered them and swiveled on his seat, frowning as he scanned the water astern and to port. He ended up facing forward, squinting over his opposite shoulder at the scintillant run of the river past the island.

You could see the stuttery breeze play along the channel. It ruffled the surface and sent off golden shimmers a second after it brushed your neck. The sun, now a deep orange, hung only a diameter or two above the forested backdrop at the distant bend.

The Luangwa definitely had a current. Even in the calm center of the eddy where we lay, and despite Just Do It's occasional replantings of his pole, it was apparent from the relative position of the dock—which was now to port rather than off our starboard bow—that we were slowly being carried downstream.

"May do, just a bit," he replied. "Want to keep a safe distance, though. Boats've been attacked by hippos."

The action had ceased momentarily. I was becoming familiar with the stately pace of most African animal life. Giraffes munching thoughtfully on roadside treetops... Cape buffalo shuffling *en masse* through the dust toward a pan... a pair of jackals snoozing inert in the late morning sunshine between tourists on a viewing platform and a herd of blithely grazing impala... those indolent lions last evening.... We'd scarcely seen a creature in energetic motion anywhere in Africa.

Except vervets and birds.

What bursts of exertion we'd witnessed had all been brief and tame, too: the gallumphing rout of the wildebeest in the Hwange darkness... the angry snorkeling of warthogs... the bolt into the brush of the spotlighted serval... the thievery of the vervets... the perfunctory flight of the zebras and impala... that scurry of baboons....

I could count the instances of real animal animation on my fingers. A far cry from the Nature-Red-in-Tooth-and-Claw TV documentaries: deadly duel for dominance, rut, hunt, stampede, harrowing escape, methodical kill, feeding frenzy... one on the heels of another, all pompously narrated and cinematically arced according to the most egregious anthropomorphic sensibility.

True day-to-day existence for the mammals of Africa is more like the cliché Navy pilots used to recite with mock-modesty in the O-Club about the experience of flying from carriers: It's ninety-nine percent boredom, one percent sheer terror. And we'd yet to be entertained by the one percent.

It would be a real serendipity, an amazing treat, I knew, if these two hippos were actually to light into each other in front of us.

But the prospect seemed, typically, to be waning.

"Looks like the younger one's got his head down," Denys said. "Sign of submission. Appears he may've decided to chuck it in. "

"No gony have to wigwag his bum, like a baboon?" Ewan inquired softly.

I smiled as soon as I'd deciphered the comment—which took a beat for mental replay. I imagined the sight. Then my imagination added a pink tutu. Like something out of *Fantasia*.

"Nah," Denys replied. His delayed response suggested a similar need for internal translation of the Scots argot. "Baboons the exception, proves the rule. Used to be said that in confrontations between members of the same species, weaker animal would surrender by exposing his privates, invite the dominant animal to have at him where he's most vulnerable. Which the victor would refrain from doing out of an evolutionary compulsion to advance the good of the species, or some such. Heard that, have you? Well, it's all rot. Take vervets, for example. Other way round entirely. Dominant monkey makes a great to-do of his... genitals, hey? Blue scrotum, bright red penis. Hops about waving 'em in his weaker opponent's face, so to speak. Subordinate monkey always keeps his own equipment modestly tucked away."

"Monkeys are creatures of such exquisite nuance," Laura murmured.

It occurred to me to wonder if Denys was slyly amusing himself with these phallic allusions. Talking dirty, as it were, in a woman's presence but in a context and in terms defensible against any but the bluest of noses.

"Agonistic behaviour goes on all the time," he continued. "Full-scale fights are less common than probably y've been led to believe, however. Participants just not keen to get themselves injured unnecessarily. Hide of a big hippo like that old herd bull may be five, six centimetres thick at the neck, but the canines on the other fellow can slice right through...."

"He's yawning again," Laura declared, her voice almost a chortle. "I love it!" She raised her camera.

"May've been premature in saying he'd tossed in the towel...," Denys allowed.

The hippo on the left responded to the challenge with harsh grunts, and then spread its jaws. You could see the high, close-set bumps of its popeyes just in front of the tiny pricked-up ears. The cheeks were lighter streaks along the dark, guitar-shaped snout.

Denys peered through his binoculars, although we were close enough to make out plenty of detail with the unaided eye. I aimed my camera between the humped shoulders of Ewan and Nigel and leaned forward until their ears were no longer bookending the wildlife scene. I shot again.

"They're so roly-poly." Laura mused. "You wouldn't think their bites would be anything as bad as their barks, with those mushy-looking mouths...."

"Quite the contrary," Denys said. "Formidable instrument of attack or defence, hippo's jaws, tusks. Old boy out there has the scars to prove it. Been in many a scrap, he has, from the look of him. See, about the head? Down along the neck? Here." He offered her his binoculars.

Laura leaned forward and accepted them. They had no strap, I noticed.

The breeze was beating at our backs. The punt's bow had been pushed around so that the hippos were now more nearly dead ahead than on our beam. The bull in the middle of the side channel was just to the right of George's epauleted green shoulder from my vantage. The animal's brown yoke did appear to be seamed—puckers of old wounds if Denys said so.

"Main enemy in the water's the crocodile," he continued. "Seize a calf or a small female once in a way, but even the largest croc's got no hope against a fully grown male hippo."

Laura had crouched forward and had rolled almost horizontally on her hip, leaning into the well between the thwarts and straining to gain a clear line of sight around Denys.

"Eh, *kapitau*. Bring us about a bit, hey?" Denys stirred the air with his finger. *Mwa. Mwa.*" He was addressing Just Do It.

Who responded, "Yes, okay, *bwana. Ndawo.*"

Immediately the bow started swinging toward midstream.

Laura's back suddenly stiffened in front of me....

"Heh!" Ewan yelped simultaneously. He bounced on his seat as if stung or shocked.

"Ooh. Sorry," Laura blurted.

She'd jerked her right hand into her lap as if she'd just touched something scalding. Apparently, I realized, she'd clapped it to Ewan's bare thigh unthinkingly, using it to brace herself to straighten. I remembered the rouge-blots of sunburn above each of his knees.

"Oh, yeh. It is bloody nipping the now," Ewan conceded.

"That's too bad," Laura said.

"Actually, it's time we headed over," Denys declared.

He bobbed his head, indicating the opposite bank and the dock.

"Getting on toward dark, and we still have a bit of a walk before us. *Kapitau! Mtsinje twa.*"

George darted a glance at Denys's back and nodded in what I took as approval. He had a firm grip on his rifle. The crewman said something to Just Do It.

"But we'll miss it if there *is* a fight," Laura objected. She had the binoculars to her face again.

"Be able to watch 'em most of the way, crossing," Denys comforted her. "Under strict orders to have you lot back safe and sound at the lodge by happy hour. Eh? And with a roaring thirst. Frankly, I'd be quite surprised if anything more serious were to come of this little jol. Soon be twilight and they'll be leaving the river to forage inland. Adult hippo needs to take in several hundred pounds of grass each day... or night, more accurately. Do most of their browsing after dark, when it's cool. Hippo gets dehydrated if it spends too much time in the sun. Same problem you have, Ewan—skin's fair, burns. Got their own natural sunscreen, though. Bright red fluid a hippo secretes when it's overheated. See a hippo in the bush looks like it's sweatin' blood, that's what it'll be. Reason they prefer loungin' about in a pool during the daylight hours."

We'd begun to gather way. As Just Do It bent to his pole—they'd been calling him *Kapitau*, but I'd surmised that it was a native adaptation of "captain" rather than his name—the punt rolled noticeably. Now there was a slight pitch as well. Our blunt prow was cleaving a wave through the sleek fabric of the eddy on which we'd been floating. It purled toward the point of the island and the hippos, who were slowly ticking aft.

"You're right, he's got all kinds of scars on him," Laura said. "Other one seems to be much smoother-skinned. Their faces sure aren't built to express anger, are they? Or whatever it is. Kind of one piggy-eyes expression. Anybody else want a look through these? It's all right, isn't it, Denys?"

"Certainly," he approved.

Both Ewan and Denys were turned sideways, watching the hippos through their zoom lenses.

"Naw, ta," Ewan said.

"'S awright," Nigel echoed, looking around at her and shaking his head. "Thanks, Laura."

"Daniel?" she asked.

"Sure," I shrugged.

She presented the binoculars to me over her shoulder, not looking back. I slipped the cord off my wrist and tucked my camera into my shirt-pocket, then grasped the binoculars carefully and took them from her.

When I twisted to face the hippos I almost lost my cap to the wind. It was perched precariously on the back of my head, and I grabbed the bill with my free hand just as it lifted to sail off into the river. I turned the cap around backwards, the way Chris would wear it, snugged the adjustable band down tight above my eyebrows and snatched my sunglasses off my ears. They hung on their string against my bare chest in the vee of my open shirt.

I spread the binocular barrels to match the wider distance across the bridge of my nose than Laura's, fitted the rubber eyecups to my eyesockets. I skimmed an empty blur of water, moving upwards in search of an object....

...And suddenly found my field of view bisected by a rust-red band on which was embossed a big, thick, loose S.

The waterline, I recognized. Muddy shoreline....

The S was a crocodile.

That's what it was. A crocodile.

I fingered the knurled wheel between the binocular barrels to resolve the image, which jittered unsteadily to the motion of the punt. `

The lines sharpened but one eye was still distractingly out of focus.

I played with the diopter-setting on the eyepiece.

A grinning reptile—bony helmet, bossed gray armor, blunt, ridged tail—emerged with breathtaking clarity from the field of ochre mud and the fuzzy driftwood background.

The tip of its tapered snout was cocked at me, as if tasting my scent across the water. The long mouth had scalloped lips that were cracked ajar, just enough to reveal a few spikes of shark-like teeth. There was an odd twist to its upper jaw at the hinge; it seemed to be leering out at the world with the evil jollity of the Joker in a Batman comic.

"The killer that smiles as it eats its prey." I'd read that somewhere. Or heard it on one of those insufferable wildlife specials.

An ugly, rapacious, prehistoric-looking creature this was, all right... the pale, cold-blooded snake-eyes slit by vertical pupils. The scaly wedge of head nothing but a vise designed for gripping and crushing. The stubby legs bent over webbed paws that trailed the tracks its claws had scritched into the soft red earth when it had dragged itself up out of the river... although at the moment this crocodile crouched on its belly as motionless, stolid, complacent as a temple Buddha.

I examined it for a fascinated moment. But nothing exhausts curiosity quicker than a stuporous crocodile—the very definition of animal inanimacy.

I panned away, across a heap of driftwood caked with dried sediment... to the little hippo.

Closer, requiring another slight adjustment of focus. Quiescent too. Just soaking its baby toes dreamily near its mother. Was it in any danger from the crocodile?

I shifted to a consideration of the guardian mother.

Muzzle more tapered than the bulls'. Rounded, snub. Though not truncated like a pig's. Still, with her pink belly and legs that's what she reminded me of.

"Are hippos and pigs relatives?" I asked Denys. I chuckled.

"Ah. Same *order*, actually," he said. "Different families."

"Really!" I exclaimed. I'd thought I was joking.

"*Hippopotamidae. Suidae.* Both *artiodactyla*, though, the order. 'Even-toed,' it means. Whatever that's worth. Covers a lot of territ'ry. Large order, you might say. Camels, giroffes, the antelopes. Cattle as well."

"Wonder if you could get a hippo to come to you by calling out 'soo-*eee*,'" I free-associated. "Sooo-*eee!* I'd never realized, but that must be what it comes from. Do they use that same call for hogs in South Africa?"

"Pig farming not within my scope of knowledge, I'm afraid," Denys replied. "Nor can I say I've ever bloody well had occasion to hollo up a hippo."

"Is that the derivation of the word *swine*?" Laura wondered. "*Suidae. Schwein.* Must be some Indo-European root...."

Woman after my own heart.

The punt was bouncing, joggling my aim. I lowered the glasses to look around.

We were in a rip where the eddy and the main current met. Our bow slapped the turbid water as Just Do It poled us through. The river was definitely getting roughed up by the breeze that was gusting stronger as darkness raced toward us across the eastern *veld*. The punt even threw up a few drops of spray as we approached mid-channel.

The encounter between the bull hippos seemed to be at an impasse, all right. They were on our quarter, contemplating each other unhappily, occasionally emitting a tentative rumble. I put the binoculars to my eyes and leaned slightly backwards to see around the broad ebony cameo of the crewman, silhouetted beside me.

It was an awkward position, and I could barely keep whichever hippo I tried to focus on within the wavering circle of magnification as the boat tossed beneath me and my abdominal muscles started to jitter from the strain....

The old bull's hump was indeed pocked and scored, suggesting many past defenses of authority.

The challenger was again airing its tonsils.

I had a pain in my neck and between my shoulder blades from trying to maintain this elbows-high crunch, this semi-situp. There was just enough space for me to wriggle around on my buttocks and hoist my right boot, only slightly muddy, onto the thwart without kicking my seatmate—who did edge outboard to accommodate.

Hugging my knee to my chest as closely as my rusted hip socket would permit, I wrestled my heel across the plank until I could drop it into the bilge in front of Just Do It. Gasping at the effort and then sighing in accomplishment, I sat astraddle the thwart, feet planted fore and aft. Now I had a much solider perch for hippopotamological observation.

And not a moment too soon. The herd bull, with a bellow of outrage, launched itself at the young interloper.

Who bawled back fearsomely and lifted its head to fend off the attack.

Gaping maw to gaping maw, in a froth of water, the two huge animals thudded together....

"Oh my God!" Laura exclaimed. "They *are* fighting!"

There was a quick oral slash and parry, tusk versus tusk, a scuffle for weight advantage, and then the squalling antagonists ricocheted apart.

I hadn't wanted to miss anything by trying to find them in the glasses. Hippo colonies on further bends of the river erupted with commentary on the duel: A chorus of distant grunts reverberated on the breeze. The waves stirred up by the combatants sloshed at the legs of the cow and calf, who fidgeted and grumbled uneasily....

The herd bull surged at the challenger again.

I clapped the binoculars to my eyes just as their mouths locked. The whitewater that streamed from the elder's gorge was tinted pink, his own blood or the other's—a leathery cheek or lip had been pierced by a cutlass incisor....

The image suddenly sheered to trees and sky. I rocked back unweighted, the thwart dipping out from beneath me as the punt wallowed to port.

I heard a loud catch of breath, followed immediately by a feminine yelp as the thwart rose to slap my newly leaden buttocks.

I lurched toward the crewman.

I threw my hand out and clamped my knees hard into the edges of the plank seat to save myself from skidding downhill and slamming against him.

Out of the corner of my eye I saw Laura unaccountably on her feet. Bent at the waist, knees buckled, her right hand pawing the air in front of her....

The punt listed to port again, action, reaction.

Denys angrily barked "Laura!"

Ewan gave a violent start and gargled. She'd clawed at his shoulder or neck to regain her equilibrium and he'd shrugged her off in pain.

She instinctively recoiled.

I grabbed for her with my left hand... succeeded only in landing a karate chop on her swinging elbow. My fingers closed on nothing....

Wordless, a look of astonishment on her face, still clinging with her left hand to the camera tethered to her neck, she swanned backwards away from me.

With a cannonball smack, Laura plunged into the Luangwa.

First there was blank shock.

Then a bubble of laughter formed in my chest. It was funny, a hilarious miscue, an unscheduled dunking.

Isn't that one theoretical explanation of humor? That it turns on a rupture of ordinary expectation, a disorienting juxtaposition of incompatible contexts? Self-possessed matron gliding along serenely in boat suddenly executes pratfall into river.

And always, I remember from a long-ago cram session for a midterm in aesthetics, comedy requires a larding of aggression or apprehension. That's why we laugh at a pie in the face, a skid on a banana peel, Wile E. Coyote's hopeful installation of the latest roadrunner-extermination device ("some assembly required") from Acme. It's why a nervous giggle can be a response to the appalling... why a husband might laugh at a wife's humiliating flop overboard.

"*Yi!*" I heard one of the Africans exclaim.

"Laura!" cried Ewan.

"Ah, Jesus!" Denys moaned.

My diaphragm had tightened to force out a guffaw. But it seized. I couldn't breathe—the apprehension had flared out of proportion.

Laura was still under.

Just Do It and his mate jabbered at each other. The latter, who'd bounced to one knee on the thwart and vised my right shoulder in his meaty fingers, leaned into me, gesticulating with his other hand inches from my face as if directing my attention over the side, as if I'd somehow failed to notice or fully appreciate what had just happened.

"*Iko iko!*" he shouted hoarsely. I swiveled my neck to follow his finger. "*Mkazi,*" I made out. "*Iko iko! Mami!*"

The punt was still rocking, almost but not quite shipping water.

I'd braced myself by the handrail. Ewan and Nigel clung dumfounded to their seats.

"Steady on!" Denys commanded.

But if the mate hadn't had me clamped under his paw I might have floundered in after Laura at that instant. It was my intellectual reflex, all right. Had to leap to her rescue....

Laura reappeared. She came up gasping and spitting, blinking her eyes open under the strands of hair plastered to her brow and straggling down her cheeks. She'd lost one barrette—the other dangled uselessly from a wet plait. She was perhaps fifty feet upstream of us.

I'd still been stupidly scanning the opaque soup nearer in. I later estimated she'd been underwater for ten or fifteen seconds at most—an eternity, of course, in the circumstances. I'd seen her go limp and sink out of sight. Then she must have kicked away from us to regain the surface. And the breeze was briskly shoving the punt downriver along with the main current. Which at just a couple of miles per hour, I'd later calculate, would itself account for the separation.

"*Mami!*" Just Do It and the mate chorused at her. "*Mami!* We are coming to you!"

"Laura! Can y' stand?" Denys called against the wind. "Bad luck! No worries! We'll have y' back aboard momently!"

Laura was freighted by boots and pants. Her uptilted chin kept dipping below the chop. Obviously she wasn't toeing bottom at the moment.

She bobbed, coughed, snorted. She'd emerged, oddly, holding her camera high, as if in triumph, as if it were a pearl she'd just plucked from a giant oyster on the river-floor—or as if she'd decided she might as well snap a few fish-eye views of us against the sunset sky while she ineptly trod water using only her free arm.

Her instinctive, ludicrous priority, I realized, was to keep her camera and film from getting wet. Wetter.

But I was processing all those details and sensations subliminally. Their significance would have to be reconstructed:

Laura, apparently, had risen off the thwart intending to take a picture of the clashing hippos over the obtrusive heads of Ewan and Nigel. The punt may have scraped across a hidden snag, or been thumped by piece of flotsam at that instant. Or it might have been her weight-shift alone that had unbalanced us....

When she wobbled and pitched overboard, Just Do It, who'd probably never lost a passenger before, had been preoccupied by the initial necessity of riding the unstable craft to submission. Now he was frantically plying his pole to bring the bow up toward her....

The crewman's urgency in pointing out the bubbly swirl Laura had left in vanishing, and his accusatory insistence now that she'd once again popped into view, wasn't simple-minded panic. Whether by instinct or instruction, he was doing exactly what *I'd* been taught to do in the Navy.

It's easy to lose sight of a small object winking on a broad expanse of water, or of the featureless spot at which a head was last seen, even if it's only in a river—especially while your own low, unstable perch is jibing.

In fact, I used to replicate the man-overboard drills I'd taken part in on the *Huckaby* later with Susan, back in those happy early days of our marriage when we'd owned a little sloop, a vintage *Bear*, and had sailed with the kids on weekends out of the Berkeley Marina. We'd heave an old mildewed life jacket into the bay and practice maneuvering to recover it while Chris and Megan, wide-eyed, swathed to their chins like pint-sized Michelin men in their own sour, drool-and-cracker-crumb-encrusted orange kapok vests, dutifully trained their forefingers at it as we'd explained they must do if they ever saw Mommy or Daddy get cracked by the boom or trip on a deck-cleat for real....

But, of course, none of those digressive thoughts entered my mind at the time. I was looking at Laura out of a welling delirium of dread.

Now that I was no longer distracted by the immediate fear that she might be drowning, I was confronted by an even more primal horror:

Laura was swimming in a river infested by crocodiles.

I'd just seen one dart into the water. Nose under. It prowled the depths somewhere nearby.

Others like the one I'd watched through the binoculars haunted the river's margins or skulked in the bottom-mud, primed to explode like so many saurian mines. Fresh in my head was how just two nights earlier a boy had detonated one almost at this very spot. Died an excruciating death for his misstep, devoured thrashing and screaming, according to Steve's awful lunch-table description....

...As had the old woman I'd heard about at the ford, dragged under and torn apart limb for limb, quartered alive in the mesozoic jaws, mangled, shredded, eviscerated by the horrible septic lizard-teeth....

When I was a child of twelve or thirteen I'd seen a grainy black-and-white movie sequence of an Amazonian cow being consumed by piranhas. It was some weird travelogue trailer, or maybe an installment in the Frank Buck "Bring 'Em Back Alive" series that accompanied the Saturday matinee feature at the local movie house. (With the Tarzan-Cheetah burlesques, "King Solomon's Mines" and "Bwana Devil"—lions springing, Masai spears flung directly at you as you flinched behind your cardboard 3-D glasses, one blue lens, one red — those movies conceptualized Africa for me.)

The unfortunate cow, of course, had inhabited another continent. As I recalled, it had been jostled off a raft while its herd was being ferried across the Amazon. Like Laura. Reminiscent of the story of Mpamvu, too.

As the cow beat its hooves to stay afloat, nostrils flared, eyes goggled in effort and terror, the water around it began to boil. And to darken with blood as the tiny carnivorous fish swarmed and flayed the animal from below, implacably stripped the flesh from its bones, harvested the soft organs from the hollows of its gut, reduced it to an anguished head on a skeleton and then nibbled out even eyeballs and tongue in a matter of seconds. In the span of a single ghastly take.

That scene, with its obvious moral for humans who might be foolish enough to bathe in the river, had had a powerful impact on me. It had lodged in my mental viscera like one of the barbed flukes I'd more recently read about that also pervade the Amazon—parasitic flatworms attracted by the warmth of fresh urine that swim up the stream into the penis of unfastidious male swimmers to wedge themselves inextricably in the urethra and slowly eat their way out. Or something like that.

Gughh. Nastier even than the schistosomes. Which only colonize your colon. Worm their way from there into your bladder, liver, kidneys....

What was I doing in this place?

Nervousness about the invisible river perils had certainly contributed to the fact that I'd yet to travel to Amazonia. Even though I'd always regarded it as one of the ultimate modern destinations—like Africa one of the few remaining frontiers for aboriginal experience.

That documentary footage of the piranhas' feast guttered in my subconscious along with the opening scene from "Jaws," fragments of nature films portraying brutal crocodilian feedings, memories of a couple of water-ski outings on the Chattahoochee River during a college spring break, when each hapless cartwheel meant a wait for the circling tow-rope among knots of basking cotton-mouth moccasins (talk about incentive to learn quickly to stay upright)....

Once when I was aboard the Norwegian freighter, in a deep funk after learning my best friend among the crew had jumped ship hours earlier in Singapore, I'd stood on the poop and watched the Moluccan shore glide by within what I judged was swimming distance.

Ahead for me was just a long, lonely passage to Cochin, and then across the Indian Ocean to Aden and up through the Suez Canal. Back to the U.S.A. within a matter of months, to resume the boring study of English literature. Or else clean latrines for two years as a draftee into the Army.

I had stared down speculatively into the warm, sapphire strait and slowly fallen into a rapture—felt the amniotic pull the sea exerts if you open yourself to it too unguardedly. I was an excellent swimmer, wasn't I? I could make it to that sugary Malay beach over there, I was sure. Make my way back down to Singapore and join my shipmate in his plan to find work in Australia on a cousin's sheep station.

I was actually about to vault the rail when I noticed a tiny, slender snake... then others... hundreds, thousands of them, in fact, writhing along on the sunstruck surface. Were they poisonous? Would they bite if I stroked through them? I had no idea (probably yes, and the venom is deadly, I was later told). But whatever, the impulse to jump was immediately quenched.

All of those experiences had reinforced in me a latent dread of the dangerous creatures lurking in strange waters.

Tropical waters, more specifically. Fast northern rivers, clear lakes, the San Francisco Bay and Delta had never unsettled me. And somehow I'd been able to master my disquiet sufficiently to dive on occasion for recreation. Not in the cold Pacific surf where the Great Whites might mistake me in my glistening black wetsuit for a seal. No indeed, no matter how much I liked fresh abalone steak pounded tender with a tire-iron and sauteed in lemon and butter.

Even in the Caribbean I was always on jumpy lookout for barracudas and sharks. Always flipping to check back between my fins for what might be sliding up behind me. And you'd never find me reaching into a sandy crevice, or even skimming too near a bulbous coral head, for fear a giant octopus tentacle or the hideous needle-toothed maw of a moray eel might pop out at me.

Thalassophobia.

No, obviously. It's not the sea itself I fear. It's what's in the sea. Under the sea. Under the water.

A particularly embarrassing handicap for a Pisces.

More than an embarrassment now. Unmanning. Utterly debilitating.

I gaped, appalled, at Laura; all I could think of was that I was supposed to hurl myself in alongside her... escort her to safety, even crook my arm under her chin, cradle her on my hip and bodily squire her to dry land. It would be like the helpful Boy Scout frog-marching the unwilling old lady across the street. But that was my lifeguard training. Doubled or trebled in exigency by the marriage bond.

No way in hell, though, was I going to jump into that river-water.

And why should I? Laura could swim. As well as I could. Would she dive in to pull me out if the tables were reversed?

Of course not. Well, that would be ridiculous—she was smaller, weaker. I had the size, the muscle. I was the man. And the man takes care of his mate. The man protects his mate.

No way in hell was I going to jump into that crocodile-water.

Laura had begun sidestroking toward us. One-armed, still favoring the camera. She was going with the current, but it was setting us away from her.

In boating you always try to come about upwind of someone who's fallen overboard—the larger sail area of your hull and superstructure will cause you to be blown down onto the smaller swimmer and create a lee for calm retrieval. But that was more or less impossible with our mode of propulsion, a pole. And though Just Do It was pumping vigorously, like one of those metronomic oil rigs you see around San Ardo when you're driving on 101, it was all he could do to keep the punt from being spun broadside to the channel between thrusts. The thermal wind was sweeping at us now unremittingly.

At least we didn't have a keel. So Just Do It was slowly winning.

The flat-bottomed punt bounced through the chop, skimmed the current, yawed closer to Laura.

Denys crouched forward anxiously and shouted encouragements: "Good job, Laura! Can't be very deep! Another month and y'd be wading! Done it many a time! Shallower a little to the bank! Chin up, we'll soon have you!"

Laura wasn't answering. She was too busy bicycling her legs, stirring the water with her right hand and spitting out unwanted nose- and mouthfuls.

The breeze flung Denys's words over his shoulder anyway.

Laura's face was impassive, blanked out by the moment's physical demands and too many simultaneous emotions, the way white results when you mix all the colors of the spectrum. Or is it brown—brown under real conditions, when earthy pigments are compounded, rather than ideal light?

There *was* a sullen cast to her expressionlessness. Beneath the pluck and determination she was embarrassed, uneasy if not actually frightened, and most of all angry... angry at herself and at me, that it had been she and not I who'd been guilty of this stupidity. Who'd committed this humiliating public foolishness.

Or so I sensed. Or maybe projected. But again subliminally, if not in retrospect.

Everything going on around me, all immediate perception, was filtering in hazily through the impasto of fear. My abstract crocodile-fear, my *ur*-fear of death by reptile—seizure, vivisection, ingestion.

I clung white-knuckled to the handrail and to the barrel of the binoculars as the primordial dread churned in my bowels. It made me light-headed, like the flu. Faint and sick. Close to blubbering, even.

Obviously there'd been many situations in my life when I'd been scared, to one degree or another. But I'd have to say that I'd never before experienced a fright so intense. *Any* emotion so overwhelming. So physical. So *visceral*. *Literally*!

...Except maybe for a quick spasm of passion, a brief *frisson* of love. Which was, in complex push-pull with duty, common sense and self-preservation, what had me immobilized. I was incapacitated by the clashing demands of love and instinct like a run-down wildebeest standing pole-axed in shock while a pack of hyenas strip it of its intestines.

If I loved Laura, could I just sit here watching till the awful moment when her death arrived?

Any second now! The invisible strike, her shriek, the hopeless, drowning entreaties, the pitifully brief struggle...? Laura! My wife! Recover her body parts stuffed in some reeking hidey-hole...!

But I couldn't fight off a crocodile.

Couldn't be expected to. Could I?

But if I really loved her, oughtn't I be willing to?

Didn't I have to?

Interpose my own body. Distract the deadly lizard if nothing else. Sacrifice my life for hers. Wasn't that what real love meant? Required?

He must have despised me, Denys. And George. Every one of them in the boat. Observing my craven inaction. My mute, passive contemplation of my wife's plight.

But all of this was happening in a span of two or three minutes. And for me there didn't seem to be any of that cinematic slowing of motion that attends instants of focused consciousness—the "zone" of sports perfection, when shot after shot arches lazily off your fingertips to float true through the gaping hoop, or the consummate movie moment when you and your lover moon-lope across a meadow of undulant rye into each other's outstretched arms.

This was the most harrowing event of my life—more than half a century of it... the most fundamental disequilibration of everything I'd ever believed, wanted to believe, about myself.

Yet the data were cascading in through my senses and kaleidoscoping within my brain as if I were watching some dadaist film-loop. Projected at manic speed.

And buried inside the reel, like frames subtly spliced to condition behavior without actually registering an image on the optic nerve, was every one of the doubts, terrors, formative memories I've described.

"Here!" Laura suddenly announced. Her voice, carried on the wind, was startlingly loud, immediate. She might have been sitting right next to me.

In fact, Just Do It's urgent surges had brought us to within fifteen or so feet of her.

"Take this," she said.

She flicked the camera strap from around her neck and with a couple of determined arm-pulls and scissor-kicks, swam up under the gunwale. Right below me. It was as if she'd been toying with us, lolling perversely at a distance she could've closed any time she'd decided to give it a serious try.

She wasn't looking at me—her eyes refused to lock on mine. Maybe she expected to encounter some kind of rebuke in them.

Denys reached out his hand to grasp her.

Instead of seizing it, she slapped the camera into it.

"Wait," she said. She reached behind her back, underwater. After a moment of fumbling she brought up her waistpack and flipped it over the gunwale into the punt.

"I'll just... upset *you* guys... if I try to get back in," she said, short-breathed, shaking her head at Denys. "Easier to swim. Meet you there!"

With that she kicked backwards, rolled on her shoulder, buried her face and churned away toward the Chibembe bank at a no-nonsense crawl.

"No!" I blurted after her. "What about...?"

But I was arguing, aghast, with the face I'd been staring down at several seconds earlier—the Laura I'd momentarily, finally, relaxed my grip on the handrail to help snatch from danger. I hadn't even mustered voice until too late.

"No," I murmured a second time, uselessly, at her receding form. At myself.

I glanced toward Denys. He grimaced.

"*Mo-tsakana*," he said. He was talking past me, at Just Do It. He waved a hand toward the swimming Laura. "*Msanga! Kwe kwe kwe!*"

"*Ndawo*," the captain grunted.

The voice made me turn my head—I glimpsed the sinewy, sweating African in his incongruous mass-market American athletic togs humping over his pole.

Then George's rich baritone sounded from the bow and I swung back toward him.

He knelt on one knee on the plank bench, ramrod tense under the olive-drab uniform, the rifle poised in front of his chest in both hands. I'd recognized a charge to the timbre, an ominous rise in the tone with which he'd spoken to Denys. And I'd caught a word—a word I knew, with its smoothly swallowed glottal: "*ng'ona.*"

"Aah, Christ," Denys muttered.

There was a peripheral flicker of motion.

My gaze darted to the side channel, behind the mudbar. I became aware again for a moment of the continuous background chuffing and bawling of the hippos. Beyond the restive cow and calf on the shoal, the two bulls collided. But the brushy crown of the islet was about to obscure their desultory combat. Not that it was any longer of interest to me. They slithered heavily apart....

I was already looking away to Laura.

We were twenty feet or so behind her, on a parallel course... keeping up now, maybe even gaining.

Her elbows crooked in and out of the brown water at a steady beat. Her flutter-kick was irregular, slowed by the boots, but occasionally producing a little rooster-tail of effort.

The boots and clothing would be a drag, would tire her soon enough, and the graceful Esther Williams cock of wrist

317

before her cupped hand sliced the water—I could've picked her out by that characteristic stroke among a poolful of lap swimmers—was less efficient, supposedly, than my claw-fingered, overhand racing reach-and-snatch. But she was strong, able. Even if she'd begun to plod a bit, I wasn't worried that she couldn't....

Wait!

I snapped my neck around to squint at the muddy brim of the islet where, I realized, I hadn't noticed the crocodile that had been lying there. The one I'd studied through the binoculars.

"Oh God! Denys!" I gurgled. "Denys! Denys! There was a crocodile over there!"

He'd stiffened at my alert.

I pointed. "But...!"

"Yeh, yeh."

"...It's gone now! It's in the river! Two of 'em!"

"More than that," he nodded. "In this river. George keeping an eye peeled. *Bwino iwe!*" he snapped, over his shoulder.

"*E*," George rumbled, "*e.*"

"Just as well she swim, actually," Denys continued immediately, speaking in an even tone. He was trying to be reassuring, to Ewan and Nigel and me. And to himself, no doubt.

"Easier vasbyting... easier just getting on with it. She'll be on dry ground almost as fast as if we were to try to haul her back aboard. Probably right, too, she is. Might easily dump the lot of us in the process. No point everyone getting wet needlessly. Not that it wouldn't be lekker enough after a long, hot day.... Ah. Beg pardon, Ewan. Don't mean to give y' the willies. Crossed this spot several times myself, though, I have. Up to my armpits. No problem. Not that I'd recommend it on a steady basis. Little higher this year, true. Bit more rain earlier in the season. Is a tiny risk, of course. One elects to run. Infinitesimal, though, really. The likelihood. That a croc. Would take an interest."

Throughout this carefully modulated rumination his eyes had been in constant squinty motion. "*Kwe kwe kwe, kapitau*," he urged finally, his voice slightly raised and peremptory.

Laura broke her rhythm, lifted her head, floundered. Her feet were sinking.... Then her shoulders rose. She'd found the bottom!

She waded and swam with her arms, pulling herself along as she hopped forward clumsily. Relief gushed through me... more or less irrationally, since she still had a wide band of river to negotiate before she could clamber out at the base of the sheer mud-cliff on the Chibembe side.

Unlike the shore we'd departed, there was only the most rudimentary fringe of beach ahead of us; it was probably why the little dock had been built for the punt. Laura would have to slog back upriver to reach it, rendezvous with us when we poled in. No paths were visible leading directly up into the mopanis that crowded the undercut lip of the channel here downstream from the dock. On the other hand, there was also no convenient perch at the water's edge for crocodiles on this side—none, thank God, lay in visible welcome.

Maybe—probably—they wouldn't lurk in ambush here either. It didn't appear to be a spot where animals drank.

She ducked her face and launched herself forward, kicking, gliding for a beat or two, then swinging into her arm-stroke again. Swimming was still more efficient than wading at the depth she was in. I hoped she was opening her eyes to look where she was headed when she twisted her neck to gulp for breath: she was going to have to thread between several tangles of deadwood and a mudcaked log that jutted from the choppy current closer in to shore.

She must have appreciated that. She stopped again after a moment, parted the sodden curtain of hair that covered her eyes—the surviving barrette clung like a butterfly that had alighted on the side of her neck momentarily—and stood. The brown water now came to her ribs, just below her bra, whose straps and seams were clearly molded by the clinging top. You could see the dark circles of her nipples. It looked as if she had been soaked in coffee. She staggered forward a few steps.

"Stay clear of the snags!" Denys warned her.

My crocodile-terror was beginning to abate. Or at least it had reached its zenith, and was ebbing with Laura's progress. Denys had offered me absolution: "Just as well...," he'd said. "Infinitesimal...."

My paralysis dissipated, too. Without conscious calculation, without even much awareness of the attending tweaks at the hip-socket, I used my right wrist and the binoculars to support my knee as I cranked my shin, ankle, boot-heel up over the thwart. That forced the crewman to sidle further away from me. I twisted on my buttocks so I sat normally, facing forward again, facing Laura more fully.

My heart was still in my mouth, though—apt cliché. The coronary lump lodged so high in my craw it almost gagged me. My molars were gritted anxiously, my muscles knotted, twitching sympathetically as I mentally mimed each of her semi-submerged swimming/plodding gains toward the bank, urged her on with my body English out of the lethal waters....

Suddenly her torso sank and her head jerked back. She yawped and slapped at the river with outflung arms to keep herself from going face-under....

"*Ng'ona! Iko iko!*" a gravelly voice shouted at my ear....

"*Yi!*"

"*Timba!*"

The world exploded.

Or might as well have. My adrenal glands had already spurted their bitter tonic: Laura in some awful distress... the crewman's grisly cry... the answering clamor of alarm from Denys, from George, from Just Do It....

And then a blast that wrenched me up off the thwart like a strawman, a marionette.

Its shock wave convulsed my body and momentarily shorted out all but the involuntary nervous circuits.

George had fired his rifle. I could smell the acrid cordite. Something terrible....

Laura thrashed, twisted toward us, rose, stumbled backwards, windmilling, sliding under again, her face stricken....

I'd soiled myself.

I felt the liquescent warmth between my buttocks. Blotting into my underpants. My precarious bowels, the horror—then that apocalyptic bang.

Ah Jesus! My sphincter had betrayed me.

"You okay, Laura?" Denys bellowed "Are you tangled!"

Blam!

Another deafening roar, from close range. George had fired again. My bones almost left my skin.

All that was left to evacuate.

I couldn't see what he was shooting at. Surely not toward Laura!

A crocodile! Had to be!

Somewhere!

Laura wallowed, face contorted....

I was sitting in my own shit. My cowardice manifest. The ultimate dishonor: "scared shitless."

It was something you only read about: I could *never* have imagined it happening to me. And yet here it was—the evidence of my ignominy squishing when I squirmed, oozing through the layers of thin cotton under me....

"On with it, Laura! Now! Now!" Denys was yammering. "Out of the river! Quickly!"

An image flashed through my mind: I was walking back from the dock with the others, through the forest, to Chibembe Lodge. I'm not sure whether Laura was in the picture. The trip would happen either way. I saw the seat of my shorts smudged with that intolerable bull's-eye stain, that unmistakable fecal splotch. The absolute nadir of shame. For everyone to witness.

It had to be washed away.

Rinsed.

Cleansed.

In the river.

Of course. The river.

Swarming with crocodiles.

Only alternative, though. The river.

Fuck it.

I tumbled over the side, squeezed my eyes shut and held my breath... settled deep into the black bosom of the Luangwa.

My boots pulled my feet down until they settled under me, into the invisible, gluey silt. I awaited the reptilian caress, the great pointed teeth slipping tenderly around a leg, an arm, the steel-trap snap....

Death was not instantaneous. I opened my eyes to a stinging underwater gloom, sprang upward to the light and air.

I broke the surface, blinked to clear my sight and saw the crocodile coming! The gray tip of nostrils...!

No. It was just my cap. Floating a couple of arm's-lengths away.

Beyond it rocked the punt. All of them goggled down at me, silhouetted against the amber sunset. George with his rifle poised. Denys's features barely discernible. His mouth seemed to be opening and closing. He was shouting, apparently. I didn't register the words. The water was practically body-temperature but I'd begun to shudder violently.

I sucked in a lungful of potential voice—the shock of immersion and the need to vent my spiraling panic had restored the capability of speech. Made it essential.

"Laura!" I howled blindly over my shoulders. "Laura! Laura! I'm coming! I'm coming!"

I lunged toward her, flailed my arms over my head, fluttered my booted feet.

Denys's binoculars were still locked in my right fist. That made my backstroke—believe me, I was committed to the backstroke—even clumsier.

I *could barely limp to the cabin, force my legs, throbbing with exhaustion and seared by random pains that radiated from my tortured hip sockets and lumbar spine, to propel me across the grounds.*

Swimming had not proved a salutary exercise.

IX. The Trouble with Talismans

What a sorry, bedraggled sight Laura and I were. But darkness had fallen and the path ran for most of the way along the bordering *msikisi*s.

We trailed in silence behind Ewan and Nigel until we reached the fork near the shower hut built for the overland safari parties. It was newly thatched—I'd seen a group of men with big *lupanga*s, machete-like bush-knives, working on it before lunch. We heard water splashing; somebody from Mamba was inside getting ready for the evening. Abluting.

Neither Laura nor I was anxious for chance encounters. Wordlessly we veered off, leaving Ewan and Nigel to plod along toward their tent in the clearing where the Bedford was parked.

Laura claimed our bathroom first, out of need.

I immediately stripped off my damp clothes. I scowled at my shorts and underpants as I stepped out of them to make sure the agitator-cycle in the river and a slip that I hadn't fought, that I'd allowed to sit me down awkwardly in the muck as we'd labored along the water's edge—with a little extra butt-wriggle for good measure before I'd heaved myself back on my feet—had done their work.

Everything was fouled and discolored. Routinely fouled and discolored. I glanced at the bathroom door and wafted the briefs under my nose. No odor except the incipient must of wet cotton saturated with river silt and still warm from body contact.

As I pried apart the swollen, grit-encrusted knots in my bootlaces I heard the shower-curtain rings clatter and the water start running. So I was going to have to take my turn after her.

I was annoyed that Laura hadn't negotiated or even announced her intention—but then, we hadn't said much to each other since I'd plowed toward her through the Luangwa.

We were both waist deep, both clambering for safe ground with the panicky, concrete-legged difficulty of nightmare.

"What are you *doing?*" she'd cried over her shoulder to me querulously. "For God's sake, Daniel! Why did *you* jump in *too?* What's he *shooting* at?"

"I'm from the government and I'm here to help you," I'd managed. I was hardly about to explain in serious detail. Best to go out with a quip on one's trembling blue lips.

"Didn't seem fair, watching you have all the fun," I managed. "We are having fun, aren't we?"

"Oh, yeah!"

"Okay. *Please,*" I'd wailed, "could we just get the fucking hell... *out*... of this... *fucking, goddamn... river?*"

I peeled off my socks, added them to the sodden heap, balled everything up, realized my camera—surely ruined—was still in the shirt-pocket. And my shorts were still weighted with wet utensils. James' address had probably dissolved, an illegible blue blot between the pulpy pages of the notebook. Too bad.

I would retrieve and dry all that stuff out later, after a shower. And a martini.

I nudged open the screen door and set the dripping bundle outside on the porch.

The river shone faintly. My eyes hadn't adjusted but I could make out a few indistinct lumps along the waterline on the opposite flat. Because ours was the last cabin and set almost on the brink of the cutbank, there was no need for modesty. No need to be concerned that somebody might be walking by to glimpse me through the doorway naked.

Good thing. I was arrestingly banded, like a Harlequin or a Hopi corn-dancer, mud-smeared from mid-thigh to ankletops and from elbows to fingertips, except where my wristwatch had been. It was turning cool outside; my balls had retreated as far back inside my baseball-taut scrotum as they could nestle, and my penis was a quarter-inch vestige of its full nine-inch male-standard glory. Uh-huh.

The plank floor glistened where I'd dropped my trou. Lacking a towel or an article of dry clothing I wanted to sacrifice, I smeared the thin puddle over a wider surface with the bottom of my bare foot. Then, coddling my back, I lowered myself onto one of the two narrow wooden chairs at the room's small oval table.

I bowed my head and squeezed my eyes, sighing, breathing in deeply, sighing. I rested my forehead in my hand, elbow propped on the bare tabletop. Eyes closed, I kneaded the ridge of bone above my eye sockets. I shivered. I could conjure my grinning, unfleshed skull.

Denys hadn't said much either, really.

"You all right, then," he'd scowled at Laura when we'd finally scrambled to join them on the dock. He'd seemed too drained or disgusted even to give the question an upward inflection. The others were disembarking; they'd all ridden escort as Laura and I had picked our way along the base of the sheer mudbank—Just Do It skillfully holding the punt offshore beyond the treacherous deadwood tufts that clogged the shoals, George with his head aswivel and his finger on the trigger of the poised rifle.

Slip-sliding ankle-deep or worse when we had to wade out into the eddies to skirt a beached log or a skeletal bush—

feeling for footing with each gingerly blind step, hoping not to trip or tangle up in in a drowned root or branch or, worse, have it suddenly lash out from under your boot, a trodden cobra, a crocodile tail... I, for one, had been desperately grateful for the armed accompaniment.

Assuming George had had time to reload.

If not, there'd only be one cartridge left in his rifle. Phenomenal marksman, he'd have had to have been in any case—and phenomenally reactive—to have done us much good if a crocodile had actually erupted.

Yow! Glom! Too late! Though it might not be the worst thing to be put out of one's misery at that point by an errant risked shot.

"Yeah, no harm, except to my dignity," Laura replied to Denys sheepishly. "I'm really sorry. It was absolutely the dumbest thing. I'm sorry if I hurt you, Ewan. I didn't mean to scratch you where you're sunburned."

"Och...," he grunted, flapping his hand in forgiveness.

"I deserved to have to swim home."

"What made you shoot? What were you shooting at?" I demanded of George, who'd just set his rifle on the dock preparatory to scrambling out of the boat.

"Yeah, that was when I suddenly got *really* scared!" Laura exclaimed.

George didn't meet my eyes or answer. I wasn't sure if he was embarrassed, deferring to Denys to explain, or filled with such scorn for my cowardice and fatuity he no longer deigned to speak to me.

"Warning shots, 'cross the bow," Denys replied. He too addressed Laura, not me. "Scatter any crocs that might be lurkin' in the neighbourhood. Did spot one cruising by."

"A crocodile?" Laura demanded.

"Mm," Denys nodded.

I winced. Laura inhaled sharply.

"Oh. Gee. God, wow," she murmured.

"Aah, well. Minding its own business, basically," Denys added quickly. "Nothing to fret about, turned out. Boys were a bit jumpy, though, with Mommy in the river. Gordon was keeping a very sharp lookout."

Denys nodded at the crewman, who hunkered by the post at the end of the dock tying off the bow-line.

"George thought it best to put a couple of rounds close to the bugger's nose. Offer 'im encouragement to move on along to a more salubrious clime, hey? Before any nasty ideas crept into that crafty loaf. They're quite intelligent, actually."

"Think it was the same one that was on the island?" I asked.

Denys ignored the question.

"Weren't y' scared when y' went in, Laura?" Nigel asked her. "Had me brickin'. Tell you that much."

"I wasn't even thinking about crocodiles, or danger, I have to admit," Laura said. "Until then. I just felt like such an idiot. Then when I heard that gun go off.... And the water was deeper there all of a sudden, too. I lost my balance. And then when there was another shot.... Frightened the shit out of me, to be honest."

With a catch of hope, I wondered if that were literally true. But the concept wouldn't bear analysis—the image was distasteful. I didn't want to think any woman was capable of such a self-abasement. Certainly not Laura. Only men shat themselves. Nigel—"brickin'." Comes, I learned, from "shit a brick." Women have babies. Get raped. Go home to beatings by their boyfriends and husbands. Swim in the Luangwa. They're stoic, they don't succumb to abject, mewling fear. Like men. Like me. The weaker sex.

Besides, it had to be a figure of speech, a cliché, or Laura wouldn't have tossed it off so readily. And yet, coming from her, the scatology was indicative of the depth to which she'd been shaken.

"That's when I dived in," I noted. "Wake-up call."

"Ah yeh. Brilliant piece of work," Denys muttered. He turned a cold eye on me. "Two in the river, add to my grey hairs. Should've realised when you started gropin' for tree-snakes what a joller you are, mate. Here."

He held out my limp, wet cap.

"Oh. Thanks," I mumbled, wondering how deeply I'd been insulted. I didn't know then what a "joller" meant in South African slang: roughly a party-guy, I'd find out. So in fact it *was* some sort of sarcastic dismissal.

"Boys fished it up for you," he said. "Y' can thank them."

I rummaged momentarily through my linguistic storage banks trying to recall how to say "thank you" in Chinyanja. "*Arigato*" was what popped up. Dismissed instantaneously, but the Japanese miscue had jammed the translation machinery. I could no longer get past it to access my minuscule Chinyanja vocabulary.

"The boys," at least, appeared oblivious to the conversation. They wouldn't feel slighted if I didn't immediately comply. *Sayonara. Danke. Takk.* Hopeless.

I took the cap and held out the binoculars in my other hand.

"And here," I said to Denys, "are these back."

The barrels were beaded with moisture but all four lenses still glittered intact, I'd determined. "I hope they aren't damaged. I don't think they are. I'll replace 'em for you, of course, if there *is* something the matter. Water got inside, or whatever."

He nodded. "Must say I hadn't counted on seeing this bit of kit again."

"I really wasn't thinking," I apologized. "When I dove."

"I'd agree with that," he said.

"Once it dawned on me, though, that I was still holding on to 'em," I blurted, "I was kind of glad." Naive candor had always been one of my hallmarks. "Made it a bitch to swim. Reason I probably looked so awkward. But they were *something*, you know? To defend myself with? Not a weapon, obviously. But better than a little pocket knife, which was the only other thing I had. So... what I started to figure... was that if a crocodile did attack, what I'd do, just about the only thing I could do, I guess, was try to jam the binoculars in between its jaws. Slam 'em in, quick, all the way back, to where the jaw-hinge is? It's what they say to do with sharks, I think. Or like biting dogs, wedge your forearm in real deep, keep the mouth propped open? So it can't close all the way to chew through." I smiled self-deprecatingly. "Anyway, that's how I decided I was going to try to save myself. And her. If it came to that."

I shrugged. "Pretty lame. About all I could figure to do, though."

"Man with a plan," Denys nodded. He smiled faintly. I chose to read it as indulgent amusement rather than outright disdain.

"Missionary-python principal, rather, hey?" he added. "Had it backward, though, mate. Idea with a croc is to clamp its jaws *shut*. Muscles that pull the jaws apart are relatively weak. Made for crunching, grinding, they are. Capable of exerting tonnes of pressure in the direction of closure...."

He did an instinctive pantomime with the heels of his hands together, clapping the binoculars against the palm of the other. "Spit these out in short order. And your arm in the bargain. See a man wrestling a croc... tourist attraction sort of thing... well, that'll be the trick of it, keeping the mouth shut. Not terribly difficult, actually, for a man of ordin'ry strength. I figgered maybe you knew that. Though I wasn't dead keen to see it put to the test on some of our larger specimens round here. Like the bugger George scared off.... Besides, when a croc lunges at its prey, it comes in with its mouth open. Aims to seize the head if possible. Wouldn't lay much on your chances if you'd actually trolled up one of our... 'reptilian denizens,' was it you called 'em? Whilst you were paddling about, playing at the bloody comics-strip hero."

"Playing at the hero." Never mind the qualifiers. My mind performed a nip-up. I was so shamelessly pleased by this deprecation I broke into a grin and flopped my head, as if in rueful acknowledgement of my ill-advised indulgence in virtue too bone-deep to be denied.

Virtue, of course, derives from the Latin for "man." Even if Denys considered me at base a hopeless imbecile, he at least accorded me that quixotic motivation, that tiny, redeeming strain of virile intent.

I had little doubt I'd be the subject of endless bar and campfire chin-sessions, the guides lowing sympathetically, the huddled tourists snickering smugly, as Denys recalled the time this silly git on one of his walking safaris had actually jumped into the Luangwa after his wife, who'd contrived to tumble overboard.

But, hey, I could live with that.

And even Laura, a hot shower and a martini having begun to assuage the agenbite of chagrinwit, seemed to accept that I'd done something grudgingly laudable. Irrational, of course. Utterly useless. Foolhardy, even (which is commendable in at least half its construction). But in its way, only fair.

"It was you who knocked me out of the boat, actually," she observed as she refreshed her tumbler from our large plastic water-bottleful of premixed gin and vermouth (roughly ten to one). "You know that, don't you?"

She'd put on a pair of teal slacks and sandals while I'd had my shower—which had gone cold before I'd finished. She was still in her bra, the écru shirt she'd chosen to wear hangered on the square back of the chair I'd perched in earlier. Her damp hair was loosely turbaned in a white towel. I'd put on a dark blue tee-shirt and was stepping into crisp faded Levis from the pile of fresh laundry.

"What?" I exclaimed. I gave the zipper on the fly an astonished jerk.

"You hit me on the arm," she explained.

Her tone was even, dispassionate. She plucked a stuffed olive from a separate plastic canister and dropped it into her clear drink. We were forgoing ice, neither of us up for an errand to the bar. I was still on my first, which she'd had waiting for me when I'd dashed shivering from the bathroom.

"You're kidding!" I exclaimed. "Where'd you get *that*?"

"It's what you did."

"You can't be serious. That's nuts! I was trying to *catch* you!"

"First Ewan gives me a shove. Which is understandable enough because I scratched his sunburn. It was an automatic reaction on his part.Accidental. But then as I'm struggling to find my balance you reach out and *punch* me. I couldn't believe it."

"*Punch* you! You were *gone*! There was no *way* you weren't going in at that point unless I could grab you!"

"Well, that wasn't the effect, was it?"

She sat on the foot of the bed.

"So it's my fault? You've gotten up on your feet, you're rocking the boat, you're flailing your arms around wildly, you're falling backwards. You were way past *extremis*, believe me, Laura. And I reach out to try to help you. Boom. So I get blamed for it."

"All I'm saying...."

"*You* batted *my* hand *away*! Is more like it."

"Whatever. Our memories differ."

"It reminds me of when we were taking care of little Squeegee. For your mother? And he was sleeping on a chair? And the mailman drove up the driveway and blew his horn and Squeegee jumped off the chair and broke his leg...?"

"Yeah, yeah. I remember. That dog was ridiculous."

"Don't have to tell me. But I'm the one who digs him out from under the couch, where he's cowering, whimpering, snarling. Biting the hand that's trying to rescue him. And I drive him to the vet...."

"I remember."

"And he never forgives me. I'm his savior, I act out of nothing but his best interests, I get him fixed up, but he shivers every time he sees me from then on, as if I'm some kind of Nazi torturer. In his pitiful poodle pea-brain, I'm the one who broke his leg."

"Mm-hm. I've heard that many times. So what's your point?"

"Ah. Right. Pretty obscure, any parallel. Since your leg didn't get broken."

"Okay. I know. If I hadn't gotten up off my seat in the first place...."

"Aaah. Don't worry about it. It's over and done with. I just don't want to be made the scapegoat if it isn't deserved. It'll make a great story in years to come."

"Wow," she nodded reflectively. "One of our guides is actually shooting at a crocodile to keep him away while I'm blithely swimming along in a river in Africa. Wait till Lisa hears that. And Chris and Megan."

"It *is* kind of amazing that it didn't occur to you...."

"Well, I was totally disoriented right off the bat. And then I was embarrassed, and all of you were close by, and I knew it wasn't deep, or that far to go to shore. And it *would* have been hard climbing in again."

I noticed the pale gray-blue amulet resting at the top of her cleavage, between the tan swell of her breasts above the clean white bra.

"And you were protected by your *nyaminyami*," I said.

She touched it thoughtfully. "If it were such a powerful protection, you'd think I wouldn't have fallen in to begin with."

"What's amazing is that *I* got through unscathed," I said. "Considering I'd lost mine. If I'd thought about that factor, I'd never have risked the plunge."

"Which was pretty weird, you know. Your doing that. I guess in some way I should be flattered."

I shrugged. I had enough grace to keep my mouth shut. Besides, I was partially distracted. Was what I'd just said true? Would superstition have outweighed shame?

"I still can't figure out what you thought you were accomplishing."

I drained the styptic martini and let the olive roll onto my tongue. I shrugged again. "Let's just say it seemed like a good idea at the time."

I crushed the mushy, hollow sphere between my back teeth. It was a cheap brand gone stale without refrigeration—the flavor released was reminiscent of kerosene.

"For various reasons," I added.

"Everybody'll know about it, of course. Nigel and Ewan'll spread the whole story around." She winced and shook her head in self-recrimination. "Now they'll all be convinced I'm the world's biggest klutz. And you're... I don't know. Some variety of loony."

"Some variety. Probably not garden."

"That's your comeuppance. For not taking proper care of the *nyaminyami* I gave you. And for pushing me in."

"Your story and you're sticking to it, huh?"

I hung my head and mugged wry resignation. "Just deserts. Thank God we didn't end up just desserts. With two esses. For crocs."

She rose. She centered her *nyaminyami*, which had pendulumed on its cord. "Mine must have been strong enough for both of us."

"Or had no effect whatsoever."

"Be careful. We've still got a dive ahead of us, in Lake Malawi. And who knows how many rivers to cross."

"Bite my tongue. Disregard anything negative I may have said or implied, Mister Nyaminyami."

She walked toward me, searching my eyes for a moment with an intensity that was unsettling. Her gaze held such unguarded depth and earnestness I almost took a step backwards and demanded suspiciously, defensively, "What!" We almost never exchanged looks like that any more except during sex, so thick were the calluses rubbed by the hurts and humdrum of ongoing marriage. She seemed about to say something. Then she touched my shoulder and gave me a quick, glancing kiss as she twisted the empty glass from my hand.

"But thanks for nothing," she said. "It's the lack of thought that counts."

"Ah," I said. "If you only knew."

"You want a refill?"

"You're not going to have another one."

"Yes I am. They're small, and after this afternoon, I think I have every reason to drink myself into oblivion if I so choose."

"Fine. Might as well hit me again then too, bartender. I take all my cues from you."

"So it would seem," she said.

We barely made it to the restaurant before they'd stopped serving. By the time we'd finished we were the only diners left. Along with our menus we were presented with a bottle of the Stellenbosch chardonnay:

"It is compliments of the managing director, sir," the waiter explained carefully.

Laura had so mellowed she simply commented, "Wow, isn't that nice," instead of subjecting the poor messenger to a grilling on the provenance of the largesse, which he probably couldn't have satisfied anyway.

For my part, I grinned benignly, sniffed the cork—"Ah, definitely cork," I approved—and took the judgmental sip. I've always been an undemanding recipient of freebies.

I had lamb curry over rice. I figured the latter would be good for my questionable stomach. And the curry was bland, although I tried spicing it up with the Major Grey's chutney and *periperi* from among the boys. Uncharacteristically, I left a lot on my plate. I was feeling my drinks, among other things. Laura went ahead and ordered *chambo*—poached, tonight.

"Can't imagine having anything other than fish," she said, "even if I did have it yesterday. Make this a totally aquatic day."

The guides had all eaten earlier, obviously—nor did we see Denys in the bar *chitenje* when we slipped past it on our way to and from dinner.

In fact, we never saw him again.

Leaving the waiters clearing and setting up for breakfast around the guttering fireplace behind us, I did spot Steve across the path, on a stool at the high counter that curved around the bar's huge central *muchenja* tree; he was shaking dice with the French machine-tool salesman we'd had breakfast with that morning.

The usual Mamba suspects were there too, in their own corner: Rory holding court, flanked by Jen, Emma, Gerhard and Mel, all of them bantering and chortling uproariously. Reg was lipping his pipe in silent contentment, warmed by the camaraderie as by a cozy pub fire. Graeme, hair slicked, had pulled up one of the round leather armchairs at Jen's shoulder and sat with a tight grin that was supposed to make him look knowing and suave, though he was obviously lost in the Mamba in-jokes and giggly London gossip that washed past him. Ewan and Nigel humped side by side with their backs to us, almost identical to the perspective I'd had on them in the punt. Ewan's neck and scalp were as red as a stoplight.

There was no sign of Nick or Renée. I imagined them in their cabin, making love. Getting as much use as possible out of its privacy and comfortable bed before they had to strike off into the bush once again.

No surprise, Alistair and Greta, the two recluses, were also absent. One in her cabin, one in his tent, no doubt.

I felt a certain urge to nip inside and join the group for a quick nightcap (though the thought of the nightcap itself made me want to throw up). Outside, looking in, I momentarily longed to assert my membership in that snug coterie, display my personability and vitality, assure all of them that Laura and I were not like Greta or Alistair, that we were neither invincibly odd nor obsolescent. We might be Americans, middle-aged, but we still had youthful *élan*.

Of course, to whom among this assortment I felt a need to prove myself was unclear. Okay, Jen, maybe. Mel, even. Emma, in a fatherly way—show the kids you're not over the hill yet. And Gerhard, I guessed, for some strange male hierarchical reason. And Rory—who reminded me, I now realized, of my long-ago cabinmate on the Norwegian freighter.

But I knew without asking that Laura was in no mood to court commentary on our day's misadventures. And neither, upon a nanosecond's reflection, was I.

No, no, no, indeed.

So we edged to the outside of the bankside path, trying to keep our upper bodies in the riverine darkness above the spray of barlight on the crescent of intervening lawn, walking quickly but not furtively, in case we were glimpsed and hailed.

(One of my pet peeves had always been the marital "we." Both Susan and Laura had the habit of imputing to me, by casual joint assertion, emotions, motives or opinions I didn't recognize or wasn't ready to acknowledge. "Speak for yourself, white woman," I used to growl, variant on an ancient Lone-Ranger-and-Tonto-surrounded-by-hostile-Indians joke. But admittedly there were times when nuanced discussion was unnecessary to gauge and accurately convey one's mate's state of mind.)

We made it to our cabin unnoticed. I braced myself on a post and looked up at the stars. The Southern Cross was masked by trees.

Laura gathered my Luangwa-soiled garments and washed them with hers in the bathroom basin, working up a thin, greasy lather from the miniature bar of hand-soap and hanging them to drip from the shower-rod with the miniature traveler's clothes-pins she'd packed along. We exchanged a perfunctory kiss in bed and rolled back to back.

"Too much, huh?" she sighed after a moment.

I had nothing to contribute to that.

We hadn't had anything overt to dread in the reactions of our fellow travelers, it turned out.

To be sure, there was a moment of good-natured razzing once we were well underway to Nsefu—the sun high, puku and impala dotting the parklands on either side of the road, here and there a distant gray haze and a faint whiff of smoke, sweetly grassy like marijuana. For the most part, though, the wildfires had burnt themselves out or had sputtered away far into the bush beyond our horizons.

We'd departed Chibembe at nine-thirty. While Laura had packed, I'd indulged in a long hot shower—one never knew when one might enjoy the opportunity next, and I was compensating for the previous night's Spartan ordeal.

As my joints loosened, I soaped and scrubbed myself with the lodge-provided washcloth three times, back and front, top and bottom, even between my toes. I shampooed twice. It was prophylaxis, not too belated, I hoped, against any schistosomes that might have glommed onto me in the river. (The microscopic, tadpole-like flukes seek open pores, apparently. And in retrospect, having survived crocodiles, I suspected the flukes were a much realer menace; the Luangwa was just about the picture of the sluggish bilharzia-breeding freshwater sump whose shallows the health-precaution advisories for Africa instruct travelers to stay well away from.)

I had another health concern, too. The ulcer on my shin didn't look good when I peeled off the soggy plastic strip I'd applied the night before—the diameter had grown and the crater was yellowish, with an inflamed border.

I squeezed some more antibiotic ointment on it and left it unbandaged to breathe. I put on a clean pair of khaki shorts, a denim shirt and river sandals—my truck-riding costume. I packed everything else away and we went to breakfast.

None of the Mamba people were there except Greta; she greeted us cordially but excused herself almost as soon as we'd brought our plates of eggs to her table. We recognized only the two young children and two older Afrikaner couples among the few other people in the room. Simon walked by outside but he was in conversation with another black African in a white short-sleeved shirt, a subordinate, I judged, and he didn't glance our way or come in.

We returned to our cabin for a final policing. Gerhard and Mel were chasing each other around the pool one last time as we passed it.

"What a great place," Laura breathed when she stepped out onto the porch and the screendoor slapped shut behind us. She scanned the river. "This'd be worth coming back to someday, huh?"

I squinted into the sun to the upriver bend the hippos frequented. I counted six zebras, a pair of waterbucks, more than a dozen impala and three crocodiles along the opposite bank, working downstream to the point where the Luangwa disappeared behind the westerly mopanis.

"Yep," I said. "Although I might want to do a couple of things differently a second time."

"Really. I can't imagine what those might be."

"For starters," I suggested, "how about flying in?"

"Ooh. You got that right!" She shuddered. "Brrr. I wish you hadn't reminded me!"

She grimaced. "I wonder if we've got more buffalo beans in store for us on the way out?"

"I hope to hell not. It did occur to me that there's a possibility. But I guess we can only cross that... that brr-itch! ...when we come to it."

"Ha-ha. Joke now," she said. "We'll see how much laughing everybody's doing if we do get into 'em again."

She sucked air through her teeth and rapped the porch railing three times with her knuckles.

Uneasy about the reception I might receive, I toted our bags to the truck and ducked quickly aboard to restow them in our allocated underseat bins. Laura draped our still-damp clothes from yesterday over the lip of the upper rack to continue drying until we got underway.

Those who'd been camping had struck their tents. Nick and Rory sat on folding stools in the shade of an *msikisi* with coffee mugs between their feet, filling out logbooks and conferring over the Michelin map. They paid no attention to us.

Renée and most of the others had wandered off to mew goodbyes to Mpamvu, who'd scuffed into the clearing with his equerries—or perhaps more correctly elephanterries—on his morning constitutional.

Laura went to join them. I, feeling surprisingly pain-free for the day-after and eager to prove conspicuously helpful, hoisted myself up the ladder into the viewing cockpit above the cab. Alistair's bald pate was below me and to the rear on the left; towel over his shoulder, he was shaving by the steel mirror affixed to the Bedford's outside bulkhead there. Being frugal, he was a diehard camper; being British of a certain age, he avoided the shower hut. Nigel had been cradling a mug of tea beside the cookfire ashes, and when I'd asked he'd agreed to pitch me up the tent stuffsacks, which were piled on the ground beside the front tire.

"Good job, mates," Rory called with a thumb's-up when I'd arranged everything neatly beneath the overhead seat-lid, replaced the cushion and descended to earth.

I was elated by his praise. I caught Laura's eye and together we walked to the Chibembe office, which opened at nine, to return our key and pay our bar and lodging bills.

The damage was remarkably light. The woman who totted it all up, worked out the currency conversion and ran my credit card through the wringer was the one we'd heard speaking Afrikaans at lunch the day we'd arrived. We chatted briefly and elicited the fact that the children we'd seen then and at breakfast were in fact hers, visiting on holiday from their school in Roodespoort where they stayed with her parents— who were indeed one of the two older couples—when the Chibembe season overlapped the academic year. I was reminded that June is mid-winter in this hemisphere.

She was amicable but without warmth.Performing a duty. She volunteered no information about her husband or her exact position on staff, and neither Laura nor I inquired directly. She supplied us with brochures and answered our questions with an authority that indicated she had some sort of ownership or management role.

"Have you been written up much in the United States, do you know?" Laura asked.

"I believe there was a mention in the... Los Angeles newspaper, was it? Or perhaps it was Texas." She shrugged. "We learnt of it through the E-mail."

"You have E-mail?"

"Oh yes. In the Lusaka office. Zambia's actually quite advanced that way. We have our own ZamNet, on the Internet. Very useful indeed."

"Well, my husband's a public relations type who sometimes does free-lance journalism on the side," Laura said, "and we were thinking that this place would make a great subject for a travel piece, back home, possibly."

I hitched my shoulder and smiled uneasily at Laura's unauthorized disclosures. I didn't want her implying a commitment that I'd follow up on a notion broached casually by the pool the morning before, nor the expectation that anything I might write on spec would in fact end up getting published by anyone.

"We would very much like to have more publicity in America," the woman said. "*Favourable* publicity, of course."

"Well, obviously," Laura agreed. "Would you expect anything other?"

The woman didn't reply.

"I just don't think too many people, in California, anyway, really know about this part of Africa," Laura said. "You always hear about Kenya, and East Africa... *Treetops*, and so on. We've had a *fascinating* time."

"You mean," I proposed to the woman, "about the boy getting eaten by the crocodile."

She tilted her head in equivocal affirmation. "A tragedy," she added after a moment. "But not something we at Zambia Trails had any control of, you realise. It was a village boy. And not precisely 'eaten.'"

I nodded. "We heard all about it," I said. "Adds color, of course."

"We do our *very* best," she said. "Unpleasant events will occasionally transpire despite the *most* arduous efforts of staff. All of our guides have Grade-One licenses, those who lead walking safaris. And every one of them has been with us for at least a previous season conducting night drives, which requires Grade-Two licensure at minimum."

"Which they get how?" I asked. I was already taking mental notes for the piece whose layout in one of the Sunday travel supplements or airline magazines I could envision— embellished by Laura's photographs, or mine, if any survived and were halfway decent.

"We administer quite an extensive examination," the woman replied. "Our experienced people do. Afraid I can't tell you all that it entails. And we screen very thoroughly before we engage our chaps."

"I'm sure you do," I said.

"They've all been very knowledgeable," Laura assured her. "Very competent and attentive. We've been quite impressed."

"I *am* glad to hear you say that. You can appreciate, then, that situations may materialise from time to time whilst guests are in the bush... that are in no way the responsibility of our guides or...." She let the statement trail off. "In any case.... We certainly hope you have found your stay... rewarding."

"Oh, absolutely," Laura declared.

Speak for yourself, white woman, I thought. Because not only had my stay been profoundly *unrewarding*—unless you consider gaining self-knowledge *ipso facto* a boon, no matter that the revelation is that you're a sniveling poltroon who can't even master his excretory functions when a certain virulent phobia is stirred—but now I realized that I, we, were the objects of this woman's veiled mistrust.

She knew perfectly well who we were, she had heard all about our untoward antics yesterday in the Luangwa. Bother the nettlesome subtraction-by-crocodile of some native fisherman from the local populace—what she was talking about, what she was concerned about, was *our contretemps* yesterday on the river. And whether, as a result, we might conceivably be the source of some negative word-of-mouth.

No wonder her lantern jaw was so rigid, her equine upper lip so stiff above an occasional, minimally polite curl. She was simply humoring a pair of manifestly unreliable characters— Americans, operating from who can imagine what deviant agenda—whose proclivities might subsequently spawn dissatisfactions that could turn against the resort.

Or so I read her. I even wondered for a moment if Denys might be in any trouble, for having allowed us to indulge our mischief on his watch. Well, he'd have to fend for himself on that account—I doubted an endorsement from us, beyond Laura's generalized praise, would carry much water. So to speak.

So I did have my back up when we returned to the truck to take our seats among the Mamba entourage for the full day's ride ahead of us.

Past Nsefu, Nick had briefed us, we'd be traveling over what promised on the map—and at least last year had proved—to be a good connecting road to the trans-Zambia highway.

"Think we'll go through any more buffalo beans?" Laura asked.

"Never say never, but less likely," Nick replied. "If it's still in reasonable nick, we'll be on tar-seal most of the way."

Barring unforeseen setbacks, then, he continued, we'd be close enough to Chipata and the Malawi border-crossing by lunchtime for the women to change into their skirts. We were slated to spend the night at a caravan park adjacent to the Lilongwe Golf and Country Club.

As he did on occasion, Rory chose to loll in the breezy back of the Bedford as we retraced the first easy leg from Chibembe to Nsefu. That portended ill, I thought—he'd already teased me about my beard and earlocks during the pre-departure briefing.

"Gonna have to let me take me clippers to y', Danny boy," he'd needled, rubbing his hand demonstratively over his stubbly crown after Nick had outlined the procedures for entering Malawi. "Do you like Nick and Em and me. The Nineties look."

All three, I'd noticed, were freshly mown. Nick and Rory had also shaved closely this morning.

"Never gonna let you in, hidin' under all that shrubbery," he'd warned, grinning.

"I'm from Berkeley," I'd muttered. "This is the way of my people."

"Ah, yeh," he'd laughed, "when they see that on your passport, the game'll be up altogether. Take you for a druggie, no question."

"Says Oakland, actually."

"Time to stop clingin' to that Sixties image, man. Need a fashion makeover. Let the wind blow free on your naked knob."

"It's as naked as I want it to get, thanks. On its own initiative."

He'd winked and pantomimed the action of the clippers. "Not too late to change your mind. I'll be waitin' for you at lunch with me tools at the ready. Bzzzzt."

"No way," I'd glowered.

But I'd worried that he was going to insist, that it was some sort of Mamba initiation ritual I'd eventually have to submit to, like the indignities imposed by King Neptune's Court when one is a Pollywog crossing the equator for the first time aboard ship.

Or maybe real unpleasantness did await me at the customs barrier—and all my companions as well, on my account—if I didn't comply.

For the first half-hour or so everyone was distracted by the excitement of departure and the anticipation of new vistas.

Greta, Alistair and Reg were riding upstairs, as per custom. Various others of us were strung out along the storage-bin tops on either side of the aft compartment, bare legs dandled outboard in the sun, searching the passing *veld* for noteworthy game (the smaller antelopes had become routine features of the landscape) and waving back at the few human figures in the little forest-bound settlements.

Again I noticed several jarringly rectangular prefab bungalows, cynosures of modernism among the neatly thatched mud rondavels in attendance, boasting all the charm and suggesting all the living comforts (minus the plumbing) of what were called here ablution blocks. Public restrooms. A couple had green roofs. I wondered if one of them was Simon's.

"So Laura," I heard at my back finally. "Enjoy your dip in the river yesterday, did you?"

Laura was sitting on the bench below me, behind my right hip, inside the compartment. It was Rory's cheery drawl I'd heard, of course. He lounged across the aisle from her, one leg up on the vinyl cushion, his shoulder against the cab bulkhead, next to but not touching Emma. They were a pair, obviously if incongruously, but they always kept whatever transitory relationship they had playfully shallow in public.

I tensed.

"I did," Laura replied after a hesitation. She'd apparently decided a dumb-show would only prolong the agony.

"What's the problem, Mamba not providin' enough Anxious Moments for you? We must be fallin' down on the job."

"You're doing just fine," Laura said levelly.

"What happened?" Emma asked.

"Laura and Dan took the walking safari yesterday," Rory informed her. "Turned it into a swimming safari, from what I hear."

I'd angled my head to better catch, and with covert shifts of gaze observe, the conversation.

"Really," Emma said. She flared her eyebrows inquisitively at Laura.

"Your guide said he about shat his pants," Rory continued. "Guy Denys it was, hey? Didn't fancy havin' his clients splashin' about amongst the crocs. According to Jen's pal Graeme last night."

"My pal," Jen objected sarcastically. She'd swiveled inward from her perch on the opposite shelf at mention of her name. "Whyever were you swimming in the river?" she asked Laura.

"I fell in," Laura admitted. "Stupidly. We were in a boat crossing on our way back home, and there were these two hippos fighting along the shore and I half-stood up to get a better picture and the boat tipped and I lost my balance. That's all."

"Oh, gosh!" Jen sympathized.

Mel, sitting to my left, exclaimed appreciatively, "Hippos fighting!" She was playing footsie over the side with Gerhard, who was next to her at the end of our outboard row. "Why is it *I* never see things like that?"

"Did your camera go in the water also?" Gerhard inquired.

"*Oh* yeah!" Laura nodded.

"It's all right, or not?"

"Who knows? We'll find out," Laura said.

"It was me shoved her in," Ewan piped up. He sat at the end of Laura's bench next to the rear door, whose top half was latched open. Renée half-reclined across the aisle from him in her favorite position already, a pillow propping her neck and shoulders, both bare feet up on the seat and a book cradled against her perfect thighs.

"Couldnay stop m'self," Ewan continued, "when she touched m' shoulder, what with the sun. Woulnay blame y' for givin" me a doing, Laura. I was daft to go and get so burnt. You as warned me, and then...."

"It wasn't your fault, Ewan," Laura declared. "I told you."

He bowed his rubicund face.

I waited for Laura to pad out the comfort she'd extended him, to level the blame at me.

Neither Ewan nor Nigel, I now understood, had said a word. The latter was peering at the countryside from the shelf across the aisle—his expression inscrutable, perhaps a smile, maybe just a squint against the brightness—willfully oblivious to what was being discussed behind him. Hard to imagine, but our two withdrawn accountants had apparently found no reason to share their interesting experiences on the walking safari throughout all the course of last night's group carousal. Could they be uneasy about their own passivity?

Whatever, had it not been for some aside between Graeme and Rory, no one else on the truck would ever have twigged, apparently, to Laura's flop and my funk.

"So how'd you come to join her, then, Dan?" Rory persisted.

My heart beat guiltily. I rehearsed answers.

"Seemed like a good idea at the time," I repeated finally. I shrugged. "Monkey see, monkey do."

"Oh, he was going to save me," Laura declared in an exasperated tone. "He thought I needed help. Rescue me from drowning. Fight off the crocodiles or whatever. He was going to hold their mouths shut, I believe was the idea. Or offer his arm as an *hors d'oeuvre*. I forget which."

"That was quite gallant of you, Daniel!" Renée said.

I couldn't tell whether the tone was ironic.

"It really wasn't all that anxious a moment," Laura insisted. "Maybe it should've been. But basically I just felt silly and wanted to get out of the water as quickly as I could. It wasn't that deep. Only for a minute when one of the guides took a couple of shots at crocodiles around us did I consider that there might be danger. *That was* a scary part."

"Jeepers. Shots? At crocodiles?" Emma marveled.

"Apparently," Laura nodded. "What we were told. I never actually saw any, thank God. At least while we were in the river."

"Oi, I'd've wet meself," Mel goggled. "Glad we didn't go on one of them, then."

"It wasn't a big deal," Laura insisted. "All's well that ends well, anyway, right?"

"*There's* a highlight you'll remember," Renée grinned. "And good on *you*, Daniel! Chivalry is not dead yet, eh? Nick should hear this...."

"Hyenas," Gerhard interrupted.

Everyone turned to follow his finger.

And so that was that. I didn't have to lie, I didn't have to stammer and parry. Reticence became me. Silence suggested modesty, suggested something to be modest about. (Oh, I had plenty to be modest about, as they say.) It suggested a gest, suggested wellsprings of strength and resolve. I came away with a certain cachet.

At least that was my sense. Renée, after all, had publicly dubbed me *gallant*—be still my beating heart. But maybe I was just relieved that nobody was sneering or spitting at me.

Whatever uptick in image I may have enjoyed certainly didn't alter the day-to-day of our factitious fellowship as we rode and read and bantered and stopped to pee and sightsaw and photographed and camped and cooked and ate and washed and flapped our way across the Warm Heart of Africa.

(In fact, we had found, a democratized Malawi had relaxed its old Puritanical strictures out of eagerness to attract more foreign tourists. The country, which had been the only black nation to maintain relations with South Africa under *apartheid*, had taken to billing itself "The Warm Heart of Africa." Our border crossing was uneventful, the document perusal perfunctory, the visual search of the storage bins and undercarriage of the truck cursory. None of the soldiers who eyed us sitting apprehensively in the back made a peep about my beard or grooming.)

In Lilongwe, Laura and I replenished our supply of gin and vermouth at a small Western-style supermarket. Then we ambled, fascinated, through the city's central market, itself carefully departmentalized: beans, tomatoes, potatoes, onions, cabbage, bananas and plaintains of amazing variety mounded artistically by their vendors, mostly women, each in distinct sections; an even larger and more fancifully displayed selection of whole dried fish—*chambo, mlamba, usipa, kampango*, the white-shirted men who stood over them were happy to differentiate—stiff silver bodies painstakingly interleaved in three-dimensional circular, helical, tic-tac-toe and herringbone patterns; ground corn, cassava and other meals in a range of grit sizes; the whole bounded by neat heaps of auto parts and gutted appliance innards; the air pulsing with the rhythms of African pop being demoed by young men selling tape cassettes and the percussive clangor of hammers on scrapmetal as the tinsmiths in their corner of the market shaped new pots and pails on the spot.

At Cape Maclear we set up on a sandy beach, under chattering palms. We drank *Carlsberg Special Brew* on the verandah of a crumbling building that had once been a private villa, its rooms converted to accommodate a dive shop, a dormitory for backpackers, a seedy bar, smelly toilets and moldy showers without hot water.

We watched the sun sizzle scarlet into Lake Malawi while tourists who'd driven up from Zimbabwe and South Africa irately scampered after vervets fleeing with plundered valuables. (One poor distraught couple's car keys.) We had *chambo* for dinner. While others, swam, sunned or hiked next day, Nick, Renée, Laura and I rented snorkel and SCUBA gear and spent hours winding through rocky underwater canyons in pursuit of flitting schools of yellow or blue-and-white-striped cichlids. And each morning at her invitation I nestled my foot on Renée's lap and let her caress my shin—tenderly frowning and dabbing at my insistent little ulcer, sprinkling antiseptic powder from her medical kit into it and deftly redressing it with sterile gauze.

Pathology hath itth privilegeth.

On the Zomba Plateau, up a steep road past old Dr. Banda's palatial summer retreat, we pitched our tents in a lush meadow among tall evergreens. At night we hiked by starlight—6,000 feet above sea level, temperature 9 degrees centigrade (48 degrees Fahrenheit), heavily sweatered and breathing sharp puffs of vapor into the chill—to the cozy KuChawe Hotel. There Laura taught the barman how to mix martinis.

(After pouring the Booth's over the Noilly Prat, he reached into his bowl of Maraschino cherries. "Oh, no, nothing sweet!" Laura recoiled. "Ah. Zest of remon?" he proposed, revealing his expertise and his native Chichewa-speaker's characteristic conflation of English "*l*"'s and "*r*"'s. Later he thanked Laura for expanding his repertoire and showed us on a cocktail napkin how to write Malawi properly, with a little roof over the "w" to signify a sound in Chichewa that also has a hint of "*v*" in it.)

We ate another high-spirited, Mamba-paid group meal in the hotel's restaurant. Before bed Laura heated a rock in the campfire and wrapped it in a towel to tuck into the foot of her sleeping bag. The grass was glazed with frost when we woke.

After breakfast Laura and I made picnic sandwiches and set out for a fern-shadowed creek whose riffles and pools I searched for flickers of trout. I was disappointed to spy none, until we came on a government hatchery upstream where we were told that someone with an unexplained grudge had recently dumped poison into the water.

We continued higher, following signs toward an outlook at the apex of the plateau, along a dirt logging road, through stands of conifers ribboned for future felling. The air had a wintry bite, the sky was slate gray, wisps of fog floated in the treetops. Bulbous crimson *amanita muscaria* mushrooms poked through the duff beneath huge, prehistoric-looking softwoods with segmented trunks, like a cross between bamboo and redwood. In fact, it felt as if we were on the Mendocino coast, perhaps during the Late Permian. The elevated, lake-influenced microclimate was utterly unlike anything we would have associated with Africa.

As were the views when we reached the edge of the escarpment, out across a dappled plain 2,500 feet below, to the tea-planted massif of the Shire Highlands and majestic Mount Mulanje jutting 10,000 feet into the distant clouds.

At Senga Bay, the last stop, we loaded up on souvenirs.

While I stood by bored, in desultory chat with the two 13-year-old boys who'd relentlessly attached themselves to us as "guides," Laura prowled roadside stalls haggling over ornately carved wooden bowls, salad utensils, Africanized Nativity figurines, chess and *bao* sets (throughout Lilongwe we'd seen men hunched over these egg-carton-like wooden gameboards, hands a blur of practiced strategy as they dipped up and distributed dried beans among the two rows of shallow *bao* cups).

With my approval Laura bought a pair of narrow-backed, two-piece, portable Malawi tripod chairs incised with leopards rampant, elephants passant and big-eared impala regardant. They were skillfully wrapped in brown paper and snugged with twine for carriage on a airplane.

And she commissioned an artisan to make a mask for us like those we'd seen decorating the bar of the Livingstonia Beach Hotel, where we were staying. It was delivered to us there that night in a paper bag—a fearsome, horse-faced apparition roughly hewn from a huge blackened bole, with glittering tinfoil eyes, snaggly chips of ivory-like plastic teeth, flowing strips of rags in muted colors for hair, and a crown of bloody, fresh-plucked seagull feathers.

Cheesy? Not a bit. The gaunt visage was frightening. It took us aback.

"Do not ret anyone outside the gate see this one," the messenger hissed nervously. "It is too powerful."

We knew what he meant. It was both appalling and thrilling, stern but menacing—a true masterpiece of folk art.

Everyone except the die-hard budget camper—Alistair, Reg, Ewan and Nigel—had rented a room at the hotel to decompress after three weeks on the road. Mamba had negotiated a half-price deal, so Laura and I popped for a luxurious detached rondavel of white-washed stucco with pole beams and a thatched roof, shaded by palms and mopanis at the end of a landscaped brick walkway between the hotel's pool and a private swatch of manicured lakefront sand.

"I've always *wanted* to stay in a rondavel," Laura exulted when we entered the circular room. "My mother told me her parents lived in one of these once."

Of course, theirs probably hadn't had a tiled floor, a capacious bathroom attached, maid service, and a wide, firm bed in which we were lulled all night by the romantic crash of surf driven ashore off the lake by a keening wind.

Stephen and Kumbo, the two local boys who'd adopted us like ox-peckers despite our protestations—they settled at our elbows within moments of our venturing outside the walled hotel grounds, day or night—coaxed us to visit a fishing village perched on a sandspit between a shallow backwater lagoon and the wave-swept open lake.

The gale was slackening but it had kept the painted dugouts ashore that morning. Men were darning nets or tending racks of drying fish while women stirred cooking pots or nursed babies and children dashed in and out of the surf. Smoke rose, laundry flapped, gulls wheeled. From a distance it looked like a mirage, or a scene from some George Lucas movie about a sand-and-water planet.

From within, as Stephen and Kumbo led us along the bustling strand between the line of wattle shelters and the prows of the beached pirogues, it *felt* as if we were on a film set. This was just too colorful, too picturesque, too makeshift, and too accepting a community; the people went about their domestic business with no more than a quick smile or a nod of friendly acknowledgement when our glances impinged on theirs. They might have been a cast assembled by the Malawi Tourist Board and directed to act blasé as the two white strangers strolled in their midst.

Later, of course, Stephen and Kumbo hit us up for payment for their services. They wanted 100 *kwacha*, an outrageous sum. I agreed to 20, still generous by comparison to what that would buy from a woodcarver down the road.

One is always confronted by this sort of moral dilemma in Third World countries. The poverty is disturbing. Everything is cheap by American standards—even the first wildly inflated price the seller throws out to begin negotiations would be easily affordable. But dickering is *de rigueur*. And to pay too much reveals one as a mark, a fool to be despised, and to be badgered mercilessly from there on out by other hucksters and beggars. Not to mention that it destabilizes the local economy.

How bad would it be, though, I thought, to inject a little chaos into this agora—personally help nudge ask-and-bid closer to parity with First World market levels? I should worry if the next bargain-hunting American or German or French tourist is inconvenienced?

On the other hand, to reward these boys too lavishly out of charity simply because they'd spent a few hours walking and chattering beside us uninvited would be to devalue the hard work of Malawi's honest artisans and merchants. Wouldn't it?

I told Stephen and Kumbo to wait at the gate, went back to my room and returned with a clean pair of athletic socks and a tee shirt to sweeten the deal. I also had them write their names and addresses ("c/o Senga-Bay F.P. School") in my notebook, a couple of warped pages along from where the ink of James's had soaked through. (His original ballpoint inscriptions remained legible, I'd been relieved to find.)

Idling with our accumulating spoils while Laura shopped, I'd asked the boys if they played football.

Oh yes, they'd declared. Kumbo, the smaller, said he was a midfielder; the more aggressive Stephen, in character, boasted that he was a striker and always scored many, many goals. But they had never in their lives, he added wistfully, played with a real ball.

I believed him, although I suspected he was angling for a donation, and I doubted it would end up benefiting local youth soccer. I resolved, when I got home, to visit the sporting goods store where I'd outfitted Chris and Megan from U-8 to U-16 when they'd scuffled for the Grizzlies, the Bay Oaks and the Mavericks; I'd buy a regulation ball and send it in Stephen and Kumbo's name to the Senga-Bay F.P. School.

(I did. Stephen wrote me back to thank me on the team's behalf, not neglecting to mention that they'd be even more effective in passing the new ball if they had uniforms to help them distinguish the sides. I didn't reply.)

A motorboat trip to tiny Bird Island was the final scheduled highlight.

Ewan, of course, was not among us, nor was Alistair. We dived off rocks, cruised in facemasks above lazing cichlids, eyed the monitor lizards that, with eponymous cormorant colonies, were the island's only inhabitants.

A couple of double-ended dugouts like those we'd seen at the sandspit village landed men who were probably looking for eggs.

That night Rory arranged a farewell dinner at a tiny restaurant called the "Top Hill." It sat in a low spot by the road. We'd passed it on our way to and from the market stalls.

The one-room, mud-brick structure was pitch-dark when we arrived. It had no electricity. Nor was there a kitchen. But the proprietor, whom Rory introduced as Peter, welcomed us ardently and lit a candle to reveal the room's only two tables pushed together to accommodate our banquet party.

Squatting over a paraffin campstove on the back-door stoop, Peter's assistant, an ebullient boy of about twelve named Gordon, handed in platters of fried *chambo*, chicken (primarily for Ewan, who'd firmly declared that he didn't eat fish), chips, rice, cabbage salad, and fried bananas for dessert. There was *periperi* and plenty of *Carlsberg*.

Nick and Renée hadn't come, but Rory had brought a couple of bottles of wine too.

Peter found a railroad lantern to supplement the candle, and we crowded shoulder to shoulder inside the halo of light, our giant caricature shadows bobbing on the bare walls, awkwardly bumping elbows, passing things, pouring for one another, comparing booty and coups scored on the day's shopping forays, reminiscing about the past three weeks, and exchanging last toasts.

"To the U.S.A. synchronized swim team," Rory proposed when it was our turn. "Show Laura and Dan a body of water and these two'll be rehearsin' a routine with the fishes and the crocs faster 'n you can say '*nyaminyami*.'"

"Hip hip," Gerhard seconded.

"Cheers," everyone acknowledged.

"Maybe we ought to say, 'Here's to *Nyaminyami!*'" Laura offered.

She lifted the amulet out of the vee of her collar for display.

"Give credit where it's due," she said. "I know Ewan's got one, and his has served him well. Never got a drop of water on him... did you, Ewan? And I survived my harrowing plunge into the Luangwa. Daniel lost his, so he had to jump in with me, as penance."

"And I drowned, unfortunately," I muttered.

"Hip hip," Gerhard said. He fished the little blue-gray stone out of his tee-shirt neck and held it up in emulation of Laura. "This is a good one too."

There was general laughter. Ewan, Emma and Mel waggled their pendants in turn, chorusing "cheers" and sipping from their bottles or glasses.

"Nyaminyami, he's our man," I offered. "If he can't do it, no goddy can."

Those who heard regarded me with incomprehension.

Stephen, Kumbo and the other children who hung out at the hotel gate to wheedle *kwacha* or ingratiate themselves as guides and factotums had trooped along with us to the restaurant. They clustered in the darkness at the doorways and windows watching us eat, shushed and shooed away periodically by Peter. Indefatigably they returned. Now as the party was breaking up they entreated us to come with them to a nearby compound to see a big dance that, they said, was being held there. Or for a small fee could be arranged.

The indefiniteness, the late hour, our satiety and Rory's warning that we'd have to walk nearly a mile uphill through the darkness damped everyone's enthusiasm.

All right then, the kids announced, *they* would dance for us.

The lantern was taken outside and in its feeble glow the children—perhaps half a dozen boys in well worn shorts and sportshirts, as many girls, taller, wearing loose print shifts—formed a circle and began beating sticks on canisters and pans, clapping, singing, stamping and shuffling.

Laura and I had paid admission to sit in bleachers and watch bravura tribal dances—Shona, Ndebele, Ngoni—performed by a costumed native troup at a "cultural arts centre" in Victoria Falls. Thi certainly didn't measure up on the anthropological exotica index to Emma's Masai wedding. The little kids in their Gap-outlet clothes, the fluting, uncertain voices, the swaying, hip-swiveling, shoulder-dipping body language were exactly what I might have seen through the chainlink fence of any inner-city schoolyard in Oakland where a boombox was playing.

Chris, Megan or Lisa, who'd all grown up with black friends, could have mirrored the movements effortlesly, given a Carlsberg or two as solvent for ethnic deference. So could Laura, for that matter. These kids were plainly working from the traditional local fakebook, however—they would suggest, confer, giggle, start in haltingly and then pick up the beat and refrain at the lead, usually, of one or another of the older girls. The three drummers, none of whom looked to be more than eight or nine years old, elaborated expertly contrapuntal rhythms on their contrived instruments.

The pure joy of the entertainers was infectious. Like the mask we'd just bought, this improvised show had an authenticity that sprang from its very corruption. The mask was moving because its incorporation of the ordinary was artful; the dance was touching because it was artless. But far from innocent. This was an entrepreneurial undertaking, Rory informed us. We were each expected to ante a few *kwacha*.

It was the last night and I emptied my pocket.

The children were still going at it when Laura and I snuck away for the peace of our beachfront rondavel.

And that was our safari.

Laura, not the world's most enthusiastic volunteer for the healing ministry, changed the bandage on my leg next morning. She wrinkled her nose and sneered but managed not to gag.

What with all the immersions, the wound had never scabbed—it was almost an inch in diameter now, sweating lymph and pus, radiating streaks of inflammation, vaguely throbbing.

I swallowed one of the antibiotic capsules Renée had decided a few days ago I should be taking (Floxapen 250, according to the label, from Elite Pharmaceutical Limited, Dispensing and Veterinary Chemists, Nairobi; for all I knew, this was a horse drug).

Then we dressed in our overseas traveling clothes, paid the hotel bill and boarded the Bedford for the final ride.

R eg was the apotheosis. The epitome. When Laura walked over to him with her remaining pen and the list she was compiling on a fresh page torn from the legal pad in which she'd been keeping a desultory travel diary, he wordlessly shook his head.

"Oh, I've got everybody else's now," she said lightly. As if that would alleviate his reluctance. "I'm gonna have copies made, and then I'll send you one, when we get home. You know, because some people thought it might be nice to be able to keep in touch."

Reg shook his head again.

"Really," Laura said, taken aback. "You don't want to give me...?"

"Not interested," he muttered dourly.

Laura flared her eyebrows but didn't argue.

X. *Kwacha* and Pens

Before rising from the table at the Top Hill we'd all burbled fondly about exchanging addresses. But somehow, not surprisingly, we'd never gotten around to it.

Now, in the glassed-in mezzanine transit lounge overlooking the ticket counters on the main floor of Kamuzu International Airport, Laura had taken it upon herself to act as group secretary. And everyone except Reg had readily scribbled a home address on her proffered notepad.

Still, whatever unit cohesiveness we might once have felt was now distinctly dissipated... filtered out as we scattered to pass one by one, with more or less tedious, worrisome scrutiny, through the sieve of Malawi immigration and customs control booths, to reassemble here in wait for our British Airways flight.

As soon as we'd walked through the door of the terminal each of us had embarked on his or her private itinerary.

Dispersed about the sterile lounge, Gerhard, Ewan and Marguerite now crouched distractedly over their luggage, fussing at last-minute repackings; Alistair and Reg sat apart on banquettes cocooned in stolid silences; Nigel paced; Emma—in a perky mini-dress and stylishly clunky shoes whose heels shaped her legs to arresting advantage (I felt something of the same carefully modulated appreciation aroused by Megan and Lisa when they displayed their voluptuous bodies at the beach or tarted up for evenings out)—was fretting to Jen and Melody about the reaction she'd get from her parents when they saw her shaved head.

Renée and Nick had appeared briefly, then vanished....

Nick hadn't taken any chances. The plane we'd all be on was scheduled to depart at 6:50 p.m., but he got us to Lilongwe by early afternoon. He parked the truck in the downtown mini-mall at whose tiny supermarket Laura and I had bought gin a week before, and he and Rory went away somewhere with the cashbox, logbooks and documents to complete the official change of command.

It was a Saturday. The parking lot was thronged by souvenir vendors and the sorts of Calcuttan beggars we'd encountered nowhere else: a wizened man without legs, a torso crudely shelved on plywood and casters, knuckle-walking frenetically back and forth below the rear door of the truck; a child with flippers instead of limbs (were the pharmaceutical companies still dumping their last stocks of Thalidomide in Africa?); another whose flesh and bones had been melted together grotesquely by fire, apparently—all entreating us for *kwacha*.

I had none left. Fortunately. These direct appeals, these calculated claims on pity—especially backed by the ragged entourages who ringed the unfortunates and studied our reactions expectantly—were extremely off-putting.

Renée had instructed us to ignore them.

"G'wan, get away," she'd shooed the beggars from the ladder as she'd lowered it.

Even so, one man had clambered up to flaunt his handless arm inside the door at us. The stump was pink, like a palm, the flesh tucked around the bone the way a tortilla is folded at the ends of a burrito.

"Here, stop that!" Renée had scolded. "Off with you, off!"

Since I'd observed her respect and sensitivity toward the people of the bush, I recognized her attitude as tough love, not mere callousness. In part she was simply enforcing the rule that safari trucks are off-limits to outsiders except by rare invitation. Otherwise a lot of loose—and not so loose—objects would vanish within quick fingers. But she was also acting in corollary to her and Nick's policy of forbidding their white First World passengers the lordly amusement of raining cheap candy and balloons on black Third World children.

At home I'd always found it hard to pass up a paper cup or an outstretched palm and a polite request for spare change. There but for the grace of God *et cetera*. I even apologized when what I dug up with my pocket-lint was only a dime, a nickel or two, a few pennies. And I didn't require gratitude. The money might go to buy crack, or malt liquor. All I wanted was the satisfaction of thinking I'd acted voluntarily.

Several California cities have tried to protect the tender sensibilities of their affluent citizens by legislating alms-seekers off the streets. The good voters of Berkeley contented themselves merely with outlawing "aggressive panhandling."

Malawi was one of the 15 poorest countries in the world, I'd read. The per capita income came to about $200 a year. The national healthcare budget was $11 per person annually. Nearly one in four newborns would die before the age of five.

So there couldn't be much of a social safety net. Nevertheless, I wondered, was there nothing for these poor wretches but to trade with such confrontational abjection on their infirmities? Rubbing our noses, as it were, in their tragic lots? *Passive* aggression, for sure.

I was relieved I could spread my hands, shrug and with clear conscience excuse myself.

"No *kwacha*. No *kwacha*. Sorry."

But Laura still had some in her fanny-pack. So after a stint of guard duty on the truck we went to check out an ice cream shop that Jen and Mel, who were replacing us in turn, gleefully reported they'd discovered a few blocks away.

Was there an irony here somewhere?

The place was reminiscent of a McDonald's—high-ceilinged and sterile, with a back kitchen visible behind railed counters where you stepped up to order from a large overhead plastic menu with garish pictures of the food.

Most of the entrees shown were Chinese. There was also an unappetizingly plain-looking hamburger, chips, and various ice cream concoctions.

Laura paid the Asian woman at the cash register for a small chocolate sundae, which we shared at a table under an umbrella on a grassy outdoor patio with a white-painted central gazebo. The ice cream was good—the first distinctly American specialty we'd eaten since leaving home and a kind of concession to, or preparation for, our imminent re-entry.

Laura had only a couple of spoonfuls. She was very quiet.

I assessed the other customers—several European expat parents, or maybe diplomats on station, giving their children a Saturday treat; a huge, multi-generational East Indian family group; a young Chinese couple; a few prosperously dressed Africans.

We walked over to the Lilongwe Hotel to use the clean restrooms. In the gift shop I thumbed through the latest issue of *Time*. It had also been three weeks since I'd read or heard any news of the world. No great detriment, as usual. There were photos of civilian atrocities committed in the latest African wars, to the north.

We saw Gerhard, Reg and Nigel at a table in the hotel coffee shop.

Laura had been in a nervous pet all morning. I could count on that on major-travel days. She was constantly reminding me to do this or that, issuing commands, reflexively nagging as we packed and readied ourselves for twenty-eight hours in flight.

On the road in from Senga Bay, Melody had pushed the buzzer for a loo stop, our last in the bush. (The women were in their skirts or frocks, the roadside vegetation was sparse and I was reminded of the first time I'd seen women pee in that charmingly basic, quite modest way. I was in Kaohsiung, aboard the Norwegian freighter, taking cigarette breaks at the rail and looking down admiringly on the hostesses who would emerge periodically in pairs from a dockside bar to hunker on the quay and chat. They were young, pretty, invariably crouched in that stereotypical Oriental posture as they conversed... and my 21-year-old hormones had fizzed and I'd been filled with wild surmise when I'd suddenly realized what it meant that the bargirls always left behind little puddles.)

When Laura returned and stood with me waiting to reboard the truck she'd suddenly demanded, "You *do* have the plane tickets, right?"

"Better hope so," I'd replied indignantly.

"I mean you didn't leave 'em at the hotel...."

"Better hope not."

"...Because I saw 'em on the bed just before we went out the door."

"Yes. So I'd be sure to put 'em in with my passport and stuff, in my carry-on bag."

"Did you?"

"Isn't it a little late to ask?"

"I just remember Japan. When you had our tickets where they were 'safe.'" Her voice dripped sarcasm. "I don't want to go through that again."

"*You* want to keep 'em? Or I'll give you yours right now."

"No, I just don't want to be embarrassed at the airport. Cooling my heels while you unpack and rummage through everything again. I don't want to miss our flight."

"You won't."

"That's what you said in Tokyo."

"And you didn't miss it, did you?"

"No, but it was a near thing. You have a way...."

"Oh, shut up," I'd silenced her wearily.

I might have known such an indiscretion wouldn't be allowed to fade without requital. Now as we headed back to the truck and the beggars, I scratched open Laura's festering grievance with, ironically, a conciliatory gesture.

We came upon a patch of buckled pavement and I tried to take her hand.

More often than not it was she who initiated hand-holding—the one sustained public display of affection she liked. Not this time.

Wordlessly she jerked her arm away.

"Excuse me?" I said.

"Let's just keep it nice and simple," she snapped. "You go about your business and I'll go about mine."

"Ah. Okay.... I guess."

I'd sensed the chill, the remoteness of the companionship she'd been extending. But I'd all but forgotten the underlying wound. Her ambush was successful.

"Whatever that means," I added.

"That means I'll be perfectly civil as long as we're in people's company, but I don't want you sitting next to me when we're on the truck again, and as soon as we get to the airport I'm gonna make sure our seats aren't together on the plane. Frankly, I've realized I'm sick and tired of being anywhere near you."

"Gee, that's nice."

"You're tired of me too," she said plaintively. "We've been cheek-by-jowl day and night for three weeks. It's too much. We've gotten on each other's nerves. It was too much togetherness."

"You haven't gotten on *my* nerves. Most of the time."

"'Shut up,' you told me...."

"Ah, yes. Four hours ago, in Senga Bay. I misspoke."

"That's completely beyond the pale...."

"I meant, 'Would you drop it, please?' You can be very annoying sometimes, Laura, you know that? When you get all obsessive and distrustful, patronizing? You were doing it to me all morning. I *have* the tickets. But you insisted on dredging up all this ancient baggage...."

"Then you ought to be very happy not to have to put up with my annoying company for much longer."

"You're not annoying. Not now. Or at least you weren't up until a minute ago."

"Well I will be. You can count on it."

"Oh, I do," I bristled. "Do I ever."

"I count on *nothing* from you, I'll tell you that. And I'm never disappointed."

"Ah. Cute. Bitch."

"Just keep away from me," she hissed. Her face raddled. "From now on. I mean it."

"Gee, I'm sorry. I thought we were married or something."

"That can be rectified. And don't worry, I intend to."

"Fine with me. Although it seems a *teensy-weensy* bit of an overreaction."

"After I've been told, 'Shut up?' Called 'bitch...?'"

"'You always hurt the one you love.'"

"In your case, for sure. Where's the love? If that's love, give me... whatever. We certainly don't have it."

"I'm sorry I said 'shut up' to you," I allowed.

"*Kwacha?* Prease, sir, give me *kwacha?*"

Three children stood against a wall and as we passed the tallest stuck out his hand.

"No *kwacha*," I told him curtly. I broke stride to pat my pockets and show him my open palms.

He grinned.

Laura had hastened her pace while I was distracted. She was now a few yards ahead of me.

"Come on, Laura," I reasoned after her. "I'm sorry I called you the 'bee' word too. I was just lashing out. Lashing back."

She didn't acknowledge.

I wasn't going to abase myself pleading for forgiveness. Get down and start knee-walking. I did have a bad conscience. There are bounds of respect, and I'd violated them indulging my anger. Although in a perverse way what I'd done had been a function of love.

This was hardly the first time—though possibly the last—that I'd allowed myself to spit out really nasty, nitty-gritty insults and vilification at her, provocations I'd never tax a stranger to tolerate, in the confidence that I'd ultimately be forgiven. Or to test the proposition. Tweak the elasticity and durability of the bond.

Certainly Chris and Megan had tried *me*. Susan had tried me. Lisa was a model child, but she'd had her moments. Isn't that what parents are for? Wives, husbands as well? Your family are the people who're supposed to love you even if you're a total shit. What the song says. Even Susan's affair had probably had an element of testing in it. If I'd been less hot-tempered, less insecure in my male dignity at that age....

But I'd met Laura, and then it was too late to mend the rip.

As for Laura's liaisons, she'd covered any tracks so thoroughly I couldn't be sure I wasn't just paranoid. Or resigned, guilty over my own two brief, conflicted moments of infidelity, conjuring a pay-back that seemed both in character and deserved.

I believed Laura loved me. But her love had a different quality from mine. It was flintier. I railed and threw foul-mouthed, squealy tantrums—soft, baby behavior, begging to be pardoned. She challenged *my* allegiance by going hard, cold, aloof, impervious. Pardon was beside the point.

Her emotional life was anthracitic, mine bituminous. I burned hot and dirty. She gave off almost no smoke at all. But she sure knew how to set me alight.

So. The marriage was over. Yes it was. Done, dead, here on a broken sidewalk in Lilongwe, Malawi. Sudden, to be sure, but the culmination of hundreds upon hundreds of aggravations. I might have been in the wrong this time, but I'd made overtures. I'd apologized. Only to be rebuffed.

Who could live with such a bitch? Such a self-righteous scold? Wringing a concession from her that she'd played any part whatsoever in straining my patience would be like distilling water from a lump of anthracite.

She was a bitch, all right. Not politically correct any more to use that term, but a spade's a spade. Queen of Spades. *Reine des Piques*. Pique, pique, pique... always pickin' at me....

I imagined us tensely avoiding each other on the plane.

Planes, rather. Terminals. Here, Harare, Heathrow, SFO. Grim, grim ordeal ahead of us, no question.

Maybe I'd get lucky. Sit next to an attractive successor *en route*. A bit younger, svelter, less moody, more giving than Laura—somebody like Renée, perhaps.

I pictured a woman with a soft pageboy that brushed the nape of her neck. Natural ash-blond with just the first glints of grey. Fortyish. Someone who'd finally, truly appreciate my wonderfulness. We'd chat, strike unmistakeable sparks, accidentally brush hands, laugh nervously.

By then I'd have managed to screw the gold ring off my third finger. Use lavatory soap to work it over the knuckle that was permanently enlarged from basketball jammings.

We would exchange names and phone numbers before leaping up together to retrieve our carry-ons from the overhead bin after landing. I'd have to give her my office phone, come to think of it.

Take a taxi or BART from SFO. Lisa was supposed to be picking us up. Let Laura do the explaining.

I'd check into... the Claremont or something. Some more or less convenient hotel.

Bleak room, start apartment-hunting immediately. Gruesome prospect. Prospects. Arrange to remove my suits, ties, shirts, shoes from the closet at home—ex-home. Empty my bureau drawers. Divvy up possessions. Boxed books, sheets, few small appliances, basic furniture. All my tools. A whole house, a lifetime's accumulations, to dispose of.

Hell, I'd let her keep most of it. Been there, done that. All kinds of stress and turmoil. But also a sense of relief. New possibilities. Free at last. Watch television in my underwear, guzzle beer surrounded by empty pizza boxes, jack off to the tits and tufts I could make out in scrambled pay-per-view porn... callooh-callay!

Already I could feel the emptiness in the pit of my gut that I'd gone around with for months after I'd left Susan. Perforating ulcer of perforated love.

We'd had a nice run, Laura and I. But all good things must come to a bad end. Or something like that.

At least this time there were no small children to take into account. No little lives to buffet and mar ineradicably. Easy come, easy go.

The whole thing was ridiculous. It was a game Laura and I played: "As If," I called it.

Maybe that was one reason we were suited to each other— we were both slightly manic-depressive. Bipolar, in the new parlance. That's a clinical term for given to living too imaginatively in the moment. Or at least too fully in its mood.

This was one of the few places we'd traveled to recently where Laura hadn't started cruising residential neighborhoods, visiting the nearest college campus to check out the administration building, reading through the job ads in the newspaper for both of us—excitedly acting as if we were relocating there.

(One of the attractions of a Mamba Safari was that it engaged us in foraging off the land, so to speak, at least tangentially experiencing the Africans' everyday Africa.)

When Laura and I had a quarrel, some escalating clash of opinion at the dinner table, we tended to wallow in the betrayal it represented. Here was appalling proof of the other's banality, obduracy and bad faith; *ipso facto,* any further relationship with a person of such fundamentally flawed character was untenable. One or the other of us would storm out of the house.

Our spats didn't reach that pass invariably, of course—just three or four times a year.

When I'd still had the *Bear,* I'd spent nights in my sleeping bag in its cramped cabin. A couple of times Laura had failed to return until next morning, and refused to tell me where she'd found refuge. I imagined the worst, of course.

Mostly, though, we screeched out of the driveway, drove off our immediate rage within a few blocks, maybe ran an errand at the drug store or the supermarket or prowled a bookstore to prolong the other's uncertainty, then sullenly marched back inside to claim our rightful share of the community property until morning, when arrangements for its division could more conveniently be finalized.

Never go to bed angry, couples are counseled.

"There were times," I'd read one wag quoted on his Golden Wedding anniversary, "when my wife and I stayed awake for weeks."

Laura and I took the opposite tack. For us, sleep— occasionally one or the other self-marooned on a couch but more often territorially huddled in our separate hollows in the queen-size mattress, painstakingly not touching—proved a great reconciler.

By morning the edge of dissatisfaction had been dulled. It was a new moment, distractingly routine: bathroom bustle, gulped coffee, pretense that everything was back to okay if Lisa put in an appearance. And pretense is the mother of intention.

Later there'd be punctilious conversation over the telephone, office to office; kernels of viability in the relationship would hint at a presence.

Cocktail hour would bring us face to face. There'd be stiff-backed acknowledgements of excess, apologies of sorts, finally a gin-flavored kiss—sincere lip pressure and maybe just the slightest flick of tongue. By supper we'd be recounting the workday.

And that night, or within a few nights, we'd make love. Heartfelt, clutching, joyous bodily union—intensified by our recent tragic divorce and wondrous recommitment.

Make-up sex.

"As If" is like a military exercise, a war game. You have to play it out in earnest to gird yourself to endure the real thing, and to present a credible deterrent. But there's always the comforting knowledge at the back of your mind that it's make-believe.

Of course, you're using live ammunition, so you could blow off your own foot. Provoke a hail of deadly return fire. Mistakenly arm and launch a doomsday device.

The danger gave it the thrill.

I trailed Laura past a row of men lounging against the wall of a building.

Past a boy who displayed a tin of oxblood shoe polish and some wadded newspaper and pertinaciously offered to shine my white tennis shoes.

Past a woman selling roasted peanuts—customers could choose to have her fill a tiny paper cone with a teaspoon or a tablespoon, the price varied accordingly.

I slowed long enough to see how her system worked. I would have bought a little coneful of her peanuts if I'd had any *kwacha* left. But I didn't want to let Laura get too far ahead of me. I'd watched the men's eyes taking her in—nothing lascivious, but still.... Africans like 'em plump.

This was a strange city. She could go to hell, as far as I was concerned; yet I remained bound by a sense of responsibility to see to it that she made it along this stretch of the journey safely.

Back at the truck, Laura ducked inside for a moment, then immediately reemerged with Greta behind her. She pointedly avoided looking at me. The two of them strode off together toward the crafts displays along the margin of the parking lot.

I found Renée and Alistair aboard reading, Jen and Mel bent over the backgammon board with Emma kibbitzing. So no additional truck-guardians were required.

I joined them anyway. I opened *Out of Africa*, which I'd started again a couple of nights earlier in Senga Bay... back under the old regime, when Laura and I were still a couple.

Dinesen's Kenya at the beginning of the century seemed altogether remote from Malawi at the close—no less foreign to this small contemporary city at the opposite end of the Great Rift Valley than the Navaho reservation that was the setting of the last mystery I'd finished.

I was still having trouble penetrating the surface of Dinesen's polished prose. I'd keep bobbing up to look around—at Renée, at the girls when one or another whooped, at the beggars peering in from their forlorn stakeout around the truck steps, at the dusty cars and pickups going by on the wrong side of the road behind the rank of vendors and their customers, at Laura and Greta and Ewan as well, moving among them—already forgetting what I'd mentally glimpsed during my shallow plunge into the world Dinesen described, of Kikuyus and Somalis and Masai and white coffee planters and the Kenyan highlands. (Rory, when he'd seen me with the book on the pool deck of the Livingstonia Beach Hotel, had playfully volunteered its opening paragraph from memory: "I had a farm in Africa, at the foot of the Ngong Hills....")

Another safari truck operated by another company pulled into the lot. *ExploraTours*, read the legend along its side.

I watched the young passengers pile out. Handsome, bearded guys in cargo-shorts, slim girls with ponytails or French braids, braless, wearing sarongs for Malawi. They looked French, or European, anyway, though they could equally well be South African or Australian.

Everything about them broadcast sex to me. Twentyish wanderlust twinned with carnal lust. Musical sleeping bags. The girls had wisps of blond hair under their arms and on their trim, braceleted bare ankles. When I was that age all the Midwestern coeds I'd known were meticulously depilated, short-haired, stiffly embraed and steadfastly saving themselves for their husbands; the contrast with the Norwegian girls I'd met at Blindern had left me with a residual Europeanness envy.

Like seagulls at a landfill when a promising new dumpster-load arrives, the beggars rushed away from us to flock around them.

I assessed the truck, a Mercedes, with a practiced eye now, comparing its setup—unfavorably—with that of the Bedford. The disembarking passengers glanced over at our rig with the same guarded curiosity. Whenever overland safari parties crossed paths, I'd noticed, there was an undercurrent of rivalry, like teams arriving at a tournament on their local school districts' yellow buses and sizing up the opposition, polite but reserved, leery of fraternization lest it be seen as disloyalty to one's own squad.

In the wake of the squabble with Laura I was jumpy and morose. It was a "squabble," I was now prepared to admit.

Since I did acknowledge a certain justice to her umbrage, I'd been playing this round with less than full commitment.

I kept twisting my face into self-reproachful grimaces as I read. Breathing off sardonic sighs.

Finally I clapped the book shut. I hoped I'd remember where I'd left off: just after the little servant boy had gotten his jaw shot away by accident. It was a sequence whose specificity and grimness had engrossed me. But then there was a divagation on the seasonal grasses of the Masai plain and the difference between European and African systems of criminal justice.

In bed the previous night I'd read two full pages before recognizing a feature in Dinesen's ruminative landscape and realizing I'd already been over the same ground.

I stood and zipped open my shoulder bag in the overhead bin, to slip the book inside for resumption on the plane.

There, shining out at me in all their glory, slotted with my passport and the Republic of Malawi Foreign Currency Declaration forms we'd filled out at the border and would have to surrender at the airport, were the two scarlet British Airways ticket folders.

O Laura of little faith.

I riffled through the book to the passage I'd been reading and sandwiched the envelopes in as a place-marker. No question, I was absolutely in the right in this dispute—in the global sense.

Which, along with a couple of unwrinkled bucks to feed the fare-machine, would get me a BART ticket for a standup ride with my luggage from Daly City to Rockridge.

I'd prefer to go home in Lisa's black Rabbit, thanks. Our little family unit still intact. Which meant it was time to swallow parochial pride and initiate the peace process.

I put on my cap against the sun and climbed down from the truck.

Halfway across the parking lot a group of children scurried up to intercept me. Trotting with them, taller than the rest, was a very skinny young man with deeply sunken eyes. He ran nimbly and with a kind of desperate purposefulness, his chin high and his head tilted as if absorbing light and sound through the skin of his face, the way an animal lifts its nose to trace scents in the air.

The children herded him to a halt him in front of me. He thrust out a cupped hand.

"*Kwacha? Kwacha?* Give me *kwacha?* You see. I have no eyes. I am a poor blindman," he announced.

"He has no eyes. He is a brindman," various of the children shrilled eagerly.

"Sorry. I don't have any. No *kwacha,*" I defended myself.

I was impressed by the quality of the young man's English. He reminded me somewhat of James back at the unnamed river in Zambia... to the extent that both were African males under the age of thirty-five.

In my defense, the physiques, haircuts and complexions were at least similar, and the blind beggar was wearing shorts and flipflops as James had been. This guy would have been handsome too had it not been for those creepily recessed sockets inset with the flattened, milk-glass vestiges of eyeballs.

By habit I pantomimed empty pockets. For the children's benefit, at least.

"Give me money, please," the man persisted. "I am blind, you see."

"No *kwacha.* I have no money, no *kwacha,*" I maintained.

Poor devil. I would have given him something otherwise, despite Renée's admonitions.

The man and his escort trailed me disconsolately for a moment, then broke away, all dashing—I saw over my shoulder when I turned at the sudden hubbub—toward a pair of girls who were just descending from the ExploraTours truck.

I homed in on Laura. Vendors beckoned and brandished their wares as I strode past. A man shoved a pair of statuettes under my nose.

"Very nice ones!" he declared. "Fifty *kwacha*."

There was no way to avoid him. I looked away.

"You rike these, hey?" he insisted.

He fell into step beside me.

"Fifty *kwacha*. Both together, only ninety *kwacha*."

I shook my head grimly. I flapped my hands beside my pockets, shrugged and muttered, "Sorry, you're out of luck. No money."

He smiled at me slyly and nodded at the ploy.

"Very excerrent, this piece. Also this piece," he said, juxtaposing the two. "Best souvenir, famous wood sculpture, yes? Made in Malawi. Fifty for one, ninety for two. Very good bargain, for you, sir."

"Not interested, thanks," I said through clenched teeth.

I judged them to be worth maybe five or ten *kwacha* apiece, if you went in for that sort of thing. The figures were almost identical, each with a large elongated head, a coil of hair above a high forehead and a flattened nose patterned with tribal scars. They had pot bellies, pendulous breasts they clutched with their cartoon fingers, caricaturishly short legs bent at the knees, loincloths of oiled twine and chokers of tiny, brightly colored cylindical beads.

"I rike your watch!" he announced. He was leering at my wrist.

"So do I," I said wryly. I hid it by reflex, reaching up to scratch my back with my thumb.

He waved one of the figurines.

"This excerrent piece I will give you for your watch."

I chuckled. "I don't think so," I said.

I'd seen it coming—and was particularly amused at being offered only *one* of the carvings for my three-hundred-dollar watch.

"They haven't any concept of what things cost," Rory had observed when I'd recounted a similar deal proposed by a *nyaminyami*-seller on the path between the Victoria Falls museum and the cloud of mist at the gorge's edge.

When I'd demurred he'd tried to get Laura to part with her hiking boots. My gunboats had been too large, presumably, for a similar offer. And when Laura had pointed out the minor matter that, never mind the disparity in value, she'd then have to walk to the falls and back shoeless, the guy had grandly said he'd let her have his own spavined rubber sandals.

There was often an air of generosity about these proposals, in fact, as if the vendors were doing us a favor to consider letting us acquire the coveted gewgaws in exchange for our clothing or accessories, since we lacked, or didn't want to part with, cash. Funny money—Zim dollars, Malawi *kwacha*—at that.

When I caught up with her Laura was fingering loops of green beads lying on a rickety table. She had a couple of small objects wrapped in newspaper cradled in her left arm.

I loitered a few feet away, close enough to make my presence felt—she would look around and see me eventually and I didn't want to risk refueling her annoyance by startling

385

her, or on the other hand by clumsily invading her personal space—wasn't that the term?—as if everything were hunky-dory.

"I'm with her," I tried to telegraph to onlookers by my attentive gaze. I composed my face in a fixed not-quite smile that conveyed, I hoped, total uxoriousness. Subtext: Pitches to me would be fruitless. She's the boss.

After a moment Laura held out a necklace to the barrel-chested man who sat in a weathered Malawi tripod traveling chair beside the table.

"How much for this one, then?" she asked.

"Ten *kwacha*," he replied.

"I'll give you five," she said.

He chortled merrily.

"Five and two pens."

"Oh, no, no, no," he replied jovially. "Ten *kwacha*, that one."

Laura laid the necklace on the table and wheeled. She saw me. Her eyes widened slightly, her only reaction.

"Eight *kwacha* and two pens," the man abruptly countered to her back.

Laura turned again. "Five *kwacha* and...." She unzipped her waistpack with her free hand and sorted among its contents. "...three pens?"

"Ret me see the pens," the man frowned.

Laura rooted up three of the cheap, plastic-capped, transparent-barreled stick-ballpoints we'd brought to barter with. An experienced Africa traveler whom Laura had pumped for tips before we'd left had told us that those would be just fine; no need to go for fancier retractable types.

Why exactly ballpoint pens were a desirable trade commodity in southern Africa I'd never determined. You certainly didn't see people passing them around in their own markets to buy bread or fish or vegetables. Nor had I encountered street-corner pen vendors recirculating the inventory accumulated in the tourist-bazaars.

Answers to my inquiries were vague: Well, pens were hard to come by here, people shrugged. But you could say that about all kinds of stuff. Did Africans put so much stock in writing?

I'd concluded that it was simply one of those strange social conventions by which cigarettes become a medium of exchange in prisons quite apart from anyone's intent or capacity to smoke them, and hundred-year-old bottles of wine-gone-to-vinegar are auctioned and reauctioned—never to be drunk—as if they were precious jewels.

The seller nodded. The pens were apparently of acceptable quality. But he held fast.

"Eight *kwacha*, two pens," he reiterated, "okay."

Laura shook her head. "Too much," she declared firmly.

She strolled away, toward a selection of incised wooden bowls nested on a square of cloth spread on the tarmac. She didn't look back at me.

I ambled in pursuit, this time drawing up alongside her at the opposite corner of the brightly patterned cloth. We both pondered the bowls for a moment. She stooped to examine a frieze of elephants *en marche* around the outside of a salad basin. She set it down again and met my eyes as she straightened.

"Hi," I said neutrally.

She didn't reply.

She sidled around the cloth away from me and bent to pick up a small ovoid wooden canister, unadorned except for a long, graceful nib rising from the turned lid. Its color was a rich walnut, the surface polished, the shape and proportions seemly.

"No longer speaking to me, is that it?" I said.

"I'll speak to you," she offered coolly. "When there's something to say."

"Acknowledging my greeting doesn't fall into that category?"

She curled her lip. She replaced the canister on the cloth and lifted its inset lid experimentally.

"Well, I'm glad we've cleared the air as to whether silence...."

"Oh, shut up, Daniel," she interrupted.

"Whoa," I murmured. I recoiled with a chuckle and a stage smirk. The irony.

"What did you come over here for? Just to keep on harassing me? Prolong the harangue?"

"No! Begin the beguine. Is actually more like it."

"I haven't the faintest idea what you're talking about."

"Harangue—beguine." I shrugged. "Wordplay."

"I don't get it," she frowned. She shook her head impatiently. "Look. Please. Can't we just give it a rest? We've been through this so many times...."

"We certainly have," I agreed.

"...I'm fed up. It's gotten awfully old. We both need a break. It isn't working."

"What isn't?"

"Us. The whole thing."

"Yeah, right. We haven't had a fight in three weeks. We've had a *beautiful* relationship up to now, I'd say. *Amazingly* good, really. Then all of a sudden, on the last day, when we're both in a let-down mode and we're all worked up anyway because of the hassles of packing, we start snapping at each other... and you're ready to call the whole thing off."

"That's right. I am."

"Look," I said earnestly. "I told you I was sorry. That's what I came over here for. To say I take full responsibility. I was the one who was in the wrong, mainly. I admit it."

"How much?" Laura said.

She was addressing the middle-aged woman who was tending this assortment, one of the few women among the vendors in the lot. Her tightly curled hair was cropped as short as a man's. She wore a voluminous dotted frock with puffed sleeves. She knelt impassively watching us.

"Ten *kwacha*," the woman answered.

Laura nodded and put the canister down.

"Did you hear what I just said?" I persisted.

"Oh, I'm sorry," Laura exclaimed, turning back to me with a look of wide-eyed, simulated apology for her momentary distraction. "What was it we were talking about?"

"Yeah. *Touché*, my dear," I acknowledged. "I believe you know exactly what we were talking about. It was kind of monumental, even. I was apologizing. And without any wibble-wobble...."

"'Mainly.' That isn't wibble-wobble?"

"Well. See? There's the proof that you *were* listening! But... okay. I rescind the 'mainly.' I'll take sole blame for this one."

"There you go again: 'For this one,'" she pointed out.

"I guess I can't help myself," I acknowledged. I made a sheepish face. "I apologize for that too. For every argument we've ever had. My fault invariably."

"Yeah," she sneered. "What's so 'monumental?' You apologize all the time. It means *nothing* to you! It comes so *easy*! And it should. You have so much practice. You have so much to apologize *for*!"

"If you say so. That certainly does seem to be the dynamic."

"You *know* I get all hyper whenever I'm getting ready to go some place."

"I do," I agreed. "That's what I just said."

"It's still no excuse for telling me to '*shut up*!' I mean, *that's*...."

"Hey," I interrupted her, "you just told *me* to shut up. I'm not all discombobulated about it. Do we need to rehash the whole unfortunate episode? You'll just get yourself worked up all over again. I *said* I was sorry. Let's just go on from there."

"Sweep our differences under the rug. The way we always do."

"Exactly."

"As if denial...."

"Denial is highly underrated!" I exclaimed. "It's a *great* coping mechanism! Psychiatrists ought to be touting it more highly. The first line of defense. When the going gets tough, the tough get defensive."

"Go into denial. You mean. If you're going to be consistent."

"Or... yeah. Exactly. Hey, it works for *me*!" I declared chirpily.

"That's open to question," she scowled. But I could see that her resolve to be angry had broken. Her mood was amenable to lightening.

"Think of all the *good* things I've done for you lately," I went on. "Accentuate the positive. Huh? Like flinging myself into the river back at Chibembe. To protect you from the crocodiles. I mean, that oughtta count for a whole *slew* of points on the credit side of the ledger. Offset all *sorts* of toad-like little lapses. *Lapsi*. Or is the plural the same, *lapsus*?"

She sighed. "I'm not keeping ledgers. Fortunately for you. But I *am* appreciative of the fact that you were so concerned over my welfare. Not that there would have been a damn thing you could have done if I *had* been attacked. Except get yourself killed or maimed too."

"Yeah, well," I muttered, "that's kind of my point, isn't it? Greater love hath no man."

But I'd suddenly lost all enthusiasm for the conversation. I was pretty confident we were back on track; with a little attention we'd probably make it through the rest of the agenda from here to home without any serious breach of the peace.

I was stung by a terrible conscience, though. Listening to the interior echoes of what had just come out of my mouth, I was ashamed. Thoroughly disappointed in myself. Once again my character had revealed itself as deficient. Nothing but runny stink-cheese, no fiber whatsoever. I'd actually invoked my performance at Chibembe as a selfless act. Meritorious conduct.

How low could I stoop? It was one thing to keep my counsel, let others throw whatever flattering light they might on my behavior. I was under no compulsion to set them straight. *Trumpet* my failings. Wear my chicken-heart on my sleeve. But it was another thing to lie. *Volunteer* so fundamental a perversion of the truth.

I harbored no ambiguity about why I'd jumped into the Luangwa. I'd done it out of abject shame. I'd fouled myself, voided my disabling fear into my underpants, spilled the evidence of my failure of nerve in a disgusting public deposition. And only my vanity had been more powerful than my fright. I'd been willing to brave death to wash away the stain, to preserve my false image—but not to save my wife's life.

Except she hadn't needed saving.

Maintain perspective.

In fact, part of my dilemma had been that I *hadn't* been able to reason out any obvious action to take. Until calamity struck she was cruising along in the river just fine. When and if calamity struck I'd be worthless at best. And calamity never struck. The crocodiles of Chibembe had posed a danger only in the space between my ears.

And yet.... In what other milieu, in what other context, does danger exist? It's strictly a function of the brain. Like the sound of a tree falling in the forest: shock waves are generated, they radiate from ground-zero—but "sound" implies a sensory receptor somewhere out there.

Life, similarly, is nothing *but* peril. The threat of harm is constant and ubiquitous: lightning bolts, meteorites, tornadoes, icy sidewalks, falling pianos, stray golf balls, banana peels, defective toasters, drunk drivers, drive-by shooters, angry coworkers, jealous spouses, terrorist bombers, virulent pathogens....

Every morning the newspapers lovingly remind us of the random menace. But most of the time we aren't afraid. And what we're afraid of is what yanks our chains. Nuclear power plants, not ladders; fluoridated water, not Kentucky fried chicken.

Risk assessment is invincibly subjective. I, for instance, felt no significant qualms about getting on that plane in a few hours, never mind that it could cartwheel off the end of the runway in a blaze of fiery avgas... spiral in mid-movie into the sea... lose a section of aluminum skin and with it the passengers haphazardly ticketed in seats beside the jagged hole—decanted along with the hissing cabin pressure into the black night at 30,000 feet.... It could be hijacked by vicious, swarthy, five-o'clock-shadowed zealots who'd pistol-whip me to death simply because the manifest identified me as American.

The slight chance, on the other hand, that a crocodile might somehow sense my bobbing presence in the muddy waters of an African river had scared me shitless.

So commonplace a figure of speech. So devastating a datum of personal history.

"What do you think about that? The little container?" Laura asked.

"Oh. Um. The one you were just looking at."

"Yeah."

"Fine, I guess."

"Should I buy it?"

"Whatever you want."

"Mostly I'm just spending down the *kwacha* I have left. I changed more traveler's checks than I should have. I'm trying to find things that'll make good presents for people at Christmas. Stocking-stuffers."

"Well, I'm tapped out. I bought everybody those tee-shirts in Vic Falls."

"I know. You're so imaginative."

"They'll like 'em. Think Chris'd be thrilled if we gave him a salad-bowl?"

"I'm giving him a *nyaminyami*."

"Yeah! He'll like that! He likes jewelry. Be useful."

"I got one for everybody."

"They'll love 'em. Tell you what. How much do you have? To spend still."

"Thirty," she said. "Thereabouts."

"That's, like, two bucks."

"Really," she said. "I've lost all track of the exchange rates."

"Want me to help you?"

"What do you mean?"

"I saw something I liked. A good present. Give me a few *kwacha* and a couple of pens and I'll share the burden with you, of getting rid of the loot."

She hitched a shoulder.

"Sure." She delved into her pouch. "How much do you want?"

I shook my head. "Ten. Eight would do."

"Here. Here's fifteen," she said.

"No! I don't need that much," I argued. But she pressed the bills into my palm. Then she scooped out a handful of pens.

"You can have the rest of the pens, too."

"*You* keep some!"

She frowned into the pouch. "Actually, I do still have a few."

I shrugged. "Okay. Whatever. A fool and her pens...."

"May be the only time you'll ever see me in so generous a mood. Take advantage."

"I think I just did." I said. "I'll meet you back at the truck."

I checked my watch. "We're supposed to be there in fifteen minutes."

"I know," she nodded. "This is going to be my last thing and then I'm gonna head on over. I'm exhausted. The haggling wears me out."

"You've gotten good at it. You're a tough mama. Tough *mami*."

"I hate it. But by now I don't care one way or the other. I'll just walk away if they don't like what I offer."

"That's the secret of negotiation, isn't it?"

"Secret of life, maybe."

"Never commit."

"No, no. Commit."

"'Only commit.' L.J. Schubert."

"...But don't *cling*!"

"Ah. '...But stay flexible.' L.J. Schubert."

"Exactly. Be willing to let go and move on when necessary."

"By George," I said. "Who'd have thought such wisdom could be packaged in so youthful a personage?"

She gave me a look of tolerant scorn. "Move along," she commanded. She dismissed me with a wave of her hand.

I turned and headed for the table with the beads.

I wasn't sure exactly which necklace Laura had admired, but all four on display were reasonably similar. The one I picked out was made of small marbles of dark green malachite with lighter swirls, strung in graduated sizes tapering to a gold screw-clasp.

The guy had seen me with Laura, but we had to repeat the ritual. When I offered him seven *kwacha* and three pens he accepted.

That left me the wherewithal, wending my way to the truck, to spring for two pairs of wooden elephant earrings and two plain wooden ring-bracelets. I bid mostly pens and still had three *kwacha* in my pocket. It occurred to me to give them to the blindman if I encountered him.

But perhaps because I was in a buying mode, I suddenly spotted the first object that had captured my own fancy since the *bao* board and the *Zambezi Lager* tee-shirt: a letter-opener in the shape of a crocodile.

The blade was its elongated, flattened, sightly curved tail. The handle was its heftier body, the splayed rear legs a grip-guard, the tucked-in forelegs a setting for the viperous head ornamenting the top of the hilt. The jaws were parted and inset with tiny splinters of ivory for teeth.

Presumably these were something else, something legal and cheap: plastic probably. In places the carving was less than fussy—but on closer inspection I saw how deft it had been, how just a notch or a couple of scores had released the reptilian form from the natural warp of the black wood.

Here again, minimalist rather than slapdash, was art; too literal a rendering could have reduced it to kitsch. (Of course, the broader the strokes with which you whittled these, the faster you could turn them out.)

I imagined this letter-opener on my desk at work, a great conversation piece. Blatant reminder to those who knew, and a prod to the curiosity of those who didn't ("*That*'s cute!" "Yeah. Got it in Malawi." "Where?") that I'd been to Africa. Intrepid traveler.

Validated chickenshit. The object would also be a constant reminder, I realized, of my moment of panic and humiliation.

In fact, my first glimpse of it resting among a group of carved kitchen utensils on an upended oil drum had been followed by a fleeting recognition of the Platonic ideal that now inhered for me in crocodile representations: the awesome living creature I'd studied through binoculars on the Luangwa. Grinning its spiky death-grin in close-up.

And then a demi-shudder, a cellular memory of the fear that had twisted my viscera and jellied my bones when I'd contemplated bathing in that slit-eyed saurian's murky domain.

But this was just an icon, not the thing itself. A bit of polished wood, a novelty. What was I going to do, go through life trying to avoid encounters with images of crocodiles? And come all unglued, mewling and puking and dribbling in my Jockeys, if I happened on one?

Hardly. I'm an American, a go-ahead guy. Not much more advanced in emotional complexity than a baboon. We'd established that.

Does a baboon who's had a near-death experience with a crocodile swear off drinking in the river?

Besides, there was a way, it was beginning to dawn on me, of conceiving the episode with a different spin.

I had, in fact, braved that water. My tale was as fantastic, as worthy of recounting for home-audience delectation, as Laura's—and *nobler*, even in its private motivation, since she'd simply plopped in by mischance and remained somehow, God knows how, oblivious to the danger. *I'd* made a considered leap despite being obsessed by the danger.

If you could call it a leap. Or "considered."

Willed, anyway. More or less. I'd acted on the ultimate naval principle, the standard memorialized in the official U.S. Military Tattoo, Mark I: "Death before dishonor."

Wonder who said that? Some commodore on Lake Erie, if I recalled correctly. Wonder if the seat of his breeches was still white at the time?

The thing was, my weakness had been physical. But not moral. My bowels had been in an uproar during the entire game-walk. And I'd always been skittish about gunshots.

On the pistol range at Pearl... even worse, when the *Huckaby's* forward turret was cranked around abeam and I was OOD on the bridge during gunnery exercises. *WHANGO!* *WHOMP!* The muzzles of the five-inch .38s, angled upward, level with my face, would suddenly spew flame and din and then recoil as the shock waves slammed against the dogged-down pilothouse panes, shivered the glass; the steel deck underfoot would tremble, asbestos flakes would leap and swirl from the overhead, my neck would retract with the painful alacrity of a stepped-on turtle's into my life-jacket collar and no matter how tightly I'd snubbed the strap under my chin, my G.Q.-required helmet (General Quarters, not *Gentleman's Quarterly*) would bucket down over my wincing eyes.

Its metal front lip gashed my nose once, so violently did I flinch. And never mind that the bridge-talker would have alerted us to brace for the detonation with the relayed command from Fire Control, "Shoot!" Oh, to be tucked below in the blip-lit, muffled gloom of CIC, where I'd honchoed happily until promotion to Ops Officer and the topside conn for these miserable ordeals.

I'd always had an overly developed endocrine response to surprise. As recently as a month or so before this trip I'd been in my office hunched over my keyboard, lost in the pixels on the screen as I searched for *le synonyme juste* to put some starch into a jejune paragraph of brochure copy, when a coworker had ducked his head around the jamb and cleared his throat.

I'd clawed my way out of my chair so wildly I'd bruised my thigh on the underside of my desk, and practically sent the poor guy reeling to the rug with a heart attack of his own. I ended up apologizing to *him* while I limped around mopping at the coffee that had spread from my overturned mug.

Soon after we were married, Susan had hung a ceramic planter on the front porch while I was at work. She'd suspended it just high enough so that I didn't notice it in the dusk until I strode onto the coco-fiber mat, key poked innocently toward the lock. Then the planter grazed my forehead—and dropped me, flattened me on my back as instantaneously as if it had smashed me flush in the kisser.

It was only my own exaggerated evasive reaction to the unexpected contact—the exquisitely refined self-protective instinct by which I'd managed to slip every punch ever thrown, before or since, at my face—that had put me down. I did, however, lie there groaning, feigning recovery from concussion, in order to milk as much penitential sympathy as I could from my diminutive new bride when she rushed to investigate the strange cry and thud outside the door.

That I'd go bananas when an elephant gun went off in my ear, then, was hardly a departure from form. Absolutely predictable. That the loosest link in my chain of self-command at that instant would be my gastrointestinal tract proved lousy luck. But nothing else. I wasn't a latter-day Francis Macomber, who'd taken to his heels when a lion he'd gut-shot had heaved itself out of the grass at him.

I'd been brooding on the parallels to that story since I'd clicked off the bedside lamp the last night at Chibembe. Both Macomber and I were American men on safari with wives to be reckoned with. We'd both confronted a primal terror in Africa. We'd both flunked the test, shown ourselves cowards.

Now for the qualifications.

Margot Macomber had lounged at safe remove watching her husband turn tail, and had despised him for it. Laura hadn't even remarked my hesitance. She'd been the one in trouble and displaying admirably uncomplicated mettle.

My failure of nerve had been an altogether private matter. I'd fallen short only of a naive standard I'd set for myself. The guide, Denys... the natives, George and Just Do It and the crewman... none of them had harbored any expectations of me, I was now pretty sure, as opposed to the white hunter Robert Wilson and Macomber's bearers in Hemingway's story. I hadn't done anything negative. Just nothing positive.

Because there was nothing *to* do.

And when I finally acted, when I tumbled to Laura's "rescue," it had made me look, if anything, like a nut case.

But I'd tumbled. Redeemed myself to myself, at least. In retrospect. Even if the impetus had been a shame as down and dirty as it gets.

So to that extent I *was* like Francis Macomber—whose redemptive bravery had been occasioned, after all, by an unsportsmanlike pursuit by car of a bunch of fleeing buffalo. And whose short happy life consisted of standing fast long enough to plunk several rifle slugs into a charging beast he'd already gratuitously wounded.

Both our manly moments were tainted at best. Maybe all valor is like that, though. Underlain by shame and guilt. Heroes always seem to have a certain melancholy about them. Only fools whose triumphs are as inane as sacking a quarterback or tomahawk-jamming a basketball—or as equivocal as slaughtering a magnificent animal or chopping down a giant primordial tree—go around beating their chests in gorilla self-celebration.

And when gorillas thump their chests, I'd warrant, notwithstanding my lack of any expertise whatsoever on the subject, and having adopted baboondom rather than gorilladom as my personal paradigm, it's out of fear:

"Oh, God, oh, God, don't attack me, please don't attack me, look how fucking *ferocious* I am!"

So Hemingway's premise, that a Francis Macomber newly emboldened by his buffalo-hunting epiphany on the African *veld* would seize control of all the other aspects of his life, that the momentary suppression of his death-fear was a watershed from which, most significantly, he'd impose new marital terms on his gold-digging, two-timing bitch of a wife... that was all the rankest romantic fantasy. From the pen of a man who'd gunned down every known trophy species, hauled in marlins, married four times, fought bulls—or at least talked a lot about it—gone *voz a voz* with the greatest writers of his generation, and ended up sucking lead from a rifle bore at 62. Not very much older than I was.

The foreshortened, sad life of Ernest Hemingway. Quit by his own hand, at least—unlike Francis Macomber, rubbed out "accidentally" from behind by the black widow Margot.

It was possible Laura would leave me. Could even happen because of the incident at Chibembe, indirectly. Doubtful it would be because I'd gone unsufferably brave on her there, though. Or because I'd funked, since she'd had no direct witness of it.

Maybe she'd be troubled by the irrationality of my hop into the river, or perhaps by some element of overcommitment it represented, evidence of a pathetic, clingy, cloying uxoriousness.

Whatever, she'd never know the real story, that's for sure. Because the ultimate lack of backbone would be for me to unburden myself to her in scrupulous confession.

In any case, I was pretty sure she wouldn't get rid of me by execution. That kind of *denouement*, like the Joycean epiphany, is for literature.

As are plot and characterization.

A lot of this interminable, solipsistic dithering about what my reaction to the crocodiles at Chibembe meant or didn't mean took place as I squirmed at enforced leisure trying to fight off cramps in the knee-space deemed sufficient for coach passengers by British Airways.

That's also when I decided that if I were ever to try to turn this trip into a novel I'd have to make up some more detailed back-stories to flesh out my fellow travelers.

Maybe it had to do with our Anglo-Saxonness, or maybe the fact that we were all modern urbanites, but we'd averaged at least two-thirds of the hours of every day for three weeks in one another's intimate company and chosen to withhold everything about ourselves but the most patchy and perfunctory bits of *curricula vitae*.

Did Reg have a wife hidden away in some over-the-garage flat in Croyden? No idea. Hell, he could be a vacationing Reg the Ripper. No wonder he didn't want to give his address.

How about Alastair? Apparently, but not certainly, a widower.

Was Jen really a divorcee? Not sure.

Greta might have a husband—and did mention two teenage sons—but it wasn't clear whether any of them lived with her in Mallorca or were in Denmark.

How about the question of whether Gerhard was gay?

I'd gotten better at decoding Ewan, but accountancy seemed to summarize his span of interests.

Melody was extroverted, so she'd made no secret of being Jewish—an exotic attribute, remarkably revealed, for this crowd. Or maybe it had been transparent to them all the time.

She was also, by eavesdropped inference from the stories she and Jen had exchanged over the backgammon board, from comfortable family circumstances. But I'd never heard her specify the business her father was actually in. Based on her accent, I imagined him to be a fat, pinky-ringed owner of something *déclassé* like a chain of pawn brokerages—and felt uneasy about the stereotype. The Dickensian anti-Semitism that produced a Fagin is another nasty trait of the British upper classes all too easily absorbed subliminally by American wannabe readers like me.

By the same token, I imagined Emma's parents to be of a certain Welly-wearing, British-green-Land-Rover-driving, weekend-gardening, horsy type celebrated in Dick Francis mysteries and the Thames TV dramas you see on KQED.

Day after day we'd sat side by side or across from one another in the back of the Bedford, we eleven chance Mamba-mates, avoiding impolitely prolonged eye contact, avoiding impolitely prying conversations, nattering as superficially as possible or withdrawing altogether into contemplation of the increasingly repetitious scenery, like so many well comported strangers on a commuter train. But give me eleven New Yorkers confined in a subway car for that length of time and I'd bet they'd know one another's birth weights. Even Laura and I, reflexively confessional Americans, had held our cards uncharacteristically—even uncomfortably—close to the vest in this repressed atmosphere.

Only the crew had shown any willingness to unbutton about themselves: Renée maybe because she was of a similar, wide-open-spaces colonial breed, Nick under pressure because of her influence and his own curiosity about relational issues, and Rory from a natural garrulousness.

What I could do, I mused, was have them killed off one by one. Alistair dragged from his tent in the night by the prowling lion at Nsefu... Nigel overrun and trampled by the charging bull elephant... Greta "taken" by a crocodile at the river ford... Reg jumped by a leopard on the fringe of bush camp... Gerhard, haplessly without a knife, swallowed by a python... Melody bitten in the butt by a black mamba at a loo stop....

I could eliminate them in inverse order to the degree to which we'd connected, and spare them according to their youth and physical attractiveness. Shallow, okay, cynical—but you've gotta give readers what they want if you're gonna sell books.

Maybe I'd let Melody survive. The venom sucked out by Ewan in an epiphany of heretofore unrealized decisiveness and capability. They'd fall in love, the *zaftig* Cockney "Jewess" and the diffident lowland Scot. Rebecca and Ivanhoe, united at last.

I'd have suspense, mounting tension, incident.... Who among us would be next to fall victim to Africa's perils? Who among us would be left, who'd be at the wheel, by the time we pulled into the Kamuzu International Airport parking lot?

A plotline.

I would also, of course, tweak my own saurophobic—my sorry, my phobic—character.

Duh, in the parlance of the day.

But I would not altogether eliminate my agony of crocodile-dread on the Luangwa. Transcending it could still be the crux. Like Francis Macomber's discovery of his moral fiber. I'd just clean up the circumstances. Get rid of that unpleasant physical business. Who wants to read about nasty bodily effusions? Unless they're animal, of course: the cloacal habits of the hippo, the sex life of the lion, the priapic predilections of the vervet and the baboon—all fair game, as it were. But you gross out nice people if you rub their faces in their own sweaty, seepy, flatulant, banal, concupiscent humanity. What does the art in *artificial* mean, after all?

So in my novelization I'd also paint myself—my surrogate—as more generous.

For example, after I'd bought the crocodile letter-opener I only had four pens left. I gave one each to the two beggars who still hovered near the truck. They thanked me but didn't seem thrilled.

The guy behind the oil drum wouldn't have sold me the letter opener for just three *kwacha* and all the pens I held in my hand, but his face had lit up immediately when I'd thought to offer him my L.L. Bean fishing cap in the bargain. It had served me well but was now dispensable. So I'd come away with a souvenir and the blindman had got nothing.

Not that I saw him again. For a second, pleased with my acquisition, I'd considered donating my watch to him if we were to cross paths before I reached the truck.

For a second. A three-hundred-dollar watch.

Don't be ridiculous.

Nick rode in the back with us, alongside Renée, to the airport. They were both in traveling mufti. It was the first time I'd seen Nick in long pants. Renee wore a light blue shirtwaist dress. It felt odd, like sharing a taxi with the ex-President and the former First Lady on Inauguration Day, after their return to ordinary civilianhood.

Emma sat in the cab for this last twenty-two kilometers with the new Captain of the Ship of Mamba, Rory.

At the airport he parked and we emptied the Bedford, bustling to drag out our backpacks and suitcases and wrapped mementos, exchanging handclasps and quick hugs, waving goodbye to Rory, straggling off to find the British Airways counter among Ethiopian Airways, Air Zimbabwe, Kenya Airways, Air Malawi, South African Airways....

Somewhere *en route* or in the confusion of the first days at home, Laura misplaced the page on which she'd collected the addresses. We never did find it.

I called my doctor from my office first thing Tuesday morning, and saw him that afternoon.

I hiked up my pants-leg, he whistled and put me on Dicloxacillin four times a day for ten days.

The ulcer healed.

Within a couple of years I couldn't remember which of the scars of a lifetime were souvenirs of Africa.

— Mendocino, California, August 22, 1997
Placerville, California, June 12, 2020

www.ingramcontent.com/pod-product-compliance
Lightning Source LLC
Chambersburg PA
CBHW022242020726
47496CB00004B/1019